DROPPING FEAR

MIKE CATALANO

OTHER BOOKS BY MIKE CATALANO
My Little Sister's a Zombie

DEDICATION
For my Mary Kay, whose struggle and eventual great triumph
inspired this story. And no, you are *not* 'Kerri.'

Prologue

"He's in the Hampstead Hall building!" Sergeant Reynolds exclaimed into the walkie-talkie mic on the shoulder of his uniform. "I'm currently in pursuit, but I need backup, now!"

The crescent-shaped moon in the blackened sky offered little illuminatory assistance on the campus grounds. The lighting around the entryway to the dormitories was the only real area of exposure, however *he* strangely chose to head right through it.

Moments later, Reynolds hustled up to the entryway of the ten-story building with two huge 'H's' hanging above the foyer. The double glass doors had been shattered, creating an uninviting welcome mat of sharp shards. Reynolds made little crunching sounds as he stepped cautiously into the foyer, gun drawn. He gazed grimly at the unmanned check-in counter slightly to his left. The tiny red droplets smeared across the glazed surface quickly caught his attention. He took one long stride forward and peered behind the counter.

"Oh shit." He frowned and reached for his shoulder mic.

Behind the clerk-side of the check-in area, disjointedly sprawled out face-first on the floor, was a skinny young man. His head resembled a crushed eggshell and a cavalcade of crimson engulfed the rest of his body. A piece of his neck bone had protruded its way out into the open.

Reynolds depressed the button on the side of his walkie-talkie and said, "Is backup on the way?"

Up on the fifth floor, a slender young man with light brown hair, dressed in a red T-shirt and matching shorts both brandishing the name N.J. University, exited his dorm room. A piece of paper was taped to his back, which read, **PLEDGE**. He placed a rainbow, propeller beanie atop his head and stretched an affixed elastic band under his chin to hold it in place. He popped on a pair of blacked-rimmed glasses with a huge wad of tape wrapped around the center.

"Joining a frat makes you retarded, Josh!" called his roommate from inside the room.

Josh rolled his bespectacled eyes and replied, "But it's the easiest outlet to beer and ho's."

"Enjoy your meeting!"

Josh closed the door behind him and headed down the empty hallway. The faint sounds of rap music and his footsteps filled the air. Upon passing the girls' bathroom, his ears perceived the gentle hissing of the showers. He stopped before the plastic sign that said, **LADIES,** and stared down at the steam emanating from the base of the door. He couldn't help thinking how cool it was living on his own in a building where wet, naked girls were separated from him by a single, rectangular piece of wood.

While lost in horny contemplation, Josh didn't notice the door to the stairwell at the end of the hall jut slightly outward. As soon as his mind shot its load, he stepped away from the steam and continued on his journey.

The elevator was located directly across from the door to the stairwell. Josh pressed the 'down' button and waited patiently, gazing at the glowing circle. Once the glow faded, a little 'ding' rang out. Little squeaks soon followed as the elevator doors parted. At the same time, the door to the stairwell at Josh's back gradually reopened. When the elevator was gaping wide, he walked in and hit the button for the ground floor and began turning around. Two swift, pounding steps vibrated across the floor. Once fully facing forward, Josh's heart let out one last excruciating palpitation as a thick metal pipe went piercing into his stomach. As if caught in a blustery tornado, his whole body swooped backwards off the floor. He came to a halt once the pointed end of the pipe hit the back of the elevator's wall on an upward angle, creating an instant dent. He could feel his entrails spilling out as his body began sliding down the impaled pole of metal. His coasting gut came to a stop when it touched the frame of the person holding the pipe. Blood dripping from his mouth, Josh awkwardly raised his head. The cloaked visage of the hulking aggressor before him began to grow blurry. His only visible features were his eyes, which intensified with fury as Josh started rolling back.

Once the 'shish-ka-pledge' ceased all movement, the pipe was gradually lowered. Josh's torso slipped gracefully off the metal and hit the floor with a thud. The masked intruder stepped back into the hallway and stared at his bloody handiwork until the elevator doors closed off the view.

Red lights were flashing outside the windows back on the ground floor of the dorm building. Reynolds hurriedly waved his backup in from his hunching position near the shattered entryway. An overweight male dorm resident with a buzz cut was crouching beside him. A symphonic row of sharp crunching ensued.

"Thanks for getting here fast," Reynolds said as he greeted the group of six cops.

"So it's really him, Sergeant?" asked a blonde officer right away. "The wrestler?"

"Oh yeah." Reynolds moved his eyes over to the front desk for a moment. "It's him." He turned to address the whole crowd. "Derek Haddonfear is in this building. Most of you should already know his story, yet I still feel the need to reiterate.

Quadruple homicide…" He paused right away, giving another glance back at the front desk. "Make that quintuple homicide, overly medicated, freakishly strong, and absolutely no remorse."

A 'ding' rang out from the ground floor's elevator, grabbing Reynolds's focus. He placed his hand on his holstered gun and turned toward the sound. The doors opened up, revealing Josh's gore-soaked body on the floor.

"Oh, goddamn it." Reynolds grimaced and returned his gaze to the backup. "You see what we're dealing with?"

The stone-faced officers gave him their full attention. He went on,

"Forget Michael Myers or Freddy Kruger… the biggest horrors of your imagination are real and somewhere inside this building. So the words *be careful* should take on a whole new meaning inside your brains. Plus, even though it's Spring Break, there's still a fair number of freshmen students residing in this building. We don't want to evacuate yet and create a panic and risk losing Haddonfear in the confusion. Questions?"

The foyer was silent. Finally, a lone officer raised his hand.

"What is it, Jake?" Reynolds asked.

"Sir, what's that smell?"

Reynolds lowered his sights down to the cringing non-officer with the buzz cut.

"Gentlemen," he began, "this is Horace. He's an RA. He was coming down for a midnight snack before you all got here. He saw the clerk behind the front desk, and shit his pants."

The expression on Horace's pale face assured the crowd that he was deathly humiliated.

"Don't worry, son," Reynolds hurriedly added. "I almost did the same." He brought his attention back to the officers. "And Horace is about to score some major redemption points by informing us of all the students still in the building. Our best shot at finding Haddonfear is by looking where there're already people." He knelt down before the boy with the stained shorts, attempting to nonchalantly hold his breath. "How about it, Horace? Who's still in the building?"

"Uh," Horace anxiously looked up at Reynolds. "No one's on the first and second floors. Two rooms are occupied on the third floor, three rooms on the fifth floor, and... uh... one room on both the eighth and ninth."

"Okay, good, son," Reynolds exhaled and patted him on the shoulder. He nodded cautiously over at the mess in the elevator. "Now tell me, what floor was *he* on."

"Josh was on the fifth floor."

"You knew him?"

Horace nodded.

"Do you know anyone else by name?"

"Yeah, just a couple."

"Tell me."

Horace rubbed the side of his peach fuzz before answering, "Well, there's Ryan, Erin, Tomas, 'Rich' Pamela, Donny..."

"Hold up," Reynolds interrupted rapidly. "'Rich' Pamela. Why do you call her that?"

"Because she's rich," Horace stated the obvious. "Her dad's the CEO of the EWC, you know, the Extreme Wrestling Coalition."

"You mean Pamela McAvoy?" Reynolds's eyes bugged out.

Horace nodded warily once more.

"Jesus Christ," Reynolds leapt to his feet. "What floor is she on?"

Horace looked back to the elevator. "Uh...the fifth."

Reynolds glared at his battalion of officers with extreme urgency.

A large gust of steam entered the hallway on the fifth floor as Pamela stepped her bare feet out from the ladies' room. A plain white towel was wrapped around her like a small, strapless sundress. Her wet blonde hair clung to her scalp and dangled straight down the back of her neck. With squinting eyes, she began traipsing through the extra thick fog across the hall, unaware of the massive dark profile standing merely three feet away.

Pamela's dorm room, #515, wasn't far away. After emerging from a puff of steam, she reached out to the door's knob and gave it a small twist. As a small creak ensued, she hurriedly entered the dark room. Using her outstretched hand as a guide, she navigated through the room and stopped at a raised platform. With the push of a button, a small desk light projected a dim haze around the dorm, revealing two twin beds. One was neatly made, while the other had mussed sheets. Pamela rubbed her eyes and reached out again at the desk. She retrieved a pair of square-ish, thin black-rimmed glasses and perched them on the bridge of her nose. The move jostled her towel loose. Her hands shot abruptly to her chest just before the white cotton dropped below nipple level. She turned to the left-ajar door and quickly kicked it shut. Though her privacy seemed to be back intact, she still tightened the towel back in place and looked back at her sheets. The disheveled bed was not a welcoming sight.

"Just one more day," she sighed. "Then you'll be in Cancun, on a beach, with a buff boy named Pedro serving you margaritas."

Pamela took a moment and closed her eyes to picture the obligatory Spring Break fantasy. A loud knock pounded on the door. Pamela popped open her eyes and instinctively clutched her towel. She took one quiet step towards the door. Another round of pounding rang forth.

"Who's there?" Pamela called out.

"Ms. McAvoy, this is Sergeant Reynolds," shouted the voice from behind the wooden board. "I need you to open up right away."

"Yeah right, Josh, I know about all your stupid pledge assignments. Go away. It's too late for this shit."

The pounding started up again only much louder.

"Ms. McAvoy, I don't think you understand," Reynolds said hastily. "We have reason to believe that you're in danger. There's a murderer loose in this building. Now, please open up!"

Pamela moved a bit faster toward her door and glanced through the peephole. Out in the hall stood Reynolds and Jake both flashing pressing expressions, guns drawn. A twinge of worry shot up her spine.

"Oh, all right," she hollered. "Just let me put something on."

Pamela ducked off to her side dresser, revealing the colossal figure that had been standing, waiting behind her the whole time.

Outside in the hall, Reynolds gave a nod to his officer, Jake.

"I think she was just in the shower," he said pointing his pistol at the set of wet footprints before the door.

"Think she's naked in there?" Jake asked slyly.

"Hey, get your mind out of…"

A shrill scream from the other side of the door cut off his sentence. Both officers raised up their revolvers.

"Shit!" Reynolds exclaimed and brought his big, booted foot up in the air.

With a smart shove, he vigorously delivered the base of its rubber sole into a section directly next to the doorknob. The locked hinges burst inward, giving way to the now lightless dorm room. At first glance, Reynolds could see nothing, but heard a distinctly gruff heavy breathing. Aiming his gun, he quickly dropped to his knees.

"Let's go!" Jake shouted and barged forward.

"Not yet, Jake!" Reynolds warned. "Stand back!"

Jake took one step into the shadows when a brisk *whoosh* went wheeling through the air. A hard *thwack* followed and the rushing officer's limbs jerked still. A juicy glob of red plopped out into the hall. Jake's body swayed backwards. Reynolds could only watch as he met the floor with the thick, metal pipe skewering his forehead. His shoulders gave a fast twitch, then nothing else.

"Goddamn it!" Reynolds moaned in despair and rapidly pointed the barrel of his gun into the darkness. "Derek!"

An answer wasn't returned. The heavy breathing had suddenly stopped.

"I know you're in here, Derek!" Reynolds called and stepped past Jake into the outer edge of the room. "It's me, you know who! Where's the girl? Come on, Derek, show me the girl! Whether you like it or not, this is all going to end tonight!"

Still no answer.

"Damn you, Derek!" Reynolds fumed. "It all stops now! I know what you're trying to do! Don't you dare hurt her! Don't you dare! If you do, I promise I'm going to shoot you...*many* times!"

The darkened dorm remained silent. Unsure of what was going to happen next, Reynolds reached one hand up to his walkie-talkie. Before he depressed the button, a faint exhale came forth. He felt a blast of air hit the left side of his face. A bulky hand brusquely shot out of the shadows directly beside Reynolds. The hand grabbed his still aiming arm and heaved it forward. As Reynolds flew outward between the two twin beds, he could hear Pamela let out a muffled scream.

She's still alive, his mind thought just before his body crashed into the floor.

Reynolds held onto his gun the whole time. Refusing to lay on the floor for a second longer, he surged to his feet. Derek and Pamela had left the dorm room, but the noise they were making was the perfect breadcrumb trail. Reynolds hot-tailed it after them, without noticing that the pipe had left the room as well. He hit the button on his shoulder walkie-talkie.

6

"All units convene on the north stairwell outside the fifth floor!" he shouted into the receiver while running. "There is an officer down in room 515. I need an ambulance immediately!" The door to the stairwell swung shut. "He's in the stairwell! Haddonfear's in the stairwell right now! Let's go people, talk to me!"

A row of static took over his shoulder speaker.

"We've got him!" yelled a voice. "The third floor stairwell was completely blocked off! He's got nowhere to go but up! We've got him on the stairs. He's heading up this way. We've…"

A string of incoherent shouting ensued followed by a couple of 'popping' gun shots.

"Hey, guys!" Reynolds called into his shoulder mic. "Come in! Do you copy?"

His query was met by an echoing symphony of screams from the other end.

"Do you copy?" he repeated.

All further noises ceased. Reynolds increased his pace, and he was soon bashing through the exit into the stairwell. He bounded up before the railing and pointed his gun down a flight—nothing. He switched his aim up to the ceiling. A tiny drop of blood fell right past him from some random, higher step. Reynolds swung his shoulders off the rail and began his ascent.

Exhaling flustered pants of determination, he rocketed up the stairwell. His heart let out a distraught wail as he came upon the source of the dropping blood. Three of his backup officers were sprawled out across the steps soaked in red. Reynolds rapidly applied his pointer and middle fingers to the sides of their throats to check for a pulse. *Strike one, strike two, strike three*—they were all out for the count. He had no choice but to continue his pursuit.

"Sergeant?" a soft voice suddenly came over his walkie-talkie.

"Jimmy, that you?" Reynolds asked between strides up the steps.

"It's me, sir," Jimmy replied. "The ninth floor is student-free, but I think something's coming my way."

"Proceed with extreme caution," Reynolds strongly urged. "Phil, Nick and Brian are all dead. I'm on my way. He has Pamela McAvoy. Got that, Jim… Jimmy?"

A steady row of static was all that answered.

"Jimmy, come in."

The static blipped into silence. Reynolds waited.

"Yessssss, sir," whispered a different, muffled voice. "Yessssss, sir…"

The static abruptly returned. Reynolds grabbed his shoulder mic.

"Derek! I swear to Christ I'm killing you tonight! I swear to Christ!"

Reynolds ripped his hand away from his walkie-talkie and made sure his trigger finger was tightly in place. His feet pounded into every step that crossed their path. Rage was now his partner. His mind strove to stumble upon some semblance of clarity,

He wants to kill her... It's definitely revenge... Why hasn't he done it yet? What's he waiting for? Me? It can't be me... I'm stopping him, damn it... Why is he heading up instead of down? It's not... not... The Drop? Shit!

The thinking session was complete. Reynolds reached the top level soon after. He darted right past the door to the ninth floor and continued straight on up to the roof. It was just one more flight. Before depressing the long metal handle of the final door, his walkie-talkie sprung to life.

"Sergeant Reynolds?" asked a voice from the receiver. "You there? Come in. We heard..."

The remainder of the sentence was rapidly muffled by Reynolds' palm. He glanced at his shoulder and then over at the door to the roof. With his eyes still fixated on the handle, he switched off the receiver.

The door made a slight squeak as it opened up an inch. Through the crack, Reynolds surveyed the surroundings. A lone orange spotlight offered the only illumination. Large rectangular vents jutted up from the roof and looked to be ideal obstacles and hiding places. The small opening disclosed nothing else. Reynolds grew weary of his peering and quickly reminded himself that a young lady's life was at stake. He also convinced himself that he was dealing with a wild animal and not a man. With his sights set to *kill*, he shoved the door out of the way and took two big steps out onto the roof. He pointed his gun outward, holding it with both hands. He aimed from left to right, back and forth like a single windshield wiper.

"Where are you, Derek?" he shouted, figuring the element of surprise was a lost cause. "I know you're up here! I know what you're thinking! It's not happening! Pretty soon there's gonna be cops surrounding the ground level! You've got nowhere to go! Don't make this worse!" He took one big gulp before adding in a subdued tone, "Just let her go."

Of course, his appeal was met with the sounds of silence. Unwilling to go quietly into the night, Reynolds kept his pistol poised and bellowed, "Derek! Show yourself now, you fucking coward!"

A delicate *thwap* emanated from the night sky. Reynolds looked up just as a billow of white swathed over his face. Once he was completely concealed within the cocoon of wet cotton, Derek stepped up before the edge

8

of the canopy that rested above the entryway. He still carried a now towel-less Pamela in his left arm.

"Son of a bitch!" Reynolds hollered while struggling within the confines of the extra large wrap.

Before he could pull the wool off his eyes, a Neanderthal-like force came crashing down upon his shoulders. His face smacked onto the floor and became even more tangled in the towel. While sorely writhing to get free, he could hear Pamela shrieking. Something grabbed hold of his right leg. An explosion of pain suddenly burst through his ankle.

"AAAAAHHHHHH!" Reynolds screamed.

He could feel the thick metal pipe dig into his skin. Derek used the pipe to lift Reynolds's right leg and drag him back a couple of feet. Reynolds tried to struggle free, but the pain was too intense. He felt his left leg being raised up.

With the pipe still protruding from his right ankle, the rest of its pointed end was powerfully driven through his left one. Reynolds screamed so loud, he pulled a muscle in his throat and almost choked. In the midst of a heinous coughing fit, he was hoisted upward by his feet. Once the towel left his face, he observed Derek standing in the orange light dressed in black from head to toe. A dark raggedy mask with white stripes outlining the eyes coated his cue ball-shaped head. The gigantic Goliath was able to curl the attached pipe upward with one hand like a dumbbell and keep Pamela's naked physique subdued with the other. Reynolds soon found himself completely upside-down with blood dripping past his face. Derek placed the pipe over the edge of the canopy and left him dangling. Reynolds tried to slide his ankles off the metal, but the pain was unbearable. He could feel the weight of his body causing the pipe to dig deeper up toward his feet. He was on the verge of passing out. His eyes began rolling back and in the process, caught sight of Derek dragging Pamela's defenseless frame towards the roof's edge. His blackout was put on hold.

"She's somebody's daughter, Derek!" he shouted, blood rushing to his head. "You know that! She's an innocent!"

The blackened colossus continued moving away. Reynolds knew he only had one card left to play.

"What about your son?" he roared.

Derek's movement ceased. Pamela remained tightly in his clutches. Reynolds forgot about his pain and hastily continued.

"Yeah, Derek, what about William? He's just an infant! He already lost his mother thanks to you. You want him to lose his father now too? I know

what happened to you, Derek. I know it's hard to see things clearly now…
but you don't want to take this any further. Do you?"

Though Reynolds's vision was a bit blurry, he was able to perceive
Derek bowing his oblong head. His grip on Pamela began lessening, causing
her to squirm violently for freedom.

"My father is going to fucking kill you!" she screamed, her arms and legs
flailing.

Derek's head snapped up from its lowered state.

"No, honey, don't say anything!" Reynolds implored. "Don't…"

It was already too late. Derek aggressively snatched Pamela up and set
his feet back in motion.

"DEREK, NO!" Reynolds called out feverishly. "DON'T! DON'T
YOU DO IT!"

His words could no longer initiate a response. Derek stepped up onto
the edge of the roof. Pamela shrieked with fright, as an impending gravita-
tional dread entered her mind from the sight below.

From his inverted position, Reynolds watched as a bright spotlight burst
up onto Derek from the ground level. He could vaguely make out a stirring
of voices clamoring up to them and inferred that more backup had arrived.

Backed by an evil glowing beam, Derek turned so that he was facing
Reynolds. He brought Pamela across his body and with two hands, lifted
her upside-down over his shoulder. Reynolds was ominously suspicious of
what was going to happen next.

The Drop, his mind miserably predicted.

He rolled his eyes upward in despair and noticed something clenched in
his hand. Apparently, his entire upended body had been so tightly tensed up
in pain that he had never let go of his gun. He looked back at Derek who
had Pamela's screaming frame raised straight as an arrow into the night sky.
His black, bulky shoulders began leaning back. Reynolds knew he had failed.
He lifted up his gun and aimed for the light's large, blacked-out center.

"Goddamn you, Derek," he scowled and squeezed back on the trigger.

Derek appeared unfazed by the barrage of bullets passing into his chest.
He merely proceeded with his initial falling-back motion, which was further
helped by the bullets. Once his body became an acute angle with the base of
the ledge, he began lowering Pamela like the hands of a clock until her
straightened position was perpendicular to his.

Reynolds ran out of bullets just as Derek 'Dropped' backwards off the
ledge out of sight. All he could hear was Pamela's one, long, fading scream.

He let go of his gun, closed his eyes, and succumbed to the tortuous throbbing just below his knees.

While careening through the air, Derek and Pamela seemed to be forming an 'L' — she the vertical top, he the horizontal base. Keeping his grip firmly on her sides beneath her arms, he pushed her face slightly past his shoulder making it first in line for impact. The nine stories went by fast as the fall concluded with a harsh *splat!*

Chapter 1

Will stared at her through a smoke-free vista from a quiet corner beside the men's room of the bar. Thankful that New Jersey had finally passed a law banning people from lighting up at all public social establishments, he crisply breathed in the beauty seated about twenty feet away. She had her back leaning against the drink-soaked bar and what appeared to be a Cosmo, in her hand. Her smooth slender legs were crossed and only covered above the knee by a clingy, black miniskirt. Will had always been a 'legs man' and the pair currently settled within his sights made it hard for him to look away. In order to seem slightly less obvious, he began moving his eyes up to her equally beautiful top half—loose pink and black striped, short-sleeved blouse, lightly tanned complexion, bright, bleach blonde wavy hair just below shoulder length, and a pair of piercing, light green eyes. Although he was at a fairly far distance and the bar was somewhat dim, Will could still decipher the precise, unusual pigment. And that specific shade of green was now apparently focusing directly on *him*.

Will was partially startled upon getting caught in her gaze, but did not awkwardly avert his own eyes. He remained standing and returned her 'viewing volley'. Normally, he would have expected such ogling behavior to be met with a staunch middle finger; however this particular woman decided to raise her Cosmo up to him in the manner of a toast. Will was instantly hooked. He nodded back to her and raised an empty hand with a playfully dumb expression alluding to the fact that he was obviously drinkless. She took a sip from her Cosmo, and with a shrug of her blonde locks, signaled for him to come over. Will's eyes nearly bugged out of his head. Before he began impishly checking if she was motioning to someone at his left or right, his mind sternly reminded him to keep cool.

With his eyes planted securely back in his skull, he nonchalantly pressed his pointer into his chest. The woman gave a single nod, topped off with a sultry smirk. Will's feet instantly kicked into high gear. His heart took on a much stiffer beat as he swiftly sauntered across the bar. He didn't stop until that smirk was right before his face.

"Hi," was his first exhale.

"Hey," she smiled back.

"Hey," he repeated. "So, um, can I buy you a drink?"

"I kind of already have one," she said, taking another sip.

"Oh yeah, you do. Sorry about that."

"Can I buy *you* a drink?"

She caught him off guard.

"Oh, um, sure," Will responded. "Thanks."

"What'll it be?" she asked. "No, wait a minute. Let me guess. Hmm, you seem like a Miller Lite man."

"Wow, yeah." His eyes got large again. "That's my favorite beer. How'd you guess?"

"Well," she reached out her free hand. "You seem to be in pretty fit shape." She gently touched his midsection. "That's usually a sign of someone who drinks lighter beers. And you just look more like a Miller man than Bud."

She removed her hand, leaving a small dent in his button-down shirt, and ordered a Miller Lite from the bartender. Will couldn't believe how forward she was being, but was certainly not complaining.

"You're pretty perceptive," he stated. "That's cool."

"So, you got a name?" she asked. "Or should I just call you Miller Man?"

"Oh, I have a name. It's... George."

"George, huh?" she grinned. "What's your last name, Glass?"

"Oh, um, yeah, ha," Will stammered. "Brady Bunch reference. I, uh, get those a lot." The subject had to be switched. "What's your name?"

"It's Mary."

"Nice to meet you, Mary."

Will extended his left hand outward. Mary clasped her French manicure around his palm and looked down at it.

"Uhm, George," she said, still shaking, "is that a wedding ring you've got on?"

Will nervously shot a glance down at the shiny silver band wrapped around his finger. He almost had to laugh.

"Oh... um... well...," was all he could say at first.

"Boy, George, you really suck at this," Mary smirked.

"Ha," Will chuckled oafishly. "I guess I do."

"That's okay. You can learn. I always keep mine in my purse when I go out."

Will's eyebrows rose.

"Oh, are you saying you're married too?" he asked.

"You catch on quick, don't cha?"

"I try."

13

"Is that a problem for you?"

"Oh, no." Will looked right into her light green eyes. "At least now we already have something in common."

A tiny, wet burst of mirth escaped her mouth, lightly spraying Will's face.

"You're funny, George," she grinned. "I like funny."

"Thank you," Will replied, delicately wiping his forehead.

The bartender arrived and set down a chilled, opened bottle of Miller Lite. Will swiftly snatched up the frosty flask.

"I'm really thirsty," he said and lifted up his bottle. "To you, Mary."

Mary clinked her Cosmo into the Miller logo.

"To us," she corrected.

Will quickly upended his bottle and dropped a hearty deluge of the amber ale down his throat. His chug continued for a good ten seconds. Once through, he returned the bottle to the bar three-quarters empty.

"Impressive," Mary marveled. "Is that the *only* thing you're good at?"

"Well, what else did you have in mind?" Will asked.

She leaned in real close to his face.

"Why don't we get out of here and find out?"

As he breathed in the sweet vodka odor on her breath, Will fell completely under her spell.

"Yes," he firmly nodded.

"Then why don't you finish up your drink and follow me," she said, placing a ten-dollar bill on the bar.

Will silently picked up his bottle and downed the final fourth of brew.

"Good boy," Mary said and hopped off her bar stool. "Shall we?"

"We shall," Will answered.

Like an eager puppy, he trailed her black skirt through the bar and out the exit. He trailed her down a sidewalk, as he followed her for a couple of blocks. He let her lead him into the lobby of a Holiday Inn Hotel. Not much was said during the trek, though more than a few flirtatious looks were exchanged.

"Hello, how can I help you?" asked the concierge at the front desk.

"Hi, we'd like a room, please," Mary said.

"Sure, and how will you be paying for it?"

"Credit card," Will apprehensively butted in.

He slammed a small, thin piece of rectangular plastic on the desk face-down.

"We'll be paying with credit card," he reiterated.

"Thank you," the concierge replied, taking the card. "And how many nights will you be staying?"

Will looked over at Mary.

"Well, what do you think, honey?" he asked.

"I don't know," she answered. "How long you gonna be?"

"I'm not sure. I can be pretty long, though."

The concierge seemed to be growing a tad impatient with their innuendo-infused banter.

"Well, why don't we start with one night," Will finally decided, "and if we need anything further, we'll just add 'em on."

"One night it is," the concierge declared and began checking them in.

In no time, Will was handed back his credit card along with another, similar-shaped plastic card. The concierge prepared to give his opening spiel.

"Checkout time is…"

"Thank you, but that's all for now," Mary interrupted, snatching up the plastic key card. "We'll sort through those minor details later. Other than that, are we checked in?"

He nodded.

"Then that will be all, sir."

Mary started stepping away from the front desk and made sure to pass Will on her way. He merely looked at the concierge, shrugged his shoulders, and got back to following the black miniskirt. Their room was on the seventh floor, which meant a trip down a hall to the elevators. Once they arrived, one was already waiting on the ground level with its doors open. Will let Mary walk inside first before slipping in right behind her. He went to push the button marked '7' and accidentally brushed lightly up against her backside. She turned her head back to him as the doors closed shut and grinned,

"A little anxious, aren't we?"

"Maybe," Will replied.

"Well, then maybe we can get a little something started right now."

She proceeded to press her round, mini-skirted ass softly into his crotch. Her hips gently gyrated into a slow, circular grind. Will was instantly aroused. Unashamed, he placed his hand on her outer right thigh and began slowly sliding his palm up to her stomach. He placed his lips right behind her ear.

"This was a great idea," he whispered.

"Shut up," Mary replied and began grinding harder.

15

Will simply shut his mouth and his eyes, and enjoyed the ride.

The elevator let out a little 'ding' upon reaching the seventh floor. As soon as the doors parted, Mary pulled her butt away and entered the hall. Will stepped awkwardly after her. Their room, #708, was close by.

"You ready to go, George?" Mary asked as she slipped her keycard in the slot above the door's handle.

"Yes!" Will excitedly quipped. "Just open the door!"

The moment the keycard was accepted, Mary jerked down on the handle and pushed. She grabbed a fistful of Will's shirt and yanked him inside the room. The door was slammed shut. The key was tossed to the floor. Mary shoved Will up against the door, dug two hands into his shirt and ripped it open. Buttons flew everywhere.

"Sorry about that," Mary apologized sarcastically.

"That's okay," Will answered. "I hate this shirt."

"Good."

A rush of ripping ensued as Will's torn top swiftly found its way to the floor. Mary pressed her lips into his bare neck and proceeded to suck away. Will blissfully rolled his eyes up to the ceiling as she ever so slightly worked her way up towards his face. He wrapped his hands around her waist and pulled her body close to his chest. After delivering a wet, full-lipped kiss to his cheek, she pulled partially away from him. Looking him straight in the eye, she began unbuttoning her blouse. Will gently brought up his hands.

"May I?" he asked.

"If you want," she answered.

"Don't worry. I don't rip."

Will started where Mary left off, slipping each pearly button through each little striped slot. It did not take long for him to notice her pink, lacy bra underneath. Her breasts weren't huge, but they were real and plump; pushed up to create two nice, curvy bulges.

With the last button undone, Will slid the flimsy top off the back of Mary's shoulders. Once her arms were completely bare, she wrapped them around his neck and pulled him in close. Will braced for impact as his chest pressed into the soft fleshy cushions. Her lips instantly found his and latched on. Will leisurely gave in to the supple sucking motions at his mouth and became further stimulated upon feeling Mary's tongue glide forward. After their tongues were formerly introduced, she pulled back before his face.

"Thanks for the help with the blouse," she smiled.

16

"No problem whatsoever," Will replied and leaned in to direct the sequel to the previous kiss.

Since sequels should never be an exact copy of the original, Will dug his hands deep into her skirted ass and lifted her up off the floor. Mary went along with the move like they were some kind of dirty figure-skating duo and smartly wrapped her legs around his waist. Her high heels fell to the floor.

Deciding that they'd exhausted enough of their energy in the entryway, Will began carrying her into the room. Their lips and hips remained locked. Upon reaching the queen-sized bed, he touched his knees into the foot of the mattress. Mary at once slid off him onto the bedspread. She lowered her hands to his belt and instantly started the undoing process. Will did not resist, but did kick off his shoes.

"Well, you ready?" Mary declared, wide-eyed, referring to the bulge forming around his lower region.

"Yes I am," Will agreed as his pants hit the floor.

"Nice boxers," Mary admired, referring to the freshly unveiled blue plaid shorts.

"They're my lucky pair."

"So you're looking to get lucky?"

"Maybe," he grinned. "Or maybe I just want some luck on both our sides."

"Hmm, lucky me."

Mary reached behind her lower back and snapped open her skirt. She stood up as the fabric around her waist began to loosen as the skirt's zipper was pulled down. Will could barely contain himself as her tanned bellybutton became exposed. The skirt continued its plunge until a matching pink pair of bikini-style panties were revealed.

"God, you're beautiful," Will exhaled.

Mary placed her palm on his chest and slid it all the way back behind his neck.

"You're not so bad yourself," she said and pulled him in for another tongue-filled kiss.

Her tug was so forceful, that Will quickly found himself falling forward like a recently chopped Redwood. Mary clung on throughout the descent and soon had her man horizontally on top. Like an acrobat, she swung her legs out and upward, and enveloped them back around his waist. With a staunch swing of her shoulders, she sent his body rolling and soon found herself the one on top.

"Whoa!" Will exclaimed. "Nice move."

"Really?" Mary grinned. "Well, what do you think about this…"

Her knees dropped downward to his feet as she grabbed hold of his blue plaid boxers. She exerted one smooth tug and down they came. Her eyes stayed fixated for just a moment.

"Oh, you *are* ready," she said and dropped the boxers to the floor next to his pants.

"Well, would you look at that?" Will pretended to be shocked.

"Funny, sexy, and modest," Mary said, placing her fingertips along the sparse elastic waist of her panties. "How did I get so lucky?"

The pink briefs were quickly whisked down her legs as she slithered back onto his lap. Will sat up and met her with an adoring kiss between her still covered breasts. Mary immediately stretched her fingers behind her back and unhooked the pink strap. Will helped her out of the bra and cast it to the floor with the rest of their clothes. The slightly lighter skin tone around the area of her breasts where the bra used to be accentuated their bareness even more. Will's horniness reached an all-time high. Sensing his fully stoked libido, Mary thrust her grinding thighs into motion. Will happily held onto her hips as the friction gave him goose bumps. They both couldn't keep from exuding long exhales of ecstatic pleasure.

"Oh my God, I'm so wet right now," Mary panted softly. "You know what to do."

"I… know… what… to do," Will replied between grinds.

He slid his feet off the edge of the mattress and grabbed onto her glistening ass. In one slick motion, he swooped up off the bed with Mary in tow. After a fast turnaround, her backside was promptly returned to the mattress.

"Here you go," Mary said from her laid-out position, spreading her legs up in the air.

"Oh yeah," Will concurred and looked downward from where he stood.

After locating her 'special spot', he took his manhood by the reigns and directed it inside. His already-enthralled member eagerly accepted its new surroundings, basking in warm, wet elation on all sides. Knees bent, he kept his thrusts constant and fast, which was how Mary apparently seemed to like it.

"Don't… slip out," she uttered, almost out of breath.

"Not a chance," Will assured, continuing his motion.

Since he was already in an ideal flow of undulation, it did not take long before something was going to *come about*.

"I think I'm gonna go," Will stated. "Oh, yes, I really am."

"Stay inside me," Mary begged. "Don't slip out."

"Okay." Will maintained his quick movements. "Okay… Okay… O… OOOOOHHHHH!"

Mary tightened her legs around his jerking body and made sure he was in close.

"Go, baby, go," she cheered him on.

After one final, tense jerk, Will collapsed onto her chest. He let out a few sporadic pants as she gave his back a little pat. He turned his face to hers and gave a small nod.

"Okay, Kerri, let's do it," he said, placing his knees on the bed.

"Just be careful, Will," she answered, squeezing her legs around his waist even harder.

Still connected down below, Will pushed his body upward, elevating her hips in the process. He was now situated in a very awkward squatting stance.

"Is this high enough?" he asked.

"Yeah," she replied, and stuck her arms beneath her lower back for extra hoisting support. "Just go grab two pillows after you get out."

"Okay, I'm doing it. Stay elevated."

Will gently lifted his butt to the ceiling and felt his lower appendage slip sensitively out of her void. He rushed toward the opposite end of the bed and snatched two white pillows out from under the spread.

"Just hold on, Ker, I'm almost there," he said, squeezing his hands under her hips.

With a hasty exhale, Will lifted her lower end high up again and propped it with his chest. Hands free, he took hold of the pillows and stacked them directly underneath her ass.

"All set," he smiled. "You're going down."

Will lowered her onto the pillow pile so that her hips were still elevated. Once the deed was done, he lied back on the bed beside her.

"Well, Ker, that was certainly different," he said. "Awesome, but different."

"The doctor did say to try doing it a *different* way," Kerri added.

"Role-playing rules! I was so caught up in it! And you—that performance was outstanding. I never knew you could be such a dirty, little girl."

"Anything to support our cause," Kerri said, adjusting her butt's height.

"Don't let any of it come out yet," Will cautioned quickly.

"Don't worry. Your little swimmers aren't going anywhere."

"I'm not worried. And I wasn't worried when we were doing it. I was so into the role-playing that I completely forgot about trying to conceive. How about you?"

"Actually, I was pretty good too. My mind was pretty clear. All I was concentrating on was making you cheat on your wife."

"Speaking of which." He lightly touched her hand. "You even took off your wedding *and* engagement ring. You didn't lose them, did you?"

"No, they're both in my purse," Kerri answered. "Like I told you."

"Very good. If you ever wanted to give up teaching, I bet you'd be a fantastic actress."

"You weren't so bad yourself, *George*. What made you pick that name anyway?"

"Probably because of the same reason you picked yours, *Mary*."

Kerri didn't even have to think.

"It's A Wonderful Life?" she guessed.

"*Buffalo gals, won't you come out tonight? Come out tonight? Come out tonight,*" Will sang, badly. "*Buffalo gals, won't you come out tonight and we'll dance by the light of the moon!*"

"Stop!" Kerri laughed.

"Okay, okay! Just don't laugh too hard. Remember that time I slipped on the KY after we'd just done it? You laughed so hard that my swimmers shot right out of you and onto my back. Gross!"

"Yeah, well, you should have elevated me right away. You didn't give your swimmers any advantage."

"I guess so. But that was way back in the beginning. I'm a lot smarter now. I know what it takes to get my swimmers to reach your egg."

"Yes, but I just wish I didn't have so much trouble getting it to implant."

"Ker, you heard the doctor. He said our biggest problem is thinking and worrying about it too much. We needed to just relax and fuck. And *that* is why we are where we are right this second."

He folded his fingers in between hers and held on tight.

"Don't worry, Kerri," he said warmly. "We're going to be all right. We're going to make it happen. You'll see. I promise you."

Kerri turned her face to him. Her light green eyes were shiny and moist.

"I hope so," she whispered. "Thanks for staying so motivated. You know it's hard for me sometimes."

"Yes I do, but we're not going to focus on the bad. We're focusing on the positive. And I refuse to stop fucking you until you have a child in your belly… and then I'll probably still continue to fuck you after that. You're pretty hot, you know."

Kerri emitted a bubbly burst of laughter and had to cover her mouth.

"God, I love your laugh," Will smiled. "I love you, too. Now I know it's totally killing my whole 'tough guy' image by saying mushy stuff like that, but I don't give a shit. Maybe that's why I know I'm ready to be a dad."

Kerri stretched out her neck slightly and gave him a soft kiss on the lips.

"I'm nothing without you," she replied delicately.

"Me too," Will confidently nodded.

"And Will?"

"Yeah, Ker?"

Her lips crept up beside his ear and said, "I hope we made a baby."

"I hope so, too."

Chapter 2

The noise caused Will to slowly start stirring. His mind gradually began to realize that his eyes were in motion. Waking up was one of his least favorite things to do. As his body began checking in for 'rousing duty' beneath the sheets, his brain wondered why the clock-radio wasn't playing. Every night before going to bed, Will always remembered to turn his alarm, which was set to 98.1, his favorite radio station, on. He never forgot to do this. The regimen was like... clockwork. Yet here he was now, awake with no music playing.

What woke me up? he wondered.

An extremely loud, mucus-filled sob immediately gave him his answer.

Kerri, his mind instantly clicked.

As if hit with a huge, adrenaline-loaded needle directly in the heart, Will threw back the sheets and pounced off the bed. The door to their bedroom was open a crack, causing the light from the hallway to peek through. Will burst through into the brightness on the second floor.

"Kerri!" he called out.

Another loud sob rang out. Will's attention was directed to the closed bathroom door. He rushed up beside it and gave a gentle knock.

"Honey," he said. "Are you okay?"

He had to wait through a procession of sniffles before obtaining an answer.

"No," was all she said.

"Can I please come in then?"

More sniffling followed.

"Okay," she ruefully replied.

Will rapidly reached out for the doorknob, and cautiously twisted it open. The bathroom gradually came into view, revealing a small, torn-up, purple box and some mangled towels along the tiled floor. Seated amidst the mess, with her arm dangling along the edge of the bathtub was Kerri. A small, skinny white stick was in her visible hand. Will knew exactly what was going on.

"Oh Ker, I'm so sorry," he said, quickly leaning down beside her.

"I'm not pregnant," Kerri sorrowfully lamented, gazing down at the tiles.

"I'm so sorry. That fucking sucks."

He placed his hand on her shoulder and rubbed it.

"I really thought it was going to work this time," she sobbed, wiping her nose with the back of her hand. "I really thought it was going to work. My period was due to come yesterday and when I didn't feel it this morning I, I just had to see if it had worked. But it didn't."

"I know, I know." Will moved his hand down to her back and continued to rub. "But it was only the first time we tried it this new way. You know that the percentage of it working is already low to begin with. The chances of us getting it right on the first try were..."

"I know, Will," she answered sternly. "But no matter how you look at it, this is *not* our first try. I don't care if we did something a little different this time. It's still the same thing. It's still been over three years and nothing! I can't take this anymore! It's making me crazy!"

A fresh set of tears quickly welled up in her eyes and wasted no time streaming down her cheeks. She angrily chucked the white stick onto the floor and covered her soaking face. Will glanced down at the stick, which landed face up displaying a lone pink line. Sometimes it was a pink line, sometimes it was a minus sign, depending on the test. Regardless, he was more than qualified to understand precisely what each abysmal symbol represented.

"I know how hard this is for you, Ker," he attempted to soothe.

"You couldn't possibly know, Will," she snapped back. "You haven't wanted it for as long as I have. It's not *your* body that's causing the problem! It's mine!"

"Come on, Ker. We don't know that for sure."

"Don't say that! We do know for sure! Your sperm was already checked out! It's fine! There's something wrong with my eggs, I know it!"

"Ker, the doctor never said that. He didn't find anything specifically wrong with you. I think sometimes for some people, it takes a little while longer to happen."

"But I *can't* wait any longer! I fucking hate this! It's not fair! And I hate my doctor, too. He's so unsympathetic. Just because he deals with infertility on a regular basis doesn't give him the right to come off as so cold and uncaring. God, I hate him so much! The one person that's supposed to be helping us!"

She buried her head in her hands as her speech turned back to incoherent sobs. Will had experienced this behavior too many times and was afraid he was beginning to get used to it.

"Hey, Kerri," he hurriedly said. "Look at me right now."

23

"I don't want to," she stubbornly resisted.

This created a touchy instance for Will; he had to remain firm enough to get her attention off of feeling sad, but he also had to exude an extreme sensitivity to keep from pushing her over the edge. And although he'd experienced her behavior like this many a time, he'd yet to master how to handle it.

"Kerri," he began gently, "I love you more than anything else in the world. And I know you love me just as much."

After a fast wipe over her face, Kerri looked up at him. The caring husband concept worked!

"I do love you that much," she said, eyes still wet. "It's just…"

"Whoa," Will held up a hand. "I know there's probably something negative you could add on to that statement, but if you don't mind, I'd really like to cut it off beforehand."

He braced himself for an estrogen-induced onslaught, but Kerri remained quiet and just looked off into the bathtub.

"I wish I didn't have to go to school today," she said.

Will's senses immediately perked up. With Kerri's last statement, he now had the power to move on to a different subject. And *any* subject other than infertility was worth pursuing.

"Well, why don't you stay home then?" he suggested. "Don't you have, like, a hundred personal days saved up or something?"

"I can't call out," she frowned. "There's testing today and I have to be there."

"Well, then maybe you should go in today." Will refused to give up on the new subject. "Besides, you'll get to hang with all your work buddies and talk about shopping or fashion or whatever you girls are into now."

Kerri gave a small sniff that wasn't accompanied by a sob. In fact, as Will peered closer he was able to notice that the corners of her mouth had nudged ever so slightly north. His intervention was working.

"Hey," he said, confidently rubbing her back, "you okay now, my little Kerri-Berry?"

She looked up to him, her partial smile still intact.

"No," she replied, "but I will be… thanks, as always, to you."

"You sure are lucky to have me," Will said without an ounce of seriousness.

The corners of her mouth inched up a little more as she daintily touched her head to his. Will wrapped his arms around her, invoking a top of the shoulders bear hug. Kerri weakly, but deliberately, squeezed back.

"I am lucky," she said to his chest. "Way more than you can possibly imagine."

"Good, Ker," Will smiled. "I feel the same way, believe me. Now, do you feel well enough to start getting ready? Or do you want to maybe go back to bed and chill for a little bit. It's all good. I'll do whatever you want."

"Thanks, babe. It's okay, we don't have to go back to bed. I know you have to get ready for work too."

"Well, all right then. And you know what? Since we're both already awake and simultaneously in the bathroom, I think we should hop in the shower together. It would really save us a lot of time. Plus, I would get to see your boobs. What do you think?"

Her lips let out a tiny giggle, which confirmed that Will's calm-Kerri-down treatment was complete.

Chapter 3

Unexplained Infertility. Will typed the words into the Google search bar on his computer screen. He hit 'enter' and soon found himself staring at a long list of online articles. He sighed and clicked on the very first one titled, 'Unexplained Infertility Tests Treatment'. It was still fairly early, and not many people were moving about the office area yet. Will was the first to arrive at his large, three-person cubicle. As he started to read the article, footsteps could be heard drawing nearer.

"What up, Will?" greeted a young man in a short-sleeved button down shirt with short, slicked-down, black hair.

"Hey, Fred," Will replied, looking up from his computer.

"Did you have a kick-ass weekend?" Fred asked as he entered the three-person cubicle, heading toward his desk in the far right corner diagonal to Will's.

"Eh, it was all right, I guess."

"Hey, dude, you sound a little down. Everything okay? Something bothering you?"

"Just the usual."

"Oh." Fred looked down for a second. "The Mrs. isn't..."

"Nope," Will answered before Fred even finished. "She took a test this morning."

"Sorry about that, man. I mean, that little thing you guys did at the hotel; that sounded like it would have worked. I mean, it turned me on just hearing about it."

Will stared at him with an unsatisfying smirk.

"Well, it wasn't meant for *your* pleasure, but thanks anyway. And it was stupid of me to think that doing that would automatically ensure us a baby."

"Stupid or not," Fred said, taking his seat, "you still had a good time. And that should count for at least something."

"Maybe, I guess. But you know what, Fred-o? It's kind of ironic. Like, way back when Kerri first went off the pill, I was kind of hesitant about having kids."

"Like how so?"

"You know, like how big a responsibility it is; how your social life is basically over and you lose a shitload of sleep."

"Yeah, that sounds pretty crappy."

"Not to me," Will said seriously. "Not anymore. It's now been over three years and I've definitely changed over that time. And it's not just because I know how bad Kerri wants it and I need to see her happy. It's more than that."

"Can you tell me? Maybe it'll sway my opinion, too."

"I just started thinking about what it'd be like to have a little version of me or Kerri resting in my arms—a product made solely of me and her. Something alive and pure. There's just something about that that seems so very cool. That's how I know I'm ready."

Fred paused and placed his pointer and thumb to his chin.

"You know, Will, that is a very profound, well-thought-out response," he finally said "You're definitely ready to have kids. And I still definitely want absolutely nothing to do with it."

"Well, you're certainly entitled to your opinion."

Before Fred could respond, another set of footsteps featuring the distinct clicking of high heels crept closer to their cube. Fred closed his mouth and looked at Will wide-eyed. Will simply shook his head. A tall, curvaceous brunette came strolling into their cubicle.

"Good morning, boys," she pleasantly greeted.

Her voice was simultaneously lofty and sultry.

"Morning, Loni," Will replied.

"Good morning, Loni," Fred added.

"So what's up?" she asked upon taking a seat at her desk in the back left corner between them both.

"Come on, Lon," Fred quickly reacted. "You know it really doesn't matter what a couple of schmo's like us did over *our* weekend. What everyone, especially those in this cube, truly needs to know about is how *your* weekend was spent."

Will slapped his brow and couldn't help shaking his head a second time. Loni simply squinted her eyes at Fred before answering coyly,

"You're not just saying that because you want to hear about naked girls and horny guys?"

"Oh, Loni, please," Fred quipped. "What kind of gentleman do you take me for? That wasn't my... oh... oh shit, Lon, you got me. What do you expect? I'm a dude, girlfriend! Plus, how many girls do you think I know that are graphic designers by day and strippers by night and on the weekends? It ain't many!"

"Loni, I know I say this to you all the time," Will jumped in, "but I'm sorry about him. He has a very limited social life."

"Hey!" Fred grinned.

"It's okay, Will," Loni calmly assured. "Besides, I kind of enjoy recounting my little nighttime stories to him. He's like some over-sexed little child. It's cute."

"See, Will!" Fred exclaimed. "She thinks I'm cute. Awesome! Now stop talking and let her continue!" He shifted his sights to Loni. "Okay, my dear, you may get back to your tales of debauchery. And please, can you make 'em extra dirty? Our boy, Will, has had a rough morning."

Loni unbuttoned her blazer, allowing her bulbous, d-cup breasts to breathe a bit.

"Well, Saturday night we had a big bachelor party come in," she began. "They were all stock brokers and money was no object."

"Bachelor party, lots of money, anything goes," Fred panted. "Great start. Go on."

"So I knew I had to get myself situated with them right from the start of the night. I walked over to their table, introduced myself and was all like, 'You gonna show Mr. Bachelor over here a good time?' And they're all like, 'Hell yeah!' So I go, 'Look for me a little later. I'll work him real nice.' Then I flashed them one of my boobs and gave it a little lick. From there those dumbasses were all mine."

"Oh my God!" Fred shouted. "That is so hot! What did you have on?"

"Just red boy shorts and a tight, white tank top. I was doing my sexy workout routine that night."

"Sweet! So did they look for you later?"

"Of course. I had them practically eating out of my hand. Right after my stage dance, one of them came up to me. He said I was perfect and that they were all set for a show."

"Show? What kind of show?" Fred was giving her his undivided attention.

"Actually, it was more than just one show. It was several."

"Tell me about your shows! And don't leave out a single detail."

Loni had no trouble resuming her story. Clearly, she was rather fond of being in the spotlight.

"Well, first of all," she started, "I walked up to the bachelor and started dancing real slow right in from of him. I could tell right away that he didn't go to strip clubs on a regular basis. He was all shy and sitting way back in his chair. Which was perfect for me 'cause I knew he wasn't going to try and grab my ass or anything."

"No ass-grabbing at the nudie bar," Fred commented. "Unless you want to get thrown out on your own ass. You got that, Will?"

"Yeah, thanks for letting me know that, Fred," Will replied with outright feigned interest. "You sure are smart."

"Why am I still talking to you? Loni, get back to the slow dancing. Were you shaking your booty up in his face?"

"Honey, I had everything up in his face. The dance lasted for, like, 25 minutes. All the bachelor's friends kept tipping me to get me to stay longer. So then I suggested to them that I take him upstairs to our special "V.I.P." room. They couldn't have pushed him off his chair fast enough. So I pull two of them aside and discuss the financial aspect of our future endeavor."

"See, Will, it's a business," Fred said. "It's all business. She never takes her eyes off the green. She bribes 'em with her boobs!"

"Hell yes!" Loni smiled. "And it worked! First I closed the deal on myself taking him up to the V.I.P. room and then I tell them for a little something extra, I'll take up two more girls with me."

Fred's mouth dropped open. Before any drool could escape, he found his voice.

"You... and two others?"

Loni merely nodded. Fred immediately began bobbing his head, silently counting.

"One, tw.... that's six boobs total!" he shouted. "Lucky bastard! What happened next?"

"Sorry, Freddy." Loni crossed her arms. "But what happens in the V.I.P. room, stays in the V.I.P. room."

"Damn it! See, Will, *that's* why we have to go see Loni dance. She never reveals the good stuff."

"Sorry, Fred-o," Will said. "But you already know I'm not one for strip clubs anymore. I'm a married man, someday I'm going to be a Daddy, it's just not right for me anymore. No offense to you, Loni, of course."

"I understand, Will," Loni grinned. "But both you boys know, you always have an open invite on my guest list."

"Damn it, Will!" Fred yelled. "Because of you, I can't friggin' go! Why are you doing this to me?"

"Jesus, Fred," Will barked back. "Why don't you just go yourself? Why do I have go with you?"

"Because, Will, I don't want to be that loser guy who has to go to a strip club by himself. That's not cool, that's just creepy."

"Don't you have any other friends you could go with?"

"Okay, Will, just forget it. I mean, I figured since you and me *both* knew Loni, then we could go together and show her our support. But I can see you're clearly against offering any kind of loyalty toward our resident graphic designer/stripper friend. Just forget it, Will! FORGET IT!"

All at once, Will burst out in a huge fit of laughter at his friend's over-the-top antics. Loni couldn't help joining in as well. Fred tried his best to keep composed, but kept releasing little giggle quivers at the sides of his mouth.

"Okay, Will, I know you've had a stressful morning," he finally said. "Maybe that's why you're not seeing clearly. I'm through talking."

He had to turn his face back to his computer in order to hide any further chuckle outbursts. Loni looked over at Will.

"Is he serious?" she asked. "Did you have a bad morning?"

Will was silent for a moment and glanced downward.

"Kerri took a test this morning," Fred called out, his back still turned. "It came up negative."

"Oh my God, Will," Loni said. "I'm so sorry to hear that. And you were so confident that it would work this time."

"Thanks, Loni," Will responded. "But don't worry about it. Kerri and I just have to regroup and try again. That's all we can do."

"What about doctors? Have you already been to a bunch?"

"Well, not a whole bunch. I mean, there's Kerri's gyno and her regular doctor. We tried going to a fertility specialist last year, but it was really expensive and our insurance only covered so much. Plus, it didn't work. We've even used up all our in vitro tries. Insurance will only cover it three times. Now if we wanted to try again, it'd cost like $10,000 and there's no way we could afford that. Nothing fucking works."

"But there's got to be other doctors. Can't you try someone else?"

"I just don't know. Kerri was so hopeful with the last specialist, and when it didn't work out she nearly had a nervous breakdown. I just think she's lost faith in doctors helping her. And I don't feel right forcing her to do anything."

"Well, my plastic surgeon, Dr. Ross," she began, pointing to her boobs, "he knows some of the best doctors in the business. Would you mind if I asked him if he knew any that could help Kerri?"

"Sure, why not. We've basically exhausted every other possible option. Thanks, Loni."

"Will, please. It's the least I can do. Just as long as Kerri wouldn't think I'd be butting in or anything. I know she doesn't exactly approve of my second job."

"Don't even worry about that. That's just how she was raised. She has no bad feelings towards you in any way."

"Yeah, she just hates the fact that you're a stripper," Fred added from his about-faced position.

Will rolled his eyes. Loni didn't seem annoyed.

"Hey, guys," Fred continued. "I know it's only 9:15 a.m., but I was just thinking... drinks after work at Uncle Mike's? I think we could really use it."

Loni and Will both looked at him simultaneously. His back remained turned.

"Well, I'm not working tonight," Loni affirmed. "So, although it's a little odd for a Monday, I guess I'm in."

"Wonderful," Fred declared. "And you, Will?"

"That actually does sound like a good idea," Will answered. "Just let me check in with the Mrs. to make sure it's okay."

"Okay, Will, you do that." Fred then turned his head back to him and smiled. "Maybe I'd better call my mother to get her permission for me to go, too."

Chapter 4

Kerri made a few intermittent squeaks as she ran her fresh piece of chalk across the long blackboard. The dates 'April 12, 1861' and 'April 9, 1865' were written out in white.

"Those are your starting and ending dates of the Civil War," she said, turning around to the class. "Both happened in April, so you should have no trouble remembering that."

"Mrs. Haddon," a male student with large ears that stuck out too far raised his hand.

"Yes, Trent," Kerri called on him

"Where did that guy surrender to General Lee again?"

"It was at Appomattox."

"Yeah, could you spell that out for me on the board? I want to get it right in my notes."

A small curdle of laughter rose up from the class as Kerri turned back to the board. While spelling out the word in white, her ears detected a brief spurting sound that resembled a cough only with words. She halted her hand before completing the letter 'M'. The noise repeated itself.

"*Nice ass...*"

Kerri heard it a tad clearer the second time and spun around from the board.

"Excuse me?" She sternly directed her stare toward Trent.

"What?" Trent cockily shrugged his shoulders.

Another bit of laughter echoed out of the class.

"Out!" Kerri immediately pointed her finger toward the door. "Right now!"

"What are you talking about?" The student feebly resisted. "Come on."

"Trent, j-just go to the office!" She had to briefly close her eyes to remain composed. "Right now!"

Trent shrugged his shoulders a second time, and stood up behind his desk. The class turned silent as he slowly walked up from his row. He looked Kerri in the eyes as he passed by her.

"I love it when you punish me," he softly whispered for only her to hear.

Kerri merely turned her head away in disgust. She didn't look back to the class until the door hit him in the ass. She was embarrassed and could feel the blood rushing to her face.

"No more outbursts," she tersely addressed the class.

To Kerri's good fortune, the bell rang shortly thereafter. She retreated quickly over to her desk as the students began filing out of the classroom. Once the room was completely emptied, she sat down and placed her hand on her forehead.

"I should've stayed home," she quietly exhaled.

A knock at her door gave her a momentary startle. She looked up fast to see a young, petite woman with dark blonde hair standing in the open doorway.

"Oh, hi, Lynn," Kerri said.

"Did I scare you, Kerri?" Lynn asked.

"No, no. I... I guess I was just a little bit on edge."

She wiped under her nose and gave a small sniff.

"Honey, did something happen?" Lynn questioned.

Kerri paused with a deep breath before answering, "Oh, nothing worse than the usual."

"Was it that little punk again? Trent with the Alfred E. Newman ears?"

"Yes." Kerri glanced down at her desk. "He's really starting to get on my nerves."

"More leering? Did he say something?"

"They're just little comments here and there. I'm probably making too big a deal out of it. It's been a rough morning."

"Kerri, if it's making you feel uncomfortable, then you shouldn't have to put up with it. Why don't you just tell Carol."

"I can't, Lynn. I've only been here for two years. I know how things work in this district. If I go public blaming some kid for harassment, then the school board makes this whole big issue about it, then the parents start talking and... well, maybe they think I brought it about somehow. You've heard those stories in the news about the older female teachers seducing their students. I, I just wouldn't want to ever be thought of that way. Plus, next year is my tenure year. I don't want to do anything that would cause them to question whether I'd be a solid employee or not."

"What could you possibly mean by that?"

"You know, they may start thinking, 'Oh, she's a little quick to judge. She's too fragile to teach high school history.' I know some districts think that way."

"Kerri, I think you worry too much. I also believe you think about things way too much."

"Ugh." Kerri ran her palms up over her forehead and on through her light blonde hair. "Why did I come to work today?"

"Oh, honey, don't be upset," Lynn frowned. "Hey, why don't you get Will to come here one day and kick Trent's ass?"

"That's not too bad an idea," Kerri half-smiled. "But Will would never do that. He really hates violence."

"Even if someone is bothering you like that?"

"Well, he'd probably find some other way to deal with it. Besides, I don't want to upset him with that. Like I said, nothing really bad has come of it."

"Yeah, Kerri." Lynn placed a hand on her shoulder. "But what if something does?"

"I, I just can't think of that right now. There are worse things."

The cell phone in Kerri's purse let out a generic ring before Lynn got a chance to respond. Kerri reached into her bag and checked the number flashing on its small screen.

"It's Will," she said, flipping up the phone. "Just give me a sec... Hello?"

"Hey, Ker, it's me," Will said on the other end.

"Hi, Will. What's up?"

"Oh, just checking in with you, I guess. How's the school day going?"

"It's okay," Kerri answered, biting her lower lip. "I've got a free period now and Lynn's here. Everything okay at work?"

"Oh, yeah, yeah, everything's fine. I just wanted to see if there was anything important we had to take care of after work."

"Uhm, nothing special. I mean, I've got a faculty meeting at the end of the day, but that's about it."

"Okay, that's cool, um..."

The phone received a bit of jostling on Will's end as Kerri began hearing a different, distanced voice.

"Ask her..." Fred struggled to whisper near the receiver, "...ask her about the happy hour."

"All right, Fred." Will finally wrestled back the phone. "Just chill out for a sec, and then I'll ask, okay?"

"I'll be good," was Fred's fast reply.

"Ker, you still there?" Will returned to the call.

"Yeah, I'm here," Kerri said.

"Well, since you got that meeting after work, would you mind if I went to happy hour with the work peeps for a little bit?"

"Oh, sure, that's fine. I was going to be a little late getting home anyway."

"Okay, cool. I won't be out too long."

"All right."

A long pause ensued over the telephone connection.

"There's nothing else you need to tell me?" Will finally said.

"Uh... no, that's it," Kerri replied.

"Okay, then I'll see you when I get home."

"All right, see you then. I love you."

"I love you, too."

Kerri pulled the phone away from her ear and snapped it shut. She placed it back inside her purse and slowly looked back up to Lynn who had her arms crossed.

"If something happens again," Lynn said, "I think you should at least let Will know."

"Okay," Kerri nodded, although she knew Lynn was lying.

Chapter 5

Will lifted up a bottle of Miller Lite alongside Loni's Cosmopolitan and Fred's bottle of Bud.

"What are we drinking to?" Loni asked. "And nobody better say *world peace*."

"Ahem," Fred cleared his throat and began, "To Monday being over, to Loni's exquisite skills at stripping, and to Will's eventual fatherhood."

The drinks were all clinked together and subsequently downed in big gulps.

"Oh, Fred, that was so sweet of you," Loni said after swallowing.

"Well, thanks, Loni," Fred replied. "I guess I'm just a sweet guy... tell your stripper friends... all of them."

"Of course I will."

"I'll drink to that," Fred shouted, hoisting up his bottle a second time.

Loni and Will did the same. All three of them returned their drinks to the shiny, wooden bar at the same time. Uncle Mike's was a fairly low-key bar-&-grill-type establishment with a single section of dining tables encompassing the designated drink-pouring area. However the scene was much louder than usual because 1) It was Monday Night Football and 2) The Giants were playing against their arch rivals, the Eagles. Though kickoff was still a good two hours away, numerous patrons in navy blue had already begun tailgating around the bar ordering wings and beers.

"So tell me, Loni," Fred sparked up some conversation. "If I may ask, how much cash did you make the night of the bachelor party?"

"Jeez, Fred," Will intervened. "That's none of your business."

"What?" Fred threw his palms up in the air. "I'm just curious."

"Do you really want to know, Fred?" Loni asked, picking up her drink.

"I wouldn't have asked if I didn't want to know." Fred grabbed hold of his brew.

"Seven fifty," she said.

"Seven... hundred... and... fifty... dollars?" Fred's jaw almost grazed the floor.

Loni silently raised one eyebrow and gave a little nod. Even Will couldn't help bugging out his eyes in shock.

"No offense, Loni," Fred said, "but I hate you."

"Don't hate the player," Loni laughed. "Hate the boob job!"

"No, Loni, I could never hate that!"

"That's very humble of you, Fred," Will added.

"I just can't believe you made that much money!" Fred marveled. "Do the other girls make that much? Did you have to work extra hard to get it? What do you make on a slow night?"

By now, Fred was delving too deeply into stripper territory for Will to bother paying attention. He truly wasn't a fan of all things regarding pole dancing. As Loni began giving Fred all his answers, Will politely turned his head up toward the TV screens above the bar. In preparation for the Monday Night Game, each station was tuned to a sports channel. The closest to him was broadcasting the beginning of a sports news program featuring an anchorman with slicked-back gray hair, seated behind a desk. The 'news box' hovering just over his shoulder was displaying the logo for the EWC—Extreme Wrestling Coalition. Will's eyes instantly became glued to the set. Although there was a lot of chatter about the bar, he was still able to hear the anchorman reporting the latest story.

'The now-defunct Extreme Wrestling Coalition had always been known for bringing forth the most menacing of characters to its sport. However, on a dark day twenty-five years ago, 'menacing' took on a whole new horrifying meaning.'

Will tightly shut his eyes and clenched his jaw, fully aware of what was going to be said next.

'On this anniversary of the night that spelled the end of the EWC, we look back on the rampaging rage that was Derek Haddonfear.'

Will opened his eyes and somberly placed his fingers over his mouth. The 'news box' switched from the logo to a picture of a face cloaked in a black mask with white stripes outlining the eyes. He grudgingly listened on.

'Determined to become the highest-paid EWC athlete, Haddonfear allegedly took to unorthodox training methods in order to increase his strength.'

The screen cut to an old-fashioned wrestling ring where a black-masked Derek was about to take on an opponent. His uniform consisted solely of a black pair of spandex-style pants and matching boots. His bare upper body revealed a somewhat muscular shape. As he charged into the center of the ring, the anchorman's voice echoed over the action.

'Seen here early on in his career, Haddonfear displayed marginal talent and agility. He wasn't the strongest in the Coalition, but he had potential. Then the transformation began. In a short amount of time, Haddonfear appeared to have put on a huge, almost impossible, amount of mass. It did not take long before the speculation of steroids abuse arose. However, no traces showed up in all of the EWC's weekly substance abuse tests. And Haddonfear continued putting on weight. His strength increased exponentially and it showed.'

The screen cut to a new wrestling match where a now gargantuan Derek was profusely pummeling his current opponent. He was relentless in his devastation. After a final, hard blow directly to his face, the bloodied opponent stumbled down to one knee. The referee in the ring tried to break things up, signaling that the match was over. Derek picked him up with one hand by the collar of his black and white striped shirt and flung him out of the ring.

'It was in the championship bout against Tony Santini, where Haddonfear took his newfound strength one step too far. After beating Santini to a bloody pulp, Haddonfear, refusing to heed to referee Glen Ackles, performed his signature move, The Drop, one last time.'

Derek hoisted Santini's limp frame up over his shoulder and began climbing the corner turnbuckles. Once at the top of the ropes, he hoisted his opponent's upside-down body straight up in the air and faced out into the stunned audience. Once the position was fully secure, Derek began leaning backwards to the ring. Will felt a strong urge to close his eyes, but didn't. He looked on as Derek brought Santini head-first back into the center of the ring. Santini's face hit first. His limbs at once went flailing downward like a collapsed marionette. Derek's landing sent a shock wave of rumbles throughout the ring. Santini's body lay sprawled out beside him.

'Upon impact, Tony Santini's neck snapped in two places. He died instantly.'

Inside the ring, Derek slowly rose up to his feet. The camera zoomed in on his masked face. His eyes, the only visible feature, were on fire.

'Tragically, the remorseless rage that had grown inside Haddonfear refused to stop. He was banned from the EWC and brought up on charges for Santini's death. However, the authorities were unsuccessful in their attempt to apprehend him. Then a true horror story began...'

The image of Derek's face on the screen turned entirely red.

'Completely out of touch with reality, Haddonfear's mind self-destructed, sending him on a violent, murderous rampage. The first victim was his wife, Sally, who had tried to convince Haddonfear to give himself up. From there, he was able to evade police long enough to commit five more murders, the last of which being the most outlandishly twisted.'

The shot of Derek on the screen faded into a picture of another man with dark parted hair and a thick mustache.

'It was Richard McAvoy who Haddonfear blamed his harsh treatment on. Apparently, McAvoy had threatened him and other wrestlers, saying that if they didn't bulk up to the level of professional body-builders, they'd be let go from the Coalition. Haddonfear's revenge was sought in the worst of ways.'

The picture of McAvoy was now replaced by a large building surrounded by police cars. Words flashed across the screen, which read, 'Hampstead Hall Dormitory of N.J. University.'

'Police had tailed him to New Jersey University where he broke into the Hampstead Hall Dormitory. Determining that Haddonfear could be trapped inside, back-up was called in. However, the police were unaware of Haddonfear's real intentions for entering the building. Upon discovering that Richard McAvoy's daughter, Pamela, was currently residing in Hampstead Hall, the small battalion of officers that had already arrived stormed the building... but their efforts were met with extreme brute force and thwarted.'

The screen interspersed clips of police officers being wheeled out of Hampstead Hall on stretchers. Their bodies were already covered up with red-stained white sheets.

'After single-handedly disposing of every officer that got in his way, Haddonfear, wearing his now-infamous wrestler's mask, seized Pamela and carried her to the rooftop of Hampstead Hall. It was there that his sick retribution was realized. Poised at the edge of the roof, Haddonfear lifted Pamela above his head in the manner of his signature move, The Drop. He then leapt backwards off the building. Pamela was killed upon impact. She was only nineteen years old.'

A black and white picture of Pamela took over the screen.

'The true reasons behind the strength Haddonfear attained, which led him down this homicidal path, still remain a clouded mystery. Richard McAvoy declined to comment on any aspect of this story and we will respect his wishes.'

The screen finally returned back to the anchorman behind his desk.

'When we return, the impossible outcome after Haddonfear's plunge off the building as well as the story behind the family he was just starting.'

Will's eyes and ears quickly perked up as the show cut to a commercial. He gave a rushed wave toward the nearby, burly bartender.

"Excuse me, sir," he called. "Could you change this channel over here to something else? I think ESPN2 is doing a retrospect on the whole Giants/Eagles NFC rivalry."

The bartender reached his thick arm up to the TV set and switched the station. Will exhaled a small sigh of relief and picked up his beer bottle.

"Thanks," he said and took a big sip.

"Hey, Will," Fred said, tapping him on the shoulder. "What about adoption?"

"Huh?" Will turned away from the TV. "What'd you say?"

"I was asking you about adoption," Fred repeated.

"Fred and I were just talking about your bad morning," Loni interceded. "And out of all the options you've tried, adopting wasn't one of them. Is that something you and Kerri would ever think about?"

"Oh." Will lowered his head slightly. "Well, we have."

"Not into having someone else's kid?" Fred asked.

"No," Will answered. "It just costs anywhere from 10,000 to 50,000 dollars, which is even more than the in vitro."

"Jesus Christ! That much? That's crazy!"

"It's just a huge freakin' process. You have to go through all this paperwork. If you're adopting from another country, you have to take trips there. And you never get to take your pick. You just have to wait until one is available and sometimes it can take years."

"Wow," Loni said. "That's pretty harsh."

"Too harsh for us," Will asserted. "It looks like for now, we're stuck relying on Mother Nature."

"Hey, Will," Fred called out. "I think I might have an idea!"

"What is it?"

"Well, how does Kerri feel about stripping?"

"Fred!" Loni slapped him upside the head.

"What? You just told us how much money you made in one night. Kerri's a good-looking girl. I bet she would be a great stripper."

"Sorry, Fred," Will said, "but I can assure you that Kerri is not the stripping type. She's way too shy."

"Really? I'm surprised. Sociological statistics usually suggest that women who look as good as your wife does are used to getting attention all their life, and normally don't develop many shy personality traits."

"Thank you very much, Doctor Phil."

Loni spurted out a fleeting laugh.

"What?" Fred looked at her. "Just because I like hearing about boobies doesn't mean I can't pick up a copy of Newsweek every now and then."

"You still continue to astound me, Fred," Will said. "And I do appreciate your sociological assessment. And you may be right, but Kerri doesn't fit into your supplied demographic."

"What do you mean?"

"I just mean that she was a late bloomer," Will explained. "Just like me."

"What are you talking about? What's this late bloomer crap?"

"Easy there, buddy. It just means that Kerri really didn't start looking as hot as she is until, like, her junior year in college. So she's still not fully used to it, hence she wouldn't be able to take the high-attention factor associated with the job of a stripper. Plus, I would never force her to resort to that."

"Oh, all right, all right." Fred took another sip of his Bud. He placed his hand to his chin, evoking a ponderous stare. "Hey, Will, I've got it. *You* could strip!"

Will glared at him irately and crossed his arms. He looked over to Loni for some endorsement of maturity. However, her returning gaze did not seem to see it his way.

"Well," she reasoned, "I *could* talk to my friend over at The Studly Package."

Will hung his head and gave it a little shake. Fred and Loni could only silently wait for his reply. After waiting almost a full minute, he picked up his noggin.

"Okay, Loni, do it," he answered, laying on the sarcasm thicker than a double-stuffed Oreo. "And while you're at it, call Dr. Ross and ask him about possibly performing a penis enlargement. I'm looking to add on a couple of extra inches down below."

Chapter 6

"I'm ovulating," was all Will needed to hear upon arriving home from work on a random Wednesday night.

Dinner was put on hold. Kerri hurriedly led Will up to their bedroom. All role-playing antics were set aside in favor of a basic 'married-couple' approach. Considering the negative results that sprung from the last hotel tryst, Kerri wasn't too keen on trying it all over again.

She waited patiently beneath the covers of their queen-sized bed as Will quickly peeled off his work clothes. Once he got down to his white socks and boxers, he headed towards his already fully nude wife.

"You left on your boxers," Kerri stated as he jumped under the sheets.

"I know," Will answered. "I figured I'd just leave them on and let you take them off to, you know, help with the mood."

"There's no time for mood."

Kerri's hands at once zipped below the sheets and latched onto Will shorts. With a swift yank, she brought them down around his ankles. Before Will could kick them off his feet, her naked body was already on top of him.

"Are you ready?" she asked.

"I guess so," Will had to answer.

Kerri proceeded to kiss his neck and grind her lower half against his. Understanding that time was of the essence, Will made sure all his bodily functions were set to go. He grabbed her ass with both hands and began sucking on her jugular. She abruptly pulled back.

"Don't give me a hickey," she said.

"What?" Will questioned. "Why?"

"I just can't be seen at school with a big hickey on my neck. It's not proper for a teacher."

"Okay, okay. No hickeys. Got it."

Kerri pressed her body back against him as Will rolled his eyes slightly. He opted to focus all his efforts on her bouncing ass by pressing it firmly into his lower body. They exchanged a few lip-to-lip, non-French kisses— no time for tongue. Will moved his right hand up before one of Kerri's breasts and softly started massaging. He pinpointed his motions closer and closer to the center, knowing that her nipple was a hot button for fast pleasure. While lightly pinching the areola area, he listened closely for the soft moaning that almost always accompanied the act.

After a short while, as predicted, Kerri's mouth opened up and exhaled a rather arousing overture. Pleased at their rapid progress, Will replaced his fingers with his mouth. The moaning continued… and continued… and still continued some more. Kerri's sound and motion seemed strangely consistent. Will looked up from her bust.

"Everything all right, Kerri?" he asked.

"Huh? What?" she awkwardly retorted. "No, everything's okay."

"Are you sure?"

"Well… I don't know. I just think I'm trying too hard. I wanted everything to just come naturally. I'm trying and…"

"Stop worrying, Kerri. I know it's tough to just kick it into sex gear at the drop of a hat. Especially right after work in the middle of the week."

"I know that and I didn't want to be that way. Oh, I'm totally ruining the mood. This is so stupid!"

"Shhh." Will gently covered her mouth. "You don't need to keep talking. I already told you that I understand. Here's all you have to know…"

Kerri kept quiet and listened.

"Okay, there's something that we both badly want," Will continued. "And all that matters right now is us doing all that is possible to get it. Just forget everything else. All that matters is *right now.*"

"I'll try. It's just been so exhausting trying to wait for the exact right moment. I'm sorry. Do you want to stop?"

"Hell no!" Will answered affirmatively. "We ain't stopping till your cherry gets a poppin'."

His rhyme scored a partial laugh from her.

"So how are you doing, you know, down there," he cautiously asked.

Kerri's eyes glanced downward.

"Oh, I guess I'm pretty wet," she replied.

"Well, seeing as how the mood is fading fast, and I'm NOT giving up, why don't we try getting in?"

"Okay," Kerri answered without much thought. "We can try."

Will at once slid his legs off the edge of the bed. He grabbed Kerri's thighs and dragged her toward him. She immediately spread eagle, keeping her heels up in the air. Will grabbed hold of his manhood with one hand and prepped Kerri's womanhood with the other.

"All right," he said. "Here we go."

"Do it," Kerri said, wincing a bit.

They'd been having sex for the past five years, yet she still felt the need to brace herself upon the moment of insertion. Will softly placed his member up before the area he had spread apart. His hips exerted a moderate push.

"Ow," Kerri quietly uttered— which wasn't much of a mood helper.

"Oh, you all right?" Will asked, putting his hips about an inch in reverse.

"Yeah, yeah. Just keep going."

Without answering, Will pressed his lower half closer again. An uncomfortable tension forced him to pull back a second time.

"Damn it," he said, looking downward.

"What? What is it?" Kerri asked.

"It's not slipping in so easy. It feels like you're all dried up. And uh… it's kind of squishing my dick."

"I don't get it. It felt wet down there before. Maybe it wasn't wet enough. Can you try again?"

"Yeah, I'll try again."

Will spread Kerri's thighs a little more and aimed directly at the hole. He gave one good thrust, but could feel right away the lack of true penetration. Refusing to give up, he finagled back and forth looking to gain his Johnson some leverage. His movements suggested a 'porno' version of Ricky Martin. He began speaking one word in between every lower-region jab,

"Why… won't… this… work…"

"You can stop, Will. Really. We don't have to do it this time."

"No way." Will shook his head. "I just need it to be a little more slippery. Where's the KY?"

"No, you can't use KY."

"Why not?"

"Because KY Jelly could kill your sperm. You're not supposed to use it if you're trying to get pregnant."

"Well then what are you supposed to do if your wife's vagina dries up…" He paused to look down between his legs, "… and your husband's dick has gone flaccid."

"Out of all the pregnancy books I've read, there's only one thing that's supposedly perfectly safe."

"What is it? Tell me!"

Kerri slapped her hand over her eyes before reluctantly replying, "Egg whites."

"Egg whites." Will somehow repeated with a straight face. "Egg whites?"

Kerri nodded, her hand still covering her eyes.

"Like, egg whites from a chicken?" Will asked. "Like, if you want to make your omelet healthy, you order it with egg whites? *Those* kind of egg whites?"

"Yes! That's what you have to use!"

"This is ridiculous!" Will threw his hands up in the air. "I can't believe we have to…"

He caught himself mid-sentence, realizing that he was about to denounce his previous declaration on "not giving up." He lowered his head in shame.

"Egg whites, huh?" he asked.

"I'm sorry, Will," Kerri answered, "but yes."

"Be right back."

Downstairs in the kitchen, the white refrigerator door was flung open. Will popped open a carton of eggs and snatched one out. He returned to the bedroom toting the egg, a small bowl, a paper towel, and a tiny yolk-separating device. Kerri remained in her sprawled out position on the bed.

"I've got to tell you, honey," he said, kneeling down before her legs. "This is definitely one of the kinkiest things we've ever done."

"Oh God," Kerri half-laughed. "Are we crazy?"

"Probably." He picked up the egg and the separating device. "But at least we're not boring."

Will cracked the egg on the edge of the bowl. While holding the broken shell above the separator with one hand, he gradually began opening it up. A light-yellowish goo dripped slowly downward. A round ball of orange soon followed and plopped directly in the center of the separator. The device held on to the ball, but let the rest of the yellowish goo pass through into the bowl. Once through, Will placed the separator and eggshell on the paper towel and set them aside.

"My dear, we have our *safe* lubrication," he said, holding up the bowl to Kerri.

"Great," she answered, inching her butt closer to the edge of the bed. "Just get it over with."

Will exhaled a brief sigh as he stared down at his bowl o' goop. They were both only twenty-six years old, and sex was starting to become a chore. Yet Will couldn't believe it was their own fault. They were trying to create something beautiful and it was taking way too long. It was beginning to have a negative affect on their lives. It had to be stopped and he only knew of one sure-fire means to do so.

"Okay, Ker," he said. "We're doing this."

Will dipped his fingertips into the bowl. The ooze inside was quite cold, which gave his wiener the willies. Nonetheless, he took up a huge, gooey clump and slapped it down on his salami. The chilling rush was like plunging one's lower half into a frigid pool for the first time. He rapidly started rubbing with the hope of creating some arousing, friction-based warmth.

"Goddamn, this is cold," he said between strokes.

"I'm sorry, Will," Kerri lamented. "You don't…"

"No time for don'ts, honey. I've already got it on me and you know what? It's actually pretty slippery; as good as KY."

Considering that the 'lubrication' aspect of their dilemma was basically solved, Will focused the rest of his efforts on handling the limpness problem.

"All right, let's go," he thought to himself. "Time to get hard again. Thinking of hot stuff… Thinking of hot stuff. Okay, what's really hot… um, girls showering in the locker room. Nice. And *Kerri*… Kerri showering with a bunch of naked girls in the locker room after cheerleading practice. Oh yeah, that's good stuff."

The image of Kerri lathering up her bare breasts with soap, surrounded by a crowd of unclothed girls doing the same thing promptly appeared in his head. Then every girl stopped soaping herself and started soaping the nude girl standing next to her because *clearly* that is what all women would normally do while showering as a bunch.

Regardless of his ill-conceived notions regarding female group cleansing, Will's powerful mind-imagery instantly did the trick.

"Honey, we're back in business," he smiled.

"Really?" Kerri asked. "That fast?"

"Yup. It's time."

He stood up beside the edge of the bed, still holding his freshly lubed member in his hand. Kerri threw her feet up and out at opposite ends of his hips. Will zeroed in on his target and pressed his tip firmly up against it. Before anyone could say 'Open Sesame,' he easily slipped right in.

"Yes!" Will exclaimed as a bead of sweat became caught in his eyebrow.

"Yes," Kerri quietly repeated, fighting back the urge to wince.

"I can't believe the freaking egg worked!" He started pumping his hips back and forth. "It actually feels really good."

"Good, I'm glad." Kerri's eyes were shut. "Just try to hurry."

"I don't think that will be a problem."

Will only needed a couple more properly placed propulsions before his inner self was ready to explode. He tensed up his below-the-waist muscles for as long as he could, hoping to build up a powerful 'sperm shot' that would have no trouble bursting up through Kerri's uterus and into her egg.

"I'm gonna go," he said once the pressure became too much.

"Okay," she answered, relieved.

Will bent down over her chest and allowed his package to detonate.

It had been an arduous after-work journey, which had most likely led to a fairly strong payoff. After ensuring his pistol was packing nothing but an empty chamber, Will readied himself for phase two of their insemination ritual. He placed a foot on the base board of the bed and rested his opposite knee on the mattress.

"I'm done, Ker," he said. "Is it all right if I lift you up now?"

"Yeah, do it." She opened up her eyes. "And Will, thanks for staying so strong for me."

"That's why I'm here, baby."

He pushed with both his legs, sending her hips on an upward angle. Once at a sufficient height, he reached for the nearest pillow.

"Okay, I'm pulling out," he said.

"Don't forget to grab a towel," Kerri added.

"It's next on my list."

Will shoved the pillow beneath her butt and hopped onto the floor.

"Now keep that ass elevated," he said, jogging toward the bathroom.

Kerri threw her hands beneath her thighs for some extra support. Will returned with a light blue towel that he swiftly scooted under her hands. The procedure was officially complete. Sporting a fresh glaze of sweat all over his body, Will flopped down next to her on the bed. His lungs sucked in a huge gust of air and then blew it all out toward the ceiling.

"We did it," he whispered.

"I just hope it worked," she whispered back and looked up at the ceiling. "I just think that hope is all we've got. It's all I can hold on to."

"Hope is definitely a nice thing to have… but it ain't all we got."

"Really? What else is there?"

"There's faith, honey. And I've got it."

"That's nice, Will." She turned her face to his. "I wish I could have it too."

"Hey, don't worry about it. I have enough for us both. So if you don't have any faith in what we're trying to do, you can at least have faith in me, right?"

"What makes you so sure?"

"You mean, what makes me so sure that we're going to get pregnant?"

"Yeah, I mean, so far nothing has happened that would lead us to believe that it could actually happen."

"Kerri, faith isn't about seeing things happening. You know that. It's deeper. It's something I just feel inside."

"Okay, I get that. I guess I just need to hear exactly where your faith is coming from."

"Because I know the kind of person you are and the kind of person I am, it seems highly logical to me that God would want us to have a kid. We're both the right kind of people. Us bringing a child into this world would probably make it a better place. That is how I feel and I'm not just saying that to make you feel better. You know I'd never lie to you."

Kerri reached her hand out to his cheek and pulled his face closer. She lightly touched her lips to his forehead.

"You're so good for me," she said, flaunting a petite smile. "I will have faith in you."

"I'm glad," Will grinned. "That's all I ask. However, I have to admit that there is one thing I'm a little worried about now."

"What is it?" Her face turned serious.

"Well, what if our kid is born with a beak?"

Kerri wiped out her look of solemnity with a big burst of laughter.

"And what if instead of crying, he clucks," Will went on. "Seriously, what if instead of giving birth in a hospital in a bed, you have to do it inside a barn in a bale of hay? I really don't understand why you're laughing so much. These scenarios are really bothering me."

Chapter 7

A scowl furrowed across Will's face as the phone on his desk let out a loud ring. He already had one foot out of his cubicle and debated whether to step back in. The phone rang again. Will looked at the empty chairs before Fred and Loni's desks. They had left right at 5 p.m., but he had to stay twenty minutes late in order to finish up an overdue layout. The phone sounded its presence a third time. Will reasoned that it was either his boss checking up on the layout or Kerri. Both were good enough reasons to pick up the phone. He snatched up the receiver in the middle of the fourth ring.

"Hello?" he said.

"Is this Will Haddon?" asked a low voice on the other end.

"Yeah. Who's this?"

"Mr. Haddon, my name is Dr. Julius Phalen. I received your number through an associate, I believe?"

"Okaaaay, maybe you did." Will wasn't sure if this was some kind of lame solicitation phone call or not, and was preparing to hang up. "And who exactly are *you*? Help me out, why don't cha?" He never did care for phone solicitors.

"Yes, of course," the 'supposed' Dr. Phalen continued, "um, it is to my understanding that you and your wife are having trouble conceiving. Is that correct?"

This was no phone solicitation.

"Oh, yes," Will answered and promptly took a seat behind his desk. "My friend, Loni, actually did put the word out about my wife and me. But you know, to be honest, I really wasn't expecting anyone to follow up."

"Well, you can be assured, Mr. Haddon, I *am* following up," Dr. Phalen pledged. "And I'd like to help you and your wife out."

"That sounds very nice, sir, but how can you help us out?"

"Why, by getting you pregnant of course."

"Yes, that would be a great help." Will deliberately rubbed his forehead. "But I have to let you know, we've been trying for over three years now. And so far, nothing has helped. And believe me, we've tried everything."

"I'm sorry it's taken you two so long, Will." Dr. Phalen paused, like he was inhaling a deep breath. "But believe me, you have not tried everything."

Will removed his hand from his forehead.

"What do you mean?" he asked.

"What I mean is you haven't tried *me* yet. Regardless of your situation, I'm quite confident that I can get you pregnant."

"Again, that does sound really nice, but I have to ask, what makes you so sure? I mean, forgive me for being skeptical and all. It's just that after semen tests, fertility drugs, injections, in vitro fertilization, we've both grown quite cynical regarding our dilemma."

"That's completely understandable, Will. After all that, how could you not be thinking, *This doctor must be out of his mind?* I've dealt with a number of couples having trouble with infertility; some even worse off than you. I know what a tough, trying process it can be."

"Yes, it really is. And I don't think you're out of your mind."

"That's good," Dr. Phalen stated matter-of-factly. "Because I'm not and I *am* going to help you."

"Please, Dr. Phalen, tell me how you can help."

"I've been developing a new kind of hormone enhancement drug that strengthens the ovaries of the female, thus leading to a much stronger implantation process. I'm sorry if that all sounds a bit too technical."

"No, that's okay. My wife and I have been through so much, I actually understood everything you just said."

"Smart boy! Very good! Sometimes it's tough laying information out so that patients can comprehend it."

"Well, I can assure you that won't be a problem with us. May I ask, is this implantation process painful in any way?"

"Oh, no," Dr. Phalen affirmed. "I do a regular in vitro fertilization. The process is practically painless."

Will closed his eyes in grief. "Dr. Phalen," he said, "there's a problem with that. We already used up the maximum number of in vitro fertilizations that our insurance will allow. And we can't afford to do it again."

Silence relayed from the other end of the line. Will waited uncomfortably for the good doctor to reply.

"Will, I still think you don't understand," Phalen finally answered. "I'm *going* to get you and your wife pregnant. It is *not* about money."

"What is it about?"

"It's about *life*, Will. And I can't put a price tag on something like that."

"But you're a doctor, aren't you? Aren't you required to bill insurance companies for all the services you provide?"

"Yes, of course, but I also feel that there are special circumstances that reach beyond the realm of insurance company billing. It's my choice. And Will, I don't want to make you feel uncomfortable in any way. I'm not forcing you to consider this procedure. If you hold the slightest bit of doubt in your mind, then by all means we will end this conversation."

Will had to add up a couple of calculations in his head. Dr. Phalen's voice possessed a sort of sympathetic charisma that didn't seem to be hiding anything. And Will really wanted to dive right in to the positive-sounding promises. Nonetheless, he would never agree to something without first talking it over with Kerri. However, he did recall that she was growing increasingly unsatisfied with her current doctor.

"Well, Dr. Phalen, I have to tell you," he began, "my wife and I have tried so much already and nothing has worked. I'm all for any new kind of process as long as it's safe and won't put us in the poorhouse. However, you're just calling me right out of the blue and hitting me with all this information, it's happening so quick and... um, I just think I need to talk to my wife about it."

"Absolutely," Dr. Phalen said right away. "I insist that you discuss everything with your wife. You're a good husband, Will. I can tell. I can also tell that you're going to make a great father. Here, why don't I give you my number? After you talk to your wife, if you feel like moving forward, give me a call and make an appointment. If not, then no problem."

"Thank you very much. I really appreciate that. Plus, we're in the 'waiting zone' right now, regarding my wife's period. So keep your fingers crossed and maybe we won't have to bother you with our problem."

"I will definitely do that. Good luck to you. And here's my number."

Will grabbed a pen and pad out of his desk and proceeded to write down Dr. Phalen's ten-digit number. Upon hanging up the phone, he raced out of his cubicle nearly knocking down the makeshift walls. He hopped into his maroon Saturn and sped out of the parking lot. The whole ride home he couldn't stop thinking about the doctor's 'your going to make a great father' comment. Truer words were never spoken. Will knew he was going to be the best dad in the world and was dying to prove it. The short session with Dr. Phalen had led him to believe that the chances of realizing that dream had now increased. However, whether or not they moved forward with this possible opportunity rested solely on what Kerri had to say on the subject. The Saturn's wheels let out a slight screech as it came to a halt at Will's home. Kerri's purple Kia was already in the driveway. Clutching the note with the phone number inside his pants pocket, Will traipsed over the lawn up to the front door. He slipped his key into the lock. Something made a loud crash on the other side of the door.

"Ker?" he called out from the porch.

A harsh thud immediately followed.

"Kerri!" Will shouted, rapidly twisting open the lock.

He burst into the house, leaving the key in the door. The noise had come from somewhere in the back. The light in the kitchen was on. Will dashed forward, his fists pumping, toward the side of the refrigerator which jutted partially out in the entryway. The hardwood floor seemed extra shiny the moment his feet stepped in. Once he realized it was broken glass, his legs hit the breaks. While skidding to a stop, his eyes detected a red, wet substance smeared across the counter and floor. His heart abruptly hit the panic button.

"Kerri!" he screamed. "Where are you?"

Will set his shoes into a frantic spin, casting glances all around him. The kitchen and its neighboring dining and living rooms appeared to be empty. Before he began pulling his hair out, a sudden, mucus-filled gasp came echoing his way. Will turned instantly toward the side the sound came from.

"Kerri!" he called out again. "Are you here?"

His query was met with another, much louder sniffle. At once his feet went bounding toward the first floor's corner bathroom. The door was shut, but there was an illuminated crack looking out at the base.

"Kerri, I'm coming in," Will stated.

Although worried about what scene was being depicted behind the door, he still brazenly flung it open. His heart let out a painful yelp as more stains of red first came into view on the tiled floor. He followed the trail towards a towel rack, beneath which sat Kerri, clutching her knees to her chin. Her face was fully flushed and extremely moist. The tears had left permanent skidmarks down her cheeks. The legs of her pants were dotted with smudges of red. She had a bloodied white wash cloth wrapped around her right hand. Although he was relieved to have found her, Will was still saddened about being able to deduce what most likely led her there.

"What happened?" he asked.

When Kerri tried to speak, her sobs only grew stronger. Her inhaling convulsions were so intense she appeared to be hyperventilating. Will rapidly stepped through the blood on the floor and crouched down beside her.

"Hey, Ker, come on now, it's okay," he tried to console even though the situation probably wasn't *okay*. "Come on, baby, you're scaring me. Please, try to catch your breath and tell me how I can help."

Kerri's gasps grew a bit erratic as she tried to regain respiratory control. After a short bout of concentration, she was finally able to swallow the large amount of saliva that had built up in her mouth. Once her throat muscles finished flexing, she parted her lips.

"No… baby," she slowly whispered. "There's… no baby. My period just came today…"

She pushed her face into her knees and emitted a big sniff.

"I know, Kerri, I know," Will said softly. "But what did you do? There's broken glass in the kitchen… and you're cut."

"I… I just got so upset." Her voice squeaked. Her face remained at her knees. "It hadn't come yet and today I thought… that it might have finally worked. Then I felt the wetness in my pants. I checked in the kitchen and saw… the blood. Then I broke the fucking glass and cut my hand."

She paused as a fresh row of tears trickled down. Will had to summon all his strength in order to keep from exploding into a heartbroken fit of frustrated rage. That would only make things worse. He instead dug the fingernails of his left hand into his side and used his right hand to lightly stroke Kerri's blonde hair. The time had come to attempt calm-down mode again.

"I love you more than anything, Kerri," he began. "You know that. If anything ever happened to you, I wouldn't want to go on living." He stopped as the mere thought of what he had just said made him ill. "Please, please don't get so upset that you wind up hurting yourself. That won't make the sadness go away."

"I know that." Kerri looked up from her knees. "Don't you think I know that? I try to tell myself every time not to get upset if my period comes. And every time I only get more upset. All I see are pregnant women everywhere; at work, on the street, on the covers of all those stupid entertainment magazines. They all have what I want and make it look so goddamn easy. But not for *me*. It doesn't get to be easy for me. I can't take it anymore. I, I think it's killing me."

"No, Kerri. Don't say that."

"Don't tell me what to do!" Her bloodshot eyes widened. "You're not me. You can't possibly know what I'm feeling inside… in this pathetic, fucking body that can't produce children!"

She smacked her palm cruelly across her face.

"Kerri, don't do that!" Will shouted.

"Shut up!" Kerri screamed back. "Just shut the fuck up! I hate it! I hate it!"

She awkwardly rose to her feet, dropping the bloody cloth to the floor.

"Kerri, wait!" Will exclaimed. "Where are you going?"

"Get away from me!" Kerri roared back. "Leave me alone! I just want to be alone!" She rapidly marched across the blood on the tiles and out of the bathroom. Will could only quietly watch. He was certain no calm-down methods would be working on this night. Kerri's footsteps were heard pounding up the stairs to the second floor. The trek was capped off with the bedroom door slamming shut. A few intermittent crashes followed. Will guessed that she was most likely throwing her what-to-do-when-you're-pregnant books against the wall, which wasn't an unusual occurrence. He closed his eyes and threw back his head so that he was facing the ceiling. He took in a deep breath and opened his eyelids on the exhale. The circular light above was shining bright. Will refused to look away, letting faint purplish blotches float through his vision. He pulled his left hand out of his side and wiped away the sweat that had formed on his forehead. The intensity of the light became too much. Will looked down from the ceiling and sluggishly hung both his arms. He caught his reflection in the mirrored vanity. There was a smear of red across his brow. The realization then set in that his left side still felt like someone was grabbing it. He glanced down at four tiny, red peck marks soaking through the hip region of his white work shirt. The sight made him feel glad; glad that Kerri wasn't the only one bleeding that night.

"Good," he said, casting a long gaze into the fabric. "Very good."

Will recalled once again how wonderful a father he would be and added on that Kerri had all the makings of an ideally nurturing mother. At this point, tears were usually the norm. However, his eyes remained entirely dry this time. The infertile scenario had been overplayed for far too long and he couldn't cry anymore. He knew that something had to change before they both went insane. A foreboding chill settled up through his spine.

"I can't lose her to this," Will assertively whispered to himself. "This can't break us. We're both good people. We are going to make a great family. I have to stay calm. I have to make this happen. I . . ."

Will discontinued his monologue and looked down at his pants. He reached into his pocket and removed Dr. Phalen's number. Holding the piece of paper closely before his face with two hands, he wistfully recollected the phone conversation he'd had just a short time ago. The pain in his heart became briefly alleviated, like a lingering strand of hope was still wafting out there in the universe. Kerri needed a sniff of that strand desperately before it was too late. Though the rest of the night would undoubtedly offer only solitude to them both, Will vowed that on the following day he would convince her to give Dr. Phalen a try.

Chapter 8

"I'm scared, Will," Kerri said, staring through the windshield from the passenger's seat of the Saturn.

"I know you're scared, honey," Will said from the driver's side. "And I know exactly what you're scared about. It ain't the doctor because we've both met Dr. Phalen and know what a great guy he is. It ain't the pain, because you've already had in vitro three other times and know it's only about as uncomfortable as a Pap smear. Now I have no clue what a Pap smear could possibly feel like, but from the doc's description, it didn't seem too bad."

Kerri gave a grin at Will's poor pronunciation of the gynecological term.

"No, the one thing that you're truly scared of," Will went on, "is the same thing that I'm scared of—it not working."

"Yes," Kerri nodded. "I'm so nervous. I mean, in vitro hasn't worked already three times. If it doesn't work this time, I'm going to be convinced that there's something wrong with me that can't ever be fixed."

"Hold on right this second, honey. What did we say we were going to promote today?" He waited patiently for an answer. "Come on, what did we say?"

Kerri exhaled a little sigh and replied, "Positive energy."

"Yes, that's right! And I'm totally going to help you. We're a team in this all the way. In fact, I'm going to help you out with how you're feeling right now. Ready?"

"Okay," Kerri said softly.

"Well, I just have a good feeling about this time. And no, I'm not just saying that to make you feel better. I mean, just look at the factors leading up to this. Some random doctor just calls us out of the blue wanting to help. I *tell* him we can't afford to do another in vitro, yet he offers to do it for *free* without any catch. Plus, he's developed this new, FDA-approved pregnancy-enhancement drug that we get to use. Doesn't that seem just too perfect for us?"

"Yes… but what if it *is* too perfect? My dad always used to tell me that there are no free lunches ever. Someone will always want something in return. I know we've met him now a couple of times and everything about him appears to check out… but what if he has some kind of hidden agenda?"

"Aw Kerri, I hate when you start getting a case of the what-ifs. What if Dr. Phalen never even called us? Where would we be then? Besides, I know for a fact why he's doing all this for us. He told me when they were prepping you for one of the ultrasound tests."

"What did he tell you?"

"Well, I was mentioning how I still couldn't believe that he wasn't billing us for the in vitro, so he quietly pulled me into his office. He then says, 'Just between you and me, there is a real reason for why I'm doing this.' So I ask him, 'What?' He tells me that he and his wife lost a child, a son, a long time ago. He didn't go into detail how or why, but made it clear that it totally devastated them."

"Oh my God. That's terrible."

"I know, and it got worse after that. See, they started trying again for another kid, but were having a lot of trouble. They were a lot older than when they had their son and I guess his wife's insides weren't working so well."

"What happened?"

"He said it took a very long time, but right when they were almost ready to give up, she got pregnant with their daughter."

"Oh, I'm glad it worked out for them."

"Yeah, me too. And Dr. Phalen was really glad. He told me that he was on the verge of losing his practice as well as his mind, and was constantly praying everyday for another child. When it finally happened, he was so grateful that he vowed from that point on to dedicate his research to advancing the process of fertility. He made it his mission to cure all couples having trouble conceiving. He also told me that he would never turn patients away simply because there was a monetary issue."

"He told you all that?"

"Yes ma'am. So now is your mind a little more at ease?"

"I think it is. Thanks, Will. I knew I married the right guy."

She gave him a light-hearted jab in the shoulder. Will looked at her with a tiny smirk.

"Yeah," he nodded, "I guess you did okay."

Kerri quietly rested her head on his shoulder. Will leaned down toward her and took a whiff of her sweet, blonde locks. The medical center was coming up on the right. Will kept his head next to hers as he pulled into the parking lot.

"Hi, guys!" Dr. Phalen greeted them the moment they stepped inside the facility. "Right this way."

Will and Kerri followed him down a long hallway with gray tiles and stark white walls. The facility wasn't hospital-size large, but more along the lines of an elaborate doctor's office. It didn't seem highly populated as well, just a couple of nurses and orderlies about. A serene silence engulfed the scene.

Dr. Phalen was the first to reach the end of the hallway and sharply turned to his left. As Will and Kerri rounded the same bend, they came upon a type of waiting room.

"This is where you get off, Will," Dr. Phalen said. "I'll take care of Kerri from this point on."

"Okay," Will said and turned to Kerri. "You ready for this, tough gal?"

Kerri gave a fast nod and wrapped her arms around him. He gave her cheek a big kiss and moved his lips up close to her ear.

"Remember," he whispered, "promote the positive."

"I will," she replied softly.

Kerri slowly let go of her embrace as they both turned to the good doctor.

"Don't worry, you guys," Dr. Phalen smiled. "In just a couple of weeks you're both going to be celebrating. I promise."

"I like your confidence, Doc," Will said. "I hope some of it rubs off on us."

"What do you say, Kerri?" Dr. Phalen looked toward her. "Let's go get you pregnant."

"Sounds good," Kerri forced a grin through her edginess.

"Very good. Will, you can just take a seat. The procedure won't take very long, so I'll have her back to you very shortly."

"Thanks, Doc," Will said. "Go work us some baby magic."

"Indeed I will," Dr. Phalen affirmed.

Will watched his wife and the doctor head off down another, much shorter hall. Kerri glanced back over her shoulder. He gave her a nice wave and then turned it into a big thumbs-up. A steadfast smile overcame her face before she turned away. Will watched them disappear through a thick, black door before walking into the waiting room. He took a seat on one of the wooden chairs with soft cushions built in around the back and base. Confident that Kerri was no longer in sight, he exhaled nervously and bowed his head. Eyes clamped shut, he folded his hands together and began to silently pray.

On the other side of the thick, black door, Kerri as well quietly asked the Lord above for guidance as she changed into her hospital gown behind a privacy curtain.

"Kerri, how are you coming along?" asked a nurse who'd just poked her head into the room.

"I'm fine," Kerri replied, stepping out from behind the curtain.

"Wonderful." She walked into the room pushing a wheelchair. "I'm Nurse Nancy and I'm just going to help get you situated before the doctor comes in. You're going to do great."

Nurse Nancy's darkish hair with hints of gray and warm smile reminded Kerri a bit of her mother. Her rate of relaxation jumped up an entire level.

"Thank you," she said, stepping closer.

"How are you feeling, honey?" Nurse Nancy asked.

"I'm still a little nervous, I guess," Kerri answered, hoping to suckle a little bit more at the pseudo-mom's teat.

"Well, I can promise you won't be feeling that way for long. Dr. Phalen is a brilliant, gentle man. He will take great care of you."

"Oh, that's nice to hear."

"Have a seat, dear." Nurse Nancy motioned down at the wheelchair.

Kerri squatted down on the chair and put her feet up on the metal footrests. Nurse Nancy placed her palms around the handlebars in the back.

"Okay," she smiled. "We're off."

As Kerri rolled through the hallway, her ears detected the low chords of classical music being pumped in. She looked up at the ceiling for speakers.

"I hear music," she said.

"Yes, I know," Nurse Nancy agreed. "Dr. Phalen likes his patients to be as relaxed as possible. During the holidays, he switches over to Christmas tunes."

"Oh, that's nice." Kerri actually thought the faint tones of strings and wind instruments added an odd, eerie vibe to the hospital's hallway.

The operating room did not seem worthy of the name 'operating'. It didn't have the cold, high-tech aura that Kerri was expecting. There weren't any lighted mechanical contraptions hanging from the ceiling or rows of liquid-filled jars or trays of sharp, metal instruments—which was a plus. The room consisted solely of a small computer with a bunch of tools wired into it, a chair, a sink, and a cushioned examination table with stirrups. The windowless setting resembled a kind of kinky office.

Situated on the examination table beneath a white sheet, Kerri quietly collected her thoughts as the spooky classical chords were beginning to fade away. The Valium tablet that Nurse Nancy had given her was beginning to take effect. The lone door to the room slowly creaked open. Dr. Phalen stepped in with a small tray of non-threatening tools.

"Hello again, Kerri," he smiled. "How are you feeling?"

"Kind of drowsy," she slowly replied.

"That's good. This procedure is very quick and you shouldn't feel a thing. I just need you to place your feet up in the stirrups. Can you do that?"

"Okay."

Kerri spread apart her legs and rested her heels down within the stirrups. Dr. Phalen folded back the base of the white sheet until her knees were exposed.

"All right, Kerri," he said, "we're all set. You just relax."

Kerri could no longer hear the doctor. Her senses had fully succumbed to the Valium and her mind was already off focusing on less medical, more positive entities. In desperate times for complete calmness, she had one particularly special memory locked away in her brain's bank. As her eyelids slowly shut, the rosy recollection was released...

Dressed in a red, hooded cloak, Kerri sat on a couch beside a sexy Strawberry Shortcake and a female devil. Music echoed in the background as well as many different conversations. Although the room was dimly lit, a frown could be seen across Kerri's face. Strawberry Shortcake was rubbing her hand. A stocky man in a bushy wolf mask walked briskly up to the couch. He lifted the snarling visage up off his face.

"What the fuck, Kerri?" he immediately exhaled. "What's your problem?"

"Her problem is *you*," snapped Strawberry Shortcake, "hitting on all those other girls!"

"Yeah, Keith, what's *your* fucking problem?" added the devil.

"Bitches, how 'bout you both shut the fuck up?" the Wolf scowled. "I don't need you answering for her."

Kerri could only stare straight toward the floor, mortified, wishing she was able to crawl beneath the couch.

"Come on, Kerri," the Wolf went on. "Answer me. Don't just sit there all quiet and shit."

Kerri closed her eyes and took in a deep breath.

"You embarrassed me, Keith," she exhaled. "Please go away."

The Wolf glared at her with a stern brow.

"Oh, no," he said. "That is not happening. I was only kidding around with those girls. Why you gotta be so damn stuck-up. Let's just go outside and talk."

"No, Keith. I don't want to. You've had too much to drink. Just... just go away."

"No fucking way. We're going outside to talk right now!"

He latched his thick fingers onto her red-caped shoulder. Kerri violently shrugged his hand off and slid a ways down the couch.

"Get off her, asshole!" screamed Strawberry Shortcake.

"Fuck you, bitch!" the Wolf growled, moving in for a second grasp attempt.

A hand suddenly shot forth from off to the side and grabbed onto the Wolf's shirt from behind. He was quickly dragged out of the range of Kerri's red cloak. Strawberry Shortcake and the devil both looked up in shock.

"What the fuck?" the Wolf exclaimed.

He spun around to see Will, wearing black-rimmed glasses and a black suit with a white buttoned-down shirt that was opened up to reveal a red and yellow "S" underneath.

"Get your fucking hand off me, super-geek," the Wolf snapped.

"Hey, buddy, you're being a bit loud," the much shorter Will calmly said, removing his hand. "You're kind of creating a ruckus."

"Eat shit and mind your own business."

"You're ruining the party." Will glanced beyond him at the girls on the couch. "And bothering these nice ladies."

"You want me to kick your ass?"

"I just want you to leave." Will kept his hands at his sides. "Now."

"I'm not going anywhere!"

The Wolf grabbed Will by his shirt, exposing the "S" on his chest even more.

"Keith!" Kerri yelled, standing up.

"Shut up, Kerri!" the Wolf ordered.

"Keith," Will coolly said, "you're being an asshole."

The Wolf was now through talking. He hammered Will across the face, knocking his glasses off. Will remained standing as he was punched in the stomach. He did not retaliate.

"Keith!" Kerri screamed. "Stop it!"

Without answering, the Wolf delivered another facial blow, sending Will onto his back. The shrieks of the girls caused a Zorro and a Frankenstein to come rushing over. They both grabbed the Wolf and dragged him away from Will.

"All right," warned the hulking Frankenstein, "you're out of here."

"No fighting in the house," added Zorro.

"Good riddance, you goddamn prick!" Strawberry Shortcake shouted after them.

"Are you all right, Kerri?" asked the devil.

Kerri did not answer her friend. She was already off the couch, kneeling down on the floor beside Will. His eyes were shut.

"Oh my God, are you okay?" she asked, picking up his glasses.

She placed a hand on his "S" and gently rubbed his chest. Will's eyes popped open and glanced up at her.

"Your boyfriend hits like a girl," he smiled.

"You're okay?" Kerri inquired, a bit surprised.

Will sat right up. "I'm fine."

"Thank you so much for coming over. I was starting to get scared."

"Well, I wasn't going to at first, but then I saw him grab your arm. That wasn't cool at all."

"Here, let me help you up."

Kerri touched her fingers to his hands and helped him up.

"Thank you very much, Ms. Riding Hood," Will smiled.

"Are you sure you're okay?" Kerri asked. "It just looked like it hurt. Here, sit down with us."

"Thank you." Will took a seat on the end of the couch. "And yes, I really am okay."

"Hey, Clark Kent," Strawberry Shortcake said. "Good job getting that asshole kicked out of here. You really are the man of steel."

"I just feel that violence is never the answer," Will replied, keeping his eyes on Kerri. "And like I said, her boyfriend hits like a girl, so it was really no problem."

"He's *not* my boyfriend," Kerri quickly assured.

"Oh, that's very good news. By the way, my name's Will."

He tried extending his hand to shake hers, but realized that their palms had never parted from when she had initially helped him up.

"Oh, I still have your hand," Kerri admitted sheepishly, but still didn't let go.

"That's okay," Will said warmly. "It's all yours. Keep it."

"Ha, thank you so much," she laughed, jokingly caressing his palm. "I'll treasure it always."

"And your name is Kerri, right?"

"You know my name?" she gasped.

"Well, I heard the Wolf and Strawberry Shortcake saying it a couple of times. I'm not psychic or anything."

"No, but you are pretty funny."

She kept his hand in hers as Strawberry Shortcake and the devil rolled their eyes, feigning nausea.

"Thanks, Kerri," Will smiled. "Kerri, Kerri… hey, Kerri… Kerri, are you awake?"

She stared at him oddly, wondering what reason he had for continually saying her name. The more she stared, the blurrier the room around his face got. He kept on calling her name as his outfit started morphing into another one. Kerri could feel something soft pressing against the side of her head and realized that she wasn't sitting up anymore. The couch was gone, replaced by sheets of white.

"Kerri, are you awake?" she heard Will ask again. "It's over now. You're all finished." A sense of reality gradually began creeping back into her brain.

"Will," she slowly said. "What's happening?"

"The procedure's over, silly," he replied, trying to stifle bits of laughter. "That Valium must have really whacked you out."

"Oh yeah, oh yeah… no, I remember. I just… just feel… a little woozy right now."

"That's perfectly normal," added Dr. Phalen, standing in the entryway of the recovery room. "And the procedure went fantastic." He stepped in a bit closer. "All you have to do, Kerri, is rest here for a couple of hours. That's it."

"You hear that, Ker?" Will said. "The operation was a success. Now we just sit back and wait."

"That's right," Dr. Phalen went on. "Wait two weeks, then come on back here. We'll do a little blood work and find out if the fertilized embryos implanted."

"Do you think it worked, Doc?" Will asked.

"Well, Will, I'm not really one for tooting my own horn, but Kerri's eggs have been treated with my new fertility drug, which so far has shown a 90% success rate for conception. So…" He held out his hand, palm-down, and depressed it two times. "*Toot, toot!*"

"That sounds good to me," Will smiled. "I know you heard that, Kerri. Our horn has been tooted. It's going to be good news, I just know it."

Kerri was still weary, but managed to display a faint smile.

Chapter 9

While driving her purple Kia through some light traffic, Kerri gently rubbed the itchy band-aid taped across the inside of her elbow. She had never been very fond of needles. The tiny prick always formed into an ugly circular, reddish bruise and the pain lasted for about a week. However, on this particular occasion, she was more than happy to roll up her sleeve with the understanding that the molecules currently in her blood possibly possessed the answer to her prayers.

The past two weeks had felt like two years. Remaining calm wasn't an easy task for Kerri. An indescribable restlessness had set up shop inside her. Fortunately, Will was always there, truly earning the title of her 'rock'. Her follow-up appointment was at 9 a.m. bright and early. She had trouble getting to sleep the night before. Will had wisely talked her into taking the entire day off from work. Seeing as how she had accumulated a large sum of personal days and was in no way in the right frame of mind for teaching students, it seemed like the right thing to do.

The Kia slowed to a stop at a red traffic light. Kerri glanced at the car's digital clock and then at her cell phone sitting in the passenger's seat. Dr. Phalen said he would be calling her as soon as he had her results.

"It shouldn't take too long," he said to her. "Maybe a little over an hour. All you have to do is think positive in the meantime."

However, Kerri's *meantime* felt more like *prison time*. Her worrisome thoughts kept her captive. She knew she wouldn't be able to function fully until the doctor called with her answer.

God I need to know! her mind screamed. *I need to know right now! Why is it taking so long? Why is...*

A loud honk interrupted her thoughts. She looked up to see that the traffic light had switched to green. The honk sounded behind her again.

"I'm going!" she shouted, looking into her rear-view mirror. "Jesus Christ, what's your problem?"

The Kia's tires emitted a partial screech as it moved on through the light. Kerri breathed in unsteadily and felt as though a panic attack was coming on. Behind the wheel of a car wasn't the right place for her. Besides she really needed a shot of fresh air.

Fortunately, she was driving through a main street in the town where Dr. Phalen's office was located. The Kia's right-turn blinker ignited as it turned off into the nearest parking space next to the sidewalk. Kerri sent the gearshift into 'park', removed her key from the ignition, and snatched up her cell phone. She stepped out onto the street and quickly walked over to the sidewalk. The temperature was a tad on the chilly side. Kerri reached into her jacket pockets and pulled out a pair of woolen gloves. They weren't very stylish, featuring faux leather tackily stitched on the inside palms for gripping a snow shovel, but did the trick when it came to warmth.

Once the outdoor air fully hit her lungs, she started to stroll down the street. The town had a certain other-side-of-the-tracks feel that she wasn't normally used to. Having grown up within the wealthier areas of Northern New Jersey, Kerri liked her fences white and picket, not chain-linked and barbed. Nonetheless, the current area only seemed slightly slum-ish; hopefully nothing to worry about. At least, nothing that could subjugate the main worry on her mind.

When is he going to call? she wondered, staring at the clock on her cell phone. It's already been forty-five minutes. *God, I need to calm down. Should I call Will? No, I promised him I wouldn't call until I got the news. Ugh, what can I do to kill the next fifteen minutes? I can't stop thinking... I... well, I do have to pee... and I'm hungry.*

She scanned across the shoddy line of shops along the main street and found a dry-cleaning business, a Laundromat, a pawn shop, and a small 7-11-esque market—that would do.

Kerri sauntered up to the single glass door of Veejay's 24-Hour Mart. A chorus of jingling bells rang out as she entered. A dark-skinned Indian man, no doubt Mr. Veejay himself, stood behind the counter and the cash register. He looked up from his newspaper and stared at her as she got closer.

"Excuse me," she said. "Do you have a bathroom here?"

"Yes," he answered in a perfect Indian accent, "but you must purchase something in order to use it."

"I'm planning on purchasing something," Kerri retorted, a bit annoyed.

"In the back, next to the refrigerated section." He looked back down at the newspaper.

Without saying thanks, Kerri headed toward the back of the empty store. She took notice of how messily all the shelves along the way were stacked. Cans were shuffled all out of place, random napkins and boxes were scattered on the white-tiled floor.

The tiny refrigerated section drew nearer. A wooden door labeled 'Restroom' resided right next to a stocked ledge of milk cartons. Before reaching the door, Kerri abruptly halted in her tracks. She reached down and lightly pressed her fingertips between her legs. It was moist. Kerri knew she had to go to the bathroom pretty bad, but couldn't have inadvertently begun peeing in her pants. She rushed forward to the restroom as a sharp pang of worry was injected into her stomach. The wooden entryway was quickly opened up. The dull light was flipped on. Kerri slammed the door shut behind her, pressing her back up against it. She could feel the cold from the neighboring refrigerated section pushing in through her skin. She closed her eyes as the humming buzz of the fridge's motor filled her ears. She didn't want to check, though the suspense was killing her. The glove on her right hand was sharply ripped off.

"Just do it," she quietly whispered, eyes still shut.

With nervous precision, she undid her belt and stretched one hand down the front of her pants. The wetness between her legs greeted her touch right away. Kerri winced as she swabbed up a damp sample onto her tips. She held her breath as her hand reemerged.

"Just open your eyes and look."

Kerri reluctantly did as she was told. The traces of red smeared across her fingers made her heart instantly sink. She tightly closed her eyes again. A harsh comprehension slunk into her skull; she was *never* going to have children. The familiar pair of tears found its way past her lashes. Kerri was waiting to hear herself scream, but found her vocal cords muted. Every muscle in her body felt numb. The humming of the motor was too much. She shoved the glove back on without washing the blood off her hand and re-tightened her belt.

The wooden door creaked open as Kerri silently stepped back into the store. Staring down at the tiled floor, she gradually made her way toward the exit.

"Hey!" called Veejay. "You didn't buy anything. You must make a purchase if you plan on using the bathroom!"

Kerri paused. She gazed lazily at the angry man behind the counter. She didn't want to get into an argument at that moment. In fact, she didn't care about anything anymore.

Without making a reply, she about-faced and strolled back into the heart of the store. She came upon a large magazine rack. Her feet stopped. She gazed up at the wide array of colorful periodicals. The headlines written in the largest type jumped out at her first. ***Angelina Pregnant Again! Britney Keeps Custody of Her Kids! Baby Boom: The Latest Hollywood Craze!***

Kerri's blood pressure rose rapidly with the reading of each baby-centric caption. Her face grew extra red and her cheeks glistened with tears. All the famous women pictured had what she wanted and they were flaunting it in her face. A severe pain was burning through the back of her head and it didn't lessen until her arms began to rise. With a grief-stricken grunt, Kerri's gloved hands lashed out. She grabbed the magazine with Angelina Jolie on the cover and callously tore it in half.

"Hey!" Veejay shouted. "What are you doing?"

Kerri didn't answer. She already had the next magazine in her grasp and gave it the same harsh ripping as the last one. She refused to stop. Mountains of mangled pages found their way to the floor as Kerri succumbed to the rage building inside of her. The magazine rack soon looked as if a tornado was blowing through it. Even ones without a baby theme on the cover suffered Kerri's wrath. She grabbed a copy of Rolling Stone and prepared to shred it in two. Her peripheral vision caught something long, yet circular coming up beside her. She spared Rolling Stone and turned her eyes a little to the right. Veejay was pointing a long-barreled shotgun at her head.

"Did you think I was just going to sit back and watch you destroy my store?" he hissed. "You stupid bitch!"

An odd aura overcame Kerri's mind as she was being yelled at; as if she was hearing and seeing everything through a clear, plastic bubble encompassing her head. She was aware of the wrongdoing going on around her, but had lost the urge to cope with it rationally.

"I'm through dealing with all the lowlifes and druggies who constantly come in and mess up my store!" Veejay went on. "The cops in this town won't do shit! So I'm taking matters into my own hands! Now you're going to pay for everything you have damaged in my store… or I'm going to blow your head off! You got that, bitch?"

Kerri's eyes stayed fixated on the obliterated magazine rack, allowing only a partial side view of the shotgun's barrel. She couldn't stand being threatened and demeaned after having her dream smashed yet again. Why couldn't Veejay understand the pain she was constantly enduring? Why couldn't anybody understand? Maybe she would be better off if he would just pull the trigger. Her brain was pounding against her skull like a jackhammer. Fresh tears dripped down her cheeks

"You hear me, bitch?" Veejay bellowed. "Pay up now!"

Kerri's hands shot forth and grappled the barrel of the shotgun. Before Veejay realized what had happened, she forcefully yanked it out of his grasp.

The leather grippers on the inside of her gloves made the extraction extra easy.

"You fucking bitch!" Veejay finally screamed.

Kerri still hadn't turned to face him, but her ears longed to shut him the fuck up. She flipped the shotgun around and sent the barrel careening forward. The cold, steel circle impaled Veejay just above his nose and remained there. Kerri tried yanking back the barrel, but to no avail. Veejay's teary eyes widened as blood spurted out in a whirlwind around the center of his face.

Unsure of how hard she had actually jabbed forward, Kerri wrapped her hands around the back end of the gun for a better grip. Her finger grazed the trigger. The top half of Veejay's head exploded into a red mushy mixture that rained all over the cash register. The rest of his body collapsed backwards onto the white tiled floor. Kerri stayed frozen with the gore-tipped shotgun still raised. Her eyes bulged without a single blink. A small haze of smoke rose up to the ceiling. What was left of Veejay's head squirted out a solitary red line onto the tiles.

Kerri finally opened her mouth and took in a long, violent stream of air. She released her tight grasp on the shotgun, letting it drop to the floor before Veejay's body. The only sounds in the store were the faint humming of the motor in the back, Kerri's deep breaths, and the gooey pieces of brain matter dripping off the counter. She was afraid to move a muscle, aware that she had most certainly brought about the end to everything. Her life was finished; it had to be. She would no doubt be continuing her baby-less years behind bars. All was lost, yet Kerri still refused to bat an eye. The numbness had taken over her whole body.

Her cell phone suddenly went off in her pocket. Its generic ring tone echoed throughout the entire store. The incessant ringing was what forced Kerri to reach into her pocket. Without looking at the caller ID screen, she flipped up the receiver.

"Hello." Her lips barely moved, making it sound more like "Ha-oh."

"Hello, Kerri, it's Dr. Phalen," the voice on the other end said.

"Oh," Kerri replied.

"Are you sitting down, Kerri?" he asked.

"No, but it doesn't matter."

She already knew what he was going to tell her and saw no point in prolonging the inevitable.

"Nothing matters," she closed her eyes and continued. "I already know."

"You do?" Dr. Phalen asked. "Did you start having some symptoms? It's still kind of early."

"What the hell are you talking about?" Kerri opened up her eyes.

"Well, it seems kind of frivolous now since you already know, but congratulations, you're going to be a mother."

Kerri's went silent as she gazed at the pool of blood forming around Veejay's body. The silence felt awkward.

"Well, Mommy," Dr. Phalen said. "Say something."

Kerri slowly opened up her mouth like a deaf mute attempting to utter her first sound. Finally, her vocal cords kicked in.

"Uh…I… I'm not pregnant," she said. "I can't be. I, I just got my period."

"Really? Are you sure?" Dr. Phalen's voice never shifted in pitch. "That isn't very likely considering the test results we just got."

"Well, Doctor, I just checked between my legs and found blood."

"I see." He paused briefly. "Exactly how much blood did you find?"

"What do you mean?"

"Well, was it a relatively heavy flow or was it more like just a touch, like spotting."

Kerri forced her mind to play back the image of her bloody fingers and recalled only a light glaze of red smudged over them.

"No, it wasn't very heavy," she replied.

"Well then Kerri, I have more good news for you," the doctor's voice grinned on the other end of the line. "Actually, it's just the same good news as before."

"What are you talking about? I still don't understand."

"Please, Kerri, allow me to explain. You see, the bits of blood you found are just the embryo implanting into the uterus. It's called implantation bleeding. It is a perfectly normal initial sign of pregnancy, especially with in vitro fertilization. Trust me, Kerri, you *are* pregnant!"

Kerri lowered the phone from her ear. She looked down at what was left of Veejay, then directed her gaze ahead to the front door of the store.

"*Kerri?*" the receiver faintly called out from her hip. "Kerri? Are you still there?"

The phone was smartly snapped shut. Kerri's feet dislodged their soles from the floor and quickly moved her forward. She made sure to steer clear of the bloodied body. Upon reaching the front door, she hurriedly turned the locking latch until it clicked in place. She flipped over the 'CLOSED' side of the hanging sign and rushed back into the medicinal section of the store. There were only two brands of pregnancy tests on the shelf. Kerri snatched the more expensive one and headed back to the bathroom beside the refrigerated section.

Paying no attention to the humming noise or dull lighting, she tore into the cardboard packaging and removed the digital 'measuring' stick.

With her pants around her ankles, she squatted over the toilet. The stick was skinny, which made it tough to get a reading. Kerri did her best to aim her stream of urine onto the designated area. Once the stick was sufficiently soaked, she brought it out and stood up. Without wiping, pulling up her pants, or flushing, she held the small digital screen up to her eyes. The box said it could take up to three minutes before the result was displayed. Kerri refused to blink. She stared ominously into the still blank screen, waiting. The stick was so close to her face that she could smell her piss on it.

"Come on," she growled. "Just get it over with."

As her mouth curved into an angry frown, something started to appear on the screen. The faint, grayish background was overtaken by a dark, circular visage. The blackened digital bits gradually came more into focus. Kerri brought the stick even closer. A little smiley face was soon staring back at her. She held the stick a ways back for a less obtrusive view. The smiley was still there. Her eyes started to twitch. Never in her life had she expected to ever bear witness to the positive pregnancy symbol. Her heart skipped three beats. She inhaled deeply through her mouth, waited two seconds, and then exhaled. For so long she had fantasized about how her reaction would be once she found out that she was finally pregnant. However, none of those fanciful reveries resided in her current state of affairs. It still couldn't be true. Kerri had to look at the digital screen again just to make sure. The smiley continued to flash its digitized grin as if to say, *Hey, you're knocked up. Congrats.*

She stepped out of the bathroom, stick still in hand, and caught sight of the bloody mess on the floor. She couldn't help wondering if she was trapped in some sort of surreal dream. Maybe she was still at the medical facility, hopped up on Valium, awaiting her in vitro treatment. Even if that was true, she wasn't sure whether she wanted to wake up or not. She quickly, but cautiously, stepped over to the corpse. While staring down at Veejay's remains, she tenderly hugged her hands around her tummy. She closed her eyes and pictured a newborn child in her arms gazing up at her with the deepest blue eyes. When her eyelids lifted back up, the vision disappeared, which sent an instant pain through her chest. Her mind had been made up.

"Cameras," she said quietly.

She cast a glance about the upper regions of the store, searching for any stray wires or video equipment. Nothing appeared to be on the walls, but that wouldn't serve as good enough.

While vigilantly avoiding the still forming lake of red, Kerri moved to the area behind the cash register. She crouched beneath the counter and sent her gloved hands sifting through a stretch of various hidden crevices. No video recording equipment of any kind was discovered, just a small set of keys, which she stuffed inside her pocket. Seeing as how the store was a tad on the dilapidated side and located in a crappy section of the town, the fact that there was no high-tech security didn't make Kerri feel too surprised, just fortunate. It also explained why Veejay was so quick to break out the shotgun.

Kerri stood up behind the counter to contemplate her next move. The cash register covered in carnage looked like it had been murdered as well. A light bulb went off in her head.

A robbery, she thought and peered closer at the register's buttons.

Having worked as a checkout clerk at a grocery store throughout high school, Kerri had a fairly keen grasp on how cash registers worked. She picked up a pen that was lying on the counter and used it to press a green rectangular button. With a little *ding*, the cash drawer at the base popped open. At once, Kerri began removing all the stacks of dollar bills. She made sure the retrieval went sloppily on purpose, scattering a couple of random ten's and twenty's on the floor.

After emerging from behind the counter, she still had a large wad of cash in her hands. There was no chance in hell she was keeping it for herself, but a robbery had to appear to have taken place. For some amazing reason, Kerri's mind was thinking quite clearly.

The bathroom, her brain instructed.

She headed swiftly back once again to the wooden door and entered. The wad of bills was tossed into the toilet, which still contained her smiley-face-inducing urine. She tore up the pregnancy test box and threw it in as well. The evidence floated about in the bowl like soup ingredients. Kerri flushed it all down, made sure the bathroom was clean, and moved back into the store. She walked down the aisle to the far left, totally avoiding the mess by the cash register. Once back at the front, she took the small set of keys out from her pocket. The store was beginning to conjure a stringently foul odor. Kerri knew that it was time to leave.

Okay, just forget about everything you just did, her mind coached. *Step out of that door and into your new life. Concentrate on how you're going to tell Will the news. You've been waiting so long to tell him this. That is your focus starting now. Just walk out that door.*

She peered out through the glass, checking for any passers-by. The coast was seemingly clear. Keys in hand, Kerri crept up to the door and carefully unhinged the lock. Without looking back, she slipped onto the outside sidewalk. The door shut behind her, still flashing the **CLOSED** sign. She quickly inserted key after key until the right one fit. The lock was snapped back in place. Kerri shoved the keys into her left pocket and began stepping rapidly away from the store. Luckily, the sidewalk was unpopulated and nary a car passed by on the street.

Get to the car, her mind commanded. *Just get to the car, right now!*

The Kia was a short, straight trek roughly two blocks down the sidewalk. Kerri did her best to travel at a brisk, yet inconspicuous pace. An old man wearing a frail leather paperboy-style hat emerged onto her path. He had just passed by the Kia on his way toward her.

Stay calm, she told herself. *He knows nothing. Just keep on walking. You're almost there.*

Her expedited advances took her past the large plate-glass window of the Laundromat. She instinctively glanced partially at her reflection.

Oh shit! her brain bellowed. *Shit! Shit! Oh no!*

A long, streaming bloodstain marked up a large section on the inside of her jacket's right arm. Kerri's first impulse was to begin batting at it immediately until the stain went away. However with the 'paperboy' man drawing nearer, she knew it was best to draw as little attention to herself as possible. So darting across the street was also out of the question.

He's coming right this way! Her head was about to explode. *Why did he have to be walking my way right at this moment? Damn it! What's his fucking problem? Son of a bitch!*

Suddenly, the pain in Kerri's stomach shifted. It still hurt, but the reason felt different. She was now filled with an ache to lash out at the 'paperboy' man. The fear had turned to a weird kind of rage. Fortunately the abrupt deletion of fear enabled her to think on a much clearer level. Her excessively jazzercising heart slowed to its regular beat. The man was now fifteen feet away and closing in fast. Kerri actually slowed down her pace a bit. As the two crossed paths, the man partially turned his head her way, like any other red-blooded American male that was walking by a pretty blonde. Kerri slid her eyes to the left and actually looked right at him. The moment their stares met, she emitted a sweet, humble smile. The man almost tripped over his feet, much like any other red-blooded American male who'd just been smiled at by a woman clearly out of his league. Kerri allowed her grin to linger on a bit longer, waiting, almost hoping, for him to make some kind of false move.

Come on, she thought through her smirk. *Do something. Do anything. Spot the blood on my arm. It's there. Ask me about it. Please… and see what will happen to you.*

The man quietly continued on his way without so much as looking back to check out her ass. Kerri gave a fast, glance over her shoulder for final verification. Satisfied, she resumed her stroll toward the Kia.

Was I just wishing for him to stop me? she wondered. *Am I out of my mind? Oh God, I have to get out of here.*

She whipped her jacket off the instant she sat down in the car and flung it on the floor in the back. After disposing of her gloves the same way, she stabbed the key into the ignition and started the engine. The Kia made haste in peeling out of its parking space. Kerri kept a tense grip with both hands on the steering wheel. Her arms couldn't stop faintly shaking. She wanted to call Will right away, but didn't feel she was in the right frame of mind to speak to him.

What do I say? I'm pregnant, uh… and I just killed a man. Yeah, that'll go over just great. Okay, forget it. I just need to get home. I'll go home, I'll lie down on the couch, I'll force myself to relax, and then I'll call him. There, that's it. That's my plan.

Chapter 10

Kerri never called Will. She made it home. She made it out of the Kia. She made it in her house. She then walked up to the couch and collapsed on the floor beside it. It took her all of roughly thirty seconds before her overworked nerves shut down and sent her to sleep. She was completely dead to the world for the next seven and a half hours.

A set of screeching tires finally stirred her senses. The following noise of a car door slamming shut broke Kerri fully free from her slumber. Her eyes popped open and took in the view of the base of the couch. Fast footsteps outside were getting closer by the second.

What time is it? she wondered, recognizing that the house had become enveloped in darkness.

A harsh thud erupted at the front door. Kerri could hear the doorknob jiggling madly. She rose to her feet as the door burst open.

"Kerri!" Will called out right away. "Are you home?"

"Yeah!" she yelled back. "I'm in here!"

Another row of fast footing overtook the house as Will went rushing into the living room. He reached for the nearest light switch. The darkness was instantly flushed out.

"Oh my God," Will exhaled upon witnessing Kerri before the couch. "I was so worried. I thought..."

"What?" Kerri asked. "You knew I took off today. I don't like when you get your nerves all worked up."

"You never called. You said you were going to call me. Then I tried calling your cell, I tried calling you at home... you never picked up."

"I'm sorry, Will. As soon as I got back home I fell right to sleep. I was just really tired."

"You went to the doctor and then came right home? You didn't go anywhere else?"

Veejay's mutilated skull immediately flashed through Kerri's mind. She gave her eyes one hard blink before answering,

"No, nowhere else."

She despised lying to him, but knew he wouldn't be able to sustain hearing the graphic truth.

"And that's it?" Will held up his palms.

"Yeah, I think so," Kerri plainly replied.

"Oh," he said, softly. "Okay, then."

Will hung his head a tad, but still didn't break eye contact. He sensed a slight standoffishness in Kerri's voice, which up until this point could have only meant one thing. Though convinced and disheartened that he once again had failed at becoming a dad, he vowed to show no signs of outer sorrow. He did not want to upset her any further. In fact, he decided to not even bring up her doctor visit that day and pretend it never happened.

"Well, um, are you hungry," he said. "I can make us some dinner if you like."

Kerri realized she hadn't eaten anything all day.

"Yeah," she said, "I'm kind of hungry."

"Okay, I'll whip something up right now."

Will looked away and took one big step toward the kitchen.

"Wait!" Kerri blurted out.

Will halted, a little startled, and almost tripped.

"What?" he asked fast. "What's wrong?"

"Nothing's wrong." Then Kerri smiled her first real smile of the day. "Nothing's wrong at all."

"You don't mean..." Will's feet changed their direction toward the living room. "...that... it..."

"It worked," she simply nodded.

"So you're telling me that you're..."

Kerri quietly nodded again. Will was unable to reply. His heart had stopped beating. He couldn't recall what had gone on at work that day. He forgot how he got home. The meal he was just planning in his head to make for Kerri had disappeared. His wife nodding her head was the only thing replaying in his mind over and over. He began walking toward her. Still speechless, the sides of his mouth curved upward and hardened immediately. He nearly plowed Kerri over before wrapping his arms tightly around her upper body.

"AAAAHHHHH!" he noisily exhaled. "I can't... I can't believe it... it happened!"

Will buried his face into her shoulder. His eyes welled up like two water balloons. Crying had never really been a trait of his before. Getting a little misty-eyed once in a while was possible, but never a full-blown sob-fest; not even tears of joy. However, this singular moment with Kerri would serve as the only exception.

"I can't believe it," was all he could repeat between rows of clamorous, but happy, weeps.

He had never been this moved before in his entire life.

"Finally... finally!" He was able to speak between great gasps. "I'm... so... proud of you... Ker!"

"It was the both of us," Kerri gasped for air, still caught up in his bear hug.

She gently rubbed his back with both hands. Will refused to let go.

"I... can't... stop... crying," he confessed to her shoulder. "I... I wish your parents could've been here for this."

"Thank you, Will. I do too."

"I just want to stay here for a little bit." He kept staring down at her shoulder. "Okay?"

"Okay, Will, that's fine," she said, trying to squeeze him back. "I've got you... I mean, you've got me."

He was unable to laugh at her little jab at his overindulgent embrace. The emotional explosion kept him from even hearing it. He merely stayed hunched over, soaking the left side of Kerri's shirt.

"I'm sorry I'm getting snot on your shoulder," Will sniveled, attempting to add some humor toward the sheepish situation.

"Shut up, Will," Kerri said. "It's fine."

The wetness near her neck didn't bother her in the least. However, her thoughts were forcefully engulfed by another feeling of vexation. She had always pictured herself swimming deeply within enormous joy upon finally discovering that she was pregnant. The image was so strong that it brought her to tears practically every time she imagined it. Yet for some reason, now that the image had come to fruition, the feelings inside her were not as she had pictured—not even close. Granted, having her dream realization stem from the gore-filled death of Veejay did offer an offsetting effect on the occasion. But guilt wasn't the real anchor currently weighing Kerri down. She felt something scary, unsettling. She was worried. But about what? If the incident at the 24-Hour Mart wasn't affecting her, then how could anything else?

Why do I feel this way? she wondered. *Why can't I be happy? I deserve this.*

Will was finally purging all of the pent-up joy he had been waiting so patiently to express. Kerri desperately longed to share in the experience that they had strove to create together. It would have been the fitting manner. It was what she had always wanted for so long.

Why don't I want it now? she wondered and then froze.

Her hands ceased rubbing Will's back. She couldn't believe the question that had just crossed her mind. What could possibly lead her to think such a thing? It wasn't supposed to be this way.

Maybe this is my punishment? she considered.

That notion did not sit well.

No, her brain continued, *that man shoved a gun in my face. Me, a woman. He was the one truly at fault. He shouldn't have brought out the gun in the first place. I was merely protecting myself and, instinctively, the baby inside me. In actuality, I was acting the role of a concerned parent. God, where the hell am I going with this—crazy? Am I nuts?*

Kerri had to halt her runaway-train head-trip before it crashed off the tracks. She couldn't understand what was causing this strange reversal of feelings and fret that something could be wrong internally. Her heart began to race as Will at long last picked his head up.

"Oh my God," he said with a sniff. "I can't remember the last time I cried like that. I really am sorry about your shoulder. I totally soaked it. Man, and they say the woman is the one who's supposed to get all emotional. Talk about a freakin' role reversal."

"Wait," Kerri quickly said. "What did you just say?"

"Freakin' role reversal?" Will asked.

"No, not that. That thing about the getting emotional. What was that?"

"Oh, I was just saying how whacked out a woman can get when she first becomes pregnant. You know, like in that one book we read that talked about all the new hormones your body takes on when there's another life inside you."

"Yes, my hormone levels double every day in the beginning. I remember." She glanced down at her tummy. "I remember."

The twinge of worry deep inside her had relaxed for the time being. An explanation for her disconcerting feelings and repellent behavior had surfaced. Kerri took solace in the understanding that a name had been given to her faceless inner demon; Ms. Hormone.

Chapter 11

The First Trimester

The red pen streaked across paper after paper, leaving a trail of check marks and grades ranging from D+ to A-. Kerri sat behind her desk, keeping her eyes pointed downward, recording every mark. The students all stayed seated behind their own desks. Some were getting head starts on their homework, while some simply stared at the slowly ticking clock. The bell would be going off in roughly three minutes. It was Kerri's last class of the day and the day was Friday, which meant that she was exhausted from a full work week. As a relaxing reward, she had deemed the last ten minutes of class 'free time for all'. The first trimester was now in full effect, and her stomach was currently sending out a steady stream of gas. She had to keep her ass pressed firmly against the base of her chair to keep any foul smells from leaking out. 'Sitting On It' was what Will referred to it as. Suddenly her nose started to wrinkle.

"A-choo!" she erupted, covering her mouth.

The vibration of the sneeze caused her to shift in her seat, releasing a silent, smelly puff from her butt. She nonchalantly moved her hand off her mouth up to her nose to prevent the escaped odor from entering her nostrils.

"Bless you," said one of her students.

Kerri looked up from her desk to say thank you to whoever spoke. Much to her chagrin, she spotted Trent, the most recent recipient of a D+, gawking at her.

"God bless you, Mrs. Haddon," the big-eared boy repeated, adding a little, smarmy wink.

Repulsed, Kerri tightly squeezed the pen in her right hand.

"Thank you, Trent," she replied with the utmost reluctance.

"Anytime." The gross grin grew wider. "And I mean *any* time."

Kerri quickly directed her sight back down to her desk before he got a chance to see her scowl. Her wrist muscles tensed up and delivered an even tighter grip on her pen. She gazed right through the pile of marked and unmarked papers, her mind focusing only on rage. The school bell went off. Kerri's shoulders jerked gawkily at the unanticipated sound.

The students collectively rose up from their desks and began packing up their books. Kerri called up enough composure in order to put on a congenial face for their departure.

"Have a nice weekend, everyone," she said softly as the students started exiting the room.

Trent kept his eyes on her all the way until he reached the exit. Kerri cautiously watched him out the corner of her eye, channeling all her anger into the grasp around the red pen. The hallway outside was bubbling over with juvenile voices anxious to get a jump on Friday night.

Once the classroom was empty, Kerri closed her eyes and took one big, deep breath.

"Thank God it's Friday," said a woman's voice from the hall. "Isn't that right, Mommy?"

Kerri opened her eyes and turned toward the door to find Lynn standing with a smile.

"Oh, you can say that again," she replied. "How was your day, Lynn?"

"It was fine," Lynn began, but abruptly switched her tone. "But, honey, what happened to your hand?"

Kerri looked down to find a pool of red gushing out from her right palm all over her papers.

"Oh, shit," she exclaimed, dropping the cracked plastic pen casing. "I think my pen broke."

"Jesus, Ker, I thought you were bleeding. Don't scare me like that."

"I'm sorry, Lynn." Kerri opened up a desk drawer. "I didn't mean to scare you. Jeez, this is messy."

She took a clump of tissues out from the desk drawer and began wiping the red up. Lynn walked over to her.

"You need a hand with that?" she asked.

"Oh, no, Lynn," Kerri replied. "That's okay. I don't want you to get all messy too."

Lynn glanced down at the crushed writing instrument.

"Honey, how did you bust that pen?"

"I'm not really sure. I was grading papers and waiting for the bell to ring... and Trent was..."

"Trent, huh? Well, that might explain it. I guess I just caught you letting off some steam."

"Yeah." Kerri held up her hand. "Caught me red handed."

"Ha, I guess so." She took another look at the spilled ink. "My God, you really must have been pissed. And that poor pen got the brunt of it. Check that out, you totally annihilated it."

"I know and I didn't even mean to."

Lynn leaned in close to her and whispered, "Too bad you couldn't have wrapped that aggression of yours around Trent's scrawny little neck."

"Hmm." Kerri paused to silently picture her hands squeezing Trent's jugular until the whites of his eyes turned red. "Too bad."

She sopped up the remaining traces of red and tossed the stained clumps of tissues into the waste basket.

"So tell me, Ker, what are we doing tonight?" Lynn asked.

"Well, some of the people Will works with want to go out for happy hour to celebrate us getting pregnant," Kerri explained. "Will really wanted me to come along, but I don't really know his work friends all that well."

"And you figured you'd bring me along to kind of even things up a bit."

"I wanted a work friend of my own to talk to."

"Well, what's the name of this place again?"

"Uncle Mike's, I think. It's by where Will works. They say the food there is pretty good."

"Pretty good food, huh?" Lynn crossed her arms and raised an eyebrow. "Okay, that's a start. However, I may need a little more convincing."

"Name it!" Kerri smiled.

"Have they got coconut shrimp as an appetizer?"

"I'm sure they do, but if they don't, I'll find a local supermarket and buy you a box of Gorton's to have all to yourself."

"All right, I like the sound of that. Anything else?"

"Uhm... yeah, of course. Uh... okay, how about this. I think one of Will's work friends is single and cute."

"Really?"

"Well, I know that he's definitely single and his name is Fred."

"Hmm, the possibility of frozen Gorton's coconut shrimp and a single, but not necessarily cute guy whose name is Fred... that sounds fantastic! I'll totally be your wing-man."

"Thanks, Lynn. I owe you."

"Anytime, my red-handed momma. Now let's get our asses out of here. It's drinking time... for me, not for you."

After Kerri packed up all her belongings, they both left the building. Since Lynn was planning on getting her 'drink' on, Kerri volunteered to drive.

The trip to Uncle Mike's was about twenty minutes with minimal traffic. Upon arrival, the Kia parked in a lot across the not-too-busy street. Will's Saturn was already there.

"I think they're all inside," Kerri said, as they approached the entryway to the bar and grill.

"Oh, I hope that 'slight-chance-of-being-cute' guy is there," Lynn smirked.

"Oh, honey, I'm so excited for you," Kerri sarcastically replied.

The two walked inside and cast simultaneous glances over toward the bar area. Neither could spot their party right away.

"There she is!" cried out a man's voice from the direction the two were staring. "There's the pregnant lady!"

Kerri and Lynn both zeroed in on the location of the shouting to find Fred maniacally waving them over. Kerri spotted Will standing right beside him and felt comfortable moving forward.

"That's not…" Lynn began.

"Uhm… yeeeah," Kerri reluctantly answered. "Sorry about that."

"There just better be coconut shrimp."

As the two made their way over, Fred freely continued with his obnoxious outbursts.

"Everyone out of the way!" he exclaimed. "Pregnant woman coming through! Please disperse! She is carrying a child and needs space!"

"Thanks, Fred," Kerri said, walking up to him. "Have you started drinking yet?"

"Of course!" Fred bellowed, giving her a light hug. "I started the second I got to the bar!"

"And you haven't stopped since," Will interjected, placing a hand on his shoulder.

Fred at once released his embrace and took a step back. Will stepped in closer to Kerri, revealing a tall red drink with a black straw in his hand.

"A Shirley Temple for the lovely lady carrying our baby," he smiled, passing the drink to her.

"Thanks," she replied, reaching out her right hand. "Just what I wanted."

"Kerri, what happened to your hand?" he asked in dismay, but not wanting to make a scene.

"Oh." She held up her stained palm. "One of my red pens burst at work. It's nothing, really."

"It happens to teachers all the time," Lynn added. "Damn defective pens."

"I got it," Will said and handed over the Shirley Temple. "You didn't get any of it on your clothes, did you? I know how you hate that."

"No, Will, I'm fine," Kerri assured. "Stop worrying about me. It's happy hour, right? Let's start getting happy."

She took a big chug from her Shirley Temple without using the straw.

"All right!" Lynn concurred with her party attitude. "Where's the coconut shrimp?"

"Good call!" Fred jumped back into the conversation. "Somebody get this woman a menu!" He slipped up beside Lynn. "Can I get you a drink in the meantime Miss…"

She shot a bemused glance over to Kerri before answering, "Lynn. My name's Lynn."

"Nice to meet you, Miss Lynn. My name's Fred. I'm drinking Budweiser. And you're drinking…"

"Vodka and cranberry." Lynn caught on right away.

"Vodka and cranberry coming right up." Fred stepped over to the bar.

"Watch out for him, Lynn," Will warned with a grin. "He's a wild one."

"Well, lucky me," Lynn smiled, "'cause I'm looking to get extra wild tonight!"

After gracing Kerri with another look of mock disdain, she traipsed up to the bar to receive her drink.

"She sure is a fun one," Will said.

"She sure is," Kerri agreed. "Do you think Fred knows she's only using him for free drinks?"

"Absolutely not," Will answered right away. "But it sure is going to be fun to watch."

Before Kerri got a chanced to laugh, she was instantly bombarded by well-wishers.

"Oh, congratulations, honey!" exclaimed Loni, administering a good squeeze. She was clearly already a good two drinks ahead of everyone else.

"Thanks," Kerri could barely eek out while held captive in Loni's cleavage.

"Mmwah!" Loni planted a great big, possibly collagen-infused kiss on her cheek. "I'm so happy for you!"

She finally relinquished her hold, allowing Kerri a moment to catch her breath. A large lipstick imprint remained on her cheek.

"Oh, let me get that," Loni said rapidly applying the base of her thumb to Kerri's face. "There, that's better."

"Whoa, Loni, easy there!" Will came to the rescue. "She's only eight weeks pregnant. We still have to be very delicate with her. She's not some cute, little doll, you know?"

"Oh, he's so protective of you," Loni said to Kerri. "I love that. That's what I need from a man."

"Well, I guess I'm a lucky girl," Kerri stated, and moved closer to Will.

"Yeah," Loni agreed. "He's definitely a keeper."

She gave Will a little rub on the shoulder, which gave Kerri reason for pause. She stared intently, watching this other woman gently caressing her husband, and felt something sharp streaming through her veins. Her arms involuntarily yanked Will closer, out of Loni's range of touch.

"Whoa," Will uttered, nearly losing his balance.

Kerri quickly wrapped both her arms around him to awkwardly cover up her jealous action. She placed her head on his shoulder and flashed a fake grin. Fortunately, her intentions flew right under Loni's radar.

"Aw, you two are so in love," she merely smiled. "Oh, we should do some shots to celebrate! Well, I know you can't, Kerri, but you can cheer Will on if you like."

"Well, Lon, I don't know," Will said. "Shots can really do a number on me and I still have to drive home later."

"Oh come on, Will. Don't be a big wimp. We're all here for *you*. You owe it to us to be a gracious guest. Now get your butt over here and take your medicine. Let's go, Kerri really wants to cheer you on. Isn't that right, Kerri?"

On the contrary, Kerri didn't want Will drinking any remotely inhibiting substances around this big-breasted baby, not even Nyquil. However, she felt too self-conscious amidst all the new people to express how she was truly feeling. These were Will's friends and she didn't feel right creating some kind of scene.

"Sure, Will," she softly replied. "Do a shot with your friends."

"Okay, you have the wife's permission," Loni beamed. "Do you feel better now? Can we proceed?"

"Fine, fine," Will said. "Let's go do the shots!"

"Yay! Hey Fred! Kamikaze shots right now! Get 'em lined up!"

"You know it!" Fred called back, already beside the bar.

82

Will watched him holding up his hand to get the bartender's attention. A cluster of his fellow co-workers began to rapidly form around the pouring area. He looked back at Kerri.

"You're sure you're okay with shots?" he asked.

"Yes, I'm su…" Kerri didn't get a chance to finish as Will was sharply pulled away from her.

"Come on, Will!" Loni said, holding onto his arm. "You have to be the first one in line!"

While being led toward the bar, Will looked back at Kerri and quickly waved for her to come after him. She tried taking a couple of steps forward, but the crowd before the bartender had grown pretty thick.

"Excuse me," she said softly, trying not to push anybody too hard.

Will was now out of her sights. There were too many people blocking her. She could only hear a lot of cheering and yelling and the sounds of shot glasses being slammed onto the bar. Loni's high-pitched, valley-girl voice was soon drowning out everyone else's. Kerri eventually had to give up and settle for standing on the outskirts.

After a good five minutes of swigging, the masses finally began to clear. Kerri could see Will standing in the middle of Loni and Fred. Lynn was up close on the scene as well. They were all laughing and drinking. None of them turned toward Kerri or attempted to acknowledge her in any way. A strange feeling of loneliness swept over her, like she was some unpopular high school girl being purposely shunned by the in-crowd. She wanted to walk forward and join them, but didn't think they'd have her. And her own husband was in the group!

What the hell are you thinking? her brain laughed. *Just go over there and stand next to Will.*

Before Kerri could set forth a foot, her eyes spied Loni getting extra close with Will once again. Her left, enhanced boob was grazing the back of his arm as she was leaning in, whispering into his ear. Kerri's pupils started to dilate. She bit down on the inside of her lip. Loni was now giving Will a little rub in the center of his back and proceeded to move her hand up and around his shoulder like they were some kind of 'buddy, buddy' couple.

Fucking kill her! Kerri's mind screamed out.

The loud thought pushed her legs into motion. She blindly took two big steps forward and bumped into the back of a random male patron. He slow turned around, revealing a half-empty beer mug and a wet blue shirt.

"Oh," she said, stepping back. "I'm so sorry. I… didn't see you."

Fortunately, the man did not appear as peeved as he could have been. Most men usually tend not to mind when a pretty woman spills beer on them.

"Don't worry about it," he said and turned away.

Kerri refused to take a moment to thank her good looks. With Loni still in her sights, her inner rage continued to flow. She desperately longed to continue moving forward, but noticed a fair amount of patrons scattered all over her path. She realized how public the place was and acting out her aggression in front of everyone wouldn't reflect positively on Will. But the rage continued to thrive. If Kerri didn't find an outlet soon, she feared a bloody spectacle would soon be occurring. The crowd kept getting louder. The room grew smaller. She could feel icy chills spreading out across her back, and frantically looked about the room. A red neon sign, which read, **RESTROOMS** soon caught her attention. The trail leading to its double doors seemed to be fairly clear. Loni's shrill laughter was still ringing in her ears. Redirecting her eyes away from the bar, Kerri charged toward the neon light.

The double doors burst open revealing two more separated doors. Kerri chose the one with the picture of a stick figure wearing a skirt. Once inside, she headed for the nearest lime-green-colored stall and barricaded herself behind it. She pressed her hands into the inner walls and attempted catching her breath. The bathroom was empty. Her brisk inhales and exhales echoed back and forth inside the tiny stall.

I want to sit down, she thought to herself. *I have to sit down.*

She turned around to the toilet and discovered that no amounts of toilet paper would ever make it a suitable seat. Loni's cackle lingered on in her mind. She cupped her hands over her ears, but could still hear it. The image of Loni touching her husband stabbed her brain over and over.

"Stop, stop, stop!" she yelled.

Her arms suddenly dropped to her sides. She balled her right hand into a fist. Her brow creased into an angry 'V' as a tear ran down her cheek. She drew back her right shoulder and sent her fist flying forward. Her knuckles crashed into the lime-green wall, leaving a substantial circular dent. Not satisfied, Kerri swung her arm back and delivered another even harder blow to the dented target. Her entire body abruptly stumbled into the wall as her fist went right through it.

Kerri waited there for a moment with the side of her face pressed into lime-green. Her legs buckled a bit in the stall as her fist unwound in the one next door. The rage was starting to unwind as well. Although she had placed herself in a rather poor position, Kerri still let out a small sigh of relief. The door to the ladies' room creaked open. Kerri's head at once perked up. She heard high-heeled footsteps drifting towards the row of stalls.

"Oh no," Kerri silently whispered.

She rose fully up to her feet and established some semblance of balance. The footsteps were getting closer. Kerri hurriedly pressed her left hand into the wall and gave a hard tug. Her right hand did not join her back in the stall. The impact of her punch had bent the aluminum wall in such a way that her arm had become nicely lodged. Unable to think, she started violently pulling and pulling. However, with each yank, a sharp piece of aluminum scraped into her skin.

Damn it! her mind exclaimed. *Why... won't... my arm... come back!*

The high heels walked past the first stall on their way to the next open door. Kerri tightly shut her eyes, clenched her teeth, and exerted a single, powerful jerk backwards. The forceful effort sent her body to the opposite end of the stall. Her arm had broken free from the aluminum wall, but was unable to escape injury. A small array of deep, crimson scratches traced her forearm all the way up to her bloody knuckles. Kerri reached down for some toilet paper just as the high heels entered the adjacent stall. She ducked out of the way so as not to be seen through the hole, and waited.

"Whoa," said a feminine voice from the other side. "That's one big hole."

"I know, right?" Kerri found herself answering automatically.

"How'd it get there?" the woman asked with a laugh.

"I have no idea."

"Well, something pretty strong must have hit it. My father used to set up stalls like these. They're double reinforced."

Kerri glanced down at her bloody hand wrapped in tissue.

"Wow, uh, yeah," she replied. "Must have been pretty strong."

"Weird stuff. Well, I've really got to go. You mind if I use this stall?"

"Oh, no, not at all. I was just finishing up. So don't worry, I'm not going to peek."

"Thank you very much," the woman chuckled.

Kerri hastily tore off her blood-soaked dressings and flushed them down the toilet. She high-tailed it out of the stall and headed for the sink area. The first available faucet dispelled a mechanized stream of cold water the instant she placed her arm under it. The sink turned a dark shade of pink as her bloody wounds were washed out. The cuts stung as she rubbed a smear of soap across them. The woman in the stall next to hers flushed the

85

toilet. Kerri darted over to the paper towel dispenser and began pumping its handle. Once a long enough wad was produced, she ripped it free and wrapped it around her wounded hand. The lock on the stall became unlatched. Kerri rushed toward the exit, tossing out the wet paper towel wrap on the way. She made it out of the bathroom before even seeing the face of her former stall-mate. All alone again, she checked on her right hand. The cuts were still there and it was a little moist, but the blood had seemed to stop flowing so heavily. Even better though, was the feeling that her rage level had sufficiently shrunk.

I can't believe how upset I got, she thought. *I really wanted to kill her. My hormones are really crazy right now. I have to start learning how to keep them under control.*

Kerri walked through the double doors and reentered the bar. Determined to not let the hormones get the best of her again, she marched up to Will and the rest of his party. He noticed her right away.

"Hey Kerri," he said, stepping away from Loni. "Where did you go? You missed the medley of shots."

Kerri was pleased to see him step away from the large chested one.

"I just had to go to the bathroom," she said, regaining a hold on his arm. "You know I go a lot more now."

"Yeah, I know you're peeing for two. You're being such a trooper through all of this so far."

He planted a sweet kiss on her lips. Kerri instantly returned the favor, making sure that Loni got a good view of it.

"Thanks, Will. I appreciate that."

She rose up her right hand and caressed his cheek. Will's eyes rolled over to her fingertips.

"Wow," he said, staring at her hand. "That pen really got you."

Kerri shot a fleeting glance toward her right hand. The blood had made it even redder than before.

"Yeah," she replied, lowering the hand out of view. "That ink sure does stain."

Chapter 12

Kerri was in the middle of another one of her after-school naps when the phone rang. Being on her feet all day was now an extra tiring task and almost always forced her to hit the couch five minutes after walking through the front door. The phone's second ring dropped her a bit from dreamland. Will rushed to pick it up.

"Hello?" Kerri could hear him say. "Hold on a second."

He crept into the living room and knelt down before sleeping beauty.

"Ker," he whispered. "Are you taking calls?"

"Who is it?" she asked without opening her eyes.

"I think it's your old gyno's office. Should I just tell them you're sleeping?"

"No." Her eyes slowly opened. "I'll take it."

He handed her the cordless phone and exited the room.

"Hello?" Kerri said into the receiver.

"Hi, Kerri, this is Nurse Warren," replied a nasally woman's voice on the other end. "We haven't heard from you in a while and Dr. Granning was just curious how you were doing."

"Oh, uhm, I'm doing fine. I'm doing great. Actually, I'm pregnant."

"Well, that is good news. Why haven't you called us to set up an appointment? It is very important for the doctor to see you early on in the pregnancy."

"Yeah, I know that." Kerri paused, a bit uncomfortable with what she had to say next. "But I kind of switched over to a new doctor."

"What?" the nurse gasped.

"Yeah, I'm sorry. I had been meaning to call you and let you know. But things have just gotten so hectic recently, I never got a chance."

"May I ask why you decided to switch doctors?"

"Yeah, sure." Kerri did not like the nurse's tone. "It's just that we didn't seem to be getting anywhere with Dr. Granning and we were just growing so frustrated and upset. My husband found out about this other doctor and special procedure he does during fertilization. So we decided to give him a try… and it worked."

She pronounced the last three words with great enthusiasm, hoping it would take Nurse Warren's mind off attack mode.

"Kerri, hold on for a second, please," was the nurse's reply.

The receiver blipped onto mute. Kerri patiently waited with the phone up to her ear, worrying about what Nurse Warren could be thinking or doing. The receiver soon clicked back on.

"Kerri, Dr. Granning is very offended that you would go off and see another doctor without telling him," the nurse said coldly.

"Well… I'm sorry about that." Kerri was caught off guard. "I didn't think th…"

"No, you obviously weren't thinking. Dr. Granning would like a chance to speak to you privately and explain why it would be a mistake going with any doctor other than him."

"Again, I'm sorry, but I don't want…"

"Listen, Kerri, Dr. Granning is a highly respected physician and doesn't deserve to be treated in this unprofessional manner by you. Now when can I schedule you an appointment to come in and speak with him?"

The muscles in Kerri's throat had lost the ability to speak. She was completely flabbergasted. Her heart began an up tempo beat and salty liquid filled her eyes. This wasn't the first time she had a bad experience with Dr. Granning's office, which was why she never really cared for them.

"I really don't feel the need to talk to Dr. Granning," she said. "The main goal was to get me pregnant and now that's done. I just don't see why I'd have to…"

"No, Kerri!" Nurse Warren hollered. "You're being unreasonable. You owe it to Dr. Granning. He deserves a chance to be heard. You can't just go around switching doctors with no good reason."

"But I did have a reason."

"That will be for Dr. Granning to decide. Now for the last time, when shall I schedule you?"

Kerri pressed her hand into her forehead and dragged her nails back through her hair. She couldn't handle the mounting pressure of the conversation. Her arms were trembling. A thick searing throb was bursting out through her chest. With her last strand of strength, she brought the receiver of the phone up to her mouth.

"Let me check my schedule," she barely eked out. "And I'll call you back."

"Okay, fine, just hurry up," Nurse Warren ordered. "The office is closing in the next forty minutes."

"All right."

Kerri heard the phone on the other end slam down. A dial tone was soon ringing in her ear. She turned off the cordless phone and placed it down on the couch. She was waiting for the tears to roll down her face. As the liquid reached her eyelids' highest level, the throbbing in her chest abruptly ceased.

I'm a pregnant woman, she thought. *I can't be made to feel upset. I'm supposed to be treated delicately.* Her brow creased, allowing the tears to flow downward. *Who the fuck are they to speak to me that way? They upset me and that could hurt my baby, damn it!*

Her thoughts were interrupted as Will reentered the living room.

"Hey, Ker, are you okay?" he asked and then noticed her salt-stained cheeks. "What's wrong? Why are you crying?"

Kerri had to swallow a big lump in her throat before answering, "It was Dr. Granning's office. And they were mad at me. They said I shouldn't have switched to another doctor. The secretary was, like, yelling at me."

Explaining the whole scenario caused her to tear-up a second time. She became very frustrated.

"Those fucking assholes," Will fumed. "What's their fucking problem? You're free to choose whatever doctor you want. It's none of their god-damn business. God, what assholes. I see why you never liked going there in the first place."

"I always knew there was something wrong with them. I could just feel it."

She inhaled heavily through her mouth.

"That's it, I'm fucking calling them back," Will asserted. "They don't talk to my wife that way. Hand me the phone."

"No, Will, please," Kerri blurted out quickly. "I, uh, took care of it basi-cally. I don't want to talk to them anymore. Please don't call them."

"Are you sure, Ker? You still look pretty upset."

"No, no, I'm fine." She stood up off the couch. "I, I just need to go out for a little bit… get some air… clear my head."

She began walking out of the living room.

"Wait," Will called out. "Where are you going?"

"I just need to go outside to catch my breath," Kerri said, still moving forward. "I want to go for a drive."

"You're sure that's all you need?"

"Yeah, I just need to go out for a sec." She threw on her coat and snatched up her keys. "I'll be right back."

"Uh, bye," Will said, just as the front door slammed shut.

The purple Kia roared in reverse out of the driveway. Kerri put the gearshift in drive, grappled the steering wheel, and slammed her foot down on the gas pedal. She zipped down the street with little concern for the people around her. Her tears had all dried up and her mind felt oddly focused. There was a pressing thought that refused to escape her head and forced her to drive even faster.

Nurse Warren was seated behind her desk, typing on a computer. She gave a fleeting glance out through the sliding glass window at the empty outskirts of the office's reception area.

"Time to lock up," her nasal voice announced aloud.

She pulled out her desk drawer and retrieved a small set of keys. When she looked back up, a darkened visage was staring back at her through the sliding glass window.

"Oh!" she screamed, dropping the keys to the floor.

"Did I scare you?" Kerri calmly asked.

"Yes, you did!" Nurse Warren's fear quickly shifted to anger. "What are you doing here, Kerri? The office is now closed."

"Well, the door was open."

"I was just about to lock up. You're going to have to leave."

"Hmm, really?" Kerri asked, placing her pointer and thumb to her chin. "I'm going to *have* to leave… just like I *have* to get a lecture from you and Dr. Granning on how I shouldn't have sought help for my pregnancy problem somewhere else, right?"

"Hey, it isn't my fault that you showed poor judgment. Now I suggest that you leave the office right now and call back tomorrow to make your appointment."

"I'm not going anywhere," Kerri stated. "Not until you and Dr. Granning apologize for making me very upset." She pounded her palm into her chest. "Me! A pregnant woman who is supposed to be caused as little stress as possible in order to grow a healthy baby! Now, you apologize right now!"

"I will do no such thing!" Nurse Warren retaliated. "Now, I suggest you leave right now before I call the authorities."

She slammed the sliding glass window shut and knelt down to pick up the dropped keys. Her acid-tongued delivery pulsed like poison through Kerri's veins. She lifted up two quivering fists and couldn't help bashing them both into the clear windowpane. Nurse Warren released a loud scream as a spider web of cracks was created. Paying no attention to the shrieks, Kerri sadistically pounded the window again, spraying shards of glass all over the place. Nurse Warren covered her mouth in fright as she was hit with an array of sharp pieces.

Inside the office a ways down the hall, Dr. Granning turned his head away from the computer screen. He plucked the tiny speaker-buds of his iPod out from his ears.

"Janice?" he called out. "What was that noise?"

No answer was returned.

"Janice!" he yelled again. "What was that? You know I'm very busy right now and don't want to be disturbed!"

Only quiet replied. With an aggravated sigh, Dr. Granning stood up behind his desk and ran his hand over his slicked-back black hair. He anxiously clicked away from the pictures of naked woman.

"What the hell is her problem?" he asked himself.

The office door slowly creaked open. Dr. Granning poked his head out and stared down the still hallway.

"Janice?" he yelled. "Are you there?"

The silence lured him fully out of his office. Frustrated, he rapidly started stepping toward the reception area. After rounding a quick corner, he arrived at Nurse Warren's area. She was seated at her desk with her back to him. Broken glass was everywhere

"Janice," he angrily said, "what the hell happened to the window? Huh? Hey, Janice."

The nurse refused to turn around.

"Janice!" he called and began walking toward her. "I want you to answer me right this second!"

He touched his hand onto the back of her shoulder. The pressure forced the chair to spin. Dr. Granning's jaw dropped as Nurse Warren's features came full circle, spraying a steady spurt of blood outward onto the floor. Thick pieces of jagged glass jutted forth from her eye, forehead, and neck.

Dr. Granning wanted to yell out, but instead only started hyperventilating. He crept up to Nurse Warren to check on the slightest possibility that she was still alive. He stopped so close before her that the spurting blood began hitting his shoes.

"J-J-Janice?" his voice shakily said.

He nervously reached out to check for a pulse in her impaled neck. His fingertips were a couple of inches away when a delicate, bloody hand shot forth from the base of Nurse Warren's desk. Dr. Granning squealed in pain and looked down to find a long piece of the broken window sticking out of the back of his calf. He stumbled forward, pushing on Nurse Warren. Her wheeled chair went rolling backwards revealing Kerri crouching underneath the desk.

"What the hell?" Dr. Granning yelled from his brand new horizontal position. "Kerri?"

Without replying, Kerri crawled out from her hiding space and slunk right up to his face.

"Hello, Doctor," she growled. "You wanted to see me?"

"What the..." was all his exasperated voice could muster.

Kerri rose to her feet and grabbed hold of his ankles with both hands. Dr. Granning screamed as he was aggressively dragged away from the reception area.

"Wait!" he hollered. "Wait! What are you doing? Stop it! Stop it right now! Let go of me!"

The strength of her movements caught him completely off guard. He tried to shake his body free, but was unable to do so. His calf left a trail of red all the way down the hall to the first examination room on the left. That was where Kerri stopped and used one hand to open the door. After flicking on the lights, she hauled the doctor inside single-handedly.

"Kerri, please, whatever you're doing," he pleaded, "just stop. Please, you're scaring me. You can't..."

Kerri's palms released his ankles and shot up to the back of his shoulders. With one swift yank, she flipped him over face-up.

"Oh, *I'm* scaring you?" she glared at him. "How absolutely terrible that must feel! It's such a wrong feeling, isn't it? Does your stomach hurt? How about your head? It's not very nice to make someone feel that way... especially if they are pregnant with a life inside them!"

"Kerri, I don't understand what you're trying to tell me, but if you could just..."

"I'm not surprised that you don't understand!"

She seized him by the shirt and swept him up onto the examining table, knocking one of the leg stirrups loose. The severed piece bounced off the floor with a metallic clank.

"Get your hands off me, you crazy bitch!" Dr. Granning yelled and began struggling with her.

Kerri's grasp remained powerfully relentless and the doctor's agitated, but futile, attempts for freedom further fueled her fury. There was a tray of medical instruments set off to the side of the table. Kerri snatched up the sharpest, strangest-looking one available and plunged it into Dr. Granning's nearby shoulder. He wailed in agony as his struggling soon ceased. Kerri grabbed his throat, closing off his vocal cords, and got right up in his face.

"I guess since I was some sad, infertile woman, I didn't deserve to choose what doctor I wanted to see," she scowled. "Is that what you were trying to say by forcing me to make an appointment to hear you tell me that I was making a mistake? That you, the doctor that *didn't* help get me pregnant, was the one I had to stay with? Basically, that I wasn't allowed to choose who could take care of me. I think that's what you were trying to say, but in case I'm mistaken, will you please tell me the real reason now?"

She eased off the squeeze on his windpipe. Dr. Granning at once emitted a fit of coughing, which Kerri aimed off to the side with a simple twist of her wrist. After his spasm was reduced to a couple of intermittent wheezes, she turned his eyes back to hers. Her stern gaze conveyed that she was still waiting for an answer to her question. He blinked twice, partially parted his lips, and exhaled. Not a single word escaped. His mouth despondently closed.

"That's what I thought," Kerri growled.

She kicked up the fallen stirrup. Her choking hand shot off of Dr. Granning's neck and snatched up the piece of metal in mid air. She twirled it around like a baton until the sharp, broken-off end was pointing forward. Without hesitation, she sent the stirrup zipping downward. Dr. Granning only had enough time to widen his eyes in shock, which helped provide a better target. The jagged, metal tip passed easily into his right eye and continued right on out the back of his head and then on through the cushiony base of the examination table. His body did a single twitch and then flopped off to the side. Kerri took a step back as his legs tumbled off the table, but did not touch the floor. The stirrup sticking through Dr. Granning's eye kept his head pinned back onto the table. Blood was dripping out of the base of the table. Kerri stayed still, taking only a few shallow breaths. She stared at the doctor's skewered face and found zero signs of life.

He's dead, she thought. *And so is his nurse.*

The realization of the dual demise sent her head into a clouded haze for what would follow. She only felt coherent for bits and pieces of the action, but still did not stop once. She understood right away that Nurse Warren and Dr. Granning were dead because of her. This immediately caused her to think of CSI, the television show. She knew how easy it was nowadays for investigators to use various pieces of miniscule scientific evidence to determine precisely who committed certain acts.

"No one can find out," she heard herself softly say.

Kerri's joints took over from that point on. Her internal 'self' sat back on the cushion-y haze inside her mind as her body did the work. The office's cleaning closet was discovered. A large jug of a cleaning agent that smelled like ammonia was removed from the top shelf. A stainless steel lighter with the engraved initials R.J.G. was found inside Dr. Granning's desk.

Then Kerri's brain turned extra fuzzy. She could vaguely make out spilling a fair amount of the jug, however her mind did not become completely clear until she was back outside standing next to the Kia. A slight smell of smoke was in the night air. Ignoring the odor, she got into her car and casually pulled away.

Will was waiting in the window of the living room as the Kia came moseying into the driveway. He watched as Kerri exited the driver's side and hurried up the front walkway. The front door was fully within his range of sight from the living room. It quickly swung open as Kerri charged inside. She didn't give notice to Will and simply rushed up the stairs to the second floor.

"Hey, Kerri!" Will called out. "Is everything okay?"

"Yeah!" she yelled down to him.

"Is that it?" He took two steps closer to the stairway. "How are you feeling?"

"Better!" was her simple reply. She kept her back to him, hiding her front from his view.

The next noise Will heard was that of the bathroom door slamming shut. A little confused, he turned around to the still open front door.

"She feels better," he shrugged and pushed the door closed.

Upstairs in the bathroom, Kerri had her back pressed up against the wooden door. She reached her left hand down and gently locked the handle. After a deep breath, she took one big step across the tiled floor. Her reflection moved into the mirror above the sink. The image instantly caught her attention. She turned to face it head on, and went into a state of shock.

"Oh God," she gasped.

The front of her brown coat was drenched in blood. She looked down to confirm the reflected sight wasn't a mirage, and discovered streaks of crimson over her pant legs, too. Without hesitation, she began removing her articles of clothing. First the coat hit the floor, revealing an equally bloody tan sweater shirt which went next. She hopped out of her pants and used her feet to push the pile of clothes off the side. Standing now in a light blue bra and matching panties, she asked the mirror on the wall if she was the least blood-covered of them all. The first thing she noticed was how large her breasts were getting—a major perk of pregnancy. She leaned in for a closer look at her oversized areolas, but was unpleasantly surprised to find tiny bits of splattered red all around her face.

The shower head let out a mighty blast as Kerri rapidly spun the Hot and Cold knobs to regulate the temperature. She soon stepped into the bathtub and shoved the shower curtain shut.

The warm, constant spray felt very soothing on her shoulders as she plunged her head fully under it. Tiny pink droplets began swirling around the drain. While staring at the base of the tub, Kerri was struck with a sudden lump in her throat. Fast flashes of Veejay at the 24-Hour Mart, Nurse Warren in her chair, and Dr. Granning on the examination table moved through her mind.

"I'm going to be a mom," she said, hoping to force her thoughts into switching. "I'm going to be a mom."

It was no use. Kerri covered her mouth with both hands as her facial muscles convulsed into a spasm of wrinkles. In no time streams of tears were running down her cheeks and mixing in with the falling warm water of the showerhead.

An extremely odd sadness had completely overcome her; one that seemed to have stemmed from happiness. The salty currents exploding forth from her eyes were actually tears of joy. She couldn't help feeling an extreme relief upon knowing that all three had met their severe demises.

And that really scared her.

Chapter 13

Kerri tightly squeezed Will's hand as they both stared up at the television monitor on the wall. The fuzzy, blotchy image on the screen appeared to be blipping in and out of focus. Suddenly something moved.

"Oh, there's a hand," Dr. Phalen smiled, still moving the ultrasound probe across Kerri's gel-covered bare belly.

"Look, Kerri," Will beamed. "He's waving at us!"

"Wow," Kerri replied, wide-eyed.

"Now don't jump to any conclusions yet, Will," Dr. Phalen added. "We don't know if it's a boy just yet... but would you two like to know?"

Will and Kerri both looked at each other.

"What do you think?" Will asked her.

"I don't know," she replied and turned to the Doctor. "Can you tell right now?"

"Not where I'm at yet," Dr. Phalen replied, gripping the probe. "But you're at your sixteenth week, so I should be able to find out."

Kerri looked back at Will. The hugely excited grin across his face easily helped her make a decision.

"Okay, Doctor," she said, nodding her head at Will. "We want to know."

Will didn't have to say a word to sign his agreement.

"All right, you got it," Dr. Phalen smiled and turned toward the television monitor.

Shadowy movement crept across the screen every time he shifted the probe. Will and Kerri anxiously waited, still holding hands.

"Can you see anything?" Kerri whispered to Will. "Do you know what he's looking for?"

"Not a clue," he replied. "It's all mushy gibberish to me."

"Will, I'm nervous. What if our baby is a bad kid?"

"Ker, what are you talking about?"

"I, I just hope he or she doesn't turn out... bad."

"Kerri, if it's one thing I know, it's that children are shaped by how their parents raise them. There's either good parents or bad parents. Guess which kind we're going to be. Trust me, it's all in how you raise them."

Everyone in the room invoked an oath of silence for the following three minutes. Kerri could actually hear the probe making squishy noises through the clear gel on her tummy.

"Hmm," Dr. Phalen finally broke the oath.

"What is it?" Will hastily asked.

"Well, it seems the little tyke is a tad on the shy side. I can't get a good look at anything. He or she is keeping his or her legs real close together."

"Is that a bad thing?" Kerri asked.

"Oh, no," the doctor assured. "This is the earliest stage during pregnancy when genitalia start to develop. If we can't find out now, we'll definitely find out soon enough."

"That's funny the baby's shy," Will said and looked at Kerri. "It's definitely my kid, then. I know I wouldn't want my business all displayed up on some big screen TV. So maybe that means we're having a boy."

"Would you like that, Will?" Dr. Phalen asked.

"No, sir. I mean, if it's a boy, great! If it's a girl, just as great! As long as it's healthy, I'll be totally happy either way."

"Well, then I definitely have some good news for you." Dr. Phalen glanced back at the screen. "It appears that other than a slight case of shyness, your baby is extremely healthy... and strong."

"All right!" Will grinned. "That's great news! Here that, Ker? It's healthy! We're keeping up that positive energy right on through the first trimester!"

Kerri gave him a smile of acknowledgement, but quickly looked over to Dr. Phalen.

"You said strong," she said. "What exactly did you mean by that?"

"Oh, well, I'm not sure," Dr. Phalen began. "It's just that as I pressed down on your stomach, I can almost feel the baby pushing back. It's like I'm disturbing naptime." He applied a bit more pressure to Kerri's belly and soon jerked the probe back. "See! There it goes again. Oh, this baby has some gumption!"

"But like you said, that's not a bad thing, right?" Will checked.

"No, sir. Looks like you two might have an athletic little monster on your hands. Did either of you play any sports while growing up?"

"Not really," Will replied. "I was never very competitive when I was a kid."

"I was always one of the last ones picked in gym class," Kerri added.

"Hmm," Dr. Phalen pondered. "Well, then how about your parents? Were they athletic in any ways?"

"I don't think so," Kerri answered.

"No," Will merely said.

"Well, that's okay," the doctor smiled. "If your baby is indeed athletic, then you both clearly won't be like those annoying soccer moms and dads that are always yelling and pushing their kids to do better."

"I can guarantee you that," Will promised.

"Good man," Dr. Phalen nodded and got back to concentrating on the ultrasound. "And Kerri, how have you been feeling so far?"

"Oh, I guess I've been feeling okay," Kerri replied.

"Okay, huh? Any nausea, aches, pains, mood swings?"

"Uhm… I don't really think so." She did her best to avoid eye contact. "I mean, I know I've felt kind of different from the increase in hormones, but other than that, I just feel okay."

"Well, I'm glad to hear that. And *you* should be glad to know that you don't have to worry about a trying, painful delivery."

"Why is that?"

"Because of the delicate nature we went about getting you pregnant, I feel that performing a cesarean section will be the most advantageous means of delivery. You won't feel a thing"

"That's good news," Will nodded.

"Oh, look closely kids." Dr. Phalen alluded up to the TV screen. "Here is your strong, beautiful baby's face."

Kerri and Will looked up at the screen. The black and white imprint of a round-ish visage stared back at them. The head bobbed slightly about like a balloon. Suddenly, the lids popped open revealing two large, black eyes.

"That's him?" Will asked.

"Or her?" Kerri added.

"That is your baby," Dr. Phalen confirmed.

"He kind of looks like an alien," Kerri marveled.

"Or she," Will jumped right in.

"I assure you both," Dr. Phalen said. "It is definitely *not* an alien."

He clicked a small button on the machine attached to the cord of the probe. A low humming sound was heard. A small rectangular role of paper slid out from the machine. Dr. Phalen ripped it free and held it up before the parents-to-be.

"Here you guys go," he grinned. "Your very first baby picture."

Chapter 14

Lately, it was only on a very rare occasion that Will was able to soak up some alone time. Between work and doctor appointments and scheduling Lamaze classes, his calendar was swamped. Considering the happy circumstances surrounding the cause of his constant activity, he really wasn't that upset. However, if an opportunity for some private relaxation ever did present itself, he was always more than ready to accept the call.

This Saturday morning just so happened to be one of those situations. All it took was a simple phone call from Lynn asking if Kerri wanted to go out baby shopping.

"Sure, honey, go right ahead," Will instructed without seeming too eager. "Go out with your friend. Get some cool shit for our baby. It'll be fun. You deserver it. Go have a good time."

"But what are you going to do?" Kerri asked. "I don't want to leave you all by yourself."

"You know what, Ker? I'm just going to sit on my ass, relax, and watch TV. It'll be great. And when you come home, then we'll do something together. And I'll be all rested."

His words couldn't be contested. Without even the slightest hesitation, Kerri called back Lynn and was out the door within the next half an hour. Will plopped down on the couch and hadn't moved since. After killing a good hour of lounge time without finding a single worthwhile show on the TV, he began to grow restless.

"This is why most people sleep in on Saturdays," he said, placing the remote on the couch cushion and standing up. "Thank God for DVDs."

Will walked up to a large wooden cabinet next to the television set, and opened it up to reveal countless organized stacks of DVD boxes. With careful precision, he started scanning row after row.

Let's see, he thought. *What do I want to watch? Hmm, nothing too intense; nothing too stupid; something fitting for right now. A-ha. That will work.*

Will reached up and extracted Kerri's copy of the movie, Love Actually. Seeing as how it was mid-November, a nice, holiday-themed movie seemed appropriate. And though many would consider the Hugh Grant-starring vehicle a super 'chick flick,' it also happened to be a very well-written comedy. Will appreciated nicely set up humor, which enabled him to tolerate the syrupy romantic scenes. Plus, there was a fair amount of 'boob shots' in the film, a clear sign that it was definitely meant to be viewed by males.

Once the DVD was inserted inside the player, Will strolled back to the couch, remote in hand. He dropped back-first onto the cushions and hit the play button. As the screen blipped from black into color, he adjusted his legs, looking for the ideal comfort position.

Right before Hugh Grant began his introductory voice over about how 'love *actually* is all around us.' Will located a spot that enabled every one of his softness-starved joints to touch a cushion. With a satisfied sigh, he settled into the flick. Then the doorbell rang. For a second, Will thought the sound came from the movie. With an, *are-you-kidding-me?* roll of his eyes, he removed his body from the ultimate cozy position and stood off the couch. He put old Hugh's voice-over on pause and angrily headed for the front door.

Who comes knocking on a Saturday morning? he wondered. *If it's a Jehovah's Witness, a magazine salesman, or an old guy looking for donations to his local Elk's Club, I'm going to become a murderer today.*

He stopped right before the door and placed his hand on the locking latch.

"Who's there?" he asked before twisting.

"This is Officers Scott and Russo, Mr. Haddon," said a deep voice from the front porch.

Without answering, Will twisted the latch and opened up the door, revealing two men dressed in dark blue. A police car was parked in the driveway.

"Hello. Is there a problem, sir?" Will said respectfully.

"We don't have reason to believe so, Mr. Haddon," Officer Scott replied. "Is your wife home?"

"No, sir, she isn't. Is anything wrong?"

"We just needed to ask her a couple of questions," Officer Russo added. "Maybe you could help us, Mr. Haddon."

"Absolutely." Will gently shoved the front door fully open. "What did you have to ask her about?"

"We had some questions concerning Dr. Roger Granning," Officer Scott said.

"Dr. Granning?" Will thought aloud. "Oh yeah, he used to be my wife's doctor. I remember. What did you want to know about him?"

"He and his secretary were found murdered three days ago," Officer Scott gravely replied. "His entire office had been set on fire, which destroyed most of whatever evidence could have been found at the scene."

"Oh my God," Will gasped. "I can't believe that. Who could do something like that?"

"We're not sure, Mr. Haddon," Officer Russo said. "Yet."

"Okay," Will began, "but I'm still not sure why you guys need me or my wife. Kerri's not a patient of Dr. Granning's anymore."

"Yes, we know that," Officer Russo went on. "We're just doing a follow-up investigation through the phone records of the office. And your home was one of the last places called before the murder took place."

Will's mind at once recounted the repellent interaction Kerri had on the phone that night.

"Do you recall anything strange happening on the other end of the line when the office called you?" Officer Scott asked.

Will looked off to the side, pretending to ponder the question. He was growing quite uncomfortable with the cops' double-team interrogation, and wanted to focus more thought onto Kerri's confrontational phone conversation.

"Gosh, I don't know," he said, still looking away. "I mean, they weren't on the phone very long. I think Dr. Granning was just checking in with her to see how she was doing. She's three months pregnant."

"Oh, she is?" Officer Scott smiled. "Congratulations."

"Thank you very much." Will was happy to take a pause from the subject at hand. "I can't wait."

The officers both nodded. Silence followed. Will knew that they were still waiting for a pertinent response to their initial question. He had to end this meeting as soon as possible.

"Anyway, regarding the phone call my wife got," he began. "Uh, it didn't last very long." He had to be as vague as possible, and still remain fully respectful. "They basically just were checking in to see how she was doing. It was actually pretty nice of them, considering we had to switch doctors."

He knew this wasn't exactly the truth, but felt it was what the officers wanted to hear.

"Was that all, Mr. Haddon?" asked Officer Scott.

"Yes, sir," he answered. "I believe that was all there was."

"All right then, that's fine."

Officer Scott scribbled something down in a small notepad he was carrying. He gave his partner a small nudge.

"Okay, Mr. Haddon," Officer Russo took his cue. "That was really all the questions we had for you today. If anything further comes up, we may come back to speak to your wife."

"Thanks for all your cooperation," Officer Scott added.

"Oh, no problem," Will said. "I'm sorry I couldn't be of more help. I hope you catch whoever did this."

They both nodded and turned to face the road. Will watched them head back to the police car, waiting to shut the door.

"So what do you think?" Officer Scott murmured to Officer Russo in the middle of their walk.

"Well, I think we can cross Mr. Haddon off the list."

"You think we'll need to come back?"

Officer Russo lowered his head and emitted a smirk.

"Oh yeah," he said sarcastically, "Because the pregnant lady did it."

They shared a good laugh before stepping into the police car. As soon as the engine started, Will closed the front door. He waited in the foyer, listening as the noise of the car got fainter and fainter. When his ears could no longer hear anything, his brain unlocked the Pandora's Box that had recently formed in his skull.

Why did Kerri come home and head right upstairs that night? he thought while scaling the steps to the second floor. *I didn't even get to see her. She just headed straight for the bathroom. God, why am I thinking all this? This is so stupid! Just go set your mind at ease and get back to Hugh Grant's monologue.*

Standing on the tiled floor of the bathroom, Will stared at the wicker laundry hamper resting against the wall. Hoping to end his worried thoughts as soon as possible, he took two big steps forward and lifted off the top. *The hamper was empty—not the answer he was looking for. His mind refused to end the search.*

You know where you have to go then.

Back down the steps, through the foyer, past the kitchen, Will rushed all the way up before the door to the basement. He didn't often frequent the lower level of the house. It wasn't finished and smelled kind of musty. All that dwelled down there was a washer, a dryer, and various storage containers. Kerri, on the other hand, visited the ground floor on a somewhat regular basis merely because she was the one who normally did the laundry. Will always liked to even off this task by doing the dishes and taking out the garbage. It was their little marriage pact.

Each step let out a rickety creak as Will descended the narrow stairwell. The washer and dryer were at the far end of the basement, illuminated by a lone, small window that just barely peeked up at the backyard outside. The flickering florescent light in the ceiling revealed a fairly clear path. Will marched straight up to the far end where a large white basket of clothes sat next to the washer. He immediately dove into the pile of articles.

Okay, what was she wearing that night? he wondered while tossing random articles left and right. *It was cold, so she definitely had on a heavier type jacket.* His hands dug deeper. *Let's see, she doesn't have that many winter coats.*

No jacket of any kind was found in the basket.

Okay, she's not washing any outerwear right now.

Will stopped digging for a second and closed his eyes. He pictured Kerri lying on the couch right before he handed her Dr. Granning's office on the phone. He saw her sitting up and holding the receiver to her ear.

It was a tan sweater, his mind clicked instantly.

Without another thought, he dove back into the basket. Clothes started flying everywhere. He soon reached the bottom of the basket, but failed to locate a tan sweater. It wasn't good enough. He had to find something. His mind had to have closure.

Now what? he thought.

His eyes moved off the empty basket, past the scattered clothing, and over to the washing machine.

In there?

Will moved up to the washer and lifted its lid. The metal, cavernous inside revealed nothing. He dropped the lid back down and turned his back to the washer, allowing the dryer to creep into his sights.

Last spot.

He slowly stepped over to the dryer and grabbed hold of the front handle. The hatch made a little squeak as it was gradually lowered. Though dark inside, it did not take long for him to notice something plush lying there. His arm shot forth into the dryer. His hand clutched a huge clump of softness and yanked it out. Will looked down at his grasp to find two articles of clothing. He moved them both up before the lone window for a better look.

"Found 'em," he nervously said.

Will placed the brown coat on top of the washer and with both hands, held the tan sweater up to his face. His eyes thoroughly scanned the fibers for anything 'non-tan'.

Nothing there, he thought. *Nothing there either.*

103

He turned the garment over to inspect the front side.

"Oh," he briefly uttered.

A clear array of dark speckles had invaded the tan. He pinched up a small stained piece of the fabric and scraped at it with his thumbnail.

"What is this?"

He mashed some of the scraped off bits between his pointer and thumb, and held them up to the light from the window. The smear on the imprints of both fingers appeared to be black at first, but upon closer inspection revealed a darkened shade of crimson. Will dropped the sweater to the floor seized the brown coat off the top of the washer. His hands tore through the thick material, turning it all about. The dark speckles were much less subtle here. In fact, they looked more like blotches.

"Damn it!" Will scowled. "What the fuck?"

He rapidly scratched his nails across the blotches, hoping to remove them. However, it was no use. The stains were very deep, some even soaked through to the other side. Frustrated, Will hurled the coat onto the floor. He slapped his hands onto his forehead and breathed heavily.

"No, no, it can't be," he unsteadily exhaled. "It's, it's something else. I just don't know... what to fucking think right now." He smothered his hands over his eyes. "What the hell am I even suggesting? It's Kerri. She doesn't have it in her to do anything like... She's too gentle and meek. And she's pregnant for Christ's sake!"

He glanced down at the spotted pieces of clothing at his feet.

"But she did come home all weird that night. She didn't even want to see me. God, I don't know what I'm saying."

His recent meeting with the two officers soon popped into his brain.

They said they'd be back, he thought. *No, they said that they* might *be back*.

He looked down at the sweater and coat again. The speckles and blotches all stared tauntingly up at him. Whether the articles were involved in something horrible or not, Will could no longer stand having them in his house. "Enough," he growled, removing his hands from his face.

Though the basement was where he spent the least amount of time, he still had a fairly good idea of what was located down there. Will ran over to a small crawlspace beneath the stairway. A deep, oval-shaped metal basin that he used when washing the cars, was dragged out into the center of the room.

"I'll be right back," he said, looking at the sweater and coat.

Will charged back up the stairway. The pounding of his feet moving all about the first floor echoed down into the basement. The stairs were once again greeted by the soles of his shoes in no time. He rushed back up to the metal basin carrying a small container of lighter fluid and a fire extinguisher. The sweater and coat were both tossed into the basin. Will popped the cap off the lighter fluid container and gave the articles a good dousing. He reached into his pocket and pulled out a book of matches. He paused for a moment and closed his eyes.

I have to do this, he thought. *Right? I have to set things at ease. This is the only way.* Though Will understood that his current actions weren't exactly morally sound, he just couldn't stop himself. When it came to Kerri, he had only one law; she stays safe, always.

Do it now.

He struck a single match and let it drop into the basin. The articles ignited almost immediately creating a mellow glow which reflected off the metal onto his face. Will picked up the fire extinguisher and waited. While he certainly felt a tad out of his mind with all that was transpiring, his brain was still working rationally enough to know not to burn the house down.

Once the basin contained nothing but black bits and a small, orange hue, Will unloaded with the fire extinguisher. The fierce, white spray did away with the burning fast, leaving behind a gray, smoky haze. He lowered the extinguisher and allowed his lungs to breathe.

It's done. Now I can...

A piercing beep unexpectedly rang out from above.

"Jesus Christ!" Will's nerves exploded.

He looked up at the ceiling to find the basement's smoke alarm flashing a bright, red light. The smoke from the basin was still going strong.

"Okay, this is out of here," Will said, kneeling down. He wrapped his hands around the outside metal handles of the basin. "Ow! Shit!"

He yanked his burnt hands back and shook them like a couple of pom-poms. The breeze helped a little. He then dove into the pile of clothes from the basket and snatched up two old undershirts. Using the makeshift potholders, he brought the smoking basin up the stairs, into the kitchen and out into the backyard. He dashed back inside the kitchen and emerged shortly after with a square-ish piece of plastic. He shook the plastic out into a big, black garbage bag. The entire contents of the basin were dumped inside. Will tied the top of the bag tightly shut and carried it over to the garbage cans lined along the side of the house. He covertly lifted the lid off the closest can and shoved the black plastic bag inside.

"Okay, I'm done," he exhaled. "It's over."

Chapter 15

Will was seated on the couch in front of the TV when the front door opened. Kerri's footsteps echoed in from the hardwood floor in the foyer. They were quickly getting closer.

"Will?" she called out. "Where are you?"

He did not answer right away.

"Will? You here?"

"Yeah, I'm in here!" he finally replied.

"Oh." She entered the room carrying a couple of plastic shopping bags with *Buy, Buy Baby* printed on them. "I wasn't sure where you were. Look at all the stuff I got with Lynn!"

Kerri hoisted the bags up in the air and walked up beside the couch.

"Wow," Will said. "That is a lot of bags."

"Wait till you see what's inside 'em," she smiled. "A lot of real fun stuff!"

"That's great, Ker." His voice didn't speak with much inflection. "I'm glad you had a good time."

"Will, what's wrong? You sound sad. Are you mad I went out shopping without you?"

"Oh, no, no. I'm glad you got to go out and do some baby things. I was just, uh, trying to take a nap before and got a little restless. That's all."

"Is that all you got to do today so far?"

"Well, I started watching a movie before, but I don't think I got to finish it."

"Oh yeah? What movie?"

"It was *Love Actually*," Will answered sheepishly.

"Will, are you kidding me? That's a pretty major chick flick right there. I mean, even with the boobs they show, it is still really girly."

"Really? How could you say that? Isn't it, like, one of your favorite movies? I thought you'd be proud of me for watching it. I wanted to get in the Christmas spirit."

"Yeah, I guess you're right," Kerri said, and then lowered her head on its side. "But I don't know. I don't think I'm feeling that flick anymore. If I wanted to get in the fun, holiday mood right this second, I'd probably watch Gremlins or that sorority movie Black Christmas."

"Ker, are you joking?" Will raised an eyebrow. "You know I hate those kinds of movies. Why would you even say that?"

"Oh, I know, Will. I'm sorry. I was just trying to think of some movies that were fun. Don't be mad, babe."

She inched her knees up to his back and placed her hands on his shoulders. Will could soon feel a soothing pressure on opposite ends of his neck.

"Wow, Will, you sure feel tense," Kerri said. "You sure there isn't anything bothering you?"

"No, I don't think so," Will answered, but pictured the metal basin in his mind.

Her sweater and jacket had already been reduced to ashes and he did not want to bring it up to her, ever. He merely closed his eyes and focused on the massaging motions.

"No, huh?" Kerri went on. "Well, maybe you're feeling a little anxious about the whole baby thing. It's all happening pretty fast. I don't want my boy to be feeling all stressed out."

"Well, I'm feeling pretty good right now," he said, succumbing fully to her circular rubbing.

"Oh, I think we can find a way to make you feel even better."

She slowly slid her hands down the top front of his chest and dug her fingers into his shirt.

"You know what, Will?" she whispered in his ear. "It's been a little while since we've fucked."

"Whoa," he gasped, a bit shocked at her use of profanity. "Uh, yeah it has been a little while."

"Well, why don't we fix that?"

Kerri aggressively pulled her arms apart, ripping Will's shirt down the center. After a few more quick yanks, he was completely shirtless. Kerri pressed hard onto his shoulders, sending his back into the cushions of the couch. She then swung her hips 180 degrees and positioned them atop his crotch. Will watched with wide eyes as she swiftly threw off her blouse, revealing a pair of inflated breasts holstered by a pink, lacy bra. She was showing the slightest bit of a baby bump too.

"My tits are so big right now," she said, sexily arching her back.

"Yeah, honey, they are," Will replied and glanced over at the floor. "I can't believe you just ripped my shirt."

Kerri instantly slapped her hand over his mouth.

"Forget about your fucking shirt," she ordered and lightly slapped her chest. "Eyes focused here."

"Okay, Ker, jeez. Are we doing another one of our role-playing games?"

"No games, Will! You're hot. I'm hot. And right now we're going to fuck."

Before Will got a chance to say *okay* or *help*, she collapsed on top of him and pressed her lips hard into his. She shoved her hand between his legs and roughly started up another kind of massage. Will was so caught completely off guard that he didn't even think to kiss her back. However, he also had stopped thinking about the circumstances surrounding the day's earlier events.

Though Kerri's very forward actions were a bit unorthodox for her, Will opted to roll with whatever she threw at him and enjoy the diversion. Their remaining articles of clothing were all eventually removed, mostly by Kerri, without any unforeseen rips.

"Here we go, big boy," she grinned, flexing her hips.

Kerri dug her nails into his shoulders and gleefully bounded up and down. Will winced from the pain while holding onto her thighs. She dragged her hands down his chest and then up to her face, pushing away some tousled blonde locks.

Will looked up at her and noticed some faint streaks of red. He moved his eyes down a little and witnessed a more prevalent shade of crimson. It did not take him long to realize that both his shoulders were bleeding. Kerri didn't seem to notice or care.

Chapter 16

Behavioral changes during pregnancy. Will typed the words into the Google search bar on his computer at work. The array of articles that popped up after he hit 'enter' touched on topics such as 'breast changes' and 'social behavior' and 'emotional adjustments'. He scanned page after page, looking out for a more sinister-sounding brand of key words. So far as he could see, nothing could serve to assuage the bothersome thoughts that had been swimming about in his head ever since the two officers came to his door three days ago.

Will didn't mention a word about the police to Kerri. The burnt-up whereabouts of her jacket and sweater were also kept mum. Will felt too uncomfortable about bringing up anything regarding that Saturday morning and didn't want to risk upsetting his pregnant wife especially without a full grasp on the situation.

"Penny for your thoughts, Will," Fred said from his desk.

Will exited the Google search page and turned around in his seat. "Huh, Fred, what was that?" he asked.

"I just said, 'Penny for your thoughts,' that's all."

"Oh. Well, I don't think my thoughts are even worth a penny right now. You may want to re-think your offer."

"You do seem a little down this morning. I mean, it is Monday and all, which sucks real hard in general. But the look on your face appears to be beyond the normal first-day-of-the-week drudgery."

"You've always been a wise young man," Will half smiled. "And I've never been too good at hiding things."

"Well, Will," Fred began, crossing his arms. "I ain't your momma and I ain't your poppa, but I am your boy… so with the hope of not sounding too Lifetime-movie-of-the-week gay, do you want to talk about it?"

"Oh, I don't know, Fred-o. It's kind of complicated and… unpleasant."

"I'm sure it can't be that bad. I've known you for a long time, Will, and you never seem to get caught up in anything too hardcore."

"I'll give you that one. I like keeping things on the calmest of levels. But sometimes things change."

"Okay, Will, you've got about ten seconds before I turn around and get back to the drunk Paris Hilton website. What exactly are you talking about?"

Will lowered his head with a little smirk.

"You know what? I really don't know if I'm even sure what I'm talking about." He looked back up. "If *that* even makes any sense."

"Oh, sure, it makes perfect sense," Fred answered with a heaping helping of sarcasm.

"I think I'm just getting worried," Will said. "I think this pregnancy is really starting to have some kind of affect on Kerri."

"Really, like what? And by the way, thanks for finally putting together a sentence with a real topic for me."

"No problem. I just think she's been starting to act a little different. I mean, I know that a woman goes through tons of changes when she gets pregnant. Jesus, all I've done for the past three years is research practically everything there is to know on the subject."

"Right, Will. Exactly. You know that all kinds of crazy shit goes down when a woman gets pregnant. It's perfectly normal. Even a monogamy-fearing fucker like myself knows that."

"Yeah, I know, but what I've seen lately from Kerri just… it just isn't like anything I've heard about before. There are times when she just seems… way more different than usual… like she's a completely different person. And I've only started seeing it recently. I'm worried that something might be wrong. If anything ever happened to her I'd…" He had to stop as the mere wording of his last sentence sent chills up his spine. "I'd just be finished forever."

Fred wheeled his chair a bit closer and leaned in.

"You've always been quite the worrier, Will," he said. "Ever since I first met you, that was the one thing I could tell almost immediately. And I'm not saying it's a bad thing. You actually care about the well-being of others way more than most people. It's refreshing. It makes me feel good. I hope that doesn't sound too gay. I'm just saying that this is your nature; to promote ease. But it's hard for a person to promote that much ease. Hence while in the process of doing so, you yourself become uneasy. You see what I mean?"

"Yeah, I do," Will nodded. "That was pretty good."

"Thanks, Will. I appreciate that, but does it make you feel any better?"

"I guess so, sort of."

"Well, that's good enough for now because I think I hear Loni coming over and I don't want her to hear us talking all personal and stuff. I've got a lothario-heavy image to keep up."

"No problem, Fred-o. Thanks for helping."

"That's why I'm here."

High-heeled footsteps sauntered their way up to the large cubicle. The big boobs arrived around the corner first. Loni followed shortly after.

"Good morning, boys," she smiled.

"Hi Loni," Will waved.

"Hellooooo, Ms. Loni," Fred added. "Were the tips plentiful this weekend?"

"Of course," she smirked and danced over to her desk. "Plus, I got a little something extra at a bar afterwards."

"Oh really? And what was that."

"A guy's number," she smirked.

"Well, well, well!" Fred crossed his arms. "So you met yourself a fella? Good job!"

"Is he nice?" Will asked.

"I think so," Loni said. "I mean, he bought me all my drinks."

"He wasn't just trying to get you drunk, was he?"

"Oh, no. I didn't even leave with him. You know I'm through with all that one night stand shit."

"Well, I'm glad to hear that."

"Hey, what do you guys have against one night stands?" Fred questioned. "They're fast, fun, and feel so fucking good!"

"Enough of that, Fred," Will interjected. "Stop filling her head with the wrong kinds of ideas."

"Excuse me, Will. I didn't know that Loni was your daughter."

"Yeah, Will," Loni grinned. "What do you think I'm your daughter or something?"

"No," Will rushed to make clear. "What I'm trying to say is a girl like Loni deserves nothing short of the best. And I'm just making sure that this is the current case."

Loni turned to him with a twinkle in her eye.

"Aw, Will, thank you," she smiled and started walking his way. "You really are the sweetest."

Will didn't get a chance to move before his neck was surrounded with two breasts as Loni wrapped her arms around him from behind for a three-second embrace. Fred's eyes broadened with jealousy.

"Your wife is one lucky lady," Loni said after finally letting go.

"Thanks," Will replied, trying not to look like he was gasping for air.

"Hey, um Loni," Fred blurted out. "I just helped Will out with some worrisome thoughts he was having about his wife being pregnant. It was *very* sweet of me." He held out his arms. "Could I get a hug too?"

Loni merely turned her head to him and showed off her plentifully curvaceous profile as she walked back to her desk.

"Sorry, Fred, honey," she playfully sneered. "I'm all out of hugs for today." She looked over to Will. "But, Will, what was wrong with Kerri?"

"Damn it!" Fred slapped the arm of his chair. "She always focuses on you, Will, you goody-two-shoes!"

"Sorry, pal," Will said before turning over to Loni. "I was just nervous about some of Kerri's behavior lately and needed to vent, I guess. It's cool. Fred actually did do a great job of calming me down. In fact, he did such a great job that I'd consider it hug-worthy."

"Hmm, really?" Loni said.

"Listen to him, Loni," Fred pleaded. "He's telling the truth."

"Wow, Fred. I'm impressed. And for your reward, I promise to hug you sometime in the near future… when you least expect it."

A content smile spread across Fred's face.

"Wow. I like the sound of that. Damn, that is exciting and sexy. Thanks, Loni."

"You're welcome, Fred," Loni said. "I'm so glad I could assist you with your morning wood."

"Baby, you're the greatest," Fred grinned, crossing his legs.

Chapter 17

The Second Trimester

Kerri's belly let out a little grumble. She stared down at the bulbous basketball that was having trouble fitting behind her desk. Her head became dizzy for a moment. She had to look up to the ceiling in order to regain focus. Her eyes moved past the classroom on their way upward. The students were all silently seated, taking a quiz.

While staring at the large, white, square tiles up top, Kerri slowly turned her head toward the clock above the door to the hallway. She wanted it to read 2:05, however was met with 1:45. With an agitated grunt, she brought her sights back to the students. Every one of them had their heads buried in the multiple-choice- and essay-answer-filled sheets of paper on their desks.

Kerri was about to look back to her belly, when her sight slipped past a pair of ears sticking out way too far. Trent was trying to secretly gawk at her. She wanted to quickly turn away, but their eyes had already locked. Trapped in his tractor-beam, her face could only emit a slightly shocked expression. Loving the attention, Trent released a satisfied sneer and lifted up his eyebrows. His mug made her sick to her stomach. She wanted to storm out of her seat and wrap her hands around his neck. The image of his eyes rolling back into his head was so soothing. Her feet aimed out from under her desk, however before she stood up, a new thought crossed her mind. Her feet crept back behind her desk. Her eyes were still in a staring contest with Trent. She gave him a sly wink and conceded her stare. The move enthralled Trent. He placed his head in his hand and maintained his smarmy sneering.

Kerri's fluctuating mind kept her occupied for the final fifteen minutes of class. When the clock read 2:02, the students began walking over to place their quizzes on the edge of her desk. A small pile of papers was forming. Kerri was pretending to write down notes in her plan book when one white sheet was set away from the pile. She looked to the left of her plan book to see Trent's name inscribed at the top of the paper. Her eyes rolled up at him.

"How's our baby, honey?" he leered.

Though insanely enraged the instant his foul breath hit her face, Kerri's brain forcefully reminded her to stick to the plan. She scraped the fingers of her right hand along the arm of her chair and could feel the wood digging into her nails. With her anger displaced for the moment, she was able to bestow Trent with a little smile and nod. He strolled back to his desk with a gratified sway.

With the clock now showing 2:04 and the second hand rapidly ticking past the number 7, Kerri stood up from her seat. She strolled down the first aisle of desks and stopped at Trent's. He looked up to her with wide, devil eyes. She gently leaned her lips down next to his extra large ear.

"I'll see you in detention after school," she softly whispered. "If you don't show up, I'm reporting you to the principal. Got it?"

"Yes ma'am," Trent replied, unable to contain his enthusiasm.

Without giving him a second look, Kerri paced back to her desk. The 2:05 bell rang just as she sat back down. The students began dispersing out of the classroom. Trent was one of the last to leave and made sure to saunter past Kerri's desk.

"Be back here in fifteen minutes," she ordered without taking her eyes off the pile of quizzes.

"Can't wait," he said, while heading toward the exit.

Once the classroom was empty, Kerri stood back up and walked over to the line of windows at her right. She stared down from the second floor at all the students and teachers rushing outside towards the parked buses and cars. People rarely stuck around once the school day was over.

Content that the building would soon be empty, Kerri turned around and headed back to her desk. She took out a white sheet of paper and touched her red pen to it. In big letters, she wrote out, *DETENTION MOVED TO SHOP ROOM. GO NOW.* She taped the note to the front of the classroom's door before quietly slipping out into the hallway. Her stomach was all tied up in knots that wouldn't unwind until her plan came to fruition.

Fifteen minutes later, Trent came gleefully stepping forward, sycophantic grin still intact. The red-lettered note immediately got his attention. He pressed his finger into the white sheet of paper while reading the note. A raised eyebrow joined his smirk as he turned away from the door. While walking back down the hall, his lips whistled a tune that resembled *Let's Get It On.*

The shop room took up a huge chunk of the rear right end of the school. Though located on the first floor, it consisted of two levels. All large cutting, melting, and sanding machines occupied the space provided on the first floor as well as a couple of huge plastic bins filled with randomly-sized pieces of wood. Tools, tables, and chairs were scattered everywhere. A black, metal stairway constructed from a criss-crossing array of elongated rods led up to the computers and screen printing devices of level two. The entire open second floor wrapped around the upper walls of the room with an extended railing for protection. The whole room was very similar to an old era factory and had an aged musty smell to match.

A brief creak burst forth, echoing all the way up to the second level, as Trent took a step inside. He gazed about the enormous open area, which received a lack of outdoor light due to the white-stained windows.

"Hello?" he called out. "Mrs. Haddon? Are you there?"

His words were met by motionless shadows. Trent reached over to the side and flipped on a single light switch. A low humming ensued, as the ancient, fluorescent bulbs attached to the ceiling slowly sprung to life. After about ten seconds, a majority of the shadows had dispersed. Trent moved fully into the shop room, keeping his eyes peeled for his teacher.

"Oh, Mrs. Haddon!" he called again. "Come out, come out, wherever you are! I'm here for my punishment!" He glanced up at the second level. "Well, are you here or not?"

The fluorescent lighting abruptly died off. Trent let out a little jump as the room became re-immersed in shadows. He turned his eyes up to the ceiling and then over at the switch by the entrance door. No one appeared to be present.

"I know those lights just didn't go out," he said, striding cautiously towards the door.

Upon reaching a distance of about fifteen feet, Trent was able to discern that the light switch had indeed been flipped downward. He crossed his arms and brought forth his trademark smirk.

"Okay, I know you're here," he said, stepping backwards into the center of the room. "So you like it better with the lights out, huh? That's cool with me, but we can't get down with my punishment until I see y…"

Trent's reversed walking halted as his back bumped into what felt like a slightly soft basketball. He spun around to spot Kerri, belly-out, standing before him.

"Jeez, Mrs. Haddon, what are you trying to do, give me a heart attack?" he coyly said.

"Maybe," Kerri slyly grinned.

"Oh, you're a very bad girl, Mrs. Haddon. I think *you're* the one that has to be punished."

"Oh yeah, Trent?" She took one step back and held up her palms. "Well, what are you going to do to me?"

115

Trent's eyes widened in shock.

"Whoa, uh," he stuttered. "I'd… I'd give it to you good and hard."

"Wow," Kerri simulated enthusiasm. "That's it?" She emitted a faint chuckle. "Good and hard? That's the best you've got for me?"

"Hey, you think you can do better? Go ahead, teach me."

Keeping her grin intact, Kerri sauntered up beside him. She placed her fingers on his left shoulder and dragged them across his back while stepping around to his right. She bent in before his conch shell of an ear.

"You know I'm a married woman," she said quietly. "A married woman who happens to also be pregnant."

"Oh yeah, I know," Trent nodded. "That's hot."

"So none of that bothers you at all, huh?" She began stroking the long outer edge of his ear. "Because I'm so fucking hot."

"I knew you were really into all the stuff I was saying to you in class," he said, closing his eyes in ecstasy. "You wanted me the whole time."

"You know me so well, Trent. I just couldn't fool you."

"That's right. So, are we gonna get down with this?"

"Oh, yes, how silly of me. I've been talking too much." She continued petting his ear while placing her other hand gently on the side of his neck. "No more talking. It's time for your… punishment!"

Kerri at once gripped her hands over Trent's head. She dug her fingernails into the soft cartilage around his ear and forcefully yanked outward.

"AHHHHH!" Trent screamed like a little girl.

He shot his eyes to the left to see Kerri dangling a bloody piece of flesh before him. Her grin was huge.

"What the fuck!" he bellowed, rushing his hand up to the gushing side of his head.

Trent felt a mushy wetness and was instantly sent into a fit of rage.

"You crazy bitch!"

He shoved her hard in the chest, leaving one bloody handprint. Kerri only budged back half a step. Dissatisfied with his initial assault, Trent stormed forward. His devil eyes burned with fury. Standing her ground, Kerri received his outstretching arms and miraculously lifted his entire body off the floor.

Before Trent knew what had happened, he was already sailing through the air toward a nearby table saw. He plowed headfirst into the machine, causing it to switch on. Kerri brushed some of the creases out of her stained blouse and began coolly walking his way.

116

"Aw, wha da fawk," Trent mumbled with his face smooshed into the floor.

His remaining ear detected feminine footsteps getting closer. He peeled his battered mug off the floor and looked over his shoulder. A tiny trickle of blood found its way into his left eye just as he caught sight of Kerri coming at him.

"Get the fuck away from me!" he yelled, stumbling to his feet.

Trent attempted sidestepping around her in order to reach the door out, but Kerri swiftly beat him to the spot. He hurriedly reversed his motions and went the other way. His efforts were foiled again. Kerri made certain to guard him extra close.

"You're not getting out of here," she coldly assured and held up his dismembered ear. "You got that?" She said into the bloody lobe.

"Oh shit," Trent whimpered, beginning to walk backwards. "You are one fucked up pregnant History teacher."

"Yeah," Kerri agreed and picked up a hammer from a nearby table. "And you should *not* have fucked with me."

"Shit! Shit! Shit!"

Trent turned and began sprinting away from her, still frantically saying *shit*. The back section of the shop room was a fairly open area offering little place to hide. All his rapidly roaming eyes could spy was the metallic stairwell leading up to the second level.

It wasn't the ideal choice, however it would allow him to gain some distance away from his female aggressor. Without a second's hesitation, he hastily staggered over to the first blackened step. His dripping ear hole left a red, spotted trail.

Intermittent clangs rang out from the stairs as Trent made his way higher without looking back. Upon reaching the top, he gripped his hand along the railing to keep from falling over. He glanced down at the first floor and saw no one. Panting violently, he turned back to the edge of the stairwell — empty.

"Where is she?" he softly asked. "Where are you? Mrs. Haddon, what are you trying to do?" He started limping backwards further away from the stairwell, still holding onto the railing. "Why are you doing this to me? You fucking stop it right now!"

The shop room remained quiet, save for the low buzzing of the table saw.

"Come on, Mrs. Haddon!" he cried out. "I'm...I'm sorry for being a dick. I just want to get out of here. Will you let me do that?"

The droning of the table saw continued, but nothing else.

"I don't care if you're still down there! I can just stay up here until someone else comes. I don't care how long it takes. So I suggest you just leave right now, Mrs. Haddon! You got that?"

The metal platform beneath his feet let out a small creak. Trent's eyes shot downward just in time to see Kerri's top half come swooping in beneath the railing. Her right hand sharply swung the hammer forward, delivering a dreadful blow to Trent's shin. The impact immediately spurt blood down to his shoe.

"Noooo!" Trent shrieked in shocked anguish, collapsing onto his back.

Kerri slipped the rest of her body onto the second level. She rose to her feet and looked down at Trent's trembling frame. Her plan was almost complete.

Trent was no longer able to fight back. Kerri knelt down and gripped her hands around the shoulder area of his shirt. She brought his body way up over her head with minimal effort. Her heels moved back until her rear was touching the railing's edge. Trent's arms dangled upside-down over the open air leading to the first floor. He looked above his head at the uninviting base below.

"Shhhhhhit," he uttered for the last time.

Kerri pressed her arms straight up in the air and let Trent dip downward. She released her grip and dropped him off her back. He did one fast flip as a rush of wind exploded through his hair.

A hard crash was emitted as his back landed first. The impact caused a strident *snap* to crack from his back. Kerri heard the crackle and turned to peer down at the first floor. The sight prevented her from saying a word or thinking a thought.

Back on the ground level, Trent blinked his eyes. He tried moving his limbs, but couldn't. He wasn't able to feel anything below his mouth. Distraught, he closed his eyes and hoped to think of something positive. Something wet suddenly sprayed him in the face. His lids shot back up.

He could already recognize the red splashed across his cheek. And the warm rain still didn't stop.

Trent squinted and stared through the relentless spurts. His eyes twitched in dismay upon discovering that he had landed square on top of the table saw. The circular, spinning blade had cut right through his back and was now bursting forth from his chest. The muffled humming of the machine's motor began fading from his ears.

A huge pool of crimson started overflowing off the table onto the floor. Trent's eyes slowly rolled back into his head as his vision grew increasingly blurry. His vital signs shut down for good the moment Kerri stepped off the metal stairwell onto the first level, hammer still in hand. She walked up to Trent's body and switched off the table saw. The blade ceased its spinning, but remained peeking out from the center of his chest. Her plan was complete.

"That will teach you," she hatefully hissed down at him.

The blood was still dripping onto the floor. Kerri gazed down at the heaping mess as a twinge of panic finally settled into her brain. She was so focused on leading Trent to his death that her actions got a bit too carried away. There were some cleaning supplies and plastic tarps that she remembered seeing near the room's entrance. Her legs at once raced in that direction.

There was a mop and bucket leaning just off to the side of the door. Kerri quickly snatched hold of the mop's handle. A throbbing spasm burst forth from her belly. She let go of the mop and fell to the floor, grabbing her waist. Her palms soon absorbed a round of repetitive pounding from the inside.

"My baby!" her mind exclaimed. "My baby's kicking! I can feel it!"

A second, sharply stabbing feeling shot out. Kerri tightly shut her eyes and gritted her teeth. She pressed her hands harder into her stomach.

"What's happening? What am I doing? I'm hurting my baby! Why am I doing this?"

She hugged her lower abdomen as tears rolled out of her eyes.

"I'm so sorry," she said aloud. "I'm so very sorry. Please forgive me. I never meant to hurt you. I…"

The door to the shop room abruptly swung open behind her. Startled, Kerri turned her head and saw someone's shoe step inside. Without another thought, she sprung to her feet, firmly gripping the handle of the hammer. The door continued swinging open. Once the slight portion of the visitor's head came into view, she moved in to strike.

The jagged back end of the hammer hurled forward and buried itself inside the left temple of the surprise guest. Kerri's hand released from the handle, leaving the hammer stuck in its point of impact. She took a few quick steps back and watched as the shop teacher, Mr. Becker, lurched into the room.

The ghastly expression frozen across his aged fifty-five year old face got closer and closer till his legs finally buckled. He fell onto his knees. Kerri watched closely as his wide-eyed stare collapsed forward onto the cold floor. The hammer remained lodged, but did little to plug up the heavy amounts of red squirting out. She took a single, extra cautious step toward him.

"Mr. Becker?" she softly whispered.

The shop teacher did not answer. His body refused to move.

"Mr. Becker?" Kerri asked a little louder.

The left side of his face could no longer be seen from the amount of blood it was submerged in.

Kerri closed her eyes and fell down to her knees.

The inside of her stomach promptly received another sadistic row of kicking.

"I know, honey," she cringed, holding her basketball-shaped belly. "I deserve it."

Chapter 18

"Will!" Kerri called from the base of the steps. "I'm going out to the grocery store! I'll be back in a little bit!"

Upstairs in the bedroom, Will slowly picked his head up off the pillow. "What?" he shouted back, eyes still half closed.

"I'm going to the store!" she hollered at the top of her lungs. "Be right back!"

The next thing Will heard was the front door slamming shut. He turned his head over to the digital alarm clock resting on his nightstand. The time was 9:14 am. Will buried his face back in his pillow. For a Saturday, it was too early to wake up. Unfortunately, now that his senses were stirred, getting back to sleep wasn't going to be an easy task.

Will tossed and turned about the bed, trying his luck on top of the sheets, then back under them. It was no use. His inability to find an ideal sleep position coupled with Kerri's abrupt exit all but ensured his 'sandman-express' ticket wouldn't be reissued.

Will turned onto his back and placed his hands on top of his head as he stared up at the ceiling. His wife was definitely the main reason why he wasn't comfortably dreaming away. She was the main reason why he hadn't gotten much sleep for the past couple of nights. Her behavior had recently become noticeably distant at times. And no matter how badly Will wanted to, he just couldn't coax himself into bringing up the tan sweater and brown coat that he'd burned to ashes.

Stop freaking out, he thought. *You still don't even know if she did anything. She's really pregnant now. And it's really taking its toll on her. She probably just needs something to cheer her up.*

Will paused his pondering and took his hands off his head. He sat straight up in the bed.

I can do that, his brain went on the moment it was upright. I can make her feel better. Hell, it's what I do. And I could definitely use the distraction. There, that's it. I'm fully awake now. It's my mission to do something that'll lift Kerri's spirits before she gets back.

He swung his feet off the edge of the bed and hopped onto the carpeted floor. Without sparing a second, his mind started contemplating what Kerri-pleasing deeds could possibly be done.

Okay, it has to be significant, but it also has to be finished before she gets back. Hmm... food? Make her breakfast? Uh, no, it might get cold before she gets here. What else?

He turned away from the bed to head for his closet, when his eyes were hit by the fresh glaze of frost coating the bedroom's two windows.

Hmm, frosted windows. His mind's wheels began turning. *It's getting colder. It'll probably snow soon. And Christmas is coming!*

The light bulb finally went fully off.

Yes! Put up the Christmas lights! What could be more festive? What could be more fun? Christmas makes everyone happy. I bet it'll make Kerri feel better. He looked again at the clock on his nightstand. *Okay, it's 9:20. She won't be out for too long. I've gotta get moving.*

Will bounded over to his closet and swung open the door.

Now, where do we keep the lights? he thought between throwing on a pair of sweats. *Let's see... last year I wound them up into big, wire-y balls and stored them in...* He closed his lids to think extra hard. *Oh yeah.* His eyes opened. *I remember. Down there.*

The stairway to the first floor was soon sounding the arrival of Will's feet. His fast-paced footing continued on through the kitchen up before the door leading to the basement. Doing his best to mentally block out all that occurred the last time he had lowered himself to the depths of the washing machine's domain, he opened the door and headed down. He hoped it wouldn't take very long. The basement was already giving off a smell even more musty than usual.

Under the low hum of the flickering fluorescent light, Will scoured the basement storage for the 'holly jolly' section. There were mountains of boxes and plastic containers to inspect and he was currently stuck in the valley.

Oh man, this is going to suck, he whined. *Let's see. Well, the Christmas stuff wouldn't be over there under the stairs because there's not enough space.* He moved further away from the base of the steps and scrutinized a new sector. *That spot's where I put the air hockey table I took apart and I don't remember anything Christmas-y over there.*

The musty smell was growing stronger.

"Oh, man, I better find these lights fast," Will said, sounding like an operator, as he held his nose.

He upped the speed of his investigating and ultimately came across a display that made him pause. A large, light green plastic container had a small piece of red felt jutting out from beneath its lid.

"Is that a part of a Christmas bow?"

Will excitedly stomped through a small swamp of storage toward the tiny, red checkpoint. Upon reaching the container, he lifted off the lid and observed a Yuletide array of bows, garland, and little stuffed snowmen. The Christmas section had been discovered. The next task would be to find the lights. He popped the top on the next closest container and began sifting through another holiday smorgasbord. No sets of strung-together bulbs were found.

"Come on," Will whined. "Where are ya?"

He wrapped his hands around a third container and ripped away the lid. A grin grew across his face. The third time was the charm.

"Jackpot!" Will beamed, gazing down at a plethora of multi-colored Christmas lights. *Okay, now I've got to bring this whole container up, check to make sure each strand works, and... and what the fuck is that smell?*

Now that his mind had stopped focusing so hard on finding the decorations, his sense of scent kicked back into high gear.

God, it stinks.

He seemed to be standing right around the source of the putrid odor and had to do away with what it was. Will knew that with Kerri being pregnant, the slightest whiff would most certainly make her sick. He followed his nose past a few boxes to a spot where the smell seemed strongest.

"Where the hell is that coming from?"

His eyes caught view of a rather large, rolled-up tarp resting against the wall. It was bulging oddly outward.

"What, did we forget to throw away the Christmas tree last year or something?" Will asked.

He took a deep breath, held it, and reached out his hands. The tarp felt like it was made of a very flimsy plastic. Will grabbed onto a dangling piece and started peeling it away. The bulge inside quickly shifted its weight and flopped forward. The side portion of a wrinkled human head and shoulders popped forth from the peeled opening.

"Jesus Christ!" Will yelled and stumbled backward, landing ass-first on a box of ornaments.

He instantly picked himself off the crushed box and backed even further away until he hit the dryer. His eyes remained locked on those of the man hanging out of the tarp. It was Mr. Becker.

"Oh my God!" he exclaimed, covering his mouth.

His heart was pounding at such an exasperated rate, that it could have jumped up into his neck. All his limbs began shaking.

What the fuck is that? he wondered. *It can't be a dead body! Oh, please God, don't let it be a dead body!* He covered his eyes and continually repeated, *Not a dead body. Not a dead body…*

Will pulled his hands partially off his face, hoping that his wish was granted. Mr. Becker continued giving him the same dead-eyed stare. He pounded the back of his fist into the dryer, creating a hollow-ish clank.

Kerri did this? He feared to think. *But she's my little, defenseless wife. She's always been so meek. This… this isn't her! It can't be! She's going to be a mother for God's sake! No! I refuse to have insanity like this in my house! The dead body has to go right now!*

He rose to his feet and trudged back through the ocean of containers and boxes. Ignoring the powerful stench, he locked his tense mitts onto Mr. Becker's tarp and yanked it away from the wall.

As Will prepared to drag the body out towards the dryer, another rolled-up tarp crashed to the floor into his view. The impact caused a scrawny arm to spill out from the plastic. Will let go of Mr. Becker and gazed forward in disheartened bewilderment. With his hope rapidly diminishing, he leapt forward to the second tarp. He seized the section of plastic at the end of the exposed arm and pulled back. Trent's face became unveiled. Will slapped his hand into his forehead as he crouched in for a closer look.

That's a young face, he apprehensively thought. *It's a student.*

His heart crumbled as he was hit with the realization that all this was really happening. Without a doubt, Kerri was clearly involved.

Will stared down at Trent and then promptly turned over to Mr. Becker. The basement's smell was now so overpowering that his nostrils had actually adapted to it. Something was bubbling deep inside him. The events that had transpired over the miniscule course of five minutes had thrown his mind into oblivion. His skin crawled. Every hair on his body was standing up. His eyes felt like they were being pierced by needles. His quivering jaw began to part. A thunderous moan of agony erupted forth from his mouth. The back of his throat felt like it was on fire as his vocal cords caused the house to shake. Tears burst downward from his eyes like reverse geysers. He tugged at his shirt until the seams ripped.

"Why?" he muttered between mucus-y gulps. "Why did it have to happen? This is not right! It's not the right way!" He wiped his face, spreading the salty wetness all over. "We're going to be parents! Our baby will not be exposed to the likes of this! My family won't turn out like…"

His voice shut down before the sentence could be finished. The idea of what could have been spoken next set Will's body into motion. He covered up Trent's face and dragged his tarp out into the open floor in the middle of the basement. He then retrieved Mr. Becker and set him down beside Trent.

Okay, he thought. *Now what?*

Will was flying blind. All he really knew for sure was that he had two dead bodies *in* his house and wanted two dead bodies *out* of his house.

Just get them out of the house now! he thought. *Once they're out, then think of where to bring them next. You will think of something. But for now, get them the hell out of here!*

He grabbed Mr. Becker's tarp cocoon and hoisted him high up over his shoulder. Will dashed towards the opposite end of the basement and went bounding up the stairway. Carrying the body came rather easy as his insides were running on pure emotion. Mr. Becker was left before the door that led out to the backyard as Will headed back to the basement.

I can stuff them both in a garbage can, he thought along the way. *No one will see the bodies on the way to the car.*

Relieved that ideas were still progressively coming to him, Will leaped down the stairwell and secured Trent on top of his shoulder in no time at all. His feet pounded back up the steps so loud that he was unable to hear the front door opening. Upon reaching the first floor, he kicked shut the basement door and prepared to move through the kitchen. Trent's tarp was pressing pretty hard into the side of his face. Will adjusted the body slightly in order to obtain a fully clear view. The moment the plastic slipped off his cheek, he instantly froze. Kerri was standing roughly fifteen feet away from him. Her face was pale and her gazing eyes were wide. Her mouth curved neither up or down; just a lifeless straight line. Will stared at her for what felt like an hour, waiting for some form of a reaction.

Come on, Ker, his mind begged. *Flip out. Ask me what the hell I'm doing. Tell me you had nothing to do with this.*

Kerri's flattened mouth refused to open. Her eyes didn't flinch. It was the guiltiest expression Will had ever seen. Severely dismayed, he slammed Trent's body into the floor, causing the tiles to crack. Kerri finally blinked.

"What... what is this?" Will held up his hands. "You, Ker? Is this you?"

Her lips pursed a bit, but remained stubbornly shut. A crack shot all the way up Will's spinal cord, causing his neck to let out one rigid twitch.

"You answer me right now!" he shouted.

The tone of his voice noticeably startled them both. He had never yelled at her before, ever. Tiny crescents of water oozed forth from the bottoms of her lashes. Her silence served as his answer.

"Why would you…" he began. "I… I don't understand. You know about me. You know my past. You know exactly where I stand. How… how could you possibly do something like this?"

Kerri stayed still, the only movement being the tears rolling down her cheeks.

"Aren't you going to say something?" Will implored. "For Christ's sake, we worked so hard at getting pregnant. Our lives weren't going to be complete until it happened. And now it *has* happened! You're going to be a mom. I'm going to be a dad. It's what we wanted! And now… *this!* It makes absolutely no sense whatsoever! What could lead you to act like this!"

Kerri's shoulders started to shake. She clenched her fists and glanced back at Mr. Becker's tarp waiting beside the back door. Her gaze briskly shifted back at Will and then down to Trent.

Will kept quiet, anticipating a reply at last. Kerri's lower lip slowly started to drop. Will leaned forward, ears perked. Kerri gradually lifted up her right arm. Before her mouth got any wider, she brutally bashed her fist across her face. Will didn't even get a chance to react as she repeated the blow a second time.

"Kerri, what are you doing?" he shouted and ran toward her.

Ignoring his advancement, Kerri rushed up to the kitchen sink. She flipped on the faucet and doused some water into her face.

"Jesus, Kerri, are you okay?" Will asked, bolting up beside her.

He gently placed his hand on her shoulder. Kerri's entire body let out a vicious spasm as her head popped up from the faucet. She turned sharply to Will and grabbed his throat. Her other hand emerged from the sink holding a large kitchen knife. She forcefully moved Will backwards until his ass hit into the stainless steel refrigerator. He started to choke as Kerri raised the knife's point up before his chin. The sheen of the blade bounced off the silvery surface of the refrigerator.

With his esophagus squeezing shut, Will glanced down into Kerri's moist, rage-filled eyes. She touched the knife's tip to the side of his neck. The pressure with which she was applying caused a pin-sized stream of blood to trickle down to his shoulder. Kerri emitted a beastly snarl and pressed the blade further. Feeling the steel penetrating his skin, Will kept his eyes locked on her and inched open his mouth.

"Do it," his voice squeaked.

His words broke through her maddening concentration. She looked away from the knife's aim at Will.

"If this is what you really want," he strove to continue, "then I want to die."

Kerri's hands started to shiver. Her eyes snapped toward the floor as she yanked away the knife and flung it back to the sink. The steel bounced off the tiles with a couple of clanks. She removed her grip from around his neck. Will expelled a brief, but vigorous, fit of coughing as a full supply of air hit his lungs.

Kerri's face had become bright red and creased into a melancholy scowl. She appeared to want to cry, but was all out of tears. Will was afraid to speak. For a moment, their heavy breathing was the only noise made. Once Kerri's breaths slowed down a bit, she was able to initiate a sentence.

"There's... something wrong... with me," she nervously frowned and placed her forehead on his chest.

"Goddamn it, Ker," Will said, placing his arms around her. "I know. I know."

"I... I just can't control myself. It's so strange..." She grabbed a taut hold of his shirt. "So horrible... What's happening to me? I thought at first it was the hormones, but that can't be... Oh, God, Will, please help me."

Holding her extremely apprehensive frame was like trying to squelch an earthquake. A disturbed sense of dread settled into the back of Will's head. This was the first crisis involving his wife that he was utterly clueless on how to solve. He pressed her body tightly against his, hoping to stifle her shaking. His eyes were beginning to water when something poked him in his stomach. Before the feeling could truly register in his head, it happened again.

"What was that?" he asked, moving back a bit.

"What?" Kerri replied weakly.

"I'm not sure."

Will stared down at her pink, clingy maternity shirt which accentuated her basketball-shaped belly. A tiny bulge jutted forth and then went back in.

"Did you see that?" he shouted.

"See what?" Kerri lowered her eyes.

"You're belly! It's moving!"

"Really? Where?"

"Right here!"

Will grabbed her hand and placed it just above her belly button.

"Now, just wait a second," he said.

The pink shirt bulged out again around Kerri's palm. Will even felt the pound through her hand.

"See!" he exclaimed. "Did you feel that?"

"Yes." Kerri slowly looked up at his eyes. "I did."

"Our baby's moving. He's alive in there… or she. God, we don't even know if we're having a boy or a girl yet."

Will lowered his head and closed his eyes. He pictured holding their child in his arms and then watching it grow up. He envisioned Kerri decorating a room with teddy bears and building blocks. She placed tiny articles of clothing on miniature hangers and hung them up in the closet. Will then imagined none of that ever happening. He saw Kerri going to jail for murder. He saw himself possibly being charged as an accessory to murder. Their baby would be taken into foster care. He thought of all this and decided that he'd rather die. Kerri was his life; it was an undisputed fact. Will now knew that his mind was made up. He opened up his eyes.

"Kerri, please listen to me," he said.

She looked up. Will gently cupped his hands around her cheeks to make sure their line of sight did not break.

"You are my wife," he continued. "And you're carrying our child. That is all that will ever matter to me in this world and it will *never* change. Regardless of whatever terrible things you may have done, I'm *still* going to take care of you. Whatever's going on, we're going to stop it."

"I w-want to," Kerri shakily exhaled. "B-but I don't know how. I'm so scared. How can we stop this?"

"We're going to focus on our goal." He took her hand and placed it back on her belly. "This is our goal. We're going to get through this for what's *here*. Because we have a responsibility. Because it's our dream to be parents. Because we need to find out if we're having a boy or a girl. Do you understand me?"

Will knew he was talking like an insane person, but no longer cared.

"Yes, Will," Kerri replied. "I don't want to be this way. I swear to God, it's not me."

"I know that, Ker, I know. I'm going to get to the bottom of it. Don't worry, I'm here to handle it."

"Okay," she nodded.

"Good. That's my girl."

Will lifted up his head, shooting two separate glances over at the bodies resting on the tiles. He looked back at his wife.

"All right, Ker," he began, "I have to get started right away, but in order to do so, I need you to supply me with as much information as possible. Can you do that?"

"What do you need?" she asked.

"I need to know the story on those two, uh, tarps over there." He pointed with both hands at the doors to the basement and the backyard. "Are people going to come looking for them? Are the police already involved? Is anybody acting like they're suspicious of you?"

"They're starting to look for them now," Kerri slowly answered. "They made an announcement at school yesterday. The police are starting up a report."

Will edgily pressed his palms through his hair.

"But nobody thinks I'm involved," she quickly reassured. "Everyone thinks that Mr. Becker kidnapped Trent and ran off somewhere."

"Really? You sure?"

"Yes, Trent has always been a real little bastard at school. He got on all the teacher's nerves, especially Mr. Becker. A lot of people aren't even surprised that he's missing."

"Okay, okay, I got it. Uhm…"

Will tried to think of another question that didn't involve how or when she committed the murders. He just needed to make sure that all the bases of their current unfortunate scenario were covered.

"So no one has spoken to you at all regarding anything?" he finally asked.

"No," Kerri reaffirmed. "We just had a big faculty meeting. That was it, I promise."

Will looked down as her words sunk in. It was enough. Thinking-time was over. He had to take action.

"Okay, that's good," he looked back up. "I have to take care of some stuff now. I'm going to be out for a little while." He placed his hands back around her face. "I need you to just go upstairs, get in the bed, and relax your nerves."

"But where are you going? I don't want to be alone. Can't I come with you?"

"No, Kerri," he replied, nicely, "you can't. I need to do what I have to do by myself. I just want you to please go upstairs and relax. Will you be able to do that for me?"

"Just tell me what you're going to do." Her voice rose to a higher pitch. "Please, I… I don't want to lose you!"

"Ker, you're *not* going to lose me. Haven't you heard a word I've been saying so far? I have to go out and take care of some things I really don't want to say aloud at this moment. But I promise, by the end of today I will be coming back home. That has to be enough for you right now. Is it?"

Kerri shut her eyes and took a deep, heavy breath through her mouth. Her lids popped up in the middle of her long exhale.

"Please, just come back soon," she demanded.

"I will, I promise. Just don't go anywhere. Stay in the house. I want to see you here when I get back."

Kerri stepped forward and wrapped her arms around his waist. Will thought he could feel his lungs caving in, she was squeezing so tight.

"Just hurry back," she said.

"You know I will." He hugged her right back. "Now, go up to bed. There's nothing more for you to see or do here. Go."

"Okay." She released her embrace. "I'll be upstairs waiting for you."

"I'll be seeing you there."

Will waved good-bye as Kerri left the kitchen. Without moving another muscle, he listened to her feet ascending the stairway. Once her steps became softened by the carpeted hallway upstairs, he ducked into the downstairs bathroom and slapped a band-aid on his neck. Once the blood was contained, he rushed into action.

A plan had already taken shape in his head back in the basement when he realized that Kerri was indeed responsible. There was a place far away down the Jersey shore that Will had discovered a long time ago when his grandparents took him on vacation. Near a rundown dam beside a river that hardly flowed was an old drainage pipe through which a stream of ocean water trickled. One day, Will was feeling upset about the circumstances surrounding his past. He went for a long four-hour walk to clear his head and eventually happened upon the spot by the drainage pipe. The area was quiet, peaceful, and desolate—just what he needed. The intensive 'alone time' made him feel better. From that point on, Will would use the healing site a number of times more and never saw another soul.

Picturing the wide, circular opening of the drainage pipe, Will stretched a pair of yellow, plastic dishwashing gloves over his hands. He looked out a window at the front, side, and back sections of his house. No one appeared to be outside. A packet of Hefty garbage bags was removed from a cabinet beneath the kitchen sink. The two tarps were both removed and replaced with several of the black plastic bags that never, ever rip. Will did his best to focus his eyes away from the blood-soaked wounds to keep his mind from attempting to reenact what Kerri had done. He grabbed his keys and rushed outside to his maroon Saturn. Once the engine was started, he drove the car as close to the backyard as the driveway would allow, wishing all the while that they'd bought a house with a garage.

Upon returning back to the kitchen, Will hoisted Mr. Becker's new Heftier body bag up onto his shoulder. He slipped out the back door and sprinted around the house toward the driveway. The Saturn wasn't equipped with a very spacious trunk, which meant the bodies were backseat bound. While balancing Mr. Becker with his right arm, Will extended his left hand towards the door's handle.

"Will Haddon!" A voice called out of nowhere. "How are you, my boy?"

Will spun around, nearly dropping the body as well as a load in his pants. Standing before him, dressed in a navy blue Adidas sweat suit, was Mr. Schofield, his seventy-two year old neighbor from across the street.

"Oh, hey, Mr. Schofield," Will said, anxiously adjusting his grip on the black plastic.

"Nice, brisk morning, ain't it?" the old man said. "Perfect for a little three mile jog."

Mr. Schofield did a little two-step dance like a boxer getting ready for a fight.

"You ever jog, Will?" he went on. "You seem pretty in shape, but I've never caught you going for a run."

Will's nerves were exploding all over the place. He didn't want to say another word, fearing he'd sound too conspicuous. However, silence would probably come off as even worse.

"No, Mr. Schofield, I don't run," he responded. "But I really think I should start. Maybe tomorrow."

"Ah, that always seems to be the problem with you young ones today— always putting things off till tomorrow. *Strike while the iron's hot!* That's what we used to say back in my day."

He abruptly stopped his dancing and glared at the plastic bag.

Will recognized the direction of the scrutinizing gaze and clenched both of his fists. He had no idea what was going to happen next, but was staying by his oath to protect Kerri regardless.

"You know, Will, I shouldn't be tellin' you what to do," Mr. Schofield said. "I apologize. I can see you're in the middle of taking care of something. What've you got inside that big bag there?"

If the truthful answer to the old man's question was *anything* other than a bloody corpse, Will would have had no trouble coming up with a good lie. Unfortunately, Mr. Becker's frozen, wide-eyed expression was burned into his brain and prevented him from thinking of another reply.

131

"Oh… uh…" was all he could say. "Uhm, actually…"

"Is that…" Mr. Schofield peered closer. "Is that clothing for good will?"

"Yes," Will answered instantaneously. "That's exactly what it is."

"I thought so. Mrs. Schofield made me empty out some of my dresser drawers last week, too. Said it was my duty to help the less fortunate."

"I couldn't agree more. That's why I have to go now. I promised the Mrs. that I'd drop off a bunch of bags before the end of this morning."

"You're a good man, Will. Well, don't let me keep you from finishing your task."

"Thank you, sir," nodded Good Will Haddon.

After a little salute, Mr. Schofield trotted off down the sidewalk. Will waited before he was a good thirty feet away before opening the door to the backseat and tossing Mr. Becker inside. He wiped a couple of huge beads of sweat from his brow and headed back to the kitchen.

Trent soon joined Mr. Becker without any further interruption. The two used tarps were thrown back down to the basement where they'd await their eventual burning in the metal basin. Will was currently interested only in making it down the shore in record time.

The Saturn zipped out of the driveway and headed off in the direction of the New Jersey Parkway. With his foot firmly pressed on the gas pedal, Will pondered about the specifics of his trip. He wasn't especially worried about locating his old 'drainage' spot or being seen once he got there. Things moved a tad slower down at the shore. Life there was much simpler than up north. All people seemed to ever look out for was high tide, which meant Will would be thoroughly safe from prying eyes.

Plus the salt water in the drainage pipe will probably do a good number on the bodies as they decompose, he thought. *Jesus Christ, did I just think that? Who cares? It doesn't matter at this point. It's all for Kerri.* He gripped the steering wheel tighter. *Just concentrate on the road… and don't get pulled over.*

Chapter 19

The waiting room at Dr. Phalen's medical facility was empty when Will walked in. He glanced up at the little opening where the secretary usually sat. The section seemed vacant as well.

"Hello?" he said. "Is anyone here?"

The room stayed silent. Will walked a couple of steps forward and peered inside the opening.

"Are they not open yet?" he asked aloud while gazing at an unoccupied computer chair. "Then why wasn't their front door locked?" He looked over at the door that led from the waiting room into the office. "Could *that* door be locked, too?"

Growing a bit impatient, Will marched up before the entryway and grabbed the handle. After a quick twist, the door popped open. He stuck his head in the long, white-walled hallway that led to the various examination rooms. The time to be discreet was over.

"Hello!" Will bellowed down the hall.

He quickly heard the sound of a door opening from around the bend.

"Yes, who's there?" called back a voice.

"Dr. Phalen? It's me, Will Haddon."

"Oh, Will, of course." The doctor came swinging around the bend in his white medical smock. "I almost forgot you were going to drop by this morning. Please, please, come in."

Will entered the hallway and strolled through the whiteness toward the end.

"Right this way," Dr. Phalen smiled, waving him into his office. "Please, have a seat."

Will sat down in the leather chair situated before the doctor's dark, wooden desk.

"Sorry for making you wait," Dr. Phalen said, squatting down behind his desk. "My secretary's running a little late today."

"That's all right," Will answered. "Yeah, the place seems emptier than usual today."

"I know. A lot of the staff took their winter vacations."

"Oh, okay." Will wasn't there to discuss the staff going on holidays. "Dr. Phalen, I really need to talk to you."

"I know, Will. You seemed very upset over the phone. How's Kerri doing?"

"It's her I want to talk to you about. I think something may be wrong."

"Really?" Dr. Phalen leaned in with intent concern. "Please, tell me what."

Will looked down at his folded hands briefly. He had to pick his words very carefully so as to not give away anything incriminating.

"Well… she, uh… she really hasn't been acting like herself lately," he said.

"Will, that is a completely normal part of pregnancy," Dr. Phalen explained.

"No, Doctor, no, it's not like that. I know about every single symptom of pregnancy. I've read so many goddamn books I could probably write one myself. What I see in Kerri now is… different."

"Different how?" The doctor brought his thumb and pointer up to his chin.

"She sometimes… just goes off in these fits of rage. And the way she does it is way too extreme to be hormonal. It's like she's a completely different person and she can't seem to control herself. I'm afraid she's going to get hurt or even worse, hurt the baby."

"Whoa, hold on, Will. Easy there. I don't want you getting all nervous now. It still sounds like Kerri is experiencing normal pregnancy changes. Remember, this is something completely new to both you and her. Some drastic alterations in mind and body do occur."

Will squeezed his hands together. Dr. Phalen still wasn't getting it. Will decided he had to delve deeper into the details.

"I see where you're coming from," he began. "But what about strength? Have pregnant women been known to exhibit unusual levels of strength?"

"Now, what exactly do you mean by that?"

"Like could someone become freakishly strong because of the huge surge of hormones or something?"

"Will, you're really reaching here." Dr. Phalen tried to hold back a laugh. "I don't think that super-human strength can ever be brought on through pregnancy." He stopped and thought for a moment. "I mean, we could say that Kerri's case is a bit special because I used my new fertility drug for her in vitro."

"Is that it? Could it have something to do with the drug?"

"I highly doubt it. The drug doesn't contain any form of steroids or anything else that could physically increase a woman's strength."

"Then what the hell could it be?" Will stood up and slammed his hands down on the desk. He looked the doctor in the eye. "I'm telling you, Dr. Phalen, something is not right."

"Okay, Will, okay. I believe you. Just calm down and give me a second to think."

Will dropped back into his chair as Dr. Phalen rolled his eyes upwards in contemplation. For the following thirty seconds, a dropped pin could have been heard.

"Well, Will, let me ask you this," Dr. Phalen said. "Does anyone in your family have a history of aggressive behavior?"

Will's ears perked up. The tiny hairs on the back of his neck grew erect. "What does that have to do with anything?" he asked timidly.

"Because sometimes, certain traits and characteristics of family members can be passed down to children. It can range anywhere from baldness to intellect to even athletic ability or strength. It can also have an affect on the woman's personality."

"But those things are passed down to the child only, right?"

"Well, the mother and child do stay connected for those first nine months. When she eats, the baby eats. You know what I mean?"

"So you're saying that since they're connected, Kerri may be taking on some of the traits that our baby has developed?"

"Yes, possibly. Is there anyone in your family with some kind of history that would pertain to Kerri's current state?"

Will paused to give off the impression that he was thinking about the doctor's question. What actually occupied his mind was the searing image of a large, shadowy figure and the name *Haddonfear*.

"No," Will lied. "I can't think of anyone in my family with that kind of history."

"Hmm," Dr. Phalen murmured. "Well, then that probably isn't the case. That doesn't surprise me though; it's a pretty outlandish explanation."

"Yeah. So, what do we do now?"

"Well, I think we should schedule Kerri for an appointment. I could do some blood work. I'll do another ultrasound to make sure everything's all right with the baby. And hopefully, we can get to the bottom of all this."

"Okay, that sounds fine."

An examination probably was the best 'pseudo' solution for now. Maybe the rage inflicting Kerri was the result of some sort of imbalance going on in her blood or head, and could be cured through medication. That was the diagnosis Will was hoping for, however that shadowy figure in the back of his head still weighed down heavily. Not understanding the full story behind the dark memory made him very apprehensive.

"Did you want to make the appointment now?" Dr. Phalen asked.

"Oh, um, let me clear it with Kerri first," Will replied fast. "Can she call you back to make the appointment?"

"Absolutely." He stood up from his desk. "I'd like to talk to her anyway. We'll figure this whole thing out together."

Getting the cue that it was time to leave, Will rose up off his chair.

"Okay, I hope so," he said. "Thanks for taking the time to meet with me."

"No problem, Will," Dr. Phalen replied. "Here, let me walk you out."

The two headed out of the office and back down the hallway. Dr. Phalen opened the door to the waiting room and held it ajar with his foot.

"Take care of yourself, Will," he said, extending his hand.

"Thanks again, Doctor," Will said and shook his hand.

"Try not to worry yourself. I have a feeling that everything will work out just fine. I mean, it's not like Kerri's killed anybody."

Will's mind abruptly burst away from the situation at hand. The hallway morphed into a dank, darkened panorama. The trickle of water was heard. Will stood ankle-deep in a soggy stream of muck, staring down at the two mounds he had just covered completely with mud. His hands were caked in black, slimy earth. The mud made the two body bags disappear entirely within the bowels of the drainage pipe and he was certain that they would never be found. Kerri's secret would lie safe beneath the coating of boggy soil. The whole process went way easier than expected, however Will did not feel relieved. He trudged through the sludge back to the wide, circular opening of the pipe. The smell was horrible, yet no worse than the stench of the bodies he'd gotten used to down in the basement.

"Will, am I right?" Dr. Phalen's voice broke into the reverie.

White walls reclaimed Will's surroundings, erasing the cavernous drain-pipe dwellings. His eyes regained their focus.

"Oh, sorry about that," he said. "I was thinking about something else just now. You know, trying to calm myself down and all."

"Well, that's a good idea. It's not as bad as it seems, trust me. Like I said, it's not like she killed anybody, right?"

"Yes, right," Will smiled with extreme reluctance.

Chapter 20

Will waited patiently in the stark gray corridor. A small nametag that read 'GUEST' was clipped to his shirt. A thick, solid metal door moved open, sending a harsh echo through the corridor. A burly police officer dressed in dark blue stepped up to him.

"Follow me, Will," he said.

Will stepped forward without speaking. He wasn't in a pleasant mood and wanted to keep it that way. Anger was weighing heavily on his heart. He wasn't looking forward to what was lying ahead.

"Right through here," the officer said over his shoulder. "And then down to the base level."

Will walked behind the officer through a large office-type setting only without any cubicles. Open desks resided sporadically throughout the room and were occupied by either men in ties or other officers. The paper-pushing hum buzzing about the workspace grew significantly less in volume once Will had fully entered the area. He turned his head out toward the village of desks. People were staring at him. He slowed down his strides for a better view. Never had so many eyes been on him. The gawking wasn't even slightly discreet.

Beginning to feel uncomfortable, Will turned his sights back to the officer he was trailing. He increased his pace. The officer looked back upon hearing the quickened steps. He noticed the circus of stares.

"Sorry about all the looks," he said.

"Oh, I hadn't really noticed," Will replied with polite sarcasm.

"You've got to understand, you're kind of like a celebrity in a weird way. We never would have expected you to show up here, even though the privilege was always yours."

"Well, I wouldn't exactly call it a privilege."

"No, I guess you wouldn't."

A caged elevator resided on the opposite end of the room. The officer unhitched the black steel door and slid it open. Once the two were inside, he hit a button on a small control panel marked 'D'.

"You ready for this, Will?" he asked.

"Let's get it over with," Will exhaled.

Without responding, the officer pulled the door shut and locked it in place. The elevator began to slowly descend. A ways off, an older man with graying hair shakily stood up from his desk. Using the aid of a silver metal walker, he took two baby steps in the direction of the disappearing elevator. His eyes delivered a formidable Clint-Eastwood-inspired glare.

The black metal cage touched down with a quick clank. The officer unlatched the door and swung it open, revealing a set of thick bars before a long dimly lit hallway. The floor featured sheet after sheet of grimy, brownish tile and the walls were unfinished brick with a door placed about every fifteen feet on both sides.

"Welcome to the dungeon," the officer said, setting foot on the tile.

Will grudgingly departed the elevator and pursued the officer up to two more men in blue standing guard beside the bars, each brandishing a fancy-looking shotgun.

"Gentlemen, we have a first-time visitor," the officer stated, holding up a ring of jingling keys. "Stand down for the moment."

Both guards moved aside, exposing a square keyhole built into the bars. The officer inserted a single key and undid the latch. A rectangular section of the bars was swung out, revealing the long hallway ahead. The officer returned the set of keys to his belt.

"Okay, Will, we're off," his square jaw grinned.

Will walked forward and passed between the two guards. Neither of them looked his way or said a word. Once Will was on the other side of the bars, the officer shut and locked the door behind them.

"Keep an eye on things for us, would ya, boys?" The officer nodded at the guards. "Right this way, Will. He's all the way at the end."

The two strolled down the dim hallway. Will tried looking into the small square window at the top center of each passing door, but only saw black.

"Not too many residents down here recently," the officer said without looking back. "But your guy, well, we like to think of him as the Grand-daddy of the Dungeon. Been down here long as I can remember."

"Mm hmm." Will wanted to save his voice for the cell at the end.

"Man, did I hear stories about this guy," the officer went on without a care. "*An unstoppable force* some called him. Said he had the strength of ten men. Apparently, he took a dive off the top of a ten-story building just to kill a girl, landed on his back, and survived. That's how they finally caught him. Kind of tough to imagine him that way now. All he does is sit in the corner of his cell. Says hardly a word. Maybe age finally caught up to him. Who knows? Maybe he's just punishing himself for what he did."

The officer's one-sided conversation lasted all the way to the end of the hall. They both stopped before the final door on the left. Will could feel his heart knocking hard on his ribs.

"Finally, we're here," the officer exhaled, removing his ring of keys again. He looked over his shoulder at Will. "Feel like turning back?"

"No, sir," Will forced himself to state. "I have to speak with him."

"You got it." He turned the key. "There'll be a thick wall of plated glass between you two. It's unbreakable. Plus, he's all chained up, so I wouldn't worry about too much movement on his end."

He pushed the door's handle downward. With a loud *click*, the cell inside became illuminated. Will heard some faint music begin playing. The officer pulled the door open with one hand and placed the other on his gun in its holster.

"Step right up," he said to Will, and walked into the cell. "Hey Derek! You've got yourself a visitor, so look alive. You might actually want to see who it is."

Once the officer was far enough into the cell, Will cautiously walked through the doorway. He was at once greeted by the opening lyrics to Twilight Time by The Platters. His eyebrow immediately went up in confusion.

"Oldies," the officer referred to the song. "Has a calming effect on the inmates or so the warden thinks; sort of soothes the savage beasts, you know?"

Will did not answer. His unflinching eyes stared through the huge wall of glass. The right side of the cell consisted solely of a king-sized mattress and a toilet. In the far left corner, crouched an oversized colossus dressed in a XXXL dark gray jump suit. Bulky silver shackles dripped from his arms to the floor. Something black and raggedy was draped over his round head.

"Okay, Will, there's a chair if you'd like to sit down," the officer said, pointing off to the side. "Don't worry about speaking too loud. He can hear you just fine through those air holes in the glass. That's all you really need to know, I think."

"What's on his face?" Will asked, eyes still focused forward.

"Oh, that. He had that with him when he first came here. It's the mask he used to wrestle in. Yeah, I know it looks pretty stupid, but they told me it had some kind of meaning in the wrestling world back in the day."

"Meaning? What kind of meaning?"

"I don't remember exactly… something like, the mask a wrestler wore became his identity. It became this big, sacred object. If a masked wrestler ever lost a match, he'd then have his mask pulled off and, like, lose his identity. At least that's how it was explained to me."

"So he just keeps the mask on all the time?"

"I heard that when he was first brought in, one of the cops tried to take off the mask. Well, ol' Derek didn't take too kindly to that gesture; put his pointer finger through the cop's eye and broke his wrist so bad that his hand was left dangling like it was about to fall off." The officer turned a glance over at the man behind the glass wall. "So the warden said it was okay to just let him keep the mask on. You know, let him *think* he's still winning. Plus, he seems to behave much better when he has it on. He really doesn't say much. I'm not sure if you're going to be able to make much conversation with him."

"I guess we'll see."

The officer began stepping back over to the exit.

"I'll be right outside this door if you need anything," he said. "But I'm sure you'll be fine." He looked back at the wall of glass. "Now you be a gracious host, Derek."

The prisoner offered zero acknowledgement, merely choosing to look at the floor. With a snide, little laugh, the officer exited the cell, closing the door behind him. The only sound that remained was the soft vocals of Twilight Time still pumping through a pair of small speakers in the ceiling. Will stood perfectly stiff and silent. Derek kept to his cowering crouch.

Deep in the dark your kiss will thrill me like days of old...

The romantic lyrics went sailing through Will's head, causing him to think of Kerri. The realization of why he was there broke through his tense hush.

"You don't know me," his voice began with a hint of a reticent squeak.

Derek did not move. His head stayed directed downward. Will took a guarded step closer.

"And this is not easy," he went on, "but I need to ask you about something very important."

No response was returned. A small bead of agitation popped in the back of Will's head. He took another step

"I really need to talk to you, uh, Derek. Do you understand that? Can you pick your head up and look my way?"

Derek continued giving his undivided attention to the ground, letting The Platters provide the only other source of vocals in the cell. Will quietly crushed his fingers into frustrated fists. He recalled all the horror the person before him had caused; how it had affected his life and how it was now conceivably affecting his wife. The influx of thoughts pushed him to march straight up to the glass.

"Were you this quiet when you killed Mom?" he shouted through the air holes. "I know I was there when it happened, but I was only an infant so I just can't seem to remember!"

Will closed his mouth and waited. His fists were beginning to shake. The black mask suddenly jerked toward the glass, flashing the faded white outlines around the eye area. Startled, Will snapped his head back from the air holes. Apparently, Derek had finally taken notice. The nasal area of the mask was sucked inward as if he was harshly sniffing.

"Now do you know who I am?" Will asked.

Derek slowly rose up to his full 6'4" standing frame, casting a long shadow that reached the base of the glass wall. The chains clanged together as he stood. Though his eyes were well cloaked behind the mask, Will could feel a powerful gaze lunging his way. His scales of frustration started tipping over to fear. Had he possibly stirred a hornet's nest?

"Yeah, it's me, William, your son," he said. "Maybe now that you know that, you'll be more inclined to help me out?"

The mask imploded again as Derek took another mighty whiff. He turned his head on a slight angle, as if somewhat confused. Will felt like they were getting nowhere, and opted for a somewhat different approach.

"You're going to be a grandfather," he stated.

Derek's head straightened up from its slanted angle.

"That's right," Will continued. "You heard me. I'm married and my wife is almost six months pregnant."

He seemed to still have Derek's attention.

"But now there's something wrong." Will looked back over his shoulder at the door to see if the officer was listening in. Once certain that the coast was clear, he leaned a bit forward and softly said, "Her mindset and her actions have turned... violent. She's not only begun hurting herself, but other people too. She's turning into a different person and I know it's completely unnatural. Do you get what I'm saying so far?"

The mask delicately expanded and contracted, showing that Derek's breathing had slowed considerably. Will didn't need a definitive, spoken answer just yet as long as his father proceeded to appear alert.

"Her unnatural actions so far remind me of what I've heard about you. I know you were on something that turned you that way. I need you to tell me everything you know about whatever it was you were on; what exactly did it do your body, how did it affect your mind, do you know if it's something that can be inherited through future generations, did it eventually wear off? Please, if there's anything at all that I can use to help my wife, tell me."

Derek persisted in doing his best impression of a statue. The stupidly childish, faded white outlining across the mask combined with the one-sided conversation as well as the blaring oldies pushed Will over the edge.

"If there's an ounce of humanity left inside your body, then you'll start talking to me right now!" he shouted. "You owe it to me, damn it! Can you even imagine the life I had growing up? Parentless? Raised by a nearly senile grandmother? Not to mention being permanently branded the son of a psychopath! By the time I turned eighteen I had to change my name for Christ's sake! You got all that? Now stop standing there and tell me what you know! You owe me!"

Derek's head bobbed down and stole another glance at the floor. Will lingered within the agitating affects of his tirade. His father's mask abruptly shot a blazing stare right at him. Will's eyes excitedly widened at the notion that his words had finally gotten through.

He took one step closer and opened up his ears. Derek's feet didn't move. He continued facing his son. His shoulders brusquely rolled back as his chin tipped upward. The front of the mask was then embedded up his nostrils as another forceful sniff was emitted. Once the black material returned to its original shape, Derek sunk back into his craven crouch. Will's proverbial last straw was drawn. He charged right up to the air holes.

"What are you, some kind of wild animal? Are you brain dead? Have you even heard a word I've said? Goddamn you!" He banged his hands into the glass as his heavy exhales fogged up the clear surface. "You've never done a single, good thing for me ever! I'm asking you just this once to take some fucking responsibility and be a father!"

Derek turned the faded white outlining of his face fully away from his son as if listening merely to Smoke Gets In Your Eyes, the second tune by The Platters that was currently emanating from the speakers. The rage splintering up Will's spine forced him to repeatedly pound his fists into the glass. The door behind him swung open as the officer came rushing into the cell. Refusing to acknowledge the man in blue, Will continued to unload on the wall.

"Whoa!" the officer shouted and wrapped his arms over the back of Will's shoulders. "This visit is over."

"You're not my father!" Will shouted through the glass as he was dragged backward. "I'm not you! You psychotic piece of shit! I hope you rot in that little fucking corner!"

The officer brought him back out into the dim hallway. As the door to the cell began to close by itself, Derek partially turned his head to catch one final glimpse of his son. As soon as the door shut, the lights and the oldies went away leaving him in constant darkness.

Out in the hall, the officer pulled Will's right arm behind his back and pressed him face-first up against the brick wall.

"Now we can't have you shouting at the inmate," he said into Will's ear. "It could cause him to get agitated and then we might have a problem. Now, are you all right, Will? Can I let go of you?"

Will breathed deeply in and out his mouth. His nostrils were pushed up against the wall. He tightly closed his eyes as his brain forced his body to regain some composure.

"Yeah," he exhaled with a nod, "I'm okay now."

"Okay then," the officer agreed. "I'm going to release my grip, and then you're going to calmly walk in front of me back to the elevator. Got it?"

"Yes, yes, I got it."

Will kept his body perfectly still. He didn't want to show a single sign of struggle.

"Thank you, Will." The officer stepped back from him and took out his ring of keys. "Now let's get back to the first floor."

Will quickly stepped out in front just as he was told. The officer locked the door to Derek's cell. After putting away his keys, he followed behind Will.

"Was that your whole purpose for coming here, Will?" he asked. "Just to yell at him? I mean, I guess I can understand."

"No," Will replied without turning around. "I just needed to ask him something."

"Did you get your answer?"

"No."

"Well, I told you he doesn't say much."

"Yes, you did."

Not another word was said for the remainder of the trip down the hallway. The two guards at the wall of bars further fueled the silence as Will and the officer passed through into the elevator. The small cage was soon ascending back to the first floor. The officer slid the door open and turned to Will.

"Do you need me to walk you back to the sign out station?" he asked. "Or can you find your way yourself?"

"I can find it myself," Will answered.

"And you're going to walk right out of here completely composed without causing any kind of commotion."

"Yes, sir. That's right."

"Very good. You take care, Will."

The officer turned his back and walked out of the elevator. Will waited till he was a good fifteen feet away before exiting the cage himself. He wanted to make it out of the battle zone of desks before all the gawking started up again. His feet prepared to establish a brisk pace when a shiny metal pole was placed down before his toes. He halted his legs and looked to his left. The pole was connected to a two-wheeled walker that stood before an older man with a majority of grey streaking through his once-dark hair.

"Excuse me," Will said. "I didn't see you there."

"Of course you didn't," the man replied. "That's because I came out of nowhere."

"What?"

"I stopped you on purpose, Will."

Will grew a bit agitated, but couldn't bring himself to yell at a man with a walker.

"Why would you do that?" he asked. "You're not looking for an autograph or something, are you?"

"No, Will," the man said.

"Yeah, I'm sorry about that. I just really hate all these people staring at me."

"Well, then would you mind if I walked you out the back way? It's much more private, so you won't get any annoying stares."

"Thanks, I appreciate that."

"Just don't walk too fast." The man said and alluded down to his left foot.

Will lowered his eyes and could easily tell that the foot was a prosthetic.

"Oh, yeah, sure," he answered hastily. "There's no rush."

"Great, it's right over here," the man said. "Oh, by the way, my name's Reynolds."

He took his right hand off one of the plastic support grips on the walker and extended it to Will.

"Nice to meet you," Will said, giving him a shake.

The two made their way toward a door in the far right corner of the room. Reynolds swiped an ID card through a slot next to the handle. A green light flashed on the slot.

"Will, would you do me a favor and get that?" Reynolds asked.

"Sure, no problem," Will said, grabbing the handle.

The door opened up to a long, empty corridor. A small glass window appeared to be waiting all the way at the end. The two casually began moving forward. Reynolds dragged his feet along, letting the two front wheels of the walker do most of the work. Will kept his pacing curbed in order to stay in sync with him.

"So, how did your visitation go?" Reynolds questioned.

"Not good," Will replied discreetly.

"He didn't say a word, did he?"

"Actually, no. How did you know that?"

"Oh, Derek and I go way back. I guess you could say we... have an understanding of each other."

Will glanced down again at Reynold's gimpy feet as an impulsive understanding came over him.

"You're the one who caught him," he said, raising his eyes back up.

"Well, I wouldn't necessarily say *caught*," Reynolds said openly and without pause. "Maybe more like *slowed down*." He once again nodded at the floor. "And he certainly didn't come quietly."

"Officer Reynolds, I'm sorry for whatever hardships my f... I'm sorry for whatever he put you through."

"Hardships, huh? Well, that was a long time ago... and I don't hold you responsible for what happened."

"I still wish it never happened."

"I can understand why. But something does puzzle me right now."

"Oh yeah. What?"

"Well, Will, you don't have to answer this, but... I just wasn't sure why you'd come back to visit him now after all these years... just out of nowhere. I hope you don't mind me asking that."

Will closed his mouth for a moment and tried to think *vague*.

"I don't mind if you ask," he finally said. "I, uh, just really needed to ask him something. Something that had been weighing down on my mind for a while. I just decided that now was the time."

"But you didn't get your answer, did you? I mean, I can only assume that because he didn't speak."

Will brought his sights forward and saw that they were almost at the end of the corridor. The conversation needed to be wrapped up.

"I got an answer... sort of," he said. "It just wasn't the one I was looking for."

"I'd hate to think that you wasted your time coming here," Reynolds said. "I'm sure it was tough working up the strength to do so."

"You're right, it was. And I really wish it could have gone differently. Maybe I should have known better."

The two reached the end of the corridor where a single glass door and a clerk at a small desk were the only things separating Will from the outside. Reynolds placed his badge down on the desk before the clerk.

"Hello, Frank, just requesting clearance to let my friend, Will, here slip out the back door," he said.

"Yes, sir," Frank replied and hit a small buzzer on his desk.

Will heard the lock unlatch inside the glass door.

"Okay, Will, that's it," Reynolds nodded. "You're free to go in peace. You take care now."

"Thanks, Officer Reynolds," Will said, holding out his hand.

"That's *Special Agent* Reynolds to you, William," Frank abruptly interrupted.

"Oh, that's okay," Reynolds attempted to hush him right away. "We're all just officers of the law here."

"Sorry, sir." Frank lowered his head.

Ignoring the clerk's reply, Reynolds took hold of Will's hand and gave it a shake.

"Nice meeting you, Will," he said.

"You too," Will answered. "Take care."

He pulled open the glass door and stepped out of the building. As the door closed, the lock automatically re-bolted. Reynolds placed his hands back on his walker. He looked at Frank and grinned.

"Nice kid that Will," he said and aimed his walker away from the exit.

While gradually moving back down the long corridor without turning around, he added,

"But the little shit's not telling me everything."

Chapter 21

The front door creaked slowly open. Kerri stuck her head inside and observed that the foyer area was empty. She cautiously tip-toed onto the hardwood and gently shut the door behind her. Without removing her long, purple coat, she dashed up the stairs. Her eyes locked onto the partially ajar bathroom door on the right-hand side of the second level. As she rapidly began moving toward it, Will unexpectedly popped out of the room to the left.

"Oh, Will!" she exclaimed, stepping back and grabbing hold of her jacket.

"Oh God, did I scare you, honey?" Will asked, holding up his hands. "I'm so sorry. I didn't mean to. I was just excited that you were home."

"It's okay, Will. I just didn't expect to see you up here. And you're home kind of early, aren't you?"

"Yes, I am." He smiled. "But I have my reasons."

"Reasons?" She forced her cheeks to grin. "What do you mean?"

"Well, I was just thinking about you and the baby... and how your checkup with Dr. Phalen went really well and how you told me you're starting to feel much better. You do feel much better, right?"

"Yes," Kerri replied plainly.

"Good. I was just thinking about the future and how great it's going to be. I wanted it to be here already for me and for you. So I did something today to sort of keep us thinking towards the future. Can I show it to you?"

"What is it?"

Will took a few steps backwards to the door he'd just come out of and placed his hand on the knob.

"Come in and see," he smiled.

Kerri folded her arms across her purple jacket and strolled toward him. Will kept his grip on the doorknob and touched his free hand to her back.

"Now, close your eyes," he whispered.

Kerri did as she was told, keeping her arms nervously over her chest. Will eased his hand into her back, sending her body forward.

"Don't worry," he said. "I've got you."

"Okay," Kerri replied. "What have you done?"

"You're about to find out. Just a few more feet and..."

Kerri heard the door creaking open. She held her breath as Will led her into the dark.

"Just one second," he said and flipped the light switch.

A low hue of brightness shone through her lids. She squinted a bit from the rapid influx of light. The smell of fresh paint crept through her nostrils.

"All right, Ker," Will said. "You can open 'em."

Kerri popped up her lids. The once-white walls had been turned into a light shade of green. A bright border of moons and stars with little smiley faces ran all around the room at the top. A wooden rocking chair resided in the left-hand corner, featuring an assortment of stuffed bears and bunnies sitting on it.

A tanned wood dresser with a cushioned changing pad placed atop its surface rested against the wall to the right. And in the far-left corner of the room, brandishing a little mobile of monkeys, was a grand crib which matched the tan tone of the dresser. Will looked over at Kerri. Her mouth was gaping.

"Oh my God, Will," she gasped. "What... how did..."

"I took off from work today," he began. "I bought the crib, dresser, and rocking chair last week, and had them delivered today. I also hired a painter to do the walls and the border. While he was doing that, I went out and got some baby toys. Do you like the color?"

"I... I think it's great." She dropped her arms down, causing her jacket to open slightly.

"Since we don't know if it's a boy or a girl, I decided to go with the Spring Mint because it's a nice, soothing, neutral color. I figured it would work either way."

"I can't believe it, but... how could you afford to get all this?"

"You know how, Ker."

"I do? Are you sure?"

"The trust fund. Remember? The one that was set up in my name after my mother died and my... father went away. Because of all the lawsuits my family had against the EWC."

"You're allowed to take money out of there now?"

"Kerri, I've been able to take money out ever since I turned eighteen. I hadn't done it yet because I wanted to save as much as possible... for the future. Do you have any idea the amount of interest I've earned?"

"A lot?"

"You bet your ass, baby! Let's just say we will never have to worry about money. And since the future is rapidly approaching, I figured it was the right time to dip a little into the fund."

Kerri looked down at her protruding belly and noticed her jacket was opened a crack. She immediately closed the purple fabric shut as if concerned she would catch a draft. She breathed in deeply through her mouth as a glaze of moisture overcame her eyes.

"Are you okay, Kerri? Don't worry about the money. It's fine. Just think of it as a late Christmas present."

"I... I just can't believe it." She looked him in the eye. "It's so... wonderful. Thank you."

"I just can't wait till this room gets its owner."

Will reached out to caress Kerri's belly. She abruptly stepped back before his hand could make contact.

"Whoa, Kerri, what's wrong?"

"I'm, I'm sorry," she stammered, clutching her chest. "I just... I think I felt the baby kick and it just startled me for a second."

"But that's a good thing. Don't let it scare you. That's our kid moving in there. It's, like, the coolest thing ever." He advanced up to her. "Can I feel it?"

"Uh, no, not right now." She took two more big steps backwards. "I... I'm just not feeling good. I think the baby's kicking too much. I'm just gonna go take a long, hot shower."

"Okay. You can just go and, uh..."

Her back had already turned to him. She briskly walked out of the new baby room.

"...get cleaned up," Will said to no one.

With her arms crossed as if hugging herself, Kerri traipsed through the upstairs hallway into the bathroom. She locked the door and finally let go of herself. With her hands even with her hips, she stepped over to the sink and gazed into the mirrored vanity. Her light green eyes were beginning to dry. She touched her finger tips to the center of her purple coat and pulled it apart.

The outer layer slipped off her shoulders and dropped to the floor, revealing dark stains of red splattered all over her clothes. She stared at the reflection of a particularly thick blotch near the lower left section of her light blue blouse. Her mind recalled the thick stream of blood which had caused the blemish.

It had squirted outward so fast from the young man's neck and caught her completely off guard. Kerri touched her pointer to her doused blouse and held it up to the mirror. While gawking at the red smeared across her finger, she recalled the scene that had just unraveled on her way home.

The Kia had stopped at a red traffic light. While waiting for the green, Kerri felt a little kick in her tummy. She looked down and pressed her gloved hand over her bulge. Tiny bumps like a calm heartbeat, repeatedly hit her palm.

"Hello," she whispered. "Are you saying hi to me?"

A blaring horn disrupted her train of thought. She looked up past the now-green traffic light at the rearview mirror. A Dodge Cougar full of rowdy teenage passengers moved extra close to her rear bumper. The young motorists were yelling and shaking their fists and middle fingers in the air.

"Let's go!" Kerri heard one of them shout. "Move!"

The Cougar moved a hair closer and actually knocked into her bumper causing the Kia to wobble. Kerri's eyes widened as a sharp pain sliced through her brow. The Cougar's horn blasted again. Kerri touched her foot into the gas and began moving forward.

The Cougar revved its engine and followed shortly after her. The road began to wind a bit. Kerri kept one eye on the road and the other on the rearview mirror. The road became narrower. No cars appeared to be coming up from the opposite lane. She squeezed her gloves tightly around the steering wheel and sharply turned to the left. Her foot slammed on the brake forcing the Kia to come to a screeching halt on an angle in the center of the road.

The tires of the Cougar left a burning trail of rubber as they skidded to a stop of their own. It did not take long for the teenage driver to sound his horn again. Kerri closed her eyes and removed her seatbelt amidst the continuous blaring. She opened the driver's side door and slipped out. She stood with her back to the Cougar for a moment. The horn ceased.

"What the fuck's your problem?" the punk behind the wheel shouted out of his lowered window.

Kerri didn't answer, but spun around and let her purple jacket drop to the ground. Her pregnant stomach lingered in the Cougar's headlights.

"You want me to run your ass over?" the driver yelled and revved his engine.

Kerri took one step directly at them. The engine roared again, propelling the Cougar forward an inch. Kerri took a second step.

"Do it, Ted!" urged the kid in the passenger's side. "Make that bitch move!"

"Yeah," Ted grinned maniacally.

He grabbed onto the steering wheel and revved the engine one last time. Kerri started advancing. Recognizing this, Ted hit the gas. The back tires of the Cougar spun erratically, creating a puffy haze of smoke. An instant later, the car lunged forward. Kerri stared into the rapidly approaching headlights as every muscle in her body flexed for action.

Ted increased his pressure on the gas pedal and stared directly into her illuminated face. A loud thud bounced off the Cougar's front bumper and Kerri disappeared. Ted instantly switched his foot over to the brake, slowing the car considerably.

"Where'd she go?" he asked, peering out through the windshield.

"She's gone," said the passenger beside him.

"Whoa!" shouted one of the kids in the back.

A gloved hand shot through the opened driver's side window and seized Ted by the chin. All the boys began screaming in shock as the Cougar continued to slowly roll. A second gloved hand entered and grabbed the top of Ted's head. The boys in the back watched through the rearview as his face was bent on an abnormal angle. As his neck emitted a shrill *snap*, his entire body was yanked out of the car through the window. The Cougar began veering off the road.

"Oh shit!" the passenger punk exclaimed and reached out for the steering wheel.

Kerri suddenly came diving through the driver's side window. She reached down in the middle of the front console and jerked up the parking brake. The Cougar stopped, however the force of her pull snapped the lever right off.

The kid in the passenger's seat shot back into the door and turned around to open it. Kerri grabbed him by the shirt collar and dragged his flailing upper body back her way. He didn't get a chance to even scream as the sharp end of the broken parking brake was shoved into the side of his neck.

Blood streamed out from the fresh wound, hitting Kerri in the side. Gasping for air, the passenger's side punk dropped back into his chair and began to convulse. The two burnouts in the back desperately tried to make it up to the front seats and out of the two-door car. They each met up with one of Kerri's hands as she came pouncing at them over the center console in the front.

She grasped the sides of both their heads and clapped her arms together. Their skulls cracked together like a pair of raw eggs. Kerri repeated this motion over and over, causing bursts of bloody yolk to spray her blouse. She did not stop until all movements ceased from their bodies. The Cougar was finally fully silent.

Breathing heavily, Kerri stepped back out onto the road. A harsh pounding broke out from her stomach. She placed her gloved hand over her bloodied belly and felt her baby joyfully sounding its presence.

Her other hand touched the kicking as well, cradling the bulging bundle in her arms. She strolled towards the Kia without looking back at the Cougar or the mess inside.

The red smear on her blouse now looked a bit dryer in the bathroom mirror's reflection. Kerri kept her eyes on it as her brain ended its flashback sequence.

She stared at all the blood and recalled that Will was under the assumption that all was well.

She then called to mind the four kills that occurred in the Cougar in most likely under a minute's time. She waited for that feeling of sadness that always accompanied the image of each person she'd done away with.

No emotions bubbled up other than an extremely weird sense of relaxation. She closed her eyes and conjured up the killings again; the neck-snap, the parking brake impaling, the double-headed smash… her lids flipped open… nothing but calmness.

She didn't speak, but kept her gaze locked on the mirror.

She couldn't stop smiling.

Chapter 22

The Third Trimester

"I could kill you, Will!" Fred bellowed upon setting foot in their three-person cubicle. "I can't believe you did this to me!"

"Uh, what?" Will asked, looking up from his computer screen.

"Oh, you know." Fred marched over to his desk and threw his coat over his chair. "You know, sir."

Will could tell right away from the overly dramatic manner with which the coat was slammed down that nothing even remotely serious was wrong.

"Fred-o, are you on something right now?" he asked. "What the heck are you talking about? Get to the point!"

"Oh, you are a shrewd one, Haddon," Fred said, squinting his eyes. "Very smooth how you work, pretending to be all cool and reserved."

"Oh, I could never be as cool as you, Fred-o. Everyone knows that. Now, about getting to that point?"

"Okay, fine." Fred stepped up to him. "You just had to let your wife bring Lynn with her to the bar that one night, didn't you?"

"Not really. Weren't *you* the one who…"

"And you just had to introduce her to me," Fred continued as if he couldn't hear Will. "Knowing full well that I was a swinging stud and that she'd be unable to resist my charms. You sly dog, you."

Will decided to play along.

"Yeah, so what if I knew all that. It doesn't make a difference now, does it?"

"I knew it!" Fred jumped back. "You were in on the whole thing from the beginning! Damn, why didn't I figure this out sooner?"

"Because that's exactly the kind of guy you are." Will smiled big. "Too slow to figure things out before it's too late."

"Seriously, Will." Fred lowered his head. "How could you do this to me? You were my co-worker, my friend."

"I did it *because* you were my co-worker, Fred. Because you were my friend." Will then realized that the game was growing a little long in the tooth. "And now, would you please just refresh my memory as to what exactly it is that I did to you?"

"Oh, fine, Will. You might as well just torture me some more by making me say it out loud." He cupped his hands around his mouth. "Here it goes! So listen up!"

"You have my undivided attention."

"Okay, well, you know how I met Lynn when we all went out to Uncle Mike's. Well, I asked her out that night and ever since then we've sort of been seeing each other."

"Sort of seeing?"

"You know, dating. I've been dating her ever since... and no one else. Me! A dude used to having a babe on each arm at least!"

"Well, that doesn't sound so bad. It just sounds like you have a girl-friend. That's actually a *good* thing."

"Oh, it gets much worse! This morning, we're lying in bed together and she looks over at me and tells me she *loves* me!"

"That's great, Fred. Congratulations."

"*That's great, Fred. Congratulations,*" Fred mimicked sardonically. "Don't give me that! I was Captain of the One-Night Stand! Now, look at what you've reduced me to!"

"Hey, if it's so damn bad, then why don't you just break up with her?"

"No! I can't do that!"

"Why the hell not?"

"Because... I love her, too! Happy? Is that what you've been waiting all this time to hear?"

"Uh... yes?" Will raised up his arms in unsure victory.

"Ho, ho, very funny." Fred crossed his arms. "This is all your fault. Hanging out with me for so long; you, with all your marriage germs. It was only a matter of time before I cracked. Oh dear Lord, how the mighty have fallen!"

Fred's shoulders slumped and his head nodded toward his feet. Will stood up in front of him.

"Don't worry," he said with mock tenderness. "It'll be okay. We're go-ing to get through this."

Fred threw his arms around him in an over-exaggerated fashion.

"Hold me," he impishly whimpered, still looking down.

Will patted him on the back and did not hear the high-heeled footsteps gravitating their way. Fred looked up from Will's shoulder just in time to see Loni walk into the cube. He at once broke away from the embrace. Will turned around to learn that the third member of their co-worker triangle had arrived, and slapped his head in embarrassment. Loni merely acknowledged them with a little nod and curtly paced over to her desk.

"Why is it when two girls are hugging, it's considered hot," Fred questioned, throwing his hands up in the air, "but if two dudes are hugging, it usually just comes off as creepy?"

Loni turned on her computer without looking their way. Will noticed that she was purposely ignoring them.

"I don't know, Fred," he tried to lighten up the situation. "It's just one of those mysteries of the universe."

They both paused and waited for Loni to provide the laugh track. Silence was all they got.

"Come on, Loni," Fred laughed timidly. "You know we were just kidding around, right? That hug meant nothing to me, honest."

She remained silent, staring down at her keyboard.

"Are you okay, Loni?" Will quietly asked.

"I'm sorry guys," she replied with a sniff. "It's just not a good day."

Fearing a deluge of more tears, Loni stood up from her seat and exited the cubicle. Fred looked over at Will.

"Must be PMS," he diagnosed.

"I don't think so," Will said, with his head turned toward the cube's exit. "I've been married for a while now. I know all the traits regarding 'that time of the month' and I'm telling you, this ain't it."

"Are you saying it's something worse?"

"Possibly. I mean, it looked like she was on the verge of crying. We've never seen her like that."

"Will, I can't deal with a hysterical woman. I'm scared."

"Don't you go freaking out on me too, Fred. You've got a woman who loves you to think about. I'm going to go see if our girl is okay."

"All right, but be careful."

"Don't worry. I've had plenty of training in matters such as this."

"Where do you think she went?"

"Elementary, my dear Fred-o." Will winked. "There's only one place the female species reverts to when solace is sorely needed."

Will jogged out of the cube and made a left down the quiet, empty hall. He stopped before the door to the ladies' room. His head turned both ways to make certain the area was truly uninhabited. After receiving confirmation, he raised his fist and knocked on the door.

"Loni?" he said, trying to remain soft yet audible. "Are you in there?"

"Yes I am," sobbed a nasally voice. "You can't come in."

"I wasn't really planning on coming in…" An idea then hit him. "Did you not want me to come in because you're upset or because you just started to do number two?"

A small, haphazard laugh broke out of her weeping—just what Will was hoping for.

"I'm just upset, Will," Loni answered. "I'm not doing *number two*."

"Oh, okay then," Will went on. "Well, I'd like to try and help you out. Maybe make you feel better. So since you're definitely *not* doing number two, then would you like to talk to me?"

"Uhm…" She let out another sniff. "…okay."

"All right, good. The only thing is, I don't want to make you shout and I don't want to make you talk to me in an open area… so I'm coming in."

Before Loni could protest, Will took a deep breath and slipped inside the pink-tiled land of the ladies' room.

"Okay, Loni," he called out once the door shut behind him. "I'm inside. Now where are you?"

"I'm in here," said a voice from the last pink stall on the left.

Will walked toward the back of the room and found a pair of black high heels peeking out from below. He knocked on the door.

"Do you want me to stay out here?" he asked.

The small circular latch near the right center of the door slow turned counterclockwise. The lock became unhinged and the door popped partially open. Will peered cautiously inside. Loni leaned back into the side wall, her eyes buried in a wad of toilet paper.

"Jesus, kid," Will began without stepping fully into the stall. "What's wrong?"

Loni lowered her wet wad of toilet paper.

"I'm pregnant," she said, facing the floor.

Will was in no way expecting to hear her response.

"Oh," was all he could say.

"Yeah, *oh*… oh shit." Loni reapplied the wad.

Will leaned the side of his head onto the opposite wall of the stall. His mind had to readjust its initial plan of attack.

"Uhm… uh… wow," he babbled. "Well, Lon, um, who is the father?"

"It's that guy I was seeing," Loni answered. "The one I told you about. The one I thought was so wonderful."

"Not so much?"

"No! Not at all! When I told him that I was pregnant he's like…" She paused to alter her voice to sound like a dumb redneck. "*Uh, you're not positive, right?*" Her voice returned to that of a sarcastic female. "No, I'm not positive! I only took, like, five fucking pregnancy tests and went to the doctor! God, what a moron!"

"I'm sorry, Lon. He does sound like a real asshole. But forget about him. What do *you* need right now? What are you going to do?"

"What do you mean, Will?"

"Like, what are you going to do now for the baby?"

"Oh God, Will, I can't... I just can't be a mom right now. I'm not ready. It's not my time. It's such a huge responsibility and I'm still so young. I don't want to be forced into motherhood because I just got knocked up by some jerk."

"So you're saying that..."

"I have to have an abortion!" She covered her eyes with her hands and continued to speak. "It's not something I'm proud of. I just can't handle it right now and this is the only way out of it."

"Hey, Lon, don't worry about it." He placed his palm on her shoulder. "I don't condemn anybody. You're totally entitled to make your own decision, especially when something just happens out of the blue like this. When are you going to go about taking care of it?"

"I already have an appointment for a consultation at the clinic downtown today after work." She lowered her hands and looked him in the eye. "I'm just so scared to go down there by myself. I don't want to get looked at with any judgmental glances. You know that people are going to do that."

"Who gives a shit about anybody else? Just worry about yourself. That's what you're doing. You're taking care of yourself."

"Really, Will? You don't just think I'm being a selfish, heartless bitch?"

"Loni, you're my friend." He placed a hand on both her shoulders. "I could *never* think that."

"Thanks, Will." She let out another sniff. "God, I still don't know if I'm going to be able to go through with this."

Will looked off to the side to think for a moment. Kerri did have a meeting after school and would be home late. The trip downtown would only take about twenty minutes. He brought his eyes back in line with Loni's.

"Would it make you feel better if I went with you today?" he asked.

"You would do that, Will? I wouldn't want to put you out or make you feel uncomfortable."

"Lon, what did I just tell you? You're my friend, got it? It's no problem whatsoever."

Loni stepped slightly forward and threw her arms around him. Her silicone breasts nearly knocked over his upper body.

"Thank you, Will," she whispered and planted a soft kiss on his cheek. "You're so good."

Suddenly, the confines of the stall felt even smaller. Will patted her quickly on the back to sort of initiate the end of the embrace, but Loni persisted. Their lower areas were dangerously close to touching.

"Uuuuhhh…" Will stepped back from the bust buttress. "Okay. Now, do you feel better?"

"Yeah, I think so," Loni answered, wiping off a bit of smeared mascara from beneath her eye.

"Good, then I think I'm going to get out of the ladies' room. That tampon disposal container is starting to really freak me out."

"All right." She laughed. "I've got to freshen up a bit."

"But we're still on for later after work."

"Yes, we are."

"Great. Everything is going to work out just fine."

"Thanks again, Will."

The door of the last stall on the left creaked open as Will popped back into the open area of the lavatory. He took two steps toward the exit door when it suddenly swung open.

"Shit," he whispered, knowing that there wasn't enough time to hide.

In walked Edna, the office's secretary—in her mid seventies, with thick glasses, and an even thicker mind. The only reason she still had a job there was because she was related to the owner and had absolutely nothing better to do. Out of all the females that could have possibly walked in on Will in the ladies' room, she was the best choice. His nerves quickly lessened as his brain worked to improvise a slick solution. First, he let Edna realize that he was there. Her magnified eyes squinted immediately.

"Edna?" he began. "W-what are you doing in here?"

"Oh, um, William," the bifocaled fogie said, "I needed to use the ladies' room."

"Well, that's great, but why are you in the *men's* room then?"

"Oh, dear Lord!" She placed her hand on her chest. "I thought I'd entered the ladies' room. Oh, dear me!"

"Oh no, Edna, you've entered the men's room!" He rushed up to her and placed a hand on her back. "Hurry, we have to get you out of here quick before someone else comes in."

Before Edna could even speak, Will had her zipping across the pink tiles toward the exit.

"Oh my!" she hollered, moving faster than she ever had before. "Oh dear!"

Will opened up the door and practically carried her out. Once back in the hallway, he used their momentum to nonchalantly spin Edna around a couple of times to further confuse her. Once their silly little dance ceased, Will directed her right back toward the ladies' room door.

"See, Edna?" he said, pointing at the sign. "It says Ladies' Room. That's where you want to be."

"Oh, thank you, Will," she gasped. "And please, don't tell anybody about this. I'd be so embarrassed."

"Don't worry," he smiled, trying to contain his laughter. "I won't tell a soul."

The drive downtown did not take very long. Fortunately at the end of the workday, most cars were exiting the area rather than going into it. Will normally hated driving through any type of urban zone, but the easy flow of traffic made this current venture virtually stress-free.

"It's coming up here on the right," Loni said, exchanging glances between the passenger's side window and the directions she had printed out from mapquest.com.

"Okay, Lon," Will nodded. "Do you see a place to park?"

"There's a lot right across the street."

"All right, nice and close."

The Saturn made a sharp left into the parking lot and easily found an empty space. Will put the gearshift in park and removed the keys.

"Are you ready?" he asked.

"As ready as I'm ever going to be," Loni nervously exhaled.

"Hey, I'll be right there with you all the way. So no worries, okay?"

"You got it. Let's go."

The two exited the Saturn simultaneously. They walked at a moderate pace across the street and up to the all-brick building of the clinic.

"We're almost there," Will said as they reached the base of the cement stairs leading up to the front door. "You're doing great."

"Thanks, Will," Loni replied and took hold of his hand.

The grip felt like nothing more than friendship, which enabled Will to calmly continue his stride. As the two began scaling the steps, his ears detected an intermittent clinking sound behind them.

"Hey there, Will!" called a voice from the bottom of the steps. "Is that you?"

Will looked over his shoulder to see an older man with a walker. He quickly let go of Loni's hand.

"Oh, um, yeah… uh," he stumbled over his words. "Hi… Officer Reynolds—oh, wait… I mean, Special Agent Reynolds."

"Please, Will, there's no need for titles or namesakes," Reynolds said.

"All right, um, what are you doing here?"

"Well actually, I was hoping I could just talk to you for a short moment."

An uneasy feeling poked at the back of Will's neck.

"Uh, why do you need to talk to me?" he asked, nodding over at Loni. "We're kind of busy right now."

"Oh, I see, please excuse me," Reynolds said. "You guys do seem like you're in a rush. Will, is this your wife?" He glanced slightly past them at the sign above the doors stating the name of the clinic.

Will and Loni both looked at each other. The Special Agent seemed to be overstepping his bounds. Will's uneasy feeling poked harder.

"Actually, this is my friend." Will felt the need to defend himself. "I'm here to give her support. Would you mind if I did so?"

"Absolutely," Reynolds nodded feigning kindness. "Believe me, I don't want to take up any more of your time than I need. Please, Will, just two minutes."

Will was filled with a strong urge to end this meeting as soon as possible. He turned to Loni.

"Would you mind if took just a quick two minutes?" he asked her.

"Of course not," she responded quickly. "I can just wait in the lobby."

"Thanks, Loni."

"Thank you very much, Miss," Reynolds added.

Loni gave the Special Agent a small half-smile before entering the clinic. Once the door closed behind her, Reynolds switched his stare over to Will.

"She's pretty," he stated.

"Okay?" Will wasn't quite sure how to respond, but decided keeping his guard up would be best. "Well, she's not as pretty as my wife."

"Oh, I'm sure." Reynolds remained collected. "Which brings me to my reason for wanting to talk."

A sharp burst of acidic worry impaled Will in the chest. His limbs went numb. The beating of his heart took a timeout. His lungs found it extremely hard to breathe. His current state said nothing short of *I'm guilty.* Will's brain harshly grabbed hold of the reins.

"Yes, what is it you want to talk to me about?" he humbly asked.

"Will, would you mind coming down here?" Reynolds questioned, gazing down at the steps. "It may take me a little while to come up to you and I want to be able to hear everything you say at a close range."

"Sure, no problem."

His joints emitted slight *snaps* as he moved forth from his scared stiffness. Upon reaching the bottom of the steps, he extended his hand.

"Nice to see you again," he smiled.

"Yeah, you too, Will," Reynolds replied and shook his hand. "Again, I apologize for interrupting anything. I really was just hoping to ask you a couple of quick questions."

"That's absolutely fine." Will forced himself to sound sincere. "What's up?"

"Well, I just couldn't get over how strange it was seeing you the other day. I mean, *no one* comes to see Derek in over twenty-five years and then, finally, someone shows up... but not just anyone. It's the man's son—the person we all least expected to drop in."

"Yeah, but so what? The visitation right was always there. I just don't get why it should come as such a shock?"

"I guess I can't really give you a definitive answer on that. All I know is if a mute doesn't say a word for over twenty-five years, I'm not expecting him to say a word ever. In my line of work, *quiet* has always been a constant."

"So maybe I was just some kind of fluke then. I mean, you don't have to expect me coming back for a second visitation *ever.*"

"Okay, I understand... but nonetheless, after that initial visit, I got to worrying about you. I thought the worry would go away, but I was wrong."

"I'm not sure what you're getting at." Will raised an eyebrow. "It was one visitation. That's all. Something was on my mind regarding my father and I had to ask him."

"Well, that's fine all the same, but to sort of set my mind at ease, I did a little bit of research."

"What kind of research?" Will tried to hide the fear growing around his question.

"Your wife's name is Kerri, right?"

161

Will didn't want to answer, but knew it would only make him appear suspicious.

"Yes, that's her name." He then pondered an attempt at turning the tables. "How did you know that?"

"At the risk of mentioning my title again, I *am* a special agent. It's my job to find out things like that. Why, is there some reason I should not be looking into anything regarding your personal life?"

Will's blood pressure started to rise. He restrained his vocal cords from speaking at a higher than usual decibel level.

"Special Agent Reynolds," he made sure to clearly pronounce the full title, "this is starting to feel like an interrogation. Are you charging me with unlawful visitation or something? Did you *follow* me here today?"

"Whoa, Will, whoa." Reynolds held up his right hand, keeping his left on the handle of the walker. "No need to get so excited. I was just looking out for you. Like I said, I was worried. Now, can I speak to you about what I found out real quick, so you can get back to what you were doing? Or should I just go, having completely wasted your time?"

Will had to remind himself that he needed to continue projecting a clear image of innocence.

"No, don't go yet," he said with subtle earnestness. "Please, say what you came here to say."

Reynolds returned his raised hand back down to the walker.

"Thank you," he calmly said. "Now, did you know there was an abduction at your wife's school?"

"Yes." Will replied instantly. He didn't know what else to say.

"A teacher and a student."

"Yeah, I know." Will's voice came back to him. "They think that the teacher took the student. My wife said that the school board had a big meeting on it."

"You don't sound too worried."

"I don't think I need to be. I mean, my wife hardly knew the teacher. He had no grudge against her. She's not worried at all. It's a pretty big school. Plus, they've got extra security there now."

Will was pretty sure that his last sentence was a lie, but figured that it sounded good enough.

"Well, I must say I'm glad you feel that way. I wish it made me feel better, though. Well, maybe it does... maybe just a little bit."

"Special Agent Reynolds, once again you're confusing me. You don't have to beat around anything here with me. Please, it's all good. You come on out and say what you've got."

"My apologies, Will. You see, after I learned of the abduction at your wife's school, I looked a little bit further into things."

"Okay, I see."

"I came across a report about a Dr. Roger Granning, your wife's gynecologist."

"Ex-gynecologist. My wife stopped going to him about a month before we got pregnant. She's pregnant, you know. Did you happen to come across that during this search you're telling me about?"

"Yes, congratulations by the way. However, back to Dr. Granning. He and his secretary were found dead at his office. The entire building was burned up. People are saying that it was possibly murder and/or arson."

"Yes, sir, I know about that, too. Two police officers came to my house a while back to ask me about it."

"Really." Reynolds rubbed the bottom of his chin. "What did they ask you?"

"They just wanted to know if my wife or I recalled any strange things going on when she used to be a patient there. It was really just basic stuff. The officers didn't even stay that long—maybe five minutes at most. No one made any more contact with us after that."

"And what did you tell them?"

"There wasn't much to say. I mean, we hadn't been to his office for so long. Actually, I think the only reason the officers came to our house was because Dr. Granning's secretary had called my wife recently to see how she was doing."

"She called your wife on the night Dr. Granning and her were murdered. There's a good chance it happened shortly after their conversation."

"Yeah, I guess so, but if it did then it would have to be purely a coincidence, right?"

"Oh, I certainly hope so. I guess that's why I felt the need to talk to you. I wanted to know if what I found out about the abduction and the doctor was just coincidental or if they were connected in some odd way. I just can't help having this feeling that the answer may be leaning towards the latter."

"Uh-huh." Will slowly nodded. "So what does that mean to you?"

"I'm not sure yet. I think it's still something I have to figure out a little bit more."

"Well, is there any way I can help you take your investigation further."

Reynolds touched his palms to the handles of the walker and leaned forward, letting his head dip downward in thought. Will waited patiently, refusing to say another word.

"You know what Will?" Reynolds picked his head back up. "I'm good for now. But in case I come across something else down the road, will I be able to find you?"

"Sure," Will answered quickly. "My wife's in her third trimester, so we're not going to be going anywhere for the next month. Do you want me to give you my phone number of something?"

"That's okay, Will. If I need you... I'll find you. Thank you very much for your time." Reynolds nodded up toward the door of the clinic. "Good luck with whatever you've got going on in there."

"I'm supporting my friend." Will still felt the urge to defend. "That's what I've got *going on.*"

"Yes, well, good luck with that. Take care of yourself, Will. And please, give my best to the wife."

"Okay, I will."

Reynolds turned the handlebars of the walker around toward the street. The instant he took his first step away from the clinic, a suffocating layer of pressure was removed from Will's chest. He took a huge, but silent, breath through his mouth to further alleviate his internal aches.

"Just relax," his mind ordered. "He's gone now. The meeting is over. Just continue projecting an air of innocence because that's exactly what you are—innocent. Keep cool."

Once Reynolds' walker touched down on the opposite side of the street, Will felt comfortable moving again. He turned back to the clinic's entrance and headed up the steps.

"Will, are you okay?" Loni asked as he entered the lobby.

"Yeah, yeah, fine," he answered fast. "Sorry about that."

"Are you sure? My God, you're white as a ghost."

Will looked down at his hands to discover an extremely pasty set of palms. The chalky tone ran straight up his arms.

"Oh, man," he uttered, still glancing downward. "Maybe, uh, maybe I need to sit down for just a second."

Chapter 23

Will had a good feeling inside as his drove home from work on a brisk Friday evening. It had been three days since Reynolds had ambushed him at the clinic and nothing had occurred since. Will could only assume that the Special Agent had exhausted all his options and given up on the search.

In addition, Kerri seemed to be exhibiting no outlandish behavior other than what would typically be expected of a pregnant woman. In fact, her pregnancy was coming along like clockwork with the baby growing and kicking on a regular basis. Will's dream of holding their child close to his chest was now close to becoming a reality. He could barely contain his heightened excitement. His foot eased down a bit further on the Saturn's gas pedal. A six o'clock dinner reservation at Uncle Mike's was hanging in the balance. Will had figured that since he and Kerri's 'going out' time was soon coming to an end, they should treat themselves to a little date night action.

The digital clock on the dashboard read 5:16 p.m. Will knew he'd be home in roughly seven minutes, which would leave him just enough time to change his shirt, slap on some more deodorant, and head out the door. An unexpected vibration from his lower left hip interrupted his mental planning process. Will reached into his pocket and took out his cell phone. Its small, glowing screen was flashing Dr. Phalen's phone number. He took his hand off the steering wheel and flipped the phone open.

"Hello?" he said.

"Will, this is Dr. Phalen," replied the voice on the other end. "I need you to come to my office right away. Kerri had a small emergency. She's here."

"I'm coming," were the only words to come out of Will's mouth before he smacked his phone shut and threw it into the passenger's seat.

He wrapped all ten of his fingers around the steering wheel and maniacally spun it to the left. The Saturn did a full 180 in the middle of the street and left a trail of burnt rubber as it skidded back in the opposite direction. The speedometer swung rapidly toward the higher increments of five as Will forced the gas pedal to hit the floor. All inclinations of dinner and Uncle Mike's were flushed out of his head. His mind only saw an image of Kerri in tears, which made his right foot push down on the gas pedal even harder.

Dr. Phalen's medical facility was precisely seventeen minutes from the point where Will's tires made their skid marks. The Saturn came to a screaming stop before the front entrance in eight and a half minutes. Will exited his car, leaving it very illegally parked, and sprinted inside. The waiting room was empty; however the secretary was visible through the little sliding glass window.

"Hi, Will," she said right away. "You can come right in. The doctor is waiting for you in his office."

"Okay."

Will charged forth through the doorway leading into the hall of examination rooms. He didn't look at the secretary, keeping a straight-on stare at the route to Dr. Phalen's office. The door was closed. Without knocking he twisted the doorknob and entered. The doctor was seated at his desk reading a chart.

"Will, please come in," he said, looking up right away. "Sit down."

"I'll come in," Will replied, walking closer, "but I won't sit down. Please, Doctor, is Kerri okay?"

"She's going to be just fine." Dr. Phalen calmly held up his hands. "She just experienced some hard contractions, but they weren't true labor contractions. She got nervous and thought the baby was coming. So she called my office. I had an ambulance sent out to her at once."

"So you're saying that…"

"She *and* the baby are going to be just fine. She just had a little scare, but it's all over now. She's resting right now in one of our recovery rooms."

Will closed his mouth. He took two small steps forward and collapsed back-first into the chair before Dr. Phalen's desk. His lungs expelled a gale force wind of an exhale.

"I'm pleased to see that you're relieved," the doctor smiled. "You *are* relieved, right, Will?"

"Uhhhh, yeah," Will gradually answered. "Wow, oh, man. Sorry about that. I was… I was just so worried. I… don't know what else to say. I mean, thank you so much for taking care of her."

"No problem whatsoever. It's my job."

"Yeah. You did a great job."

"Okay then. Now, would you like to go see your wife?"

"Definitely."

"Then let's go."

Dr. Phalen stood up and walked out from behind his desk. Will trailed him all the way out of the office. They made a sharp left and traveled down a different section of the hallway. Will had never been down that way before. The two came upon the last door on the right all the way at the end.

"Just speak to hear in a calm, soft tone," Dr. Phalen said before gently opening up the door.

The recovery room resembled that of a regular hospital room with two beds, a freestanding privacy curtain and a cushioned chair. Kerri was under the covers of the bed that was furthest from the entryway. Her head was turned away from the door and Will couldn't see her face.

"I'll leave you two alone," Dr. Phalen whispered. "Feel free to stay as long as you like."

"Okay, thanks," Will replied.

The doctor exited the room, allowing the door to quietly close behind him. Kerri's body had yet to move. Will took one step toward her.

"Ker," he began with a tender tone, "are you sleeping?"

She didn't reply. He advanced another step.

"Kerri, I'm here now. You can wake up if you want to." He continued his progression. "Or you can just keep resting. It's fine with me. I came here as soon as the doctor called…"

He cut his sentence short as her face came into view on the other side of the bed. Her eyes were wide open and aimed directly at the blank white wall. She didn't acknowledge his presence.

"Oh, you're awake. Are you okay?"

Kerri let out a slight sniff and nothing more.

"Hey, Ker, what's wrong?" Will rushed up beside the bed and kneeled down right in front of her. "Does something hurt? Should I call the doctor? What? What's the matter?"

Her shiny, light green eyes finally made contact with his.

"A cop came to our house today," her voice partially cracked. "He was asking me all these questions about you."

The whirlpool of worry that Will had just escaped swept over him again.

"What was his name?" he grimly inquired.

"It was R…" Kerri paused to think.

"Reynolds?" Will finished her sentence.

She nodded. "He said he knew you."

"Yeah, well he…"

"He said he saw you the other day," she interrupted, still looking at the wall. "He said you were at this medical clinic in the city with some *gorgeous* brunette."

167

Will closed his mouth, completely unprepared for what she said. He felt like an idiot for thinking that the issue with the Special Agent was over and done with. His hands clenched into fists.

"Was he right?" Kerri asked, turning to face him.

"Right about what?" Will asked, still in shock

"Did he see you with another woman? And was it Loni?"

"Oh, hold on, Ker." He suddenly realized that her concern was placed on the wrong scenario. "First of all, yes, I did go with Loni to a clinic in the city, but only because she was afraid to go there by herself. Anyway, we have to find some way to deal with…"

"Why did you have to go with her? Couldn't she find someone else to go with? What are you, like her secret little boyfriend or something?" Her eyes widened and her brow creased. "Are you cheating on me, Will? Is it because I'm just some big, fat pregnant woman?"

"No, no, Kerri, never! I… I just went with Loni because… she needed to… well, she was…"

"WHAT?"

Will exhaled a large breath.

"She got pregnant," he finally admitted. "And she didn't want to keep it."

Kerri's facial muscles instantly stabilized. She didn't voice a response, so Will felt obligated to continue.

"She had to go to the clinic to schedule an abortion. She was all freaked out at work when she told me about this. She was afraid to go there alone so I offered to take her. I'm so sorry I didn't tell you, but after all we went through trying to conceive… I just didn't want to trouble you with it."

"Oh…" Kerri simply said.

Will didn't utter another word, figuring that she had to be saying something more. Kerri's lips, however, remained in the shape of an 'O' and did not change. Will had to know what was going on in her head.

"Are you upset?" he asked with utmost caution.

Her light green eyes rolled down to the bed sheets. Her 'O'-shaped mouth closed shut.

"Ker, I'm sorry I didn't tell you. It really is nothing. She's just my friend and she needed some help. I understand if you're mad at me right now. Just please know that was never my intention."

For the following thirty seconds, Will was forced to endure the most discomforting of silences he had ever faced.

"Is she going through with it?" Kerri asked, looking back up at him.

"What?" Will said, relieved she wasn't yelling.

"The abortion. Is Loni going through with it?"

"Oh, uhm, yeah, she is."

"Okay, I see. Can I ask when she's going through with it?"

"Uh, I think she has an appointment at the clinic for next Wednesday. But why do you…"

"Wow, they can do it that soon, huh?"

"Yes, but Kerri, I still don't understand…"

"Some girls can just get pregnant in an instant and then end it almost as fast. It's so weird that it can work that way."

"I know that, Ker, but…" He lowered his voice. "We've got bigger things now to think about."

Completely ignoring his words, she took hold of his hand and placed it on her belly.

"How could anybody want to get rid of this?" she plainly asked.

Will looked down at the rounded bulge and let his palm absorb its supple yet firm feel. He couldn't wait to find out if they were having a boy or a girl.

"I have no idea," he replied. "I guess, maybe some people just have a different outlook on life."

"Well, I think those people are wrong."

"I'm just thankful for what we have, Ker. And I don't want to jeopardize anything, which is why we have to do something about this special agent guy hovering over us."

"Oh, hmm." Kerri glanced away at the wall again. "Don't worry about him. It didn't seem like he knew anything. He said he was, like, just doing a quick follow-up after talking to you."

"Did he bring up Dr. Granning or the missing people from your high school?"

"Yes, but he only brought them up because he said he was concerned about us."

"That's what he said to me, too."

"See, then we have nothing to worry about. Stop thinking so much, Will. Everything's going to be fine."

"Oh, Ker, I really want to believe that. I just can't help weighing all the facts in my mind before making sure we're in the clear. Are you saying that it didn't feel like an interrogation when Reynolds was talking to you?"

"No, not at all. I already told you, he was just checking in on me. That's really how it seemed. Now stop thinking about him. That's all over. I start my maternity leave next week and then in just one month, we're going to have our little bundle of joy."

Will blew out a huge gust of relief and lowered his head. Kerri slowly sat up in the bed. She spread her fingers out along his left shoulder and began a soothingly deep massage.

"That feels really good," Will said, closing his eyes.

"You know what's going to feel even better?" she said, nudging her face closer.

"What?"

"Seeing the face of our baby for the very first time."

She placed both her arms around his neck and pulled him in for a hug. Will buried his face into her neck and breathed in the sweet smell of her skin.

"I'm sorry again if I made you upset," he whispered.

"It's okay, Will," she replied, staring straight outward. "But you're not going back with her on Wednesday morning, are you?"

"No, no, no. I'm through helping her. And, actually, her procedure's scheduled for Wednesday night at, like, 7 p.m. I'm not going anywhere except work for the next month, in case our baby decides to come early."

"Okay," was Kerri's sole response.

She did, however, make a firm mental note. *Next Wednesday, 7 p.m.*

Chapter 24

Loni groggily parted her eyelids just slightly. She wasn't ready to receive a full-on vision yet. The small slits she was peering out of revealed the ceiling of a small, dimly lit area, which was most likely the clinic's version of a recovery room. Her eyelids opened a bit more. She wanted to sit up, but the rest of her body wasn't yet receptive to any forms of movement. A numbness was flowing through her limbs, giving off the impression that the procedure had only recently been completed. She remained horizontal in the twin bed.

The abortion is over, she thought as a strange lightheadedness swept over her. *The baby is gone.*

Loni shut her eyes in sorrowful relief. A fast, but loud sob escaped from her lips. Embarrassed, she swiftly shut her mouth. Her ears listened for signs that anyone heard her. Fortunately, no one seemed to be lurking about. In fact, she couldn't hear a single sound at all.

"Hello?" she faintly called out. "Is anybody there?"

She didn't receive an answer.

"Hey!" she tried again. "I'm a patient in here! Is someone out there?"

Loni couldn't understand why a nurse or orderly wouldn't at least be near a patient that had just been out of surgery. Then she remembered something the doctor had told her at the very beginning of her first consultation. He said that her procedure was not a major surgery. He also told her that she wasn't even going to be put to sleep for the process.

Wait a minute, her brain sounded off. *If I wasn't going to be put to sleep... then why did I just wake up here?* She tried sitting up in the bed. *And why can't I feel my legs?*

Her eyes moved off the ceiling and began scanning the rest of the room. The lone door was cracked open, allowing in only a minimal amount of light from the outside hallway. The lamp on a small side table next to the bed was turned off and out of her reach.

This is crazy, she thought. *Okay, retrace your steps. You walked into the clinic. Changed into a hospital gown and then...* Her mind drew a blank. *What happened next? Why the hell can't I remember?*

She closed her eyes again and desperately attempted to extract the previous events from her psyche. Her thoughts could only muster an extremely clouded haze. She began to grow more woozy as if she was about to pass out.

"This is bullshit," she said aloud and attempted to prop herself up against the pillows underneath her head.

Loni's upper body was able to reach a forty-five degree angle, which enabled her to see part of the floor. There was a long, red streak smeared across the tiles. Startled, she collapsed back onto the bed.

"What the hell is that?"

She forced her arms to hoist her shoulders up even higher. The smear soon came back into view. While rising, Loni followed the crimson trail towards the foot of her bed. She leaned off to the left for a better sight angle and quickly discovered the decapitated head of her doctor at the starting point of the smear.

"Oh my God!" Loni screamed.

The doctor's right-side-up face was aimed her way. His eyes both pointed awkwardly upwards. A silver scalpel lodged in at the top of his skull stuck straight up. The rest of his body was missing.

"Help!" Loni shouted. "Please, someone! I need help in here! There's a fucking head in here!"

She tried to close her mouth and listen for a reply, but her lower lip refused to stop quivering. Suddenly a slow set of footsteps came echoing in from the hallway. Loni pressed the back of her shoulders up against the pillows. She stared with fearful anticipation at the cracked entry to the room. A shadow appeared in the doorway, blocking out most of the light.

"Who's there?" Loni timidly asked.

The door creaked further open, revealing a short, shaded figure.

"Who are you?" Loni nervously blurted out.

The darkened silhouette turned sideways while entering the room, revealing a large, rounded bulge around her stomach. Loni watched as the figure waddled up to the lamp on the table and flicked it on.

"Hello, Loni," Kerri calmly greeted.

Loni couldn't answer back. She was too busy taking inventory of the seemingly endless splotches of blood all over Kerri's green maternity dress.

"Well, you sure do look surprised," Kerri continued. "I was wondering when you were finally going to wake up." She looked down at the head. "The doctor said he would only be able to put you out for about a half hour, but I think he may have been lying."

"K-Kerri, w-what are you doing here?" Loni gradually stuttered.

"Oh, I don't know." Kerri looked back up from the floor. "But what I'd really like to know is, what are *you* doing here?"

"I... I don't understand. What do you mean?"

Kerri leaned in before her face. The glow from the lamp illuminated manic creases coming out around her eyes. Loni pressed even further back into the pillows.

"It's a simple question, Loni. I want you to tell me your purpose for being here."

Loni could tell that she was dead serious. Their faces were a mere six inches apart. Loni couldn't stand feeling Kerri's warm exhales on her chin. She hoped that replying would get her to take a step back.

"I w-was here," she began. "T-to g-get an... abortion."

"I see," Kerri nodded. "So what you're telling me is you had the miracle... the *gift* of a child's life inside you and you just decided to have it sucked right out. Is that right?"

Loni bit her lower lip as tears welled up in her eyes.

"I had a choice," she sobbed. "And I made it. I just wasn't in the right place to have a baby yet."

"That's it?" Kerri asked. "It's that simple for you?"

"There wasn't anything *simple* about it."

"Well, Loni, I've got to disagree with you. It is very simple. First you have a life and then, you end it!"

"Shut up! Just shut the hell up! What are you, some psychotic fucking bitch? Help! Somebody, please help..."

Loni's eyes rolled briefly upwards as a burning pain protruded from the back of her head.

"There's nobody out there that can hear you now," Kerri stated, still calm. "And I don't think you're really in the right position to be raising your voice. But you *are* in the perfect place to learn a lesson. You know I'm a teacher, right? I'm sure my husband may have mentioned that to you at least once or twice while you were hanging all over him."

"You are fucking insane!" Loni screamed.

"I'm insane?" Kerri knelt down and snatched the scalpel out from the doctor's head. "I'm not the one who just gave up the chance to be a mother! I'm not the one who just ended a newborn's life like it was nothing! It was so easy, wasn't it? It's okay, you can tell me!"

"It wasn't easy! Just, please, go away! Leave me alone!"

Another shooting twinge cracked through her skull.

"Ow!" Loni screeched, pressing her hand into the side of her head.

Kerri dove forward and pressed the point of the scalpel into Loni's cheek.

"Do you want me to show you how easy it is to end a life," she whispered into her ear.

"No, please, no." Loni tightly shut her eyes, sending down two wet, salty rows.

Kerri traced the scalpel's blade down the trail of one of the tears. Loni was unable to move. She kept here eyes closed as the sharp edge found its way to the side of her neck.

"Can you feel that?" Kerri asked. "Can you feel how *simple* it is? Just one easy push..." She added more pressure to the scalpel's handle. "And then a swift slash. That's all it takes. We can watch your blood spill all over the sheets. Will you watch with me, Loni?"

Without opening her lids, Loni merely shook her head. Kerri pressed her lips into her ear.

"You sure are one hot, sexy woman with your long hair and your fake tits," she hissed. "You just love that center of attention thing, don't ya? All eyes always on you, right, Loni? Wouldn't want to give up that body of yours for the sake of a child, huh? Jesus Christ, you make me sick." She slowly moved the blade back up to her cheek. "Now, you open up your fucking eyes or I'm going to cut them both out."

"Oh God!" Loni wailed, popping back her eyelids.

"Thank you, Loni. That wasn't so hard, was it?"

"W-why are you doing this?"

"I'm just trying to educate you, Loni, while I still have the time to do so. You have to understand the importance of your mistake... and face the consequences."

"No! No! Please! You can't do this! You're... you're going to be a mother for God's sake!"

Kerri paused briefly. Her eyebrows formed a sharp 'V'.

"And so were you," she growled. "But you already made your choice. And now I've made mine."

"Please don't kill me!" Loni whined and brusquely slipped into a fit of uncontrollable coughing.

A small burst of blood shot out of her mouth and onto the tiled floor. Loni wiped her lower lip and gazed down at the red on her fingertips.

"*I'm* not going to kill you," Kerri assured. "That was never my intention for coming here. I wanted to stop you from making a huge mistake... but I was too late. The doctor was already finished… but I still had to do something."

Loni coughed up another tiny bit of blood. Her eyes were soaked.

"What did you do?" she asked meekly.

"It wasn't really me that did anything." She looked down to the floor. "Before your doctor became about five feet shorter, I asked him to do one last thing for me." Her eyes moved up to the sheets on the bed. "Tell me, Loni, can you feel your legs yet?"

"No." Loni anxiously tried to kick her feet. "Why?"

"Can you feel *anything* from your fake breasts down?"

"No, I can't!"

"The doctor said you would begin regaining feeling in about a half hour after you woke up."

"Why? What's happening?" Another dizzy spell came over her. "Something's wrong… what is it?"

"I had a choice to make too, Loni. You ended the life of your child by having it removed from your body. So I had the doctor put it back."

Kerri pointed to the sheets.

"What the hell are you talking about?" Loni asked.

"Now, mother and child are back together as it was supposed to be."

Loni's arms shot forward. She grabbed hold of the sheets and threw them off her body, revealing a bloodstained hospital gown draped down to her ankles. She quickly lifted the gown up past her stomach.

"AAAHHHH!"

Though it made her head throb, Loni couldn't stop screaming. Her eyes stayed locked on the fresh row of blackened stitches across her lower abdomen.

"I'm sorry if the stitches look a little rushed," Kerri offered. "The doctor was a tad nervous during the procedure."

Loni's shrieks turned back to coughs as she began choking on the blood that kept coming up in her throat.

"The doctor kept telling me that stitching an aborted fetus back inside a woman was a bad thing, but I just knew that you would want it to be that way."

"Fuck you!" Loni exclaimed, spraying a faint, red mist.

"And you want to know what's funny?" Kerri paid no attention to Loni's scorned profanity. "The doctor said it was going to be unbelievably painful once your anesthetic wore off. So I asked him exactly *how* painful it was going to be. Know what he said? *More painful than child birth!* Can you believe that?"

Loni was unable to answer. Tears continued to leak from her eyes and blood continued to drip from her lips.

"Speechless?" Kerri went on. "I guess I can see why. Well, why don't you take whatever amount of time you have left and think about the meaning behind all this? I hope you're able to come to the right conclusion." She waved her hand. "Good-bye, Loni."

Kerri turned around and strolled out through the half open door. Loni could only look on in defeated awe. When the footsteps outside her room could no longer be heard, she moved her sights back to the base of her stomach. The curved line of craggy stitches frowned back at her. Some movement a short distance away rapidly grabbed her attention. She moved her eyes off the stitches over to her foot.

Her toes had begun to wiggle. Upon recognizing the activity, she immediately attempted to lift herself out of the bed. Kerri's aforementioned pain then settled in. Loni felt as though thousands of needles were being pressed steadily into her abdomen. A bizarre gurgling sensation shot all the way up through her chest. Both her feet began twitching back and forth as the slicing hurt increased.

"Oh God!" Loni screamed as her hands shot down and clenched hold of the sheets.

Her body began to convulse uncontrollably. She could no longer take a deep breath. Her eyes rolled upwards until both irises disappeared, leaving nothing but white.

Her torso abruptly jerked into a tightly clenched spasm. It felt as if all her muscles were on the verge of imploding. A jarring snap came crackling forth. Loni's hands released their grip on the sheets.

She didn't make another move.

Chapter 25

While walking down the long hallway towards his cubicle area, Will stared down at the thick 'baby names' book in his hand. Kerri had yet to make up a list of her favorite boys and girls names, so he was going to surprise her by coming up with his own roster of possibilities.

Over the cubicle walls, Will could see the light above Fred's desk was on. He hid the baby book inside his jacket before entering, not wanting to receive another lecture on how his mighty manhood was turning into *sap*hood.

"What's up, Fred-o," he said, walking into the cube.

Fred did not respond right away. He was hunched over in his chair, staring down at his desk.

"Hey, what's the matter, buddy?" Will asked. "You feeling okay? You know today's a Thursday, not a Monday, right?"

Fred emitted a rather loud sniffle and feebly wiped his nose. Will knew right away that something was wrong. He'd known Fred for over four years and had never seen him even close to crying.

"Shit, Fred, what's wrong?" Will said and began walking toward him.

Fred kept his gaze locked on his desk. Will started to worry.

"Dude, I've never seen you like this," he stated. "Please, tell me what's up and whatever it is, I'll help you out. Please, Fred, you're kind of scaring me."

Fred wiped his hand across his nose and then his eyes before looking up.

"Will… it's… Loni," he said and immediately looked away as another sobbing onslaught came over him.

"What, Fred? What about her?"

Fred closed his eyes and dug his fingers into the back of his head.

"I… I can't fucking say it," he restlessly exhaled.

"What is it?" Will knelt down before him. "Please let me know. Is it something really bad?"

"Yes." Fred couldn't look him in the eye as his voice shook.

"Fred." Will lightly placed his palm on his shoulder and glanced over at Loni's empty chair. "Just tell me, man. Where is Loni?"

Fred exerted a single deep breath. His eyes remained fixated on his keyboard.

"She's... dead," he said as if still in disbelief.

Will's hand slipped off Fred's shoulder.

"That's not funny, Fred."

"It's true."

"No it's not. Tell me where she really is."

"Damn it, Will!" Fred turned right toward him. "It is fucking true! She is dead!"

Will looked into his friend's moist, widened eyes and felt extremely uncomfortable. Fred was definitely not lying.

"Oh, God," Will said as Kerri's face flashed across his mind. "How did it happen?"

"Did you know Loni was pregnant?" Fred asked.

"Yeah. She told me last week, but didn't want me to tell anyone else. She didn't want to keep it."

"She was killed at an abortion clinic. They think it was some kind of sick pro-life activists or something. Everyone at the clinic was killed like some fucked-up, bloody massacre."

Will brought his hands up to his head and recalled that Kerri had been out late last night allegedly baby shopping with Lynn.

"Fred, this is probably the wrong time to ask, but I just need to know one thing. Were you with Lynn at all last night?"

Fred glared at him in confusion.

"Yeah, she came over right after school," he replied. "She was with me all night."

Will shot up to his feet.

"Did she talk to Kerri at all last night?"

"No, dude. And that I know for a fact because she just said to me that she was wondering how Kerri was because she hadn't heard from her in over a week."

"Over a week?" Will took two steps backwards.

"Yeah. Is she okay?"

"Fred, I..." He took two more steps backwards. "I have to go right now."

"Wait, why do you..." Will was already out of the cubicle. "Hey, Will! What is it?"

Fred popped his head up over the wall and was only able to catch a trail of ruffled sheets of paper drifting to the floor.

Will dashed out of his office building and up to the Saturn. Within seconds, the back tires were spinning into a smoking frenzy. Keeping one hand on the steering wheel, he whipped out his cell phone and dialed his home number. It rang twice.

"Hello?" Kerri answered on the other end.

Will gritted his teeth hard together, as a convoluted mixture of anger and fear flowed through his veins.

"H-hi, Ker," he said. "I, uh, I was just calling to see how you were feeling."

"I'm just fine, Will. How about you?"

"Oh, I'm okay." He had to keep his voice at a normal tone. "You know me. I just know we're near the end of this third trimester and I... just had to hear your voice and make sure everything was all right."

"Is that really all, Will?"

"Well, yeah... basically. I mean, we, uh, didn't get to talk too much last night. You know, you got home kind of late and all because you were out with, um..."

"Lynn," she had no trouble answering right away. "I was out with Lynn last night... shopping for our baby."

Will lowered his head and forcefully clenched the steering wheel. His ears could easily decipher that she was lying. He wished that he could just hang up the phone.

"Yeah, I knew that. It's just that, you usually tell me how you're coming along at night and I just remembered now that you didn't. I'm sorry if that sounds kind of stupid. I guess I'm just a big dork sometimes. I'm going to hang up now."

The line was perfectly silent on the other end. Will waited, not ready to snap his cell phone shut.

"Thanks for checking up on me," she finally replied. "I'll see you when you get home?"

"Yup, I'll see you then. Bye."

Will collapsed his phone and hurled it onto the passenger's seat. He pressed his foot onto the gas pedal and kept it there until the Saturn's speed matched that of his racing heart.

You have to make it right, Will, his brain repeated over and over the entire trip. *You have to make it right...*

He was soon coasting into the parking lot at Dr. Phalen's medical facility. No other cars were present. Will rushed out of the Saturn, having once again parked it illegally right before the main entrance. He shoved his palms into the glass doorway and was met with great resistance. He tried a few more pointless shoves to no avail.

"Hello?" he called out, pounding his fist into the glass. "Dr. Phalen? Are you there? Anybody?"

No answer came from inside. Will cupped his hands around his eyes and peered through the glass.

"I don't think anybody's there," said a voice behind him.

"Jesus!" Will exclaimed, spinning around and losing his balance.

He dropped to his knees, forcing his eyes to become level with the top bar of Reynolds's walker.

"Whoa there, Will," the special agent smirked. "Why so jumpy?"

"I… I didn't think anyone else was here," Will replied, taking a couple of short breaths.

"Actually, I don't think there's anyone else *in there*." Reynolds leaned his head to the side and looked past Will at the darkened glass door. "Were you fixing to meet someone?"

"I was looking for my wife's doctor. That's all I was…"

Will's initial shock had dissipated, enabling his mind to clearly comprehend the condescension oozing forth from Reynolds's words. He rose up to his feet, regaining a two-inch height advantage over the Special Agent.

"Were you following me again?" he asked, dong very little to conceal his anger.

"Who were you meeting here, Will?" Reynolds retorted.

"I already said I was looking for my wife's doctor. What's the matter? Didn't you hear me?"

"I heard you just fine, but I didn't believe your answer."

"Why don't you believe me?"

"Because the building you're standing before isn't a medical office anymore."

"What are you talking about?" Will looked over his shoulder. "Of course it's a medical office. I've been taking my wife here for the past eight and a half months. Trust me, it's okay."

"So you don't know that this building has been abandoned for the past two years? I mean, don't get me wrong, it *was* once a medical facility, but then I believe it was bought out by some developer. I can take you to the station and show you the records."

Will wasn't sure if he could trust him anymore. Perhaps Reynolds was merely filling his head with false information to get him to give away something.

"Special Agent Reynolds, why did you follow me," he asked, "again. Is it about my father?"

"Will, do you know a woman named Loni Tate?"

Will bowed his head and had to quickly remind himself to put a lid on his current feelings of wrath. He looked Reynolds in the eye.

"Yes, sir, I do know her. And yes, I know about the horrendous thing that happened to her."

"Yes, it was unspeakably horrendous… and how did you find out about what happened to her?"

"I just found out at work." A pang of frustration pierced the back of his neck. "God, what's with all the questions? What do you want from me? My good friend was just murdered! I don't know what…"

Will had to cut his speech short as tears started welling up in his eyes—real tears! He covered his palm over the top half of his face in an effort to regain some composure. Regardless of the exact reason that brought forth such emotion, the display actually worked to help his cause.

"Hey, take it easy, Will," Reynolds said without his accustomed accusatory tone. "I didn't come here to upset you. I've just been seeing some really out-of-the-ordinary things recently and the one thing they all seem to have in common is you. If you're telling me you aren't playing a part in all this, then there's a very good chance that you or your wife could be one of the next victims."

Will kept his hands over his eyes, but could tell that the situation was gradually tipping to his favor. He figured his and Kerri's best chance at escaping incarceration would be to play the Special Agent's game.

"What can I do?" he asked, lowering his hand. "How can I help you get the answers you want?"

"First of all, tell me who you're really meeting here."

"Special Agent Reynolds, I'm telling you the truth." Will pointed a finger back at the glass door. "I came here to talk to Dr. Phalen. His office is in there."

"Wait a minute. Dr. *Julius* Phalen?"

"Yeah. You know him?"

Reynolds's eyes lit up. He placed his thumb and index finger to his chin like a professor pondering a particular equation.

"Uh-huh," he nodded. "I know him." He then cast two fleeting glances to his left and right. "Say, Will, I could really use a walk. Would you mind joining me?"

"Uh, sure. Where do you want to walk to?"

"Oh, just over this way. I parked on a side road not too far away. We can just head over there if you don't mind."

181

"No, I don't mind. That's fine."

"Great. Let's go."

Reynolds steered his walker away from the glass door. Will followed him up on the left side. They seemed to move at a deliberately slow pace.

"So Julius Phalen is your wife's doctor?" Reynolds asked.

"Yes," Will answered openly. "We were having trouble getting pregnant and he was the one that finally helped us."

"Helped you? So your wife is now pregnant?"

"Yes. Very. She's due in just a couple of weeks."

"That's great. Soon you'll have a new baby."

"Yes, sir, hopefully."

"Hopefully, huh." Reynolds turned his gaze straight ahead. "Will, how long has your wife been seeing Dr. Phalen?"

"She started seeing him fairly recently. I mean, my wife got pregnant only a couple of weeks after her first visit. So, I guess it's been about nine months."

"And your wife's last doctor was Roger Granning, right?"

"Yes, he was."

"Why did your wife decide to switch doctors?"

"Well, we just weren't getting anywhere with Dr. Granning. It had been three years of trying with absolutely zero to show for it. My wife was getting more and more distraught every day. She wanted a baby so bad and it was killing her that nothing was happening. We were growing desperate. I was willing to do whatever it took to get her pregnant. Then one day, I got a phone call from Dr. Phalen."

"Just out of the blue, like that? You hadn't heard of him beforehand?"

"No, but a very high-profile doctor that Loni went to apparently put the word out that my wife and I were seriously looking for a medical method to help conceive. Dr. Phalen said he had a sure-fire way to help us out. He sounded like a normal, upstanding person and, like I said, we were willing to try anything, so we met with him for a consultation. And that's basically how we came into contact with him." Will stopped walking to look Reynolds in the face. "Is it okay if I ask how *you* know him?"

"Sure, it's okay… but you might not like it."

"Why would you say that?"

"Here's why, Will—Dr. Julius Phalen used to be a medical analyst for the EWC. He and your father have a past."

"So what? That doesn't really mean anything. They were involved in the same business, big deal. It was a really long time ago."

"No, Will, it's more than that." Reynolds exhaled tersely. "Your father murdered Julius Phalen's son."

Will closed his mouth and let his mind take over for the moment. He recalled Dr. Phalen explaining his reasoning for wanting to help him and Kerri; that he and his wife had lost a son long ago, and how it completely devastated him.

"That really happened?" he asked.

"Yes," Reynolds answered. "I'm afraid so. It happened a little bit before your father was caught."

"Why... why did my father..."

"No one knows the real reason why. After his capture, your father never said another word. He just took his punishment, that's it. Personally, I think Phalen had something to do with the illegal muscle-enhancement drugs your father was taking, but that was never brought into light. All everyone really cared about was putting Derek away forever."

"And that was all they got."

"Yeah, but that wasn't all Dr. Phalen got. He and his wife received a huge cash settlement from the EWC."

"So he was compensated."

"Well, yes and no. Apparently, all the money in the world couldn't help his wife move on from the death of her son. She hung herself one night in their bedroom. Dr. Phalen woke up to it."

"Oh my God. Is this really all true?"

"I have no reason to lie to you, Will." Reynolds began moving forward again. "It's all on record. You can look everything up if you want to."

"I don't mean to doubt you, Special Agent Reynolds." Will set his legs back in motion as well. "I've... just tried to distance myself from all things related to my father for so long. I wanted it all blocked out of my head."

"I can understand that, Will." Reynolds glanced down at the handlebars of his walker. "There are things we all wish we could forget."

"Yeah, I guess so."

"Will, I hope you don't mind me saying this, but every once in a while I wish your father wasn't locked away in that cell... just so I could, I don't know... do a better job taking him in."

"I don't mind at all. I can totally relate to that. Sometimes I can never forget fully."

"Yes... but maybe your doctor is having trouble forgetting some things too. Where is your wife right now?"

"She's probably home resting." Will didn't want to speak too much about Kerri.

"I want you to go right home to her. If something's going on and Phalen is involved, he may be targeting you through her or even worse, your child."

"What can I do? I mean, if Dr. Phalen does have some kind of vendetta towards me, I don't want to just sit back and wait for something to happen. For Christ's sake, my wife is due in just a couple of weeks and he *is* going to be the one delivering for us."

"That shouldn't necessarily be true. What hospital are you registered at?"

"We're not registered at a hospital. We…" Will reminded himself to keep his descriptions vague. "Because we had a lot of trouble getting pregnant, Dr. Phalen said he wanted to take extra close care of us when we finally did conceive. He said that considering my wife's insides, the safest method for birth would be for him to perform a c-section. It would greatly reduce the chance of complications. We're supposed to be delivering at his facility right here."

"Hmm, I see. Did you have an appointment with him today?"

"No, I just was, uh…" *Don't say too much*, warned his brain. "I just knew I had to sign some insurance paperwork for him. Since I was in the area, I decided to try and drop by."

"So he didn't know you were coming today?"

"No, I usually call him first… but he *does* always answer the phone when I call. Hey, maybe I should call him and set up an appointment. Then I could try and find some answers when I get there."

"That doesn't sound like a bad idea. How soon could you set up an appointment?"

"Probably pretty soon. I mean, he always seems pretty receptive whenever I call him. I bet I could have something set up either by tomorrow or the next day. Should I come back to your office to, like, put together some kind of game plan or whatever needs to be done in a situation like this?"

Reynolds looked up ahead to see that they were nearing his car, an unmarked black Dodge Charger.

"Uh, I think we should keep all discussion of this matter between you and me," he said. "Most people back at the department don't invest much time in things concerning Derek. He's been locked up for over 25 years now, which would definitely file him under the category of 'old news'. Hell, most of the people there now either don't know or don't care why he's even there. Is that okay with you, Will? Can you work with me on this?"

"Absolutely. Whatever it takes."

"Excellent." Reynolds reached into his pocket and took out a white business card. "Here's my number. If you find out anything at all, call me."

"I will." Will glanced briefly at the card before putting it away. "Is there anything else I should know?"

"No, I think that's it for now." Reynolds took out his car keys. "You know how you can reach me."

He hit a small button on the keychain, unlocking the door. His movements with the walker turned a tad awkward.

"Do you need some help?" Will asked.

"That won't be necessary, Will, but thank you," Reynolds replied. "It's going to take more than permanent nerve damage and a prosthetic foot to keep me from functioning regularly."

"Well, that's definitely the right attitude." Will waved his hand. "I'll be in touch."

"Take care of yourself, Will." Reynolds opened up the driver's side door. "And please, take care of your wife too."

"Yes, sir, and thank you."

Will watched as Reynolds aptly folded up his walker and dispensed it in the back seat of the Charger. He then smoothly slipped into the driver's side and closed the door. Will waited for the car to start before giving one final wave and turning around. He rapidly went over the conflicting views in his mind while briskly walking back to Dr. Phalen's 'alleged' office.

So Special Agent Reynolds may now be at least partially on my side, shifting the blame over to Dr. Phalen. But Dr. Phalen may have some kind of grudge against me through my father. Then why would he actually help Kerri and I get pregnant? His feet increased their pace. *What if Reynolds is using him to get to me? Christ, who am I supposed to trust? What if Kerri really did kill Loni?* He moved into a full-on sprint. *What if Dr. Phalen really did do something to Kerri? What about our baby?*

Will did not think another thought before reaching the Saturn. Tensely situated behind the steering wheel, he peeled out of his illegal parking spot. His head was throbbing, which left him no choice but to concentrate solely on his driving for the time being. The objects along the side of the road zipped by like rides in an amusement park and helped to soothe his aching mind. The Saturn was soon pulling into its driveway at home next to the Kia. Will stepped out onto the pavement and noticed right away that the front door to his house was slightly open. A jarring crash, like the breaking of glass, came echoing out from the inside. Will's headache instantly returned. His legs went into overdrive.

"Kerri!" he called out, leaping over the front stoop. "Are you in there?"

Upon entering the first floor, he immediately heard a row of clamorous activity coming from the kitchen area. Will hurried toward the back of the house. The closer he got, the clearer the noises became. There was the pounding of feet and a bunch of irregular gasps.

"Kerri!" he yelled. "What the hell's going on..."

Will passed through the entryway to the kitchen and quickly spotted two figures locked in a hold to the left in the corner. Their backs were turned to him, though he could easily discern that one belonged to Kerri. The second party's identity was hidden.

"Kerri!" Will called out.

She swiftly spun around, revealing the flushed, wrinkled face of their neighbor, Mr. Schofield. Blood trickled down from a gash on the right side of his head. Kerri had him in an extra tight chokehold. Large pieces of broken dinner plates were scattered on the floor around them.

"What are you doing?" Will exclaimed.

"He was looking at me funny, Will," Kerri rushed to say while adjusting her grip. "He knows! I can tell!"

Her sudden shift in focus to Will triggered a slight lapse in her grip. Mr. Schofield repositioned his feet and was able to slip his neck out from her arms. As soon as one of his knees hit the floor, he dove away from Kerri. Will stood frozen as the flustered old man silently dashed right past him.

"Don't let him leave!" Kerri shouted.

Will was unable to respond, transfixed in a daze of disbelief.

Wary that he would be of no use, Kerri snatched up a broken piece of plate with a big, sharp point, and darted forward. Will didn't even think of reaching out to stop her. She cut through the dining room and spotted Mr. Schofield moving towards the front door.

"Hey!" she barked at him. "Get your ass back here!"

Her words startled Mr. Schofield, causing him to turn her way. The movement somewhat slowed down his stride. He looked back at the open doorway leading to the front lawn just as Kerri pounced upon him like a tiger attacking an antelope.

Before their bodies hit the floor, she knocked the back of her hand into the front door, slamming it shut. The two crashed aggressively into the hardwood. Mr. Schofield's chin hit first, causing his false teeth to dance across the floor. Kerri reigned as the one on top and raised back the piece of plate.

"Help!" Mr. Schofield hollered at the flooring, preventing any chances of a loud reverberation.

Wholly ignoring his plea, Kerri plunged the broken point downward. Will hastily stepped into the hallway from the kitchen.

"Kerri!" he wailed. "No!"

His cries were too late. Focused completely on her aim, Kerri drilled the plate straight through the back of Mr. Schofield's neck, prompting all his limbs to at once go limp. Sensing the chore was finished, she stood back up and brushed off her pregnant tummy. Will stepped cautiously toward her.

"Kerri, how could you..." he began, but stopped to look down at the old man.

More than half of the plate had impaled him. A tiny spec of the point protruded out through the front of his neck. The penetration had most certainly severed his spinal cord for his arms and legs were sprawled out like that of a rag doll. His eyes remained open and tiny streams of blood fell from his mouth. Will fanatically threw his forearms back onto the top of his head.

"Damn it, Ker," he exhaled. "You... you said it was... over. Why would... I can't believe..."

Kerri merely stood with her arms at her sides like a child anxiously preparing to be grounded.

"Why are you doing this to me?" Will begged. "This is our life!" He pointed at her stomach. "*That* is our child! Can any of that get through to you any more?"

Kerri looked off to the side as if waiting for his speech to end. Will's exasperation shifted to anger.

"Are you going to answer me?" he yelled. "You never changed, did you? All those things you told me back at Dr. Phalen's office — you were lying the whole time. So that means..." He grabbed his forehead and looked down at the floor. "You really did kill Loni too."

Kerri picked up her head, but still did not make eye contact.

"Jesus Christ!" Will began moving rapidly forward. "You really did!"

"I couldn't stop myself!" Kerri shrieked.

Will halted on his heels. Kerri stared him down as tears rolled out of her raging eyes.

"I... I..." she stuttered. "I *can't* stop."

Without another word, she spun her popped belly away from Will and grabbed hold of the front doorknob.

"Kerri, wait!" Will called out, extending his hand.

He raced after her, hopping over Mr. Schofield in his pursuit. Kerri was already inside the Kia by the time he made it onto the front lawn. The engine rapidly sprung to life.

"Where are you going?" he called, running up to the car.

He placed his hands on the purple hood. Kerri hit the gas. Will's palms quickly slid off as the Kia sped in reverse out of the driveway.

"Stop!" he yelled. "Please, wait!"

As the Kia turned parallel with the road, Kerri glanced back at her husband in the driveway. He was standing still, a heart-broken expression plastered across his face.

Though it pained her to see him that way, her mind simply couldn't convince her body to get out of the car. She turned away from him and pressed all the way down on the gas pedal.

Will watched as the Kia briskly disappeared down the road. The exhaust from the engine left an eerie haze of fog. His nostrils accidentally breathed in the noxious fumes, sending him into a gagging fit. He dropped down to one knee and covered his mouth. Once all the harmful exhaust was expelled from his lungs, his brain took stock of the harsh hand he'd been dealt.

My wife, my child, my life... he pondered. *I'm losing them all. Goddamn it, get a hold of yourself. You just... you... have to...*

He rigidly rubbed his fingers over his eyes. He was losing his mind as well. His ears detected the sound of a car coming down the street.

"Kerri?" he said, peeling away his fingers.

A light green station wagon cruised casually past him. The female driver inside stared confusedly at him. Her perplexed gaze caused Will to realize the conspicuousness of his crouching position.

He remembered the newly dead old person lying face down in his foyer and concluded that attracting attention wasn't necessarily at the top of his to-do list.

You've come so far, his brain prepped for a pep talk. *It can't all be for nothing. I... I have to find a way. I have to help Kerri. I need to... call Dr. Phalen right now.*

He rose to his feet. An extreme lightheadedness overcame him. His right foot stumbled forward toward the house, followed clumsily by his left. A sharp pressure clotted up the inside of his chest.

Go! his mind urged.

Will scurried swiftly, if uneasily, up to the front door. He stumbled over Mr. Schofield while entering the house, nearly crashing into the floor. After regaining some semblance of balance, he shakily continued on to the kitchen. He grabbed hold of the cordless telephone resting on the counter. Leaning his elbows on the laminate, he dialed the doctor's number.

"Hello?" answered Dr. Phalen after two rings.

"Dr. Phalen," Will exhaled. "I... need to talk to you."

"Is that you, Will? Is anything the matter?"

"Yes... I mean, no... I mean, yes it's me and no, nothing's the matter really. I... I just really need to talk to you."

"Okay, Will, what is it?"

"Uh..." Will rubbed the side of his head and cast a glance over at Mr. Schofield lying before the still slightly open front door. "Not right now, Dr. Phalen. I can't talk right now."

"All right. Well, then do you want to come in to the office when you're ready?"

"Yes, that's what I want. I'm just a little busy right now. I'll call you back when I can come in."

"That's fine with me, Will. Are you sure it isn't anything urgent that you need to talk about?"

Will quickly picked himself off the counter as his ears detected the hum of another automobile coasting up the street. A nervous pulsation came hammering forth from his heart.

"No, not urgent yet," he rushed. "I'll... I'll call you Dr. Phalen. Thanks."

"Okay then, Will. Take care."

Will hung up the phone and flopped away from the counter. His vision started to blur as he headed for the front hallway. As the pounding in his head grew louder, he stretched out both arms. The front door slammed shut.

After turning the lock, Will staggered backwards and succumbed to his brain's throbs. He landed on his back right beside Mr. Schofield. His last thought was that the old man needed to be disposed of. Then, everything went black.

Chapter 26

The Saturn slowly pulled into a legal parking spot at the medical facility. Will stepped out of the driver's side and took a deep breath. One full day had passed before he had the time to meet with Dr. Phalen. Within that span, he had forced himself to perform a number of dire acts, the messiest of which centering on Mr. Schofield's eradication, as well as developing a 'master strategy' for whenever his bleak situation came to an end. Kerri had yet to return home or contact him.

Will entered the empty waiting room and was greeted right away by the nurse through the opening in the wall.

"Hello, Will," she smiled. "Dr. Phalen is waiting for you. Come right in."

"Thanks," Will rushed to say and marched straight toward the entryway.

"He's in his office."

Will jogged down the white, quiet hallway and came to a halt before Dr. Phalen's door. He gave one loud knock.

"Come in," called the doctor's voice.

Will opened the door and stepped inside.

"Ah, Will," Dr. Phalen smiled. "Please, sit down. I'm glad you're here. You sounded a bit upset on the phone yesterday."

"Yeah, well, I was a little upset," Will conceded. "I still am."

"What's bothering you, Will? Whatever it is, I promise you, I will take care of it."

"I'm not so sure if you'll be able to help me out on this one."

"Try me. I'll do whatever I can."

"Well…" Will hung his head. "It's Kerri… she's gone."

"What do you mean *gone?*"

"She just left. Remember back when I told you how she had changed… how she wasn't herself anymore after she got pregnant?"

"Yes, I do."

"Well, I don't think it's her hormones. I think it's something much worse."

"Really, huh?" Dr. Phalen folded his hands. "Explain it to me."

"Well… it's like I'm living with another person." Will tried to keep his description as restrained as possible. "She… doesn't seem to be thinking of the baby anymore. She's so reckless and brutal. I can't believe I'm saying this, but I'm actually scared of her."

"Hold on, Will. Now, I can see that something regarding Kerri has gotten you very flustered. But I still can't get a clear picture of what *exactly* that something is. Can you give me a real example of what you're talking about?"

Will restlessly rolled his eyes up to the ceiling. It felt as though Dr. Phalen was purposely keeping him from getting anywhere.

"Jesus Christ, Doc, why are you always telling me to *hold on*? I'm telling you that something is wrong with my wife, *your* patient. She left the house yesterday and hasn't been back. I assure you, it is cause for concern!"

The phone on the dark wooden desk let out a ring. Dr. Phalen silently held up a finger of patience to Will as he reached for the receiver.

"Yes?" he said and then paused.

Will could hear some faint mumbling on the other end of the line. Dr. Phalen placed his free hand on the mouse of his computer and clicked once.

"Well, I'm in a meeting right now," he said. "But, yes, go through with it. I'll talk to you later."

The receiver was promptly returned to the phone and Dr. Phalen looked away from his computer screen.

"I want to help you, Will," he said. "But I need to know precisely what it is I'm dealing with. Now, are you going to tell me what the real problem is with Kerri or not?"

Will covered his face and frustratingly leaned forward.

"I already told you," he said into his palms and then looked up, "she left home and didn't come back. I can't exactly say what the problem is, but something is very wrong!"

Dr. Phalen stared at him deeply before leaning back in his chair. He turned his gaze back to the computer screen and shook his head.

"I see you have a tendency for being difficult," he smiled. "Just like your father."

Will's jaw hardened. He glared scathingly at the doctor.

"What did you say?"

"Basically what you wanted to say." Dr. Phalen's grin remained intact. "Only it was taking you way too long to call it to my attention. I wanted to hear you say it first, but I really couldn't wait any more."

"So you *did* know my father."

"You don't sound too surprised, Will. The look on your face isn't quite how I imagined."

"Well, to be honest with you, Dr. Phalen, something was *already* called to *my* attention a short time ago."

"Really? That doesn't come as too large a shock to me. What, with all the fame and publicity your father acquired, even though it was a while ago… I, for one, did not forget."

Will's eyes glanced downward for half a second at the bulge made by the cell phone in his left pocket. He contemplating contacting Reynolds immediately, but still hadn't gained any answers regarding Kerri.

"Uh, well, Doc, if you do have a recollection of who my father was," he began, "then perhaps you could please finally fill me in on why my wife's behavior has changed so drastically."

"I'm sorry, Will, but all information regarding Kerri will be revealed to you in due time." Dr. Phalen leaned back in his chair, his grin shifting slightly to a smirk. "It's *my* turn to start receiving some answers."

"What are you talking about?"

There was an unexpected knock on the office's door.

"Come in!" Dr. Phalen called out, looking over at the door.

As the handle turned counterclockwise, he moved his eyes back onto Will. A large, burly, bald-headed orderly dressing in dark blue scrubs entered. His darkly stubbled puss frowned down at Will as he walked to the back corner of the office. He did not speak a word.

"Who's this?" Will asked.

"Uh-uh, Will, your time for asking questions is over," Dr. Phalen stated. "I'd appreciate it if you listened closely."

Will looked back at the orderly standing still as a statue. He had a feeling that if things didn't start becoming clearer, his chances of finding Kerri were through. Though his nerves were beginning to rattle, he couldn't let it show.

"Okay, Dr. Phalen," he coolly replied. "My ears are open."

"Very good," the doctor grinned. "I see you also catch on quick, *another* trait of your father's—which brings me to the real reason for you being here. As you seem to already know, your father and I once knew each other. You may also know that he was responsible for the death of my son, which then led to my wife's tragic suicide."

"Yes, I did learn that, but only just recently."

"That I believe." Dr. Phalen pointed at him. "Because I highly doubt you would trust your wife in my care after learning such knowledge. And if you knew what I'm about to tell you, I'm one hundred percent positive you would *not* still be sitting so calmly in that chair."

"What you're *about* to tell me?" Will questioned, reaching in his left pocket.

"It's time for you to learn more... about your father... about what drove him to become a killer."

By Will's wide-eyed silence, Dr. Phalen could tell he had his undivided attention and thus continued.

"He was one over-the-top competitor, your father. I met him the second day I started in the Medical/Training Syndicate of the EWC. He came to me all in a tizzy asking about strength and body enhancement supplements. He said he was going to get fired if he didn't start showcasing more strength in his bouts. Apparently, steroid use was pretty commonplace in the EWC and your father was well aware of this. However, he had to have something more. I was against it at first. It wasn't the reason why I became a doctor."

"Oh, really." Will's rage was starting to creep back into his system. "And what exactly is this '*it*' you were so against?"

"My supervisor told me not to question anything regarding the wrestlers' training methods," the doctor went on, ignoring Will's query. "The owner of the EWC, Richard McAvoy, he wanted his wrestlers to be the best by any means possible. He called all the shots and if anyone disobeyed, they were terminated at once. I had a wife and son to support. Not to mention a pile of medical school bills to pay. I couldn't afford to lose my job... so I agreed to do it to the best of my ability. I told your father that I'd help him."

"What? How did you help him? Just tell me!"

"I created a particular muscle enhancement drug just for him. Actually, I came close to creating it. I wasn't through testing its effects when your father came asking for it. He said he had been scheduled for a bunch of tough matches for the forthcoming month and needed something to ensure he'd do well."

"So, what, did you poison him or something?"

"Your father took the enhancement drug without my consent. Whatever happened to him, he did it to himself." Dr. Phalen slammed his hand down on his desk. "Don't even try blaming me for *his* subsequent actions! I never wanted any of it to happen! And after not hearing from your father again... I thought it was over."

"How much of the drug did he take?" Will was becoming more engrossed in his father's evil origins.

"Only one injection, that's it. He started winning all his matches and growing in muscle mass as well as strength. Everything seemed to be stable.

Then, about a year and a half later, out of the blue, your father came bursting into my office, complaining about soreness all over his body and constant feelings of heightened aggression. I tried telling him that the drug he took wasn't fully tested and that he shouldn't have taken it. He then threatened to hurt me and my family if I didn't find a way to fix him before his next match."

"Why didn't you just go to the cops or McAvoy?"

"I had done something illegal by creating that drug, so that ruled out going to the authorities. I asked my supervisor about talking to McAvoy, and he told me that would only be a good idea if I was looking to get fired. He said your father was now generating so much money for the EWC that McAvoy would most certainly side with him. You see, I was trapped... so I decided to take matters into my own hands and deal with the situation my way." Dr. Phalen opened up his nearest desk drawer and extracted a small syringe. "I made this."

"What's that, another muscle enhancing drug?"

"Actually, it's the exact opposite." He tapped the glass tube of the syringe. "The serum inside here is a muscle inhibitor. Once injected, it will cause any muscle or internal organ to rapidly deteriorate. I call it Achilles' Heel. It was the only way I could stop your father... but I never got the chance to give it to him... and my wife and son paid the price."

Dr. Phalen lowered his head, but still kept a tight grip on the syringe. Will didn't know what to say. He chose to quietly stay seated, knowing that the time to phone Reynolds was nearing.

"And now, Will, finally," the doctor said, looking back up, "*you're* the one who is going to help me give it to him."

"What the hell could you possibly mean by that?" Will asked.

"For so long I've waited. I was never able to get close enough to him. All outside visitors were restricted from his cell... except for family members."

"Yeah, Doc, I see where you're going and there's no way I'm going to be your little delivery boy. What even makes you think that I would..."

"Do you love your wife, Will," Dr. Phalen interrupted as he opened up another desk drawer. "Actually, you don't have to answer that. I already know." He pulled out a manila folder and tossed it on top of the desk, causing the edge of a photograph to slip partly out.

"What's that supposed to be?"

"Go ahead, Will, take a look. It's one of the reasons why you're going to give me what I want."

Will reached out and collected the folder. He opened it up to find a collection of 8X10 inch color photos. The top image consisted of a street block showing part of a building in flames. A purple car was parked next to the sidewalk on the same side of the building. Recognizing the body of the auto, Will flipped to the very next photo, which featured a zoomed-in shot of the purple car and a body with long blonde hair walking up to it.

"Recognize her?" Dr. Phalen asked.

Will turned to the proceeding photo and confirmed that it was Kerri stepping into her Kia. He tightly closed his eyes in disdain, though he wasn't exactly surprised at the revelation.

"That is your wife outside the burning office of Dr. Granning," Dr. Phalen informed. "In case you haven't already guessed, she is the reason for the fire. If you keep flipping through the photos, you'll also find captures of Kerri inside the shop room of her high school wrapping up the dead bodies of a student and a teacher. Flip a little further and you will see her in the act of murdering a group of teenage boys inside a Dodge Cougar."

Will gazed briefly at each image and then tossed the folder back on top of the desk.

"How did you get them?" he asked.

"Because I knew where your wife was at all times. I was able to keep a tab on her just in case her actions got a little... out of the ordinary."

"How did you do that? What, were you following us all day?"

"Not *us*. Just Kerri. And it was much simpler than you think. Upon performing her in vitro fertilization, I also implanted a tiny microchip that I was able to use to track her down wherever she was. They use the same kind of technology on dogs nowadays. See here."

He held up a tiny, square-ish, remote-control-looking device with a small, flashing red light.

"You son of a bitch!" Will hopped out of his chair. "You put a damn microchip inside my wife?"

He took one step forward and felt a pile-driver of pressure come down on his right shoulder. Before Will knew what had happened, his ass was back in his seat. He glanced up over his head at the big, bald orderly staring down at him.

"Thank you, Clarence," Dr. Phalen smiled. "As you can see, Will, my employee Clarence possesses a fairly great abundance of strength. He also happens to have an even greater grudge against your father. So if I were you, I wouldn't make any further sudden movements. Understand?"

195

Will kept his eyes on Clarence's fiery face and could feel his fingers digging into him. He looked back down to the doctor.

"I understand," he said.

"Good. That's enough, Clarence, thank you."

The orderly released his grip and took two steps backwards.

"First of all, Will," the doctor went on. "I can assure you that the tiny microchip is completely harmless. Your wife's current behavior, however, is far from harmless as you've clearly noticed."

"So you were the cause of that, weren't you? You injected her with the same drug you gave my father."

"Not quite, Will. Actually in a metaphorical sense, *you* did."

"How could that be possible? Was it the fertility drugs she got injected with? But that was way before we even met you. Was it…"

"Hold on." Dr. Phalen held up his hand that was still holding the tracking device. "You're thinking too deeply. The real reason is much simpler. In fact, you basically already came to the conclusion yourself."

"I already came to what conclusion?"

"Once your father was finally apprehended, I was able to obtain a small sample of his blood. Upon studying it closely, I was able to learn that the high steroid levels of the muscle enhancement drug had reworked his DNA. That DNA was automatically passed on to you, Will, the moment you were conceived. However, you don't show any signs of extreme rage or strength… and neither did your mother."

"Why would you say my mother?"

"Don't forget, Will, your DNA was a part of hers for nine months. You both became one on a number of levels, however the affliction of your father remained dormant. But I always had this strong hunch that there was still something more to be researched. And after running tests on Kerri and observing her recent behavior, I've come to a new conclusion."

"What's your new conclusion, Dr. Phalen?" Will subtly pressed his palms into the arms of his chair.

"That like baldness or the gene for having twins, the affliction skips a generation. I'm afraid that your baby boy is well on his way to taking after grandpa and Kerri in experiencing the harmful effects of it."

Will's eyes grew wide.

"Baby boy?" he uttered.

"Oh." Dr. Phalen gently covered his mouth. "Did I just let that slip out? Well, at least I kept it quiet for this long. You know, I…"

"I thought you couldn't tell."

"Excuse me, Will?"

"You said you couldn't tell if it was a boy or a girl. I thought the baby was positioned in such a way that you couldn't see between its legs."

"Oh, Will," the doctor condescendingly nodded at him. "I've been a doctor for a very long time. After week sixteen, I can spot a baby's sex from a mile a way. However, I did not want to tell you and Kerri the sex of your baby because I didn't want you both to get any more attached to him than you already were."

Will squeezed the wooden right arm of his chair.

"What did you say?"

"I said I couldn't have you and your wife getting too attached to the child in case my conclusion regarding the affliction was true... which it is; meaning that the child must be taken care of before the mindset of your father takes effect."

"Taken care of?"

Dr. Phalen held up the syringe containing the Achilles Heel serum. Will's grip on the arm of his chair tightened. The wood started to splinter. He rose up again to his feet, leaking a small mist of sawdust from his right hand.

"You're not going to..." his words were cut short as a thick palm was slapped onto his shoulder from behind.

Will closed his eyes in disdain as his body was pushed back down to the chair. He no longer had a choice. Right before his ass returned to the seat, he tensed up his legs and pressed his hands on top of the chair's arms. His decent abruptly halted. Clarence's palm slipped forward off his shoulder. Recognizing that the orderly had lost his balance, Will sprung back up and bopped him in the nose with the back of his head.

As Clarence's chin flipped up to the ceiling, Will's left hand seized his neck and kept him from falling to the floor. His right hand shot downward and squeezed hold of the orderly's balls. With an angered grunt, he hoisted Clarence's massive body up over his shoulder with surprising ease. Will pointed the orderly's dazed head outward like the tip of a javelin, and started running to the back of the office. Before he was about to run out of room, he released Clarence, sending his face crashing into the wall. The orderly's unconscious frame landed on the floor followed by a dusty collection of wood and spackle. Will turned around and glared at Dr. Phalen, still seated behind his desk. Both remained momentarily silent.

Finally, Will stormed forward, knocking over his chair. He leapt up onto the doctor's desk and stepped across the array of photos. Dr. Phalen jumped up from his seat and backpedaled into a corner. Will charged right up to him, grabbed his neck with one hand, and lifted him off the floor. Dr. Phalen's mouth began feverishly gasping for air. Will brought him down to eye level.

"Goddamn you," he growled. "I haven't lost my temper ever since I first learned who my father was and what he had done. I fucking hate violence and I vowed to *never* stoop to it even though I *knew* I was able to…"

"Y-you… were…," Dr. Phalen tried to speak between coughs. "What… did…"

"See, Dr. Phalen, you were only half right with your little affliction theory. Yes, my father's rage did seem to skip me, but as you can see right now, the strength decided to stay." He raised the doctor up higher. "Now I don't know exactly what it is you're trying to blackmail me into doing, but I can assure you, I'm not doing it. So, here's the thing; you can either destroy whatever evidence you have on my wife and never come near us again or…"

Will applied even more pressure to the doctor's neck to ensure he fully understood what the second option was. Dr. Phalen's face grew red as his coughs turned to hushed heaves.

"I'm not condoning the actions of my father," Will went on. "But Kerri takes precedence above all other things in my life. Don't make me kill you. Just swallow this grudge you have against my father and walk away."

He loosened his grasp slightly and waited to hear a response. Oddly enough, Dr. Phalen didn't rush to speak. Instead, the ends of his mouth curved up into a sly, sadistic smile.

"What's your problem, Doc?" Will asked.

After expelling a brief cough, Dr. Phalen simply replied, "Look at the computer screen behind you."

Keeping his grip firmly intact, Will slowly glanced over his left shoulder. The screen on the doctor's desk was playing a full-sized black and white video recording of a light-haired woman strapped into a hospital bed. Her eyes were closed and she did not move. Nurse Nancy, Dr. Phalen's employee, stepped into view and looked straight into the camera. Upon recognizing her face, Will concentrated his eyes closely on the woman in the bed. His lids immediately winced shut. He turned back to the doctor and re-tightened his grip.

"Where is she?" he hissed.

"What makes you think I'd tell you that?" Dr. Phalen's voice squeaked.

"Because…" Will applied another heaping dose of pressure around his neck.

The doctor's eyes rolled back as his lips emitted a sporadic row of choked laughter.

"Go ahead," he murmured. "I don't care anymore. Just be prepared to watch Kerri die if you do."

Will's sights shot back to the screen. Nurse Nancy was holding up a large syringe.

"My nurse is prepared to give Kerri and your son one full injection of Achilles' Heel," Dr. Phalen continued. "You kill me, then you kill your wife and son. I'll take from you what your father took from me."

"Bullshit," Will snarled. "That's bullshit. I bet your nurse doesn't know your true motivation for doing this. I bet if she knew, she wouldn't listen."

"Quite the contrary, Will. She's fully aware of my motivation. In fact, *her* motivation is the same as mine. The same can be said for Clarence as well."

"You're talking out of your ass, Doc. Don't think you're going to get your way out of this."

"I'm telling you the truth. I have no further reason to lie at this point. Both Nancy and Clarence have ties to your father."

Will brought Dr. Phalen's face up before his.

"I still don't believe you," he scowled.

"Are you familiar with your father's case?"

"I've been trying to forget it for over 25 years."

"Then maybe you'll remember a wrestler named Tony Santini that your father killed in the ring. He was Clarence's brother." The doctor nodded over to the fallen giant at the end of the room. "And Nancy, she had a cousin that went to New Jersey University named Josh. You probably also remember what your father did to him in the hallway outside his dorm room."

Will kept his stare on the computer screen as Nurse Nancy gave a little nod to the camera as if she'd been listening the whole time. She kept the syringe raised up high in her hand.

"You can end all of this very shortly," Dr. Phalen promised. "You can take back your wife and son. They aren't my main priority."

Will looked down at Kerri's strapped-in, sedated body and his eyes started to water. He slowly lowered the doctor's feet back down to the floor and released his strangling grasp.

"What do you want?" he asked softly.

"All you have to do," Dr. Phalen began, "is pay a visit to your father."

"Then what, shoot him up with Achilles' Heel?"

"No, Will. Though I'm sure you wouldn't care at this point, I don't want *you* to kill your father. The honor of annihilating Derek Haddonfear belongs to me. And Clarence and Nancy deserve to be there to witness it."

"So what else could you possibly need me for?"

Dr. Phalen moved cautiously back to his desk and reached his hand into the still-open top drawer. Will anxiously took a step at him.

"Don't be alarmed," the doctor assured. "I'm merely retrieving the tool for your task."

He held up a smaller, skinnier syringe.

"This is a minute, concentrated dose of the initial muscle enhancement I created for your father," he explained. "Now, I'm ninety-nine percent sure that Derek's strength has remained intact. It's only lying dormant. I can only assume that with time and age, he has merely accepted his fate of incarceration and given up. What he most likely needs, is something to remind him of his power." Dr. Phalen tapped the covered point of the syringe to his temple. "*That* is all I ask of you."

"Okay, Doc," Will said, hugging his chest. "So I do this task for you. Then what?"

"Then all you have to do is return here as fast as you can and I will tell you where to find Kerri. She will be slightly drowsy, but unharmed. If you're not back within twenty-four hours, she will die. If you tell the police what is going on, she will die. If you do *anything* other than the task I've requested, she *will* die."

"Okay, I understand. No deviating. It won't happen. So when I do administer your drug and make it back here... then what?"

"Then, you and your wife walk away and never hear from me again."

"And I'm supposed to just leave here right now and trust you on your word?"

"Yes, you can either do that or kill me in this office right now... because like I said, if I can't have Derek, I can't handle it anymore. I'm done."

Dr. Phalen held out his arms. Will scrutinized his eyes and detected enough desperation to make a decision.

"Okay, give me the syringe." He held out his hand. "Are you going to be coming with me on this?"

"No, I won't be joining you." Dr. Phalen extended the syringe out half way.

"Well, will any of your cohorts be coming along?"

"No, Will, just you. No accompaniment will be necessary."

"Then how are you going to know if I actually do what you want?"

"Oh, don't worry about that. If you're able to inject your father with this syringe, I will know. I've included a special tracking diode within the serum that will tell me when it has been administered as well as how large the body of the injected subject is."

Will reached out and accepted the syringe.

"What if I can't do it?" he asked.

"Then you can save us both a great deal of trouble and just kill me now," Dr. Phalen smiled. "Unfortunately we both know that doing so won't save Kerri. But let's not talk about you failing. We should be fostering a much more positive demeanor. I think you're going to perform fantastically, especially now that I see you possess such a strong talent that I was originally unaware of."

Will placed the syringe in his left pocket right beside his cell phone.

"I'll be right back," he declared. "Make sure you're here."

"Just call me when you're on your way," Dr. Phalen grinned. "I know you have my number."

Will nodded straight-faced and moved out from behind the desk. He exited the office without looking back and headed down the stark white hallway.

He burst through the door to the waiting room, sending his feet into an all-out sprint. Though the meeting with Dr. Phalen did not go precisely as planned, enough events did occur that enabled him to keep his master strategy still on schedule.

Reynolds's number was already dialed by the time Will sat down inside the Saturn.

"Hello?" the Special Agent answered after one ring.

"Agent Reynolds, it's Will."

"Will! I was hoping to hear back from you. Your timing is impeccable."

"Yes, sir, I, um… I think I may have some information to tell you… soon."

"How soon?"

"I need to ask a favor first."

"What favor?"

"I need to try and speak to my father again. I think I know a way to get an answer out of him. Hopefully that answer will help the both of us figure things out."

The other line went silent for the moment. Will could only hear a few short breaths coming through.

"That's it?" Reynolds finally asked. "You want another visitation?"

"Yes, and I would like to see him tonight if you could make it possible."

"Well, by your voice I can tell that your need is urgent. Are you sure you don't want to tell me something right now?"

"Please, Agent Reynolds, I just really need to see my father tonight. I will speak to you as soon as I'm done. Can you make that happen?"

The other line observed its second moment of silence. Will began erratically tapping his fingers into the steering wheel.

"Okay, Will, I'll get you in to talk to your father."

"Thank you, sir," Will exhaled. "Thank you very much."

"No problem. Just don't forget to come and see me directly afterwards."

"Okay, I'll do that."

"When will you be arriving?"

"How soon can I come?"

"All I need is about five minutes to get your name on the visitation list. After that, you can come by whenever you want."

"I'll be there in fifteen minutes."

"Okay, great. When you get here, meet me at that back entrance I let you out of last time. Even though there are less people here than the last time, I don't want you to endure any annoying stares from the office area."

"Got it, thanks," Will said, turning the key in the ignition. "I'll be seeing you very soon."

Chapter 27

Will jogged as discreetly as possible down a slender alleyway toward the back entrance of the detention center. He arrived shortly at the glass door to find Reynolds standing behind his walker, staring out at him. The Special Agent gave a small nod off to the side and the door was buzzed open.

"Please come in, Will," he greeted. "I understand you're in a rush."

Will hopped up a small set of stairs and entered the building. Once inside, the clerk, Frank, hit a button to shut the glass door.

"Welcome back, William," he greeted with a slight grin.

Will didn't even acknowledge him.

"Thank you again, Agent Reynolds," he said. "I'm in a rush. Are we going to be able to see my father now?"

"*You* are going to be able to see him. *We* aren't. I have nothing new to say to Derek."

"Right, I get it. Well, I'm ready now."

"Great, let's go." He slapped a sticker reading 'GUEST' on the side of his chest. "Do you have any idea about how long you'll be? I just want to give Frank over here a possible return time, so that he's the one here at the exit when you're leaving."

"Hopefully, I won't be very long at all."

Reynolds looked over at the clerk.

"How about it, Frank?" he asked. "Feel like sticking around for a little while?"

"No problem, Special Agent," Frank replied.

"Well, Will, then I guess we're off." Reynolds pointed his walker back down the long hallway. "I'm sure you remember the way."

The two headed off toward the office area. Reynolds slid along the walker at a quicker rate than usual. Will recognized the swift motions and was more than happy to keep up. The conversation was kept to a minimum until they reached the elevator which led down to the dungeon. The same officer from the last visit resided before the elevator's door.

"Hello, Officer Carey," Reynolds greeted. "Would you please take Will down to visit with his father?"

"Yes, sir," the officer nodded.

"Thank you." Reynolds turned to the GUEST. "Okay, Will, see you when you come back up."

"Fine," Will agreed.

"Right this way, Will," Officer Carey said, unlatching the black steel door.

As Will followed him into the elevator, Reynolds pushed his walker toward a small surveillance room located behind the last row of desks. Inside, an old man wearing a pair of bifocals sat before a wall of television screens.

"Good evening, Bob," Reynolds said. "Are we all set?"

"Yup," Bob answered, flipping on a monitor. "Pull up a chair and make yourself comfortable. Sorry I'm fresh out of microwave popcorn."

"That's okay. Don't worry about it."

"I just like being hospitable." He continued fiddling with a small control panel beside the screen. "Whenever folks come in here to see a show, a snack just makes for a more enjoyable experience."

"I see where you're coming from and I appreciate it. It seems that only the older guys around here know how to do things right and with passion. We're a dying breed, Bob."

"Well, I ain't dead yet. Now, let's get to your show."

Bob clicked on a switch on the control panel and looked up at the monitor. The picture flickered briefly before displaying a black and white image of Derek hunching over inside his cell. The raggedy, black mask was still cloaked over his face.

"Here we go," Bob smiled.

"Thank you very much," Reynolds said, grabbing a seat. "Can we get some volume too?"

"Of course." Bob turned up a small dial. "Any particular reason why you have such an interest in this old soul up here?" He tapped two fingers upon the screen. "We normally don't hear too much out of him."

"Yes, I know. I guess I just had a feeling that things might not be so quiet this evening."

Reynolds nonchalantly glanced out of the room at Will entering the caged elevator. Satisfied, he turned his gaze back to the screen and Derek.

Behind the steel bars, Will watched as Officer Carey closed the door.

"Going down, Will," he said, hitting the button marked 'D'.

Will silently braced himself as the elevator jerked itself downward. They arrived at the dungeon fast. The two heavily armed guards from the last time resided at their posts before the bars separating them from the hallway.

Officer Carey unlatched the elevator door and casually slid it open.

"You know the drill," he said, looking back to Will.

"Yes, I do."

The officer stepped right up to the two guards.

"Evening, gentlemen," he said. "We have ourselves a returning guest. Please stand down."

The guards both stepped to their respective sides, allowing Officer Carey a clear path toward the keyhole in the bars. He raised his giant, jingling key ring and unlocked the bars.

"Hey, Will, you comin' or what?" he turned around and asked.

Will surveyed his surroundings and realized that he was still standing inside the elevator.

"Yes," he merely stated, worrying his lack of movement would seem suspicious.

He hopped out onto the brownish tiled floor and moved up between the two poised guards. Neither gun-toting soldier made eye contact with him, sticking to their high-alert stances. Will took note of their considerably sized weapons before passing through the opened bars. He had a bad feeling that the dungeon would soon become very messy.

"So you've returned to the scene of the crime," Officer Carey joked while closing the bars behind them. "I have to admit, I was a little surprised to hear you were coming back so soon." The lock made a loud click as he turned the key inside it. "There we go, nice and secure."

He jiggled the bars a bit to further exemplify their stability before leading the way down the dimly lit hallway. Will followed closely behind him and could feel the syringe jostle slightly in his pocket with each step. He wondered why no one had searched him this time around, but was thankful for it. His brain then reminded him that he had entered the building in a different manner for this current trip.

"Like I said, I was kind of surprised to see you back here already," Officer Carey went on. "What with the way things ended last time. Now, I don't have to expect a repeat performance from you this time, do I?"

Will wasn't listening. "Excuse me, sir?" he said.

"I just wanted to know if you'd be calmer during your visit this time. I'm not going to have to restrain you like before, huh?"

"Oh, uh, no, sir. I'll remain as calm as possible… this time."

"Aw, that's too bad. I was kind of hoping to practice my choke hold tonight. Oh well, better luck next time, I guess."

Will closed his mouth and kept it shut. He was through conversing with the officer. The time had come for him to begin psyching himself up for the task residing in his father's cell.

Okay, just try to keep cool, his mind begged. *Just go in there, say what has to be said, and get him the syringe. Do it fast. Get it over with. Then be prepared for anything, but most of all, protect yourself. Stay alert. And don't forget to call Dr. Phalen if you make it out of here… I mean, when you make it out of here. Stay focused on fully achieving everything that has to be done to save Kerri. You have no other choice. You'd be dead otherwise anyway.*

The subsequent jingling of the keys announced their arrival at Derek's cell. Officer Carey unlocked the last door on the left and pushed down on the handle. A burst of light illuminated the inside of the cell. Will could already hear the faint echo of whatever oldie was starting to play.

"Right this way, Will," Officer Carey said. "And just as a precaution, I'm going to stick around this time instead of waiting outside. That's not going to be a problem for you, is it?"

"No," Will replied, though it was a lie, "not at all."

"Good, then let's go say hi."

Officer Carey stepped aside and held the door open. Understanding that it was now or never, Will walked into the cell and was greeted right away with 'I Only Have Eyes For You' by the Flamingoes. He looked through the thick glass wall at Derek, still crouched in the corner wearing chains around his wrists. Officer Carey soon joined them, letting the door to the cell shut behind him.

"Believe it or not, Derek," he called out, "you actually have a repeat visitor." He turned to Will. "I'm just gonna stand back over here. You go ahead and have your visit."

Will watched him saunter over to the far end of the cell. He paid close attention to the black pistol resting in the holster on the officer's hip.

Once Officer Carey was situated in an observation stance, Will turned toward his father. He took one step at the glass wall. Up near the ceiling, the small security camera flashing a tiny red light captured every action and transferred it directly to Reynolds' screen.

Derek's head was aiming at the floor, yet Will sensed that he could tell who was there. The Flamingoes' melodic tune continued to flow gracefully from the speakers in the room.

"Dad," Will inadvertently said too soft, "it's me again."

Derek did not produce any moves of comprehension other than budging the nostril region of his mask in and out with each breath. Will glared at him through the glass, taking particular note of the collection of air holes.

"It's your son," he continued a bit louder. "And I really need to talk to you again. I hope you'll be a better listener this time around."

Will cast a fleeting glance back at the officer standing in the corner with his arms folded. He knew his subsequent explanation and actions had to be swift before Carey got a chance to thwart the plan.

"My wife, your daughter-in-law, is in trouble," he cautiously said. "And that trouble is a direct result of you."

Derek's gaze remained tilted downward.

"I know you don't want to say anything. I know you're content to just sit here inside this cell until the day you finally die, and that used to be fine with me. I wanted you completely deleted from my life. I wanted absolutely nothing to do with you ever... but at this point in time, I'm forcing myself to put those feelings aside. Something has come up and you're the only person I can turn to."

Derek still declined to look at him. Will couldn't hold back any longer. He had to hammer the final nail into his coffin regardless of Officer Carey's inevitable repercussions. He placed his hand in his pocket and gripped the syringe.

"Do you remember Dr. Julius Phalen?" he asked.

The movement around the nostrils of the black mask ceased.

"He was one of your doctors in the ECW," Will went on. "He was the one who made you what you are. You have to remember."

The mask imploded as Derek took one deep breath in and then slowly let it out. He still seemed stubbornly reluctant to communicate.

"You killed his son!" Will blurted out. "Remember now? I know *he* does! And he's taking out his vengeance toward you through me!"

"Hey, easy there, Will," Officer Carey cautioned.

Derek's cloaked head turned toward the glass.

"Yes!" Will exclaimed. "Good! You do hear me! What you started is not over! Dr. Phalen is still out there causing pain to your family. Can you just sit there and do nothing about it? Huh?"

"Hey, Will, take it down a notch," Officer Carey tried to butt in. "Or we're through in here."

Will refused to give the officer an iota of acknowledgement. His eyes stayed on Derek.

"You don't have to stay trapped in that cell," he exclaimed. "I know about your strength. You have to use it." Will hurriedly pulled the syringe out of from his pocket. "And *this* will help you do so. Dr. Phalen said it was a concentrated dose of the drug that made you this way."

"Hey! What the hell are you doing?" Officer Carey barked. "What is that? Put it down right now!"

Will raced up to the glass. Carey darted after him. Will knew he had lost the element of surprise.

"If you want to get out of here," he rushed to say, "then you'll inject yourself with this right now."

He pointed the syringe like a dart and pushed it through one of the air holes. The clear, slender tube landed needle-first on the floor and skidded to a stop right by Derek's feet. The black mask turned to look at the cell's new object. Officer Carey pounded into Will's back, pressing his face up against the glass wall.

"I warned you not to try anything stupid!" the officer snarled, grabbing Will by the back of the neck. "Now you're in big trouble."

With his cheek still becoming one with the glass, Will gazed into the cell. The syringe was no longer on the floor. As Officer Carey dragged him off to the exit, he caught sight of Derek standing upright and jamming the needle into his arm.

"You've got some balls pulling something like that, you little shit!" the officer yelled, slamming him into the exit door. "Now, I'm placing you under arrest! You like that?"

Will could hear the rattling of handcuffs at his backside. His right wrist was quickly shackled in metal, which helped awaken him out of his state of submissive apprehension.

"Give me your other hand!" Officer Carey ordered, gripping his left wrist.

At once, Will shot his arms outward from behind his back, taking the officer with him.

"What the hell?" Carey cried in disbelief.

Will spun around and grabbed him by the back of the neck. In one rapid motion, Officer Carey was lifted off the floor and planted face-first into the door of the cell. Will stumbled a couple of feet backwards and waited for him to hopefully drop. Carey turned away from the door, showcasing a fresh, bloody gash across his forehead. He glared at Will with wide eyes full of confused rage, and removed his gun from its holster.

"You son of a bitch," he snarled, in a bit of a daze.

Will was too distraught to move and merely stared into the barrel of the gun. As Officer Carey began pulling back on the trigger, a loud crash sent an explosion of broken glass directly into him. Will covered his face and hit the deck. Gazing through a small gap between his forearms, he watched as a huge dark mass swept in right behind the shattered glass and grabbed Carey by the head. With a furious twist, the officer's neck was smartly snapped in two. His flopping body was then tossed out of the way like a pile of laundry.

Derek, now completely chainless, took one step toward the exit door and then halted. He slowly turned his gaze over to Will, still lying on the floor. Will was breathing so heavily, he was unable to utter a word. From the constantly shifting shape of Derek's mask, he was apparently suffering a similar respiratory act. His shrouded visage looked up off of Will to the small security camera near the ceiling. The oldies music flowing from the speakers was cut abruptly short as a ringing alarm ignited immediately. The shrill siren echoed throughout the entire building.

Back on the first floor, officers and random employees scrambled about, turning the office area into quick chaos. Inside the small surveillance room, Reynolds ogled the black and white TV screen in astonishment. He slapped his hand to his brow and shook his head. Bob glanced at the heightened activity outside and then back to the Special Agent.

"Excuse me, sir," he said, "but are you, uhm, smiling?"

Reynolds quickly looked up from the screen.

"Oh, no I'm not smiling," he rushed and then rethought his answer slightly. "Not really."

His eyes drifted back to the screen. Derek and Will were still engaged in a staring contest. Suddenly, the gigantic dark one grabbed his head and began shaking it violently as if his mind was about to explode. He turned away from Will and zipped over to the cell's exit door.

"Bob, I think you should leave the building right now," Reynolds said. "I think this show is about to get too violent."

"Figures," Bob replied, throwing on his jacket. "The one time I forget to provide the popcorn. You take care, sir."

"You do the same."

As the old man exited the room, Reynolds placed one hand on his walker and rose to his feet. He hurried out into the commotion where officers were already donning riot gear and attempting to set up a blockade around the elevator.

"Special Agent Reynolds, you shouldn't be here," yelled a random cop in a black, round helmet. "Derek Haddonfear just broke out of his cell and is trying to escape."

"I don't think trying is the appropriate word," Reynolds said, again looking to hide his grin. "And yes, I'm leaving the premises right now."

Back down in Derek's cell, Will watched as his father plowed like a linebacker into the exit door, bursting it off its solid metal hinges. As both Derek and the door entered the dingy hallway, Will slowly stood up. He brushed the shards of glass off his clothing and ran over to check for signs of life within his father's latest victim. Officer Carey's head was twisted so far around it was almost on backwards. Will knew there was nothing he could do and rushed over to the now door-less exit. His mindset was now focused fully on making it back to Dr. Phalen's office and finding Kerri. He leapt out into the hallway just as a loud barrage of gunshots started ringing out. Will instantly dove back into the cell. He could hear the two guards shouting from their position behind the wall of bars.

"He's coming this way!" hollered one in a deep, husky voice.

"Shoot him!" bellowed the other.

Will cautiously poked his head out at the base of the cell's exit and viewed his father charging toward the bars. Derek was carrying the door to his cell horizontally in front of him like a large shield. The guards continued to blast away with their weapons, however every bullet was blocked by the large, rectangular piece of steel. They moved past the bars and entered the hallway, hoping to score a kill at close range. Derek's speed seemed to multiply the closer he got. The deflected bullets began bouncing all about the dim corridor.

"I can't hit him!" yelled one of the guards.

"Don't let him get to the elev…"

The second guard's words were stifled as Derek quickly reached them both, serving up a double head-on collision with the steel door. The impact pushed their bodies backward with a tremendous force toward the wall of bars. Derek concentrated all his hulking pressure on the upper section of the door, not letting up for a second. The backs of the guards' heads were instantly crushed into the bars. Like a couple of exploding melons, their skulls sprayed a mess of blood and brain matter onto the steel caged elevator.

Derek let the now nearly headless guards drop to the floor, but held onto the door. He passed through the bars and walked into the elevator. After taking a fast glance upward, he pushed the button for the first floor and placed down the door to his cell vertically so that it was between him and the elevator's entryway. As the cage began to rise, Will reentered the hallway.

Shit! he anxiously thought. *How the hell do I get out of here?*

His legs immediately moved him forward as if they already knew the answer to his question. Though Will was afraid to admit it, his head already knew the answer as well—there was only one way out of the dungeon and it resided just beyond the wall of bars. He ferociously increased his acceleration, as the steel cage was about to disappear upwards. His body zipped passed the two deceased guards, through the wall of bars toward the now empty elevator shaft. He took one enormous leap and latched his fingers within a thin stretch of railing beneath the base of the steel cage. The elevator lifted him up and away from the dungeon.

"Someone's coming up!" Will heard someone call out as he neared the first floor.

The sound of firearms being cocked followed shortly after. Will looked up through the railing at his father standing, eagerly awaiting.

"Stop!" barked a bunch of officers just as the elevator came to a halt on the first floor. "Drop the… door!"

Derek responded to the orders by stampeding forth from the elevator. The initial barrier of lawmen was plowed over like a set of bowling pins, causing their weapons to discharge sporadically.

The man in the mask continued his quest for the exit, acting as a wrecking ball for anyone who got in his way. The riot gear did not protect people much from the pain. Derek's movements were so swift that the aiming officers still on their feet had trouble lining up for a shot.

Back beneath the elevator, Will deemed that he had waited long enough and it was time to escape with the help of the diversion his father was currently creating. Keeping his grip on the railing, he swung up his legs and pressed his feet into the base for leverage. Once secure in his slightly inverted position, he thought back to the last time he'd attempted to bend metal. It was at a park over ten years ago. A little boy had gotten trapped inside the jungle gym and started to cry. No one was around to help him. Will just happened to be walking by on his way home from school. Since he couldn't fit between the bars of the jungle gym, he proceeded to pull them apart with ease. The shocked boy was then able to crawl out to freedom. Will told him that the bars were probably old and rusty, making them easy to manipulate even though the jungle gym had been set up for less than a month. He felt great knowing that he'd used his father's strength to do some good.

The flashback soothed Will's mind, allowing him to forget all the commotion going on above and focus on the task at hand. Keeping his feet and hands on the railed base, he threw his shoulders back and emitted a forceful grunt. The metal began to separate. Will continued to pry until there was a gap just big enough for him to slip through. He reached his hands up inside the elevator and pulled in the rest of his body. He stared out the opening of the cage at the fresh carnage on the first floor. Fortunately, most of the action had gravitated away from the elevator's area.

Around the center of the office, Derek continued knocking officers over with the steel door in the midst of avoiding an onslaught of screaming bullets. One overly eager cop was actually able to catch him by surprise by hopping up onto his back.

"You're going down now," the cop scowled and flung his hand onto the front of the black mask.

He dug his fingers into the fabric, attempting to rip it off. Sensing the removal of his identity, Derek took one hand off the steel door and slapped a grip upon the appendages over his face. The mask stayed put and the cop's fingers were pressed into a bloody paste.

"Fuuuuck!" the cop screamed as a wet rupture of red hit him in the eye.

Derek dropped the wounded cop to the floor and established a better hold on the steel door with both hands once again. The bullets were still blazing around him. One lucky shot finally entered his shoulder, forcing him to drop one end of the door. Thinking they'd gained an advantage, the troops converged on the wounded giant.

"Place your hands behind your head and get down on the floor!" ordered the lead officer.

Derek tried keeping his body still, but couldn't seem to stop his head from gyrating about.

Will was ready to make his departure, but assumed his window of opportunity wouldn't be open for long. He gingerly stepped out from the elevator and turned towards the door that led to the exit in the back of the building.

"Hey, there's Haddonfear's kid!" someone abruptly called out.

About half of Derek's captors looked over to the elevator. Without wasting a moment, his massive shoulders performed a quick twist, enabling his one hand to fling the steel door downward like a Frisbee. The thick rectangular slab took one hop off the floor and coasted at top speed into the besieging officers, lopping off their legs just below the knee. Derek proceeded to grab the remaining two cops on feet and hoisted them up in the air simultaneously. Holding one on his left side and one on his right, he pushed their wriggling frames high over his shoulders. Without missing a beat, he vigorously thrust his body backwards and introduced the office to the return of The Drop *times two*!

"Dad, no!" Will shouted feebly.

Both officers faces smacked into the floor. Their necks snapped in unison. Will watched the entire display in disgust while continuing to hurry toward the door out of the office. He wasn't looking straight ahead and therefore, couldn't avoid the riot-gear-garbed officer that just got in his way.

"Stop!" he yelled, pointing a long rifle forward.

Will turned his eyes forward. He waited for his heart to let out a startled, obligatory yelp, however another type of blind instinct inherently took over. Before the officer could bark another command, Will had yanked away his rifle and lifted him up off the floor.

Without slowing his pace, he carried the officer with him, as a second man in riot gear descended upon his path. The door to the exit was a mere fifteen feet away. Unable to steer clear, Will cocked back his arms and sent his 'carry-on' apprehender soaring headfirst into the chest of the one on foot. The lane to freedom became clear in an instant. As both officers collided into a nearby desk, Will flung open the door and left the room. He sprinted down the long hallway, using the thought of Kerri to replace the harsh visions his eyes had just witnessed. The glass door to the outside was getting closer, though the alarm continued to blare throughout the building. Will braced his fists for the possibility of punching through the glass if the door was locked. While balling up his palms, Frank popped promptly out from behind his small desk, aiming a small, silver pistol.

"Going somewhere, William?" he questioned.

The soles of Will's shoes came to a squeaking stop. He frantically glanced about the confining walls of the hallway. There wasn't enough space for him to perform any fantastic feat of strength to break free and avoid a bullet. He glued his eyes to the pistol and placed his hands in the air.

"Please, Frank," Will begged. "I have to make it out of here. It's for my w…"

"Were you followed?" Frank asked, cutting him off.

"What?" Will kept his palms raised.

"I said, were you followed. Is anyone else from the department back there coming this way?"

"Uh, no. Nobody followed me. Two officers were going to stop me from going, but... I, uh..."

"It's okay if the cat's got your tongue." He lowered his gun. "Special Agent Reynolds told me not to talk with you that much."

Will was still confused. He didn't know whether to speak or move or just remain quiet.

"Well," Frank said, shrugging his shoulders, "what are you waiting for?"

He stepped out of the way toward his desk and pressed the small button on top of it. A buzz sounded, unlocking the glass door. Will put down his arms, but still stayed frozen.

"I... still don't understand," he uttered.

"William, there's nothing further for you to understand," Frank stated. "I'm just following orders and I'm sure you can guess from whom. Now, *I* understand that for you, time is of the essence, correct?"

Will nodded.

"Then I suggest you get going."

Frank pointed back at the still unlocked door. That was more than enough for Will. He shook his feet awake and moved forward past Frank.

"Thank you," he quickly said.

"It wasn't me," Frank replied. "But good luck anyway."

Will yanked open the glass door and bounded down the small stairway onto the alley's pavement. The moment the cool outside air flowed up through his nostrils, the reality of his accomplishment finally hit him. He had made it out alive.

I can't believe it, his mind marveled.

A newfound sense of confidence rejuvenated his battered body. The parameters of his plan came rushing back into his brain. While running, he reached into his pocket and pulled out his cell phone. Dr. Phalen's number was on speed dial. He picked up after one ring.

"Will, is that you? Wow."

"It's me," Will breathed heavily into the receiver. "My father took the steroid. He's out."

"I know that already. I don't mean to sound so surprised at your success, but I feel that we may have underestimated you a little bit. Fascinating, don't you think?"

"Where's Kerri?" There was no way in hell Will was going to engage in any chitchat.

"Of course, Will, of course. All you have to do is come back here to my office and I will take you to your wife. That's it. Trust me, the hard part for you is over. Just hurry, please. Oh, and I can trust that you didn't speak to the authorities regarding our deal, can't I?"

"I didn't say a word. I made good on my promise, so you better make good on yours. I'll be there in under fifteen minutes. I just want my wife back and nothing else. Be ready."

"I definitely will. See you in under fifteen."

Will snapped the phone shut and began pumping his arms and legs in unison at an increased rate. Way off on the other side of the building, he could hear some loud crashing which was most likely the result of more 'Derek damage.'

The noise forced him to realize the current and forthcoming consequences of setting a seemingly unstoppable killer free.

Jesus, he gravely thought, *what have I done?*

Chapter 28

The maroon Saturn screeched to a stop a mere three feet away from the front door to the medical facility. In case something went wrong with the retrieval of Kerri, Will was planning on making a rapid escape and wanted nothing left to chance.

He entered the building to find Dr. Phalen waiting for him in the lobby.

"You are punctual, Will," he said, glancing down at his watch. "Now, if you will just follow me, we'll take care of my end of the bargain."

"Good," Will answered. "Lead the way."

Dr. Phalen turned around and headed for the door leading into the white hallway.

"I just need to make a quick stop at my office to pick something up," he said, holding the door open. "It won't take long."

"No way!" Will asserted. "You take me to Kerri right now! No more stalling!"

"First of all, Will, your wife is much closer than you think. And second, I'm not trying to stall or waste time. I have too much invested *beyond* you and your wife to do so. Now, if you please just walk this way, I can pick up the device in my office and we can move on."

"Fine. I'm *right* behind you."

The two power-walked directly up to the office at the end of the hall. The door was wide open. Will watched as Dr. Phalen sauntered over toward his desk and picked up what appeared to be a long, rectangular remote.

"Tell me, Will," he said, slipping the device into the pocket of his white coat, "What was it like seeing Dad again?"

"Are you seriously asking me that?" Will asked, glaring.

"I was only curious. That's all."

"That's all, huh? You force me to set free a virtually super-human killing machine and knowing how I felt seeing him is all you care about? He's probably out there killing more innocent people right now! Let me ask you, Doc, how does that make *you* feel?"

"Oh, I highly doubt Derek is out there killing people. Unless, of course, someone gets in his way, thus preventing him from reaching his new goal."

"You know what, Doc? You really stopped making sense a long time ago."

"My apologies, Will. You've always been such a large part of my grand scheme that sometimes I forget you're still unaware of a great deal." He stepped back to his desk. "I should show you this as well."

"No, Dr. Phalen, I don't care. Just take me to Kerri. That's all I need to know from here on out."

"Actually, Will, you really should know this. It may come to affect your wife's liberation."

"Jesus Christ! Another challenge? That's it! I've had it! Let's go!"

"I understand your agitation, Will. I should have made you clear of this before. Here, it won't take long." He turned his computer screen toward Will. "See that green flashing dot right there?" He pointed to the screen. "That is your father. Thanks to you, I'm now able to track his movement. Inside the serum you gave him was a special diode which, when injected, sends a signal directly to this computer. The serum also now receives a signal from this remote." He removed the rectangular device from his coat pocket. "It's somewhat similar to the way I kept track of your wife, only a little more complex. Right now it is sending a sharp, homing pulse directly into your father's brain, drawing him here. You see how that green dot keeps getting closer to that big square over here?"

"Yeah, I see it."

"The big square is this building and as you can plainly see, your father should be arriving shortly." The doctor tapped on the square. "Which means we'd better get moving."

"So that also means that Kerri is somewhere in this building, right?"

"Yes, that is true."

Will's eyes immediately lit up.

"But don't get any ideas," Dr. Phalen quickly warned. "Remember, if anything happens to me, she dies instantly. Got it?"

"I'm through playing games. I just want my wife and to leave here as soon as possible."

"I'm glad we're in agreement." He slid the remote back into his pocket. "Now let's get going."

Dr. Phalen briskly stepped out of the office. Will stayed right beside him. They traveled down the opposite hallway towards the recovery room where Kerri once stayed. Upon reaching the end, Dr. Phalen took out her small, square tracking device. The little red light was flashing at a much faster rate.

"See?" he said, holding the device up. "She's close by. We're almost there."

He hurried into the recovery room, sending the red light into a tizzy. Will rushed after him.

"Is she in here?" he asked.

"Not quite," the doctor replied, moving over to a bed in the right corner. "Would you mind giving me a hand with this?"

"All right." Will jogged up to the bed. "Now tell me why."

"You'll see." Dr. Phalen placed his hands on the mattress. "Now push."

With Will's assistance, the bed's metal outer frame scraped across the tiled floor like nails on a chalkboard. He kept his eyes pointed downward and watched as a circular hatch became revealed. Dr. Phalen stopped shoving and grabbed hold of the handle at the center. The hatch creaked open to display a dark, descending stairwell.

"What is this?" Will asked.

"This is an extremely old building," Dr. Phalen answered, crouching down and reaching into the darkness. "It was constructed with a fairly elaborate bomb shelter."

"This is a bomb shelter?"

"Correct. Ready to go down?"

Will heard the flick of a switch. As Dr. Phalen pulled back up his arm, the hum of fluorescent lighting came following after it. In a flash, the stairwell became softly illuminated and divulged a deep descent.

"Going down," Will stated. "After you."

Without answering, Dr. Phalen stepped into the hatch and began heading downward. He looked back at Will.

"Leave it open, please. I'll be expecting company once you and your wife are gone."

"That's right," Will assured. "Once we're *gone*."

The floor swallowed them up fast. Once underground, the stairwell became quite narrow, allowing forward advancement to only one body at a time. Will made sure to stay on his toes just in case Dr. Phalen attempted to make a run for it. A square florescent light was placed at the side about every fifteen feet. The stairs were composed of solid, manmade concrete, but the walls appeared rather crude as if chiseled out of rock.

Deeper and deeper into the hatch the two traveled until the descending slope ended at the beginning of a short tunnel. This was also the end of the florescent lighting. Will squint his eyes up ahead and was able to discern a spec of lightly shimmering brightness.

"Not much further," Dr. Phalen said and began striding toward the spec. "Soon this will all be over."

His voice echoed off the tunnel walls. Will instantly developed a strong suspicion that the doctor was indeed telling the truth; that this all would be over very soon. As the tunnel grew darker, he observed the red light of Kerri's homing device flashing through Dr. Phalen's white coat. The glow was blinking out of control.

"Exactly how much further?" Will anxiously asked.

"Just right up ahead," Dr. Phalen answered, pointing. "Once we make it to the light, you'll be able to see her."

Will knew exactly who "her" was. He zipped up to Dr. Phalen and pressed a hand into his back.

"Then shouldn't we be moving just a little bit faster?" he rushed to say. "Your *company* will be arriving soon. You said so yourself."

Will pushed along the doctor just hard enough to quicken both their paces at the same time. Dr. Phalen didn't say a word as they moved out of the tunnel and into the light. The sudden flood of illumination burned Will's eyes. He roughly rubbed his sockets before examining the new surroundings.

"Welcome to the heart of the shelter," Dr. Phalen said behind him.

Will first noticed that they were standing on a small metal loft that featured a winding staircase leading downward. He gazed out at the environment below past streams of awkwardly wrapped electrical wires and a handful of dangling spotlights. At the bottom of the fairly sized bunker, he was able to make out a bunch of desks covered in high-tech-looking computer equipment. His eyes focused on one particular machine that looked like a heart rate monitor.

"Kerri!" Will called out and darted down the staircase.

Dr. Phalen simply watched him go. Will refused to glance back for his permission to advance. He had been dying to see his wife's face again for the past forty-eight hours and now that she was within reach, nothing would stand in his way. He bounded down the spiraling steps so quickly that his head became dizzy. His hand shot out and gripped a thin metal banister for balance. He kept his grasp intact the rest of the way down.

Upon departing the stairway, Will's continuing momentum sent him crashing into a nearby gurney. He landed on his knees and the bed on wheels went rolling across the floor, making a high-pitched squeak. The noise ceased once the gurney collided with the outstretched arms of Clarence. The husky orderly, now sporting a nose wrapped in white bandages, sent a sharp, pissed-off stare over at the bunker's newest visitor. Will noticed the disgruntled gaze and hastily jumped to his feet.

"Back off, man!" he yelled. "Don't make me hurt you again because I will if I have to!"

Clarence let out a loud, moist grunt like a bull preparing to charge.

"Stand back, Clarence!" Dr. Phalen called out from the staircase. "He is only here to take back his wife! Because of him, we are now going to be able to kill Derek Haddonfear! He is not to be touched!"

Clarence looked up to the stairwell. Dr. Phalen projected an expression of extreme sternness. The orderly angrily grated his jaw, but obeyed the request by taking a step backwards. Once fairly sure that the threat had been restrained for the moment, Will pressed on, maneuvering around a maze-like assortment of freestanding privacy curtains.

"Kerri!" he yelled. "Where are you? Call out to me!"

A response wasn't returned although his ears did perceive the beep of the heart rate monitor getting louder. He frantically followed the noise until he came before an extra large freestanding curtain projecting the shadow of a bed. Fed up with the obstacles, Will knocked over the structure of metal bars and white fabric. The curtain dropped, revealing Nurse Nancy standing beside a motorized hospital bed. Stretched out beneath the sheets with her eyes shut, lay Kerri. Her eyes were closed and a long, clear IV was hooked up into her arm.

"Ker!" Will exclaimed and dashed up to the bed. "It's me! I'm here!"

"Easy, Will," Nurse Nancy said, holding up a hand. "Don't jostle her too much. She's asleep right not and shouldn't be aggravated."

"Shut up!" he barked back at her. "Don't tell me what to do. Get the hell away from me! Move!"

He stamped his foot harshly in her direction, hoping it would scare her away. Nancy kept her mouth shut and casually backed off. Will crouched down beside the head of the bed. He feverishly suction-cupped his lips onto Kerri's cheek. Her skin felt soft and cool.

"Kerri?" he whispered into her ear. "Can you wake up? Can you hear me?"

Her sole reply came in the form of some light breathing through her nose. Will gently wrapped his fingers around her arm.

"That's okay," he said. "Whether you can hear me or not, I'm still taking you out of here."

Will brought his other hand across her body with the intention of pulling out her IV. He made it about halfway to the needle, but hastily stopped. A hot pinching sensation was taking over the back of his neck. He watched as his hand fell onto Kerri's covered chest. His shoulders began to tingle. A strange lightheadedness overcame him. He began sluggishly drifting backwards.

"That's right, Will, just relax yourself," Dr. Phalen fiendishly murmured from behind him. "Lean back slowly. I've got you."

Will felt an increased painful pressure at the back of his neck.

"That's it," the doctor went on. "Good. This is going even easier than I expected."

Will's panic button went off at once. He forced his hand behind his neck and grabbed hold of Dr. Phalen's wrist. He heard a slight cracking of glass, as his hand became wet. Dr. Phalen took a step back.

"Damn it," he uttered. "I guess I spoke too soon."

Will touched the back of his neck and felt something sharp jutting forth from it. He promptly yanked the foreign object out and held it up to his face. It was a broken syringe.

"I'm sorry about that, Will," Dr. Phalen said. "But I needed to have you incapacitated when I told you this. I'm afraid I have to go back on one of my promises. The rage Kerri is experiencing is most likely because of the monster growing inside of her—a monster that I helped create—a monster just like your father." He shook his head. "And I just can't bear being responsible for releasing another Derek Haddonfear out into the world. Believe me, Will, in due time, you and Kerri will come to understand that what I'm about to do was the right decision."

Will slumped down onto his knees. His head wobbled back and forth like a drunken pendulum.

"Wha... wh..." he stuttered. "What are you doing?"

Dr. Phalen bent down on one knee and leaned in towards him.

"I'm doing what needs to be done," he said. "I'm removing the child from your wife's uterus and destroying it."

His words sent raw numbness beyond the contents of the syringe, throughout Will's body. He began to choke on the massive lump welling up in his throat. Unable to coax his limbs into motion, he merely shook his head from side to side as tears dribbled down both eyes.

"Nnno... d... don't," he had trouble saying.

"Will, I have no choice," the doctor sadly replied. "It is for the greater good. I'm very sorry. You and your wife are still making it out of here. What I've given you is just a heavy muscle relaxant. I just couldn't have you disrupting the surgery, especially after witnessing your abilities." He raised his hand and pointed off to the side. "You see that steel door over there? It opens up to a ramped tunnel that leads all the way up to the parking lot outside the building. Once Kerri is safely stitched up, I'm locking the two of you on the other side of that door. You will be able to wheel her straight up and out of here. You can begin rebuilding your lives, I promise."

His eyes turned upwards as Clarence appeared beside the bed. Dr. Phalen rose back to his feet.

"Take him to the other end of the room, please, Clarence," he said. "I don't want him watching the procedure."

Will was dying to leap off the floor and snap the doctor's neck in two. He tried coercing his body into action, however his muscles refused to function. The feeble attempt used up whatever juice was left in him. Unable to retain balance, his frame toppled over. With the side of his face pressing into the cold floor, he lost the capacity to speak and could only listen on.

"Go now, Clarence," Dr. Phalen ordered. "He broke the syringe before I could give him the full dosage. He's going to regain movement much faster than anticipated. That means we're now extremely pressed for time and I'm not setting your nose a second time if he gets up and breaks it again."

Clarence emitted another terse grunt and knelt down. Will felt the orderly's mammoth hands grab underneath his arms. Clarence hoisted his body up off the floor and began dragging him backwards. Will watched past his outstretched, floppy legs as Dr. Phalen wheeled a tray of medical instruments up before Kerri's bed. Her eyes remained closed.

A long stretcher topped off with a white cushion was parked up against the wall on the other end of the room. An array of tan leather straps dangled at its base. Clarence dropped Will's limp body down on the stretcher and snatched up the straps. Each thick band of leather was immediately tied down extra tight. Once Will was fully secured, Clarence leaned in real close to his face.

"Who are you gonna hurt now?" he quietly scowled, exhaling a spray of grimy breath.

He drew back his fist and with a forceful whoosh, dispensed some hard payback down on Will's face. Elated over the mighty blow, Clarence rose up his paw a second time.

"Clarence, what's taking so long?" Dr. Phalen called from the opposite end of the room. "I need you over here!"

The orderly looked over his shoulder and irritably lowered his arm. He rapidly stood up from the stretcher and walked off, disappearing behind another freestanding curtain. Will looked on in a clouded stupor as blood trickled out of his nose onto the white cushioning.

"Jesus, Clarence, how long does it take to strap an immobile body into a stretcher?" Dr. Phalen asked, moving Kerri's IV drip bag slightly further away from the bed. "Will isn't going to be laid up for that long which means I'm going to have to rush this surgery… which means I needed you here five minutes ago!"

Clarence lowered his large head and let out an apologetic groan.

"All right, Clarence, it's okay," the doctor went on. "There's no time for sulking. Just please come over here and help Nurse Nancy turn Kerri onto her side. I have to administer the epidural so I can begin surgery."

Clarence slumped over to the bed as Nurse Nancy pulled the sheets down off of Kerri. Dr. Phalen picked up a large syringe from the tray of tools and squirted a tiny droplet forth from the needle. Satisfied, he placed it back down and walked over to Kerri's IV bag.

"Grab her by the legs, Clarence, and push her body up on its side," the nurse instructed.

As the orderly did what he was told, Nancy undid the back of Kerri's gown. With a yellow sponge, Nancy swabbed the bare spine in a circular motion.

"She's all set, Doctor," she said after several rotations.

"Excellent," Dr. Phalen said and reached for the adjustment valve of the IV drip.

"Doctor, what are you doing?"

"I'm lessening the anesthesia in preparation for the epidural. You know that."

"Yes, but… why?"

"Nancy, I don't want to cause her to overdose."

"But… what if she wakes up? It's not worth the risk. I saw the pictures of all those things she's done and…"

"Please, Nancy, try to remain calm. You must understand that we aren't out to kill Kerri or Will. Neither of them has caused the losses of our loved ones. Our only goals are to end the evil before it is born and execute the man responsible for our pain. We are not the *monsters*."

"I understand that, Doctor, but I'm just a little worried."

"There's no need."

Dr. Phalen stepped away from the IV bag and towards the instrument tray. He picked up a silver contraption in the shape of an elongated pistol and brought it before Nancy.

"This is what I'm going to use to take down Derek," he explained. "It's loaded with 20 rounds of needles containing my Achilles Heel serum. It will allow me to shoot at him from a safe distance." He handed the gun over to her and walked back to the IV bag. "If the worst case scenario occurs with Kerri's surgery, we can resort to it. One shot is all you need."

"Well, I hope it doesn't come to that," Nancy replied, gazing down at the weapon in her mitts.

"Let's just get through this surgery as quick and efficient as possible. Derek will be here before we know it."

He turned the small valve at the base of the IV bag counterclockwise. The drip at once ceased. Dr. Phalen hurried around to Kerri's bare back and picked the epidural up off the tray. Nancy and Clarence stood on opposite sides of him.

"Okay, guys," the doctor began. "I need you to hold onto her tight. I'm sticking this needle into her spine and she has to be perfectly still."

Nancy held onto Kerri's shoulders while Clarence kept a grip on her legs. Dr. Phalen knelt down and aimed the needle forward. He breathed vigilantly in and out while drawing the syringe closer. With a prolonged exhale, he gently touched the point into her skin. Kerri's eyes instantly popped open. Because she had her back turned to the others, they didn't see it happen.

"I'm going in right now," Dr. Phalen said.

Kerri's hand briskly shot around her back and grabbed his hand. With a shocked gasp, he let go of the syringe, sending it crashing to pieces on the floor. Nancy let out a piercing shriek. Kerri increased the pressure of her grasp and, without looking, jerked the doctor's hand hard to the left, leaving it perpendicular to the rest of his arm. Dr. Phalen bellowed in pain as he stared down at part of his bloody wrist bone sticking out of his skin.

"Nancy, get the gun!" he hollered out.

The doctor turned his head to find his nurse fleeing the scene for the steel escape door. Before he got a chance to curse her out, Kerri sat up in bed, refusing to release his hand. She looked him dead in the eye and wrapped her free hand around his neck.

"Die," her lips snarled.

Dr. Phalen's feet zipped up off the floor as Kerri sent him hurling into the nearest wall. The impact cracked his skull, forcing his brain to shut down for the moment. Kerri swung her feet out from under the sheets and hopped off the bed. The silver gun was roughly pointed in her face.

"You're dead, bitch," Clarence grumbled.

Kerri's arms instinctively sprung outward and pushed the orderly's aim clear over her left shoulder just as a small pointed dart shot forth. The 'mini syringe' zoomed past Nancy and hit the steel door. It burst into a thousand pieces, sending a barrage of shards at her face. She discharged an agonizing wail and covered her eyes. She dropped to the floor as a mixture of tears and blood fell from her cheekbones.

Clarence frantically shook his arms back and forth, attempting to get free. Kerri's hands easily maintained their hold. She jerked her wrists downward, ripping both the orderly's arms out of their sockets. His mouth discharged a severely enraged grunt as he glared down at his two appendages dangling like a couple of limp dicks. It took Kerri but a single shove to send him flat out on his back. She snatched a scalpel up from the tray of tools and pounced on top of him. With her hospital gown draping over his mid-section, she gleefully plunged the sharp tip of the blade deep into his chest. More than half the scalpel, including part of the handle, entered Clarence. A geyser of blood spurted straight up into the air, dousing part of Kerri's forehead. She ravenously hungered for more. The scalpel was ripped forth from the fresh wound and rammed back into a new region of flesh, creating another similar red eruption effect.

Clarence's blood-spewing mouth was wide open as his eyes began rolling upwards. Kerri continued her frenetic motions until every last ounce of life had leaked out of his body. She gradually stood back up, her hospital gown dripping in dark crimson, and wiped some of the splatter from her eyes. As the initial rush of the kill began fading away, her ears detected an ongoing metallic squeak. Kerri turned sharply to the right and spotted Nancy pulling at the circular handle of the steel door.

"Oh God!" the Nurse exclaimed, glancing over her shoulder.

Kerri zeroed in on her latest target and marched forward. Nancy maniacally tried to force the handle to move, but was met with strong resistance.

"Come on, open!" she screamed at the steel.

The handle emitted a paltry creak and budged about an inch. The flame of hope that ignited within Nancy's eyes was promptly extinguished as Kerri seized the back of her neck. The nurse's hands went flying off the door's handle. Kerri spiked her into the floor back-first just like a football. Nancy bounced a good two feet into the air before landing for good. Her body stiffened up tight upon witnessing Kerri directly above her, bloody scalpel raised.

"Please... no!" Nancy pleaded. "Don't... don't kill me!"

She began to sob uncontrollably.

"Shut up!" Kerri snapped, halting her advancement. "Don't you dare ruin this!"

She took a small step forward and shortly caught sight of the bulge on her red-stained gown below. Her pacing halted as a microscopic pinch emanated from somewhere deep inside her head. She clenched her eyelids shut, immediately longing for the petite pang to go away. The vision of a tiny silhouette with pudgy arms and legs appeared in her mind.

"Go away!" she growled aloud. "Not now!"

Kerri smacked her palm into her forehead, but the image still remained. Frustrated, she began pounding herself repeatedly. Nancy could only watch on in frightened confusion. However, her gaze became pulled off of Kerri and onto the steel door right behind her. The circular handle was turning on its own.

"Stop!" Kerri continued to shout. "No more!"

She hoisted the scalpel up high and drove it down into her arm. Her eyes burst open, releasing a bevy of tears. The steel door abruptly swung open and knocked her out of the way. Nancy looked into the exit to find Reynolds standing alertly with one hand on his walker and the other pointing a black gun.

"Where's Will?" he asked and hurriedly hobbled into the shelter.

"He's... he's on the other side of the room by the stairs," Nancy answered, still frozen.

"Take me to him right n..."

"She's right there!" The Nurse screamed, pointing her finger.

Reynolds glanced to his right just as Kerri came barreling into him. He lost his hold on the walker and hit the floor hard. The gun went skidding out of his hand. Nancy's body at once became cured of its inertia. She vaulted to her feet and made a mad dash for the other side of the room. Kerri paid no attention to the nurse's escape, directing all her efforts onto Reynolds.

"You," she said firmly. "I know you. The cop who tried to make me think my husband was fucking his coworker."

Reynolds didn't reply right away, attempting in astonishment to wrap his mind around her blood-soaked demeanor instead.

"Jesus Christ, it was you," he finally uttered. "Will didn't... you killed everyone. Everyone?"

"And here you are," Kerri frowned, moving closer, "again."

His tipped-over walker got in her path. She picked it up with one hand and flung it into the opened side of the steel door. Reynolds shielded his face as he was hit with a shower of broken metal bars. Kerri accelerated her steps and prepared to make another unorthodox incision. Reynolds focused vigilantly on the shining tip of the blade. He snatched up one of his walker's dismembered bars. Kerri dove at him. He took his best swing. The metal connected with her hand, sending the scalpel out of sight into the heart of the bunker. Kerri's empty fist pounded down onto Reynold's chest, inflicting minimal damage. She briefly looked off in the direction that her weapon had traveled before turning back to the man beneath her.

"The scalpel's gone," she said and swiftly choked her palms around his neck. "You think that matters?"

Reynolds grabbed his throat and attempted to fight her off. Kerri calmly channeled her rage into her squeezing hands.

Meanwhile on the other side of the room, Nancy zealously hurried to the base of the spiraling stairway. From his horizontal and locked position, Will anxiously watched her come his way. He had heard all that had gone on around the steel door, but couldn't see anything.

"What happened?" he yelled at her. "Where's my wife?"

Nancy was far too engrossed in her escape to heed his words. She breezed right by him and bounded up the darkened pewter steps. Will had to turn his head in order to follow her movement. He paused suddenly.

I can move my head! he thought.

His brain immediately sent a signal down to his arms, ordering them to rise. His latent joints let out stiff cracks as his right hand wriggled its way out of the leather straps. He grabbed onto the base of the stretcher and, with a stalwart grunt, pushed his chest upward. The upper section of straps snapped in two like flimsy rubber bands and shot down onto the floor. Will sat straight up in the stretcher and could feel a rush of blood flow through his body. Not looking to waste another second, he hopped onto his feet and rushed back to the other end of the room.

"Kerri!" he shouted. "Are you here?"

His apprehension escalated when no answer was returned. He kept his eyes opened extra wide, preparing to spot the slightest of clues that would lead him to her. Desks, curtains, chairs, and anything else that dared get in his way were sent careening through the air. Soon, two bodies writhing on the floor came into view. The first distinguishing mark that Will noticed was the abundance of blood on Kerri's hospital gown.

"Hey, Kerri!" he called. "I'm coming!"

Kerri looked up at him. His over-exerted motions startled her. She picked Reynolds up by his neck and held him out in front like a shield. The special agent was gasping for air and struggled to find his footing.

"Kerri, wait!" Will exclaimed. "Don't do anything!"

His wife silently replied with a menacing scowl and shoved her shield up against the wall. Pressing her palm into his jugular, she lifted his head high above hers.

"Damn it, Ker!" Will barked, still moving forward. "Put him down! No more killing!"

He stormed right up to her backside, hoping to use his own strength to gently overpower her. As Will was about to attack, Kerri glanced back over her shoulder. Her free hand shot forth and secured a surprise hold around his neck. Will unwittingly halted his advance and began exerting an erratic breathing pattern very similar to Reynolds's. He latched onto her wrist and attempted to free his throat, but quickly learned that her strength was far greater than his. In the blink of an eye, he joined Reynolds in his elevated status. Kerri gazed glumly into his eyes as tears once again touched down on her cheeks.

"Please, don't make me do this," she strained through her teeth.

Her double-grip grew tighter. Reynolds silently closed his eyes, appearing to have accepted his fate. Will didn't want to concur, but could feel his throat closing up fast.

"D-don't, K-ker," he wheezed. "F-f-fight."

"No, I can't!" she cried. "This is what I want." She increased the intensity of her five-finger vice. "*This* is what I want!"

Will got a foreboding hunch that he and Reynolds were going to die. He could think of only one more thing to say.

"Pleasssssse," he uttered. "For our *son...*"

Kerri's jaw stiffened up. Her brow became creased. Reynolds opened up his eyes. Will could no longer speak. He lightly nodded his head to enforce the fact that he was being truthful. His fading gaze focused straight upon Kerri. Her entire face began to quiver. Will felt her vibrations pass through his throat. He knew that she was about to give in to her primal urge.

"I'm sorry," she remorsefully grunted.

Her voice destroyed whatever was left of Will's hope. He simply closed his eyes and waited for the Grim Reaper's touch.

A tremendous jolt went shooting out through Kerri's body forcing her hands to exert one more malicious clench. Will kept his lids sealed, refusing to witness the expression on his wife's face as she killed him.

It's really over, he sullenly thought.

A second after his mind spoke, the grasp on his neck seemed to abruptly lessen. A loud, horrid wail came clamoring out of Kerri.

"AAAAAAAHHHHHHH!" she exclaimed over and over.

Will opened his eyes just as Kerri began lowering him and Reynolds back to the floor. He glanced downward and noticed a small moat of murky liquid around his wife's bare feet. Her legs glistened with moisture. Both her hands released their holds and clutched onto her stomach. Reynolds toppled over, unable to find a device for support.

"Kerri!" Will said the instant his vocal cords recovered. "What's wrong? What is it?"

"Her water just broke," Reynolds informed him. "She's going into labor right now."

"What?"

"I've seen it before, Will. You need to get her back into the bed or your baby could get hurt."

Will watched in a stunned stupor as Kerri sunk to her knees, writhing in pain. He then noticed a swirl of blood swimming within the murky fluid.

"Will, did you hear me?" Reynolds asked. "You have to get her onto that bed before the pain gets any worse."

Kerri's agonizing moaning grew more strident. Once a second small stream of blood touched onto the floor, Will woke up from his bewildered trance.

"Okay, okay!" he exclaimed. "I've got her." He bent down, placing his right knee in the embryonic fluid. "Come on, Ker, I'm putting you in bed."

Kerri was too busy cringing in anguish to resist. Without waiting for her to reply, Will scooped her up in his arms and took three giants steps over to the bed. The sheets were quickly stained light pink once Kerri's bottom was laid down. She continued to fidget uncontrollably.

"Try to hold her down!" Reynolds shouted, trying to pick himself up off the floor.

"It's not easy," Will said, attempting to gain leverage upon Kerri's wriggling torso. "She's strong as hell!"

"Let's go, Will! Do you want to lose your wife and son? I can only help you out if you get her to stop moving and lie down!"

"Okay!" Will shoved his palms into Kerri's shoulder. "Damn it, Kerri, you have to hold still! Please!"

He summoned all his metal-bar-bending strength and routed it into his upper body. Kerri's backside budged a bit closer to the mattress. Reynolds climbed to his feet with the assistance of one of the longer pieces from his broken walker. He hobbled over to the bed.

"AAAHHHH, IT HURTS!" Kerri screamed.

She continued to struggle against Will's forceful pressure, grabbing at his constrictive arms. Her peripheral vision caught a glimpse of Reynolds creeping up beside her. Her hand jumped off of Will and clasped back onto the Special Agent's throat. His crude crutch fell over as she pulled him into the bed. Their sights became locked.

"You," she scowled, "are going to die."

Reynolds soon felt that familiar boa constrictor squeeze. He rapidly grabbed her hand and gnashed his teeth.

"Sorry, honey," he fought to utter under his breath. "You already had your one chance."

Though Reynolds was showing much more spirit at the start of this second chocking go-round, Kerri wasn't exhibiting any signs of intimidation. Her nostrils flared as she keenly directed all her might into her five fingers. In the midst of his feeble resistance, Reynolds nodded over to Will and silently mouthed,

"What're... you... waiting... for?"

Understanding immediately, Will thrust another spurt of tension into Kerri. Her shoulders gave way at once. Realizing he had gained the upper hand, Will vigorously drove her into the mattress. Kerri's legs straightened and spread apart, releasing a watered down stream of red. Will glanced down at the sopping sheets. He brought his face directly up to hers.

"Please, Kerri," he said, "let me help our son."

Though she declined to answer him, he was able to detect a bright, albeit distant, glint of hope deep within her pupils. His wife was still in there somewhere and it was time to bring her out. Keeping his right forearm on her chest, he reached his left hand out and attempted to free Reynolds. Kerri's hips let out a violent twitch that almost shook Will off the bed. Her lips parted wide and gave birth to another deafening shriek. Will almost had to give up on his hold in order to cover his ears.

"Jesus Christ, Ker," he cried. "What's wrong?" He looked back down at her legs. "Is it the baby?"

He shot a glance over at Reynolds's flushed face. The Special Agent awkwardly nodded his head. Will leapt toward the base of the bed. Kerri was unable to get off her back, but still kept her grip on Reynolds.

"Oh God," Will murmured gravely upon viewing the crimson-coated bottom of the hospital gown which was sticking to the tops of Kerri's knees.

He reached out his trembling hand and touched his thumb and pointer finger to the wet fabric. Holding his breath and failing to drown out Kerri's constant screaming, he gently lifted up the gown.

"Holy shit!" he said, eyes bulging. "Holy shit! Oh my… holy shit!"

The slime-glazed head of his son was staring back at him. Kerri abruptly expelled her most ear-piercing scream yet. The baby's head was pushed out even more.

Will nearly fell backwards as the boy's head got much closer to his face. A faint *wha-wha* came echoing throughout the bunker.

"Oh my God!" Will exclaimed. "The baby's coming!"

Kerri's head perked up off the bed. Her knees bent. Her shrieks turned to concentrated grunts. Her right hand remained affixed to Reynolds's throat. Will was having an extremely difficult time preventing his mind from freaking out. He had never witnessed a live birth before. His sole knowledge on the subject stemmed from movies and TV shows. And all he really learned from those mediums was that the process was very painful. Although he was also able to infer that keeping the baby's fragile body protected was always a top priority. Nonetheless, his remedial understanding of the field of obstetrics would have to suffice for the time being. He reached his hands out toward the baby's head and slipped ever so slightly back into the long dormant calm-Kerri-down mode.

"Listen to me, Kerri," he began. "I know the real you can hear me. And I want her to remember what our main goal was a long time ago. I want her to know that we are on the verge of finally accomplishing it right now."

Kerri turned her watery gaze over to Reynolds's asphyxiating face.

"I know you hear me," Will went on. "Looking away won't help. This is happening whether you like it or not. For our son's sake, you're going to have to do it right." He took a deep breath. "So, what do you say, Ker? Let's accomplish that main goal."

Kerri's knees began to shake. Keeping her grip on Reynolds intact, she threw her head back into the mattress and dispensed one final, gut wrenching screech. Will arduously compelled his sights to stay engaged on his child during the clamorous crescendo as glass beakers around the bed began to burst. The computer screen tracking Derek's movement developed a large crack. The extended shriek went on for at least forty-five seconds until Kerri's vocal cords were torn. The backs of her knees returned to the bed.

Her breathing, though erratic, was beginning to settle. Will was unable to speak. He could only stare downward in amazement at the tiny, crying, gooey being squirming in his arms. His mind opted to supply the commentary.

I can't believe you're finally here, he thought. *You came out so fast. We've been waiting so long for…*

His inner monologue became interrupted as Kerri's shoulders sprung up from the bed. She jerked her body toward her unbroken strangle hold on Reynolds, causing the baby's umbilical cord to come fully into view. Mother and son were still connected and Kerri's brusque motion threatened to yank the baby out of Will's arms. Already immersed in his new role as protective father, Will instinctively picked the nearest scalpel up off the floor and sent the blade slicing into the cord. A surge of dark pink sprayed up from the incision into his face. Kerri's limbs exerted a slight twitch. Her grip on Reynolds lessened. Will continued cutting until his son was free. The moment the separated cord fell to the bed, so too did Kerri's hold around Reynolds. The Special Agent dropped to the floor and began rapidly catching his breath. Holding the baby's face close to his chest, Will carefully wiped away the sticky, excess gunk. Using the scalpel, he cut out a small section of the sheets and swathed it around his son. His ears detected a soft moan coming from Kerri.

"Kerri," he began, sliding off the bed—baby in tow, "I'm here, Ker. What's wrong?"

Lying flat on her back, she exhaled two wispy puffs.

"I'm…" she said. "I'm so… tired, Will."

They both simultaneously recognized that her tone had changed. Kerri rolled her eyes upward, closed the lids, and opened her mouth into a huge yawn.

"Are… you okay?" Will tensely asked.

Her mouth closed and her eyes did not open. Her face was painted in pale. The bloodied region between her legs was soaking through the bed.

"Kerri!" Will called out. "Hey! Wake up right now! Kerri! Do you hear me? Open your eyes right now and look at your son!"

Her lids suddenly popped up. She raised her head a bit and peered down at her two boys.

"Hi," she muttered weakly.

"Hey," Will exhaled with measured relief. "Does it hurt?"

"Mm-hmm… but it's a different pain now."

"What do you mean? Why different?"

232

She glanced down at her red, wet hands.

"It's gone," she said. "I can't feel it anymore. I think it's gone."

"What's gone, Ker?" The answer came to Will's mind a second after he spoke. "Oh... you mean the..."

She sat up and slowly nodded her head. Will closed his eyes and gracefully touched his forehead to hers.

"Thank God," he whispered, exhausted. "I wasn't sure if I'd ever get you back. Is it really you, Ker?"

"It's me. I'm so sorry, Will. All that I've done... I... I can't make up for it. It was so horrible."

"I know, Ker. I know. But it *wasn't* you. I know it is hard to understand, but trust me, it's true." He held up their baby. "I think it was the only way we were able to get him."

Kerri gazed down at the miniature infant whose cries had turned to coos. She brushed some of the slimy fluid away from his face.

"Oh my God, Will," she said. "He's so beautiful. Do I deserve him? I've wanted this for so long."

"Don't think anymore. It's all over now. I'm taking you and our baby and we're leaving for good. I've already made arrangements."

"Arrangements?"

"I don't have time to explain right now. We just have to go."

Reynolds placed his hand on the bed and quickly pulled himself up.

"Go where?" he asked.

Will and Kerri both turned cautiously toward him. The Special Agent gently rubbed his neck.

"Where are you two going?" he asked again. "I'm sure you're leaving this place right here, but where after that?"

Will gripped onto Kerri's side while still maintaining his hold on the baby.

"Special Agent Reynolds, I'm so sorry for what my wife and I have done," he said sincerely. "You have to understand that we were acting under extreme duress. Dr. Phalen did something to Kerri. He made her this way, I swear. I can even prove it. All the information is up in his office."

"Damn it, Will, just hold on a sec," Reynolds barked. "Regardless of what was done to you and your wife, we are all in the middle of an extremely sensitive situation that has to be dealt with the right way."

"I understand that, I do. But you know about my father and the people that were involved with him. It's because of him that we got thrown into this situation to begin with."

"Yes, Will, I know. But we've got multiple acts of manslaughter here and it would just be impossible for me to let something like that go."

"Please, sir, we have a child now. It's all we ever wanted. We thought it was never going to happen and that's why we went through Dr. Phalen's whole process. He used our longing to be pregnant and took advantage of us. It's not our fault!"

"Okay, Will, okay. I know your concern. The best bet for the both of you right now is to come with me. Let me take you and Kerri in and I promise to make sure you're both given the fair chance to tell everyone there what you're telling me now."

Kerri looked up to Will and then down at their child. Tears welled up inside her eyes.

"I think he's right, Will," she said. "I'm so ashamed of all that I've done. It's not fair for me to just walk away." She placed her hand on the baby's forehead. "I want our boy to understand right and wrong. We have to go with agent Reynolds. What else could we do?"

"You're right, Kerri, that's good," Reynolds agreed. "Listen to her, Will. She wants to do the right thing."

Will turned silent. He needed a moment to think clearly without any vocal interruptions. His idea of what would serve as 'the right thing' for their child was still a bit clouded.

"Please, Will," Reynolds said, "don't make this hard for you both."

Will did not look at him. He kept his gaze on Kerri and their son—his new family.

"I'm sorry, Special Agent Reynolds," he started, "but..."

A high-pitched alarm began blaring on and off. Will looked over at the cracked computer screen. The monitor was flashing a bright green glow in sync with the alarm.

"What's happening?" Kerri asked.

"I don't know," Will replied, failing to remain calm.

Reynolds pressed his palms into the mattress and forced himself up.

"Let's not stick around here to find out," he said. "Okay? Will you come with me?"

A ways off on the floor next to the wall, Dr. Phalen stirred back into consciousness. He cracked one of his eyelids and glanced down at the beeping side pocket of his white coat. A red radiance shone intermittently through the fabric. He reached into the pocket and removed Derek's rectangular tracking remote. The beeping got louder. His eyes widened.

"Come on, Will," Reynolds persisted. "Time is running out."

"Let's just go, Will," Kerri intervened. "I don't want to stay here anymore. I want our baby to be safe."

Reynolds turned to scope out the room for his gun when a distant scream rang out from above. All three of them shot their eyes sky high. The wail increased in volume as it traveled closer. Will grabbed hold of Kerri and yanked her off the bed just as Nurse Nancy came crashing through the messy assortment of raised wires and lighting. She landed with a hard splat on the floor about a foot away from the mattress, spritzing the sheets with even more red. Will lost his balance and had to let go of Kerri in order to protect the baby as he fell onto his back. Having difficulty without his walker, Reynolds collapsed out of harm's way.

"Will, what's going on?" Kerri hollered from her knees.

Will was unable to answer. He could only gaze up through the mangled array of sparking wires and broken lights at the large dark mass looming at the top of the metal stairway. He immediately lifted his back up off the floor and looked over to Kerri.

"We have to get out of here right now!" he ordered.

"Okay, okay," Kerri replied, clearly in pain. "What is it?"

"It's my father."

Will didn't have to say another word. Kerri shoved her weakened body up off the floor. He did the same. The sudden flush of movement pushed Derek to begin descending the stairway. Will held onto the baby with one arm and supported Kerri with the other. They rushed past the fallen agent.

"Come on, Reynolds!" Will shouted down to him. "We really have to be leaving now! My father's here!"

"I'm not surprised," Reynolds said, reaching for the nearest metal pole.

The three adults were all soon upright and attempting to make haste. Their escape, however, was abruptly brought to a halt as Dr. Phalen stepped out in front of the steel exit door.

"Nobody's leaving," he stated, aiming the black syringe-loaded gun directly at them.

Will at once turned around to face Kerri, protecting both her and the baby from the direction of the gun's barrel.

"Put that down, Phalen," Reynolds warned. "Whatever sick situation you've got planned here, it's all over."

"It's not over at all! I've waited too long!" He glanced upwards briefly and clenched the gun tight. "This is my life now! There is nothing else!"

A row of clangs echoed down to them from the stairs. Will tried to access a view from above, but the flickering wires were too cumbersome. He locked eyes with Kerri and gently passed her the baby.

"Get ready to leave," he mouthed under his breath.

Kerri reluctantly nodded, firmly holding onto the child. Will looked away from her toward Dr. Phalen.

"Get down on the floor!" the doctor ordered. "All of you!"

Kerri began kneeling. Because of Reynolds's shoddy metal crutch, he was already half way there. Will remained upright.

"Let's go, Will," Dr. Phalen said, motioning the gun. "You're not ruining this for me."

"Are you going to kill me, Dr. Phalen?" Will asked. "In front of my newborn son? Is that the kind of monster you want to become… just like my father?"

"Shut the hell up! I'm *nothing* like that! You're father is an abomination! I'm doing the right th…"

Will sharply lunged forward, deciding that mid-self-righteous-speech would serve as the ideal time to attack. He pushed the gun aside with his left hand and grabbed the doctor by the neck with his right. Reynolds gained a fair sense of balance and hobbled toward them both.

"Easy, Will!" he shouted. "Don't do anything stupid!"

Will was only paying heed to his five fingers around Dr. Phalen's neck and how good it felt tightening them.

"Look at me, Dr. Phalen," he sneered. "You're *not* going to hurt my family any more."

Will kept his sights secured on the doctor's glazed pupils, searching for a sign of surrender. On the contrary, Dr. Phalen simply gazed past him and smiled. The floor started to shake. Will heard a row of rumbling coming up behind him. He glanced over his shoulder just as Kerri and Reynolds were aggressively shoved aside. A giant, black blur stampeded directly into him. An instant later, Will found himself soaring through the air away from Dr. Phalen. He landed at the base of one of the numerous freestanding curtains.

"Derek," Dr. Phalen uttered, staring through the eye holes of the darkened mask before him.

He promptly brought the black gun back in front of his face. Derek grabbed hold of the barrel as if it was a child's plaything and yanked it out of the disobedient doctor's hand. He scrunched his fingers together, sending the weapon into a mangled mass of black splinters. The piece dropped to the floor, releasing a small collection of 'syringe bullets'.

"No!" Dr. Phalen shouted. "It's not supposed to be this way! This can't be happening!"

Derek slapped his hands over the sides of his head as if suffering from a massive migraine. He tore into Dr. Phalen's white coat, ripping apart the pockets and soon extracted the beeping tracking remote. Deciphering the device as the source of his pain, he crushed it into the doctor's forehead. The beeping at once ceased as well as Derek's aching mind.

"You're supposed to die!" Dr. Phalen exclaimed, now blinded by the busted device.

Not offering a verbal response or explanation, Derek grabbed hold of the doctor's coat and swept him off his feet. Dr. Phalen let out a scorned scream as he was planted back-first into the floor. Derek snatched up Reynolds's makeshift metal crutch. Dr. Phalen lifted up his head and said, "Go to hel..."

His sentence was cut just short as Derek plunged the hardened, hollow pole down into his throat. The tip of the crutch became embedded into the floor, keeping the doctor from rotating off his back. Derek nodded down and observed as Dr. Phalen choked on his own blood. Once all the twitch-ing ceased, he moved his vision over toward Kerri and Reynolds. The Special Agent was flailing about like a fish out of water without any nearby means of standing support. Kerri laid a little ways off, her fresh birth wounds kept her from holding onto the baby. She had her legs pulled up in a fetal position with her newborn wriggling a good three feet away.

"Will!" she blindly called out. "I can't move! I can't get him!"

Derek wrapped his thick palm around the skewered metal bar and lugged it up out of Dr. Phalen. Reynolds realized in which direction the dark behemoth was headed.

"Where're ya going, Derek!" he shouted. "You're going the wrong way! You never killed me! I'm the reason why you got caught! Because of *me*, you were locked up in that cell for all these years!"

Derek stopped moving and turned slightly away from Kerri.

"That's right, Derek!" Reynolds went on. "You never killed me! Why don't you come over here and try again?"

Derek rotated his huge shoulders fully toward the Special Agent. Though the black mask shaded most of his face, Reynolds knew he was staring at him.

"Good, that's right!" he yelled. "Get over here and finish it!"

Derek's feet remained planted. His colossal chest expanded and con-tracted. The soft cry of his new grandson became the sole sound inside the room. Derek inhaled deeply, but his chest suddenly froze. Reynolds pushed his upper body off the floor in order to attain a better view.

"What's the matter?" he asked. "I'm right here. Come on. Don't you want to kill me?"

Derek finally allowed his lungs to exhale and promptly turned his back to the Special Agent. Reynolds watched as the hulking heap stepped back onto his path toward Kerri.

"Derek! You come back this way right now!" he bellowed. "No! You're not doing this to me again! Get back here you son of a bitch! If you don't kill me, I'm going to kill you!"

Unfazed by the threat, Derek continued his steady stroll. He passed Kerri by and kneeled down before the defenseless baby.

"No!" Kerri cried. "Get away from him!"

Derek dug his hands beneath the baby's sheet wrappings. Though his mitts were like a pair of bear paws, he gracefully hoisted him up off the floor.

"Noooo!" Kerri shrieked.

Without turning her way, Derek held the child up before his masked face. Surprisingly, the baby was silent. Derek slanted his head onto a partial angle, as if unable to fully comprehend what was in his hands. His contemplation process became interrupted by a barrage of fast-paced footsteps. He spun around in just enough time to latch onto the wrist of his own son. Will instantly dropped to his knees in agony as his father's crushing grip snapped a couple of bones. The unbelievable pressure forced him to let go of the single 'syringe bullet' he had planned on driving into the back of Derek's neck.

"Don't drop him!" Will yelled, motioning his free hand up at the baby.

Derek looked over at the peaceful child still perfectly secure in his one arm. A blast of blood immediately shot forth from his shoulder. The fresh gash forced him to release his grip on the baby. Kerri screamed in fright as her son plunged towards the floor. Will tenaciously extended his free arm. The wrapped sheet touched down on the inside of his elbow. He brought in his forearm like a sprung mousetrap.

Derek's gash also caused him to let go of his son and grasp for whatever was at his backside that made him bleed.

"Will!" Kerri screamed, unable to view what happened.

Will frantically glanced down below his shoulder at their child clutched securely to his chest.

"I've got him, Ker!" he called out. "I've got him!"

From his lowered position, Will spotted a pair of legs plus a metal rod standing behind Derek. He poked his head partially around the side of the wounded leviathan to find Reynolds. The Special Agent had his pistol pointed directly into the back of Derek's shoulder.

"Get the hell out of here, Will," he ordered.

"But what about…" Will had to stop mid-sentence as Derek picked Reynolds up.

"Take your family and go!" Reynolds roared, his body flailing like a windsock. "Now!"

Will didn't feel right leaving him, but knew protecting his wife and son had to be his highest priority. Derek flung Reynolds across his chest, preparing to hurl him like a shot-put. For a brief instant, Will locked sights with the Special Agent and time seemed to stand still.

"Thank you," Will said softly.

Reynolds merely nodded. Understanding that it would have been completely stupid to speak any further, Will grasped his child and darted off. He reached Kerri shortly and moved the baby into his right arm. His determination enabled him to look past whatever bones were painfully broken.

"Come on, Ker," he said, crouching beside her. "We're leaving."

"Okay," Kerri agreed right away.

"Good."

Will easily lifted her off the floor with just his left arm.

"Can you walk on your feet?" he asked.

"I'll try," Kerri said and took a step. "Owww!"

"Okay, okay. Forget about walking. I've got you. Come here."

He single-handedly hoisted her up over his shoulder. Once certain he had a good semblance of balance, Will took his family toward the steel exit door.

"Just hold on tight, Kerri," he shakily said.

"What about the baby?" she asked.

"Don't worry. I've got him. And I'm not letting go for anything. We're heading out that door. It's the only way out. Just focus on that door. Got it? Don't look back for a second."

"But, Will, how can we not?" Kerri hurriedly asked. "Where are we going from here? How do we fix… everything?"

"We can't. I'm sorry, Ker. All we can do from this point on is restart our life together. It's all we can do… for our son."

"But how?"

"You just have to trust me. I emptied out the trust fund. We're going to be fine, I promise. I have a plan. All I need for you to do is just, please, trust me. Will you do that, Kerr?"

Kerri plunged her face down into his chest. "Yes, I will trust you," she said, listening closely to the hyperactive beating of his heart.

The steel door was still partly opened from when Reynolds first arrived. Will used his foot to kick it open the rest of the way, revealing a long, dimly lit ramp. Keeping Kerri and their baby buried deeply in his upper body, he turned his head back at the bunker. Derek had Reynolds elevated and inverted in preparation for The Drop. Will grudgingly averted his eyes back to the ramp and departed the bunker.

"Fuck you, Derek!" Reynolds exclaimed, thrusting his fist downward into the rounded top of the black mask.

The pounding did little to deter Derek from his objective. He began leaning back and, with a minor hop, smashed the Special Agent's face into the floor. The move set Reynolds free, sending him somersaulting a good ten feet. He landed face-up with a fresh, dripping gash slanting across his forehead. Recognizing that his prey still showed signs of life, Derek marched toward him. The thunderous steps caused Reynolds to pick up his head. Though quite dazed, he was able to notice right away that his prosthetic foot had come loose and drooped gawkily off to the side. An immense blur in black was advancing closer. Feeling strangely calm, Reynolds detected a small, shiny object out the corner of his eye.

I really hope that's my gun, he thought almost jokingly.

It took no more than a simple rotation of his head to make his hope a reality. Reynolds tossed out his hand and reeled in the gun. He sat straight up and wasted no time in pumping out a stream of bullets. Some of the shells shot wide, but most found their way into Derek's chest. Reynolds continued pulling the trigger until an empty clicking noise filled the room along with the still sparking wires above. Derek remained on his feet, proceeding without even losing a hint of steam. Reynolds looked down at his impotent revolver and frustratingly flung it forward.

"That had to have hurt at least a little, Derek!" he shouted. "It's okay, you can tell me."

An answer wasn't returned.

"No?" Reynolds went on. "Not even the slightest sting? Well, then I guess we're just going to have to try harder."

He started casting turbulent glances all about his surroundings. His head swung to the left, to the right, and then finally upwards.

"We'll try harder, Derek," he uttered without looking down.

Reynolds remained perfectly still, but kept a sharp eye as a large shadow appeared over him. Derek hastily extended his arms downward and plucked the Special Agent off of the floor. Reynolds squirmed in agony as his sides became immersed in a vice of relentless pressure. He threw his head back and cried out loud all the way up to the ceiling. Derek quietly refused to relinquish his monstrous bear hug. Something popped around the middle of Reynolds's back. He knew that time was running out. His mind blocked out the unbearable forces squeezing his sides. He lifted his face upward and observed a tangled clump of vibrating wires leaning against the edge of a broken spotlight. His view was then switched toward the floor and his dangling prosthetic foot. He gave his leg one sharp kick back. The sudden shift loosened the prosthetic foot, sending it up in the air. Reynolds heaved out his hand and snatched it. The retrieval happened too fast for Derek to take notice. Without pause, Reynolds launched the foot upward. It collided hard with the spotlight, causing the collection of live wires to spill. Reynolds gazed with gleefully wide eyes at the sparks raining down on him. He wrapped one arm around the back of Derek's neck and reached the other up high. His face was pressed against the ear region of the black mask.

"Good-bye, Derek," he whispered.

One of the wires landed within Reynolds's palm and stuck to it like a magnet. The Special Agent clenched his fingers around the throbbing strand as the intense voltage sliced through his body. The current passed rapidly into Derek as the rest of the wires poured down. Though Reynolds could feel every muscle in his body spasming out of control, he was able to take a strange comfort knowing that the curse on the world known as Derek Haddonfear was finally at an end.

Rest in peace... was the last thought that went through his mind.

As Reynolds's vision turned to black, his electrified frame stayed permanently stuck to Derek's. Swirls of smoke rose out from their meshed-together mass. The sparks turned to flames. Derek struggled to free himself from the burning implements, but was unable to regain control over his convulsing limbs. The unyielding electric pulsations brought him down to his knees as the fire swept across his upper body. The inferno engulfed the black mask, searing off the white outlining around the eye holes. All means of resistance had evaporated from Derek's psyche. He sharply wrenched his blazing head back and collapsed face-first on the floor. All movement within the bunker serenely ceased.

Chapter 29

The sun shone brightly through the small window above the kitchen sink. A fresh haze of steam became revealed as it passed through the beams of light. A small stack of pancakes resided atop a circular wooden table situated beside a white refrigerator. Kerri stood before a matching white stove, working with a frying pan full of an egg, ham and onion mixture.

"Mmm, something sure smells great," Will smiled, entering the kitchen area.

"I sure hope it tastes just as great," Kerri replied.

"Oh, I'm not worried about that. Not in the least."

"Well, I'm glad." She glanced past him. "Is he coming in for breakfast?"

"Oh, yeah. He's just upstairs grabbing one of his toys."

"Oh, really? I thought I heard him playing outside just now."

"Nope, he was with me in the computer room. I was checking my email."

A smirk overcame Will's face.

"Why are you looking at me like that?" Kerri asked.

"Because I have news for you," Will said, stretching his grin. "Through an email I just got."

"Well... tell me!"

"Okay, here it is... Fred and Lynn are pregnant!"

"Oh!" Kerri covered her mouth with both hands. "Oh my God! That's so wonderful!"

"Yeah, and strange too. I mean, it's so weird picturing Fred now as a father. He was just so different the last time I saw him. I had only recently gotten used to seeing him as someone's husband."

"Lynn always did have a way of bringing out the greatness in guys." She lowered her head a bit. "I really miss seeing her."

"I know, Ker. I miss a lot of things too. But this..."

"Oh, I totally understand, Will. I'm not complaining." She picked up her head. "I don't have the right to complain in any way. I'm so thankful we have him and we're all together. You're both the best things that ever happened to me. I'm sorry I sounded ungrateful."

"There is no need to apologize. It's been five years. That is a very long time to be away. And let's not forget that we didn't exactly leave willingly.

And we lived there for a real long time. So it's okay to say that you still miss the people and things that we left behind."

"Yes, Will, you're right. I guess that sometimes I just... I don't know. It feels like not being able to go back to our old life is our penance... for what I did."

"I'm sorry I can't change the past. You know I would if there was some kind of way."

"I don't think it has to do with changing things. It's just that sometimes I wonder what it would have been like if things went back to normal. But then I remember that normal consisted of just the two of us."

"Yeah, we're much better as three." He walked up toward the stove and wrapped his arms around her. "Much better."

Kerri didn't wait to place a kiss upon his lips.

"I love you so much," she whispered. "I'd never want you to think that I didn't appreciate all that you've done for us."

"Well, don't worry because that would never happen. It's not so bad living down here really, is it?"

"Not at all. The house is great. The weather's always warm."

"And we're expanding our linguistic horizons. Seriously, my Spanish fluency is getting really good. I was actually able to carry on a conversation about fishing with this guy at the market the other day. I'm a muy bueno muchacho!"

"I'm so proud," Kerri laughed. "You always know how to make me smile."

The hardwood floor in the other room let out a loud creek and was soon followed by some light footsteps. Will hurriedly grabbed hold of Kerri.

"Quick, give me some sugar before the little tyke gets in here and sees his parents making out," he quietly said close to her face.

Kerri didn't get a chance to reply as Will smothered his lips over hers. He playfully placed his hand on her butt and had just enough time to give it one good squeeze before a young boy with dark parted hair, dressing in a t-shirt and shorts, entered the kitchen. He carried a toy action figure in his hand.

"Oh, hey buddy, what's going on?" Will said in the manner of a teenager who'd just got caught with his girlfriend in the back seat of his car.

A tad confused by his father's abruptly forced question, the boy merely shrugged his shoulders.

"Are you being the strong, silent type today, little Billy?" Will asked.

The boy nodded his head and half-smiled.

"Well, that's okay, dude," Will smiled. "I see you got your action man there. Do you want to play?"

Billy looked down at the toy and then back to his father. He shook his head.

"Mommy made you pancakes, honey," Kerri intervened. "Do you want to sit down and have some?"

"Yes!" Billy enthusiastically responded.

"So *that's* it!" Will jumped back in. "The boy is hungry for his breakfast!"

"Yes, I am!"

"And do you want to do 'airplane' on the way to the table?"

"Yes!" Billy threw his arms up in the air. "I wanna fly!"

"All righty then! Let's see those wings!"

His son lowered his arms until they were perpendicular with his body. Will jogged up beside him. Kerri couldn't help beaming with glee at the interaction between her two boys.

"Pilot to co-pilot," Will began, kneeling down. "Are you ready for take-off, sir?"

"Ready!" Billy nodded.

"Three... two... one!"

Will grabbed hold underneath Billy's arms and hoisted him up off the floor. The boy laughed joyfully as he soared through the kitchen.

"Be careful," Kerri said as the two zipped past her.

"Don't worry, Ker," Will replied. "We're professionals!"

"Yeah, Mommy," Billy added. "We're propepinals!"

Kerri covered her mouth, failing to suppress her laughter. Will hovered his son over the wooden table, which featured three place settings and a chopping board with a hefty kitchen knife and some onion remnants on top of it.

"Okay, Captain Billy, we are about to begin our pancake descent," Will smiled. "Please fasten your seatbelt and make sure that your tray table is up and in its locked position."

"Where's the tray table?" Billy asked.

"I don't know, son! It's just something that all pilots say when they're about to land their plane!"

Will touched Billy down in the chair situated before the plate of pancakes. The boy placed his action man on the table.

"Now, are you going to want some syrup?" he asked.

"Yes, I want some syrup," Billy responded.

"Honey, where is the syrup?"

"It's coming out right now," Kerri answered, stepping up to the refrigerator.

Billy's eyes lit up as his mother placed down a bottle of Senora Jemima next to his plate.

"Thanks, Mommy!" he exclaimed

"Enjoy, honey," Kerri grinned. "I made them especially for you."

"And did you make something especially for me?" Will hopefully asked.

"The omelet's on the stove," Kerri said. "Can't you smell it?"

"Oh yeah. I can certainly smell those onions and the melted cheese!"

"Get ready to enjoy then."

Kerri walked back over to the stove, spatula in hand. After a couple of fast flips, the eggs were properly folded. She slid the steaming creation onto a plate and brought it over to her husband.

"Ham, cheddar, and freshly chopped onions," she said. "Your favorite."

"Aw, thanks Ker," Will said. "It looks and smells awesome!"

"Well, then dig in while it's hot."

"Don't mind if I do."

Will picked up a fork and plunged it down into the omelet. He raised a cheesy, yellow piece and placed it inside his mouth.

"Oh, honey, this is fantastic," he raved. "Thank you so much for making it for me."

Will lowered his fork for another helping and waited to hear his wife's humble reply.

"Will!" Kerri shouted in a tone that was the exact opposite of what he was expecting.

Will dropped his fork on the table and saw that his wife was pointing. He rapidly spun his head in the direction that her finger was aiming, and saw Billy grasping the thick kitchen knife. The boy lunged the sharp tip forward halfway towards him and grinned with glee.

"This will hurt, won't it, Daddy?" Billy beamed.

Will wiped the smile off his face and lowered his chin closer to the knife's point.

"Yes, son, it would hurt very much," he said with grave honesty. "And that is why you can never do something like it again."

Billy put his grin on pause.

"But why?" he asked.

"Because your last name is Haddon," Will replied. "And your first name is William... just like me. And I would never do something like that."

"Are you sure?" Billy bobbed the blade closer. "It could be something very fun, Daddy."

Kerri covered her mouth, her eyes starting to glisten.

"No, son," Will said stoutly. "There is nothing fun about that at all. It is something very bad and it makes Daddy very upset. Do you want that, Billy? Do you want to make Daddy very upset."

The base of the knife jiggled slightly in Billy's hand. Will gently touched his left cheek to the point, keeping his eyes solely on his son.

"Do you really want to push that knife any further?" he asked with utmost seriousness. "And make Daddy very angry?"

Billy stayed momentarily silent and stared into his father's eyes. He looked down at the knife.

"But I want to push it," he naively responded. "I want to."

"Billy, we have talked about this before," Will said sternly. "Hurting people is wrong. We don't hurt people. You got that, son? I want you to make me a proud father. But I can't be proud of you if you do things like this. Do you understand what I'm saying?"

The boy's lips stayed sealed. Will refused to move his face away from the knife's tip. He creased his brow and glared down at Billy.

"Drop it," he growled.

Billy immediately hit the blade down into the table and released his grip.

"I'm sorry, Daddy," he frowned.

Will at once wiped the anger off his face. He placed his hand beside Billy's temple and kissed his forehead.

"That's okay, buddy," he whispered. "You're still learning."

Will slid the knife along the wooden table until it was out of his son's reach. Kerri let out a loud half-sob. The sudden outburst forced both Will and Billy to look her way.

"It's all right, Ker," Will said. "It's over. Everything's going to be okay, I promise you."

"What if it's not?" Kerri asked, shielding her sad face from Billy. "What if it's like the doctor said?"

"No, Ker, it won't be that way."

"But how can you be so sure."

"Because, it's all in how you raise them. Children are a product of their environment. We are good parents and we will raise a good son. I know that I'm one hundred percent right."

Kerri smeared her hand over her eyes, creating a bit of a moist mess.

"I need to get a tissue," she said and stood up from the table.

Will quietly watched her scamper over to the kitchen counter.

"What's wrong with Mommy?" Billy asked.

"Oh, she's okay," Will answered. "She just doesn't want to see you do bad things. And I think the onion made her cry."

"Why would an onion make Mommy cry? What did it do to her? Did it hurt her?"

"No, no, it didn't hurt..." Will paused to restrain his laughter. "Onions can't hurt people. It's just that when you peel them, they, like, uh... actually I'm not really sure why."

Kerri smiled behind the tissue draped over her mouth upon hearing her boys' silly banter. Keeping her back turned to them, she blew her nose and wiped away all traces of wetness. After one calming deep breath, she was ready to head back to the table.

The floor in the other room let out a small creak again.

"Honey, Mommy's all right," she said, turning back around. "You don't have to leave."

Kerri took one step toward the table.

"What are you talking about, Ker?" Will asked.

Kerri looked in the direction of his voice to see that he and Billy were both still at the table. She took another step forward past the entryway to the kitchen. Something large was looming in her peripheral vision. She turned her head to the side and emitted a shocked shriek.

"Ker, what is..." Will called out, rising up from his seat.

He was unable to complete his sentence as a massive, black entity entered the kitchen and swept Kerri off her feet.

"Billy, you leave the kitchen right now!" Will ordered while rushing over to his wife.

Kerri's back slammed into the row of cabinets beside the refrigerator. Before she got a chance to scream a second time, a large, callused hand grabbed hold of her neck. Tears burst from her eyes.

"NO!" Will shouted.

The intruder turned and looked directly at him. Will's heart sunk as an army of chills ran down his back. The frayed black mask was now full of tattered and torn openings, revealing random patches of reddish, burned skin. One eyehole had completely ripped open, displaying an all-white pupil. A broken-off steel chain was dangling and clanging around the leviathan's neck. With a hulking free hand, he held up something small and square with a rapidly flashing red light.

Observing the object, Will was instantly brought back to Dr. Phalen's office. He could have killed himself for forgetting about the tracking diode inside of Kerri. However this wasn't the time for suicide out of frustration.

Will summoned his inherent, inherited strength and lunged forward, hands drawn. Derek dropped the tracking device to the floor and shot out his fist. The huge, clenched ball connected with Will's nose, sending him into a stunned, stumbling daze. Before he hit the floor, Derek grabbed him by the throat and threw him into the cabinets next to Kerri.

"Don't... please... just don't," Will fumbled to speak as his head dangled drunkenly forward.

Derek jostled him brutishly back and forth like an abusive parent, literally. The harsh shaking actually brought Will back to consciousness quicker, as a fresh stream of blood trickled forth from his nose. He glanced over at his wife. The hand over her throat prevented her from speaking. The tears washing over her face said enough. Will stared Derek directly in his one white eye.

"Let... her... go," he mustered to speak through his throat's vice.

Derek tilted his head to the side, attempting to comprehend the words. He turned to Kerri and without waiting a second, lifted her up off the floor by her neck. Her eyes soon began rolling upward. Derek turned back to Will as if looking for a showing of disapproval.

"Don't!" Will exclaimed. "For Christ's sake, she's your daughter-in-law! Let her go! How could you..."

He stopped speaking and let his mouth remain open. His eyes couldn't help looking past his father. Derek rotated his head to view precisely what Will was looking at. Billy was standing nervously before them. The thick kitchen knife was back in his hand. Will was unable to say a word. The pressure around Kerri's throat prevented her from speaking as well.

Billy's shaking hand raised the knife into a pre-stabbing position. Derek at once lowered Kerri to the floor and released his grip, allowing her only a couple of brief seconds to catch her breath. He grabbed hold of the chain around his shoulders and swung a single rotation of the links around her neck. In a flash, he tightened the two loose ends of the chain around Will's waist without breaking the hold around his son's own neck.

Billy took one large step closer to his parents, still brandishing the blade. Derek turned his burned, partly masked gaze directly onto the boy.

"Don't you do it, Dad," Will was able to squeak above the choke.

Without acknowledging the request, Derek reached out his one free hand, palm up. Billy stared down at the sickly callused appendage and then over to his knife. His grip tightened around the handle. Will wanted to yell at the top of his lungs, but instead chose to wait. Kerri could only send a storm of tears raining down upon her neck's chain. Derek crumpled his fingers slightly, beckoning to Billy. The boy glared up at his grandfather with confused fear. Will looked deep within his son's eyes, and prayed for him to do the right thing. Billy returned his father's stare and slowly pushed the knife forward. He gently released the handle into Derek's hand as two thin rows of tears ran down his cheeks. A huge smile strangely grew across Will's face.

"Good boy, Billy," he beamed. "Good boy. Daddy's so proud of you." He turned awkwardly to his wife. "Did you see that, Ker? See, I told you. It *is* how you raise them."

Still muted, Kerri nodded her head and tried to smile. Derek closed his fingers around the handle of the knife and turned away from Billy. He pointed the tip of the blade at Will's face, preparing to strike.

"Do you know who this is, Billy?" Will asked out of the blue.

"No," the boy quietly answered.

"This is your grandpa." He nodded at Derek. "Remember, we talked about him?"

"Yes. He's the one with the big muscles."

"That's right. He's real big and strong, just like your action man."

Billy gazed up at his grandfather in awe.

"Well, son," Will went on. "Say hello."

"Uhm..." Billy shyly began. "Hi, Grandpa."

Derek turned his devilish eyes down toward the boy. His hold around Will remained intact.

"Daddy told me that you were the greatest wrestler ever," Billy continued, a tad more comfortable. "I like your mask."

Derek moved the knife up to his head and pointed its tip at the frayed black fabric encompassing his face. Will was ecstatically shocked to view his father actually communicating with his son.

"Well, Grandpa's had a long trip, Billy," he said. "I bet he's really thirsty. See if he wants a drink."

"Grandpa," Billy said, keeping his eyes on the mask. "Do you want something to drink?"

Derek looked over at Will and immediately tightened his chokehold. Kerri let out a scared squeal as Will aimed his sights up at the ceiling. Satisfied, Derek turned back to the boy and slowly nodded.

"Great!" Billy beamed. "I've got just the thing."

He stepped up beside the refrigerator and opened it up. Will watched out of the corner of his eye as his son disappeared behind the white door. The sound of bottles clanking together filled the kitchen. Moments later, Billy moved out from behind the door, letting it swing shut. He held a gigantic, dark green, plastic mug, at least 32 ounces, in both his hands.

"Here, Grandpa," he said, holding up the beverage. "This is for you. I hope you like it."

Completely captivated by his grandson, Derek placed the knife on top of the refrigerator. He lifted his free hand up to the bottom of his mask and began pulling the black fabric upwards. Will held his breath as his father revealed just a hint of the severely disfigured lower region of his face. The skin was so badly burned that lips couldn't be distinguished. A long, black, horizontal slit was the only evidence of a mouth.

Derek reached his hand down. His thick, charred fingers fit easily around the container. Billy kept his arms perfectly steady as the mug was lifted up out of his hands.

"It's lemonade, Grandpa," the boy smiled. "It's nice and cold. I made it just for you."

Derek cautiously raised the mug up to his face, keeping his eyes on Billy and his hold on Will and Kerri. Before taking a sip, the mask turned towards Will.

"Do whatever you want to me," Will pleaded. "I don't care if you kill me. But *don't* do a thing to him…" He nodded at Billy. "…or her." He nodded to Kerri. "Please, let them go… Dad."

Derek snarled his slit of a mouth, clearly displeased with being told what to do. Will kept his sights on the mug as the vice around his neck tightened. His father brought the drink right past him. Will lowered his focus to the mug's base. Fully in control of the situation, Derek began tilting the drink towards his non-existent lips. Will's arm at once shot out.

"Run, Billy!" he yelled upon extracting something taped to the base of the mug.

His son did as he was told and sprinted out of the kitchen. Derek realized that something was amiss and prepared to snap Will's neck in two. However, his son, though not the stronger one, was indeed the fastest. Will took the slender, taped object and rammed it into his father's exposed jugular.

The poison entered Derek's system almost instantaneously, causing him to exert an involuntary jerk. He dropped the lemonade to the floor and yanked the foreign object out of his throat. He gazed down at the miniature, empty syringe as the Achilles heel worked its way throughout his system. His legs buckled. Will could feel the clasp loosening around his throat. His placed his hand over his father's and easily moved it off of him. Derek's eyes were opened wide in utter shock.

"I didn't want it to come to this," Will whispered. "But *I'm* the one with the family now. And I know the sacrifices that have to be made to be a husband and a father."

Derek dropped down to his knees. Will made sure that their eyes remained fully linked. Still chained to her husband, Kerri could only look on in awestruck suspense.

Derek's shoulders started to convulse uncontrollably. He was about to topple over. Will grabbed him by the collar of his sanitarium jumpsuit, prolonging his descent. He moved his face up about three inches away from Derek's.

"I will never think of you as father," he coldly affirmed.

Just before Derek's eyes began rolling over, a fading glow within them exposed ever so briefly that he understood what the words meant. Will released his hold as the darkened giant collapsed on his back, sending a long, jagged crack through the hardwood floor. Kerri rapidly wrapped her arms around her husband and buried her sobbing face in his chest.

"Oh, God," she bawled. "Is he... dead?"

"Oh, yeah," Will assured, staring down at the fallen, oversized mass. "He's dead. The syringe worked fast." He kissed the top of her head and glanced over to the kitchen's entryway. "Billy, are you there? You can come back in now. Everything's fine."

The patter of little feet soon reverberated as Billy returned to the kitchen.

"Daddy! Mommy!" he joyfully exclaimed and gave both his parents a huge hug.

Will and Kerri both knelt down in order to be closer to their son.

"I'm so proud of you, buddy!" Will beamed, kissing the top of his head. "You did so great; just how we practiced!"

"Mommy loves you so much!" Kerri gushed, pressing her cheek to his.

Billy turned his eyes down to Derek.

"But what about, Grandpa?" he asked.

"Grandpa is done visiting," Will fielded the answer right away. "He's just taking a little nap now and by the time you and Mommy get back, he'll be gone."

"Mommy and me are going somewhere?"

"Yes, buddy. You're going for a nice, long walk to the beach. Mommy's going to get you some ice cream."

"Really?" The boy's eyes became elated.

"Absolutely. You better get your shoes on."

Billy looked over at Kerri.

"Really, Mommy?"

Kerri could only nod her head and say, "Mm hmm."

Will grasped the metal chain which still connected him to his wife. He applied a forceful squeeze that instantly broke apart the links.

"Wow," Billy marveled. "How did you do that, Daddy?"

"Because I'm strong," Will smiled and patted the boy's shoulder. "Just like you."

"Really? Me too?"

"Yes, but there's something very important you have to remember."

"What's that?"

Will placed both hands on his son's shoulders and stared him right in the face.

"You have to remember that even though we're strong, we are only allowed to show it and use it at certain times"

"I don't get it."

"That's okay, buddy. You don't have to get it right away. All you need to know is that not everyone is as strong as us. So most of the time, we need to hide it so they don't get sad because we're so much stronger than they are."

"Oh, okay. I can hide it. Like a game?"

"Sure! Just like a game. It'll be so fun."

"Okay, Daddy, we'll play, but... when do we show our strong?"

Will looked up at Kerri and then back to Billy.

"We can show it whenever Mommy is in trouble and needs us."

"All right. Is that it?"

"No. You can also use it whenever a good person is in trouble."

"What's a good person?"

"People like you, me and Mommy. Nice people who don't deserve to be in trouble. That's who you use your strong to protect. Got it?"

"Yes, Daddy, I get it. When does the game start?"

"It starts as soon as you and Mommy step outside to go get ice cream. So you better hurry!"

"Okay!" Billy jumped straight up. "I'm getting my shoes on!" He scampered out of the kitchen. "Come on, Mommy!"

"O... okay, honey," Kerri said. "Mommy will be right there."

She rose to her feet, still keeping her arms around Will. He could feel that she was still shaking.

"It's over, Ker," he whispered. "It was the last possible thing we had to worry about. Now, it's all over. We can finally move fully on. Please, tell me you feel the same way."

Kerri picked her head off of his chest. She placed her hands onto his face and pulled his lips to hers.

"I do, Will," she softly said. "Thank you for saving our family. You're the best thing that ever…"

"You don't even have to say it, Ker," Will interrupted. "I know. Believe me, I know." He tenderly kissed her forehead. "Now take our boy out of here. I'll take care of this." He nodded at the hardwood. "It'll be fast, I promise. Okay?"

"Okay."

Kerri placed her arms around him for one more squeeze before stepping away out of the kitchen. Will waited patiently, listening closely. As soon as the front door slammed shut, he bent down on the floor just above Derek. He gazed at the frayed, black mask which still partially revealed the bottom of his father's mouth. The all-white eyeball displayed a fresh, shiny glaze.

"It's over," he confirmed to the body.

Will gingerly reached out his hand toward Derek's face. A wave of morbid imagery flashed through his mind as to what sort of gory, ungodly features lurked beneath the black fabric.

None of the thoughts scared him.

He vigorously dug his fingers into the top of the mask and ripped it off.

Afterword

First off, thank you for reading this book. It's the first book I've ever had published and serves as a definitive example (at least for me) of a dream coming true. I once heard that writers should write what they know. Well, a long time ago, something my amazing wife and I knew was the state of infertility. That was what inspired me to start writing this book. Since then, we have thankfully been blessed with two incredible sons. I've come to learn that all things truly happen for a reason (even the bad ones) and can somehow lead to great things. I hope that you, as a reader, come to the same understanding.

Once *Dropping Fear* was published, I was lucky enough to form a strong bond with my publisher, and have since put out a children's horror novel called *My Little Sister's A Zombie*, which I'm now developing into a series of books. The sequel is coming very soon. These books are meant to entertain as well as promote a positive message of acceptance towards others. I'm very proud of them.

From there, what can I say? I love my family, I'm hoping to one day make writing books my day job, and I love taking everyday scenarios and writing about them with a horror-themed twist. I have two horror novels coming soon: *Dead at the Jersey Shore* and *McCray's Gonna Get You* from Living Dead Press and its many imprints. If you liked *Dropping Fear*, you'll definitely enjoy them both.

Thank you again for supporting my dream!

Mike Catalano

THE PLACE TO GO FOR ZOMBIE AND APOCALYPTIC FICTION

LIVING DEAD PRESS

WHERE THE DEAD WALK
www.livingdeadpress.com

Where the Dead
Never Sleep

UNDEADPRESS.COM

My Little Sister's a
ZOMBIE!
jhb '10
Mike Catalano
Jason Bailey